ANNIHILATION SQUAD

'You IN PARTICULAR should know what is at stake,' the Colonel whispers. Even in the darkness I can see the angry glint of his icy eyes. 'We must succeed.'

'Why?' I say, stepping out of his grasp. 'Why the frag are we so Emperor-damned important? I don't believe your crap about us being the only ones who can do this.'

'There are currently those in the Inquisition who are working on a more drastic solution to the von Strab problem,' he says, the words quiet and clipped. 'We are to be the last attempt at a covert conclusion.'

I can tell where the Colonel is going with this. 'They want to destroy Acheron?'

Also by Gav Thorpe

• THE LAST CHANCERS •

13TH LEGION
KILL TEAM

• OTHER WARHAMMER 40,000 TITLES •

ANGELS OF DARKNESS – A Dark Angels novel

• WARHAMMER TITLES •

The Slaves to Darkness Trilogy
Book 1 – THE CLAWS OF CHAOS
Book 2 – THE BLADES OF CHAOS

A WARHAMMER 40,000 NOVEL

The Last Chancers

ANNIHILATION SQUAD

GAV THORPE

In memory of Steve Hambrook

A BLACK LIBRARY PUBLICATION

First published in Great Britain in 2004 by
BL Publishing,
Games Workshop Ltd.,
Willow Road, Nottingham,
NG7 2WS, UK

10 9 8 7 6 5 4 3 2 1

Cover illustration by Kenson Low.
Map by Stef Kopinski and Dan Drane.

A CIP record for this book is available from the British Library.

ISBN 1 84416 075 0

Distributed in the US by Simon & Schuster
1230 Avenue of the Americas, New York, NY 10020, US.

Printed and bound in Great Britain by
Cox & Wyman Ltd, Reading, Berkshire, UK.

See the Black Library on the Internet at
www.blacklibrary.com

Find out more about Games Workshop
and the world of Warhammer 40,000 at
www.games-workshop.com

IT IS THE 41st millennium. For more than a hundred centuries the Emperor has sat immobile on the Golden Throne of Earth. He is the master of mankind by the will of the gods, and master of a million worlds by the might of his inexhaustible armies. He is a rotting carcass writhing invisibly with power from the Dark Age of Technology. He is the Carrion Lord of the Imperium for whom a thousand souls are sacrificed every day, so that he may never truly die.

YET EVEN IN his deathless state, the Emperor continues his eternal vigilance. Mighty battlefleets cross the daemon-infested miasma of the warp, the only route between distant stars, their way lit by the Astronomican, the psychic manifestation of the Emperor's will. Vast armies give battle in his name on uncounted worlds. Greatest amongst his soldiers are the Adeptus Astartes, the Space Marines, bio-engineered super-warriors. Their comrades in arms are legion: the Imperial Guard and countless planetary defence forces, the ever-vigilant Inquisition and the tech-priests of the Adeptus Mechanicus to name only a few. But for all their multitudes, they are barely enough to hold off the ever-present threat from aliens, heretics, mutants – and worse.

TO BE A man in such times is to be one amongst untold billions. It is to live in the cruellest and most bloody regime imaginable. These are the tales of those times. Forget the power of technology and science, for so much has been forgotten, never to be re-learned. Forget the promise of progress and understanding, for in the grim dark future there is only war. There is no peace amongst the stars, only an eternity of carnage and slaughter, and the laughter of thirsting gods.

ANNIHILATION SQUAD

ARMAGEDDON SECUNDUS

0   250   500

KEY
1. Crash Site
2. Cerberus Base
3. Mouth of the Chaeron
4. Infernus Quay
5. Diabolus forge
6. Averneas forge
7. Acheron Hive

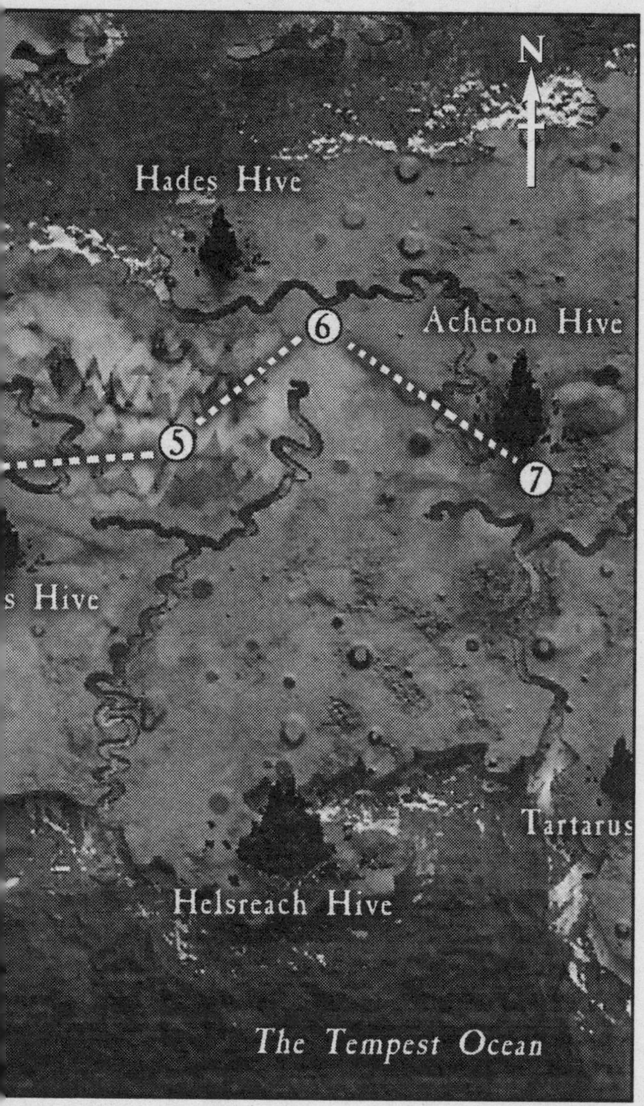
N
Hades Hive
6
Acheron Hive
5
7
s Hive
Tartarus
Helsreach Hive
The Tempest Ocean

IMMATERIUM

CHAPTER ONE
PUNISHMENT

THE IMMATERIUM. WARP *space. It is a seething mass of roiling emotive energies, a kaleidoscope of colours and textures that reflect mankind's passions and fears. Sharp red waves of anger crash against blue whirlpools of despondency and soft purple clouds of passion. It is scattered with flickering pinpricks of white, a firmament of souls, the spirits of the living that resemble tiny stars of energy: miniscule, fleeting and soon forgotten. Here and there, like a candle in an insane wilderness of crashing colours, burns the soul of a psyker. The turmoil feeds its fire, giving it strength.*

Through the tempest of feelings surges a ship, its harsh lines obscured by a miasma of fluctuating forces. Its Geller Field pushes back the burning energies of the warp. Its eagle-beaked prow tears through hope and despair, the stubby wing shapes of its launch bays cut across love and hate, leaving wispy trails of rage and disappointment.

Behind the ship drifts a shadow, an empty tide of nothingness that consumes the disturbed energies, and feeds upon them. The cloud is more than a shadow; it is a shoal of emptiness made from thousands of warp-entities – daemonic sharks of the Immaterium that prey upon the energy of mortals. They gather around the ship, flickers of protective power flash along its length as they attempt to break through. But they are flung back by the psychic shield.

The Geller Field brightens and dims under the assault of the daemonic creatures; its power waxes and wanes. Around the vortices of its warp engines, a brief tear opens, and the energy of Chaos seeps in, a lone shadow flitting through the momentary break in the warding fields.

It passes effortlessly through the steel hull of the ship, seeking a host. It can feel its life-force dripping away, leeched from its invisible, incorporeal form now that it is cut off from the sustenance of warp space. It slips into a wide, low chamber, its unreal eyes spying the sleeping forms of humans. They look like grey, flat silhouettes. Their life force is weak, lacking in nourishment. A freezing black hole engulfs one of the rough pallets and the daemon veers away, terrified of the shadow that could consume it.

It then detects warmth, a glow of power, from further up the chamber. Drawn instinctively towards the source of energy, it speeds up, flitting back and forth, basking in the heat. Coiling around itself, it luxuriates in the sensation before dissolving itself into the energy until its whole being is fully encompassed.

* * *

WARP-DREAMS

It's a dream. A nightmare, in fact. I can tell, because I know I went to sleep on my bunk as normal, wrapped in a thin grey blanket, and there's no other way I could have ended up plummeting down a chasm into a roaring inferno. But it's not really a nightmare, because I'm calm about the whole thing. I should have been terrified as I plunged down into the fiery depths, falling through smoke, my skin burning from my flesh, the flesh blowing away from my bones as ash.

It's a warp-dream, horribly real in every sensation, more lifelike than life itself. Everything is sharper, clearer, more bright and focussed. Through eyeballs that have long since exploded into steam, I can see the cracks and crannies of the chasm wall, and small red eyes peering back at me through the fumes. The wind that screams into my cindered ears is sharp and loud. The flames that lick up from below, bursting forth from a river of boiling magma, are searing hot.

So why is there no pain? Why am I not afraid?

I don't feel as if I'm dying, just changing. I was once a clumsy, pain-ridden, emotional husk of a body, but now I am unfettered by its restrictions and my soul is allowed to burst free. Wings erupt from my back, and suddenly I'm soaring on the thermals, swooping and diving amongst the rising flames.

I laugh, though there is no sound. I delight in the freedom, the ease of movement as I climb upwards through the smoke and then kick my legs back and dive headfirst towards the inferno. The heat washes over me like a soft caress; the blistering heat is like the warm touch of a lover awakening me.

It feels beautiful, and I feel beautiful to be experiencing it.

And then something shudders within me. Something casts me free in the same way that I freed my own body. It takes my wings with it and soars up out of sight, leaving me falling towards the flames.

The terror starts then. It wells up from the pit of my stomach and a scream is wrenched from my lips. My horror bursts forth in a wordless screech as the heat blisters my entire being. Unimaginable pain infuses me; every fibre of my soul suffers vibrant agony.

Perhaps this is damnation. Maybe this is the Abyssal Chaos that I am doomed to be thrown into once my mortal life is ended. To know joy, liberty, and then have it taken away as I am damned for my sins – that is true torture.

I WAKE WITH sweat coating my body. With a shuddering gasp, I take in a lungful of the warm, stale ship's air. I hate warp-dreams. This one has been plaguing me for several weeks, although it's the first time I've had the sensation of fear. Usually it ends with me soaring majestically out of the chasm and disappearing into a halo of pure light.

Reality crashes into my senses, and for a moment I feel a disassociation with everything around me. For a split second it feels like I'm watching it from behind my own eyes. And then everything feels normal again.

The bunk throbs with the vibrations that come from the ship's deck. The air is filled with a steady humming from the machinery that keeps us alive in this hostile environment. The snores and heavy breathing of the other Last Chancers accompanies the relentless droning of the ship's systems, and I sit up and listen, trying to detect some oddity, some change in the eternal harmony that would have woken me. It all sounds normal though. I thought perhaps we might have dropped from warp, after all we must be somewhere near our destination.

We've been travelling for nearly a year now. A single, long, virtually impossible warp jump. I've never heard of such a thing before, I didn't even know it was possible. Usually a ship will jump into warp space for a short time, and then jump back into the real galaxy a week, or perhaps a month later. Ships that jump further get lost, or are destroyed. I've heard tales of ships that got caught in warp storms, only to emerge five hundred years later, their crews aged by just a few months. And I've also heard of ships that have disappeared for only a week or two, and are then found drifting, the crew nothing but ashes, the ships' logs showing that they died of old age.

Given a choice, I'd rather not travel in the warp. The strange dreams aside, it has got to be one of the most dangerous things a man can do.

But I don't have the choice, do I? I'm a soldier in the Last Chancers. Known as the 13th Penal Legion to everyone else. We're all here because we deserve to be. Each one of the thirty people sharing this chamber with me is being punished for their crimes. I murdered my sergeant because of a woman. Topasz, who lies to my left, is a thief who stole from the officers' mess of her regiment. Keiger, the bearded man to my right, hung his own squad for supposed insubordination. Looters, heretics, mass-murderers, rapists, thieves and all the other scum of the Imperial Guard end up here, doomed to spend their short lives fighting to their grisly deaths in battle.

Well, most of them are. We're different. We're Last Chancers. Our commander, the ice-hard Colonel Schaeffer, has other plans for us. We've got one mission, and that's it. It'll be tantamount to suicide, mark my words, and there are some here who'll wish that they'd chosen the firing squad or hangman's company before we see the thing through. Death is almost as certain this way as it is on the executioner's list.

But we're here because we're too good to waste. We're prime meat for the grinder that is the Emperor's wars. We're specialists, survivors, experts in our fields, and that means the Colonel has chosen to give us our Last Chance. If we finish the mission, we're free to go. Pardoned of all crimes, our souls absolved of our sins so that we might once again be part of the glorious Imperium of the Immortal Emperor of Terra.

Except me, of course. Even amongst these miscreants and frag-headed stains on humanity, I'm even more special.

I'm the Last Chancer who never got away. I'm too stubborn to die, but too mean to stay out of trouble. I'm useful for the Colonel to have around, for sure, and though I used to make his life hell and cause him no end of trouble, I've kind of got over that now. I'm just like the lifers in the other penal legions, except that by following the Colonel I'll see more fighting, more danger and more ways to end up dead than any long-serving veteran in other regiments. I had my Last Chance and I blew it. Now I have to live with it.

The lights flicker on to show that it's now morning, ship time. Obviously it's all artificial, and I swear the Colonel makes the days longer and longer so that we have to work harder. I know I did when he entrusted me with training the last squad. That didn't go so well in the end, and so although I'm still Lieutenant Kage, the rank is now more honorary than it ever was.

The others begin to wake. The chamber is filled with groaning, yawning, stretching and farting. Another day begins.

OUR DAYS START with the slop-spilling contest that passes for breakfast, and a compulsory punch-up between Kein and Glaberand over the seat nearest to the heaters. On the way out I count the cutlery, including the spoons, to make sure nobody's smuggled out anything that could be used as a weapon. It's bad enough that we give them guns to train with. Who knows what they'd do if they were let loose with a fork.

After we've all completed the cautious obstacle course that is a spin around the ablutionary block, it's back to the bunkrooms to see who's stolen what last night. Topasz has managed to acquire half a field rations pack – which nobody owns up to owning since we're not supposed to have any yet – a spare heel from a boot, two decks of playing cards and a small ball of string. After a year, everyone sleeps with their meagre valuables – the odd brooch, chain or ring – on their person or under their pillow. During the theft inspection, Goran and Venksin get into a fight, and Goran wins hands down because he's a big brute of a man. I send Venksin down to the med-bay to see if it's worth getting his ear stitched back on.

After this, and the odd argument, scuffle or back-biting comment, I lead the platoon down to the small stores room to gear up for training. Two commissariat provosts, even meaner and leaner than Navy arms men, guard the door to the armoury. They eye us through the black-tinted visors of their helms, shotguns held across the carapace armour on their chests. Anyone would think we were a bunch of criminals that might try and take over the ship. Nobody's had that idea since Walken got his head blown off by these two about six months ago. I give them a wave. No reaction.

Behind his worn counter sits Erasmus. His bespectacled eyes peer at us across his stores ledger, his quill-skull hovers over his left shoulder. He's not the fattest man I've seen, but there's a definite softness to him, like butter that's been left out too long and is starting to melt. His small, fidgety hands play with the corners of the ledger. I notice that his nails are caked in grease, and his fingertips smeared with red ink. He smiles at me as I walk in.

'Lieutenant Kage, how are you?' he says in his thin, stammering voice. 'Wh-what'll it be today? Close quarters? Knives and bayonets? Or perhaps rifle drill? Or maybe heavy weapons training? I still have that Phassis-pattern grenade launcher for you to try out, but you're not interested in that, are you?'

Erasmus, or Munitorum Armourer-scribe Spooge as he is known officially, has a way of making every sentence a question. I have no idea how he does it, or if he's even aware of it, but it's impossible for him just to make a statement.

'Grenades and demolitions, dummies only,' I tell him and his smile turns to a pout.

'Dummies?' he says. 'No live charges? How will your men learn if they use decoys and dummies all the time? I mean, I know there was that poor business with Morgan the other week, but do you think the others will stop being so sloppy if they're using dummies?'

The 'poor business' he's referring to was the premature detonation of a faulty grenade Erasmus had supplied. Stephan Morgan, a first class soldier as far as I could tell, excepting his predilection for finding alcohol everywhere and anywhere and being drunk on watch, was blown into so many pieces it took four servitors to clean up the mess. I've got another scar on my ripped up face as a memorial to his bloody death. The only other thing that marks the occasion is a small entry into the ledger. I can't read much, but knowing the Departmento Munitorium, it probably says something like, 'Grenade, fragmentation Mk32, faulty, item unavailable for inspection.'

'Dummy charges and fake grenades,' I tell him again. He looks at me and nods, before whispering something to the quill-skull. It hovers over his shoulder, the polished bone gleaming in the yellow light of the storeroom, and a dripping pen extends from its whirring innards. The scuttlebutt maintains that the skull is actually from Spooge's father, who died in service to the Departmento, and Erasmus inherited the position. Along with his father's skull, of course, now refitted as an auto-scribe. At Erasmus's promptings, it scribbles squarely across the ledger, leaving dribbling blots as it goes. Little wisps of smoke bubble from its machinery-filled eyes. When it's finished, Erasmus gives it an affectionate pat. It returns to its position, hovering just above the armourer-scribe's shoulder.

'Please wait while your munitions are being prepared, if you don't mind?' says Spooge.

One of the provosts opens the armoury door and I see a servitor tottering away between the racks on six skeletal, artificial legs. Its arms have been replaced with a lifting hoist. Scraping and clanking, it works its way along the shelves, picking out crates and canisters. It loads them onto the flatbed back of another servitor, doubled up under a heavy plate. There are tracks where its legs were that grind across the grated floor. Its withered arms are bound across sagging breasts, life support tubes have been driven into its ribcage. The monotonous hissing of artificial lungs reverberates through the air. Drool hangs from its slack lips. The servitor's blank eyes look straight through us as it trundles out of the door, coming to a halt just in front of me.

'Load up,' I tell the squad, trying not to wonder who the servitor was before she was changed, or what affront against the Machine God she had committed to earn the wrath of the tech-priests.

Geared up, we make our way back along the ship, passing through humid, pipe-filled corridors above the engine rooms to the training deck. It was a loading bay once, but as it is the largest space on the cramped ship, it was turned to a more useful purpose. Seventy-five metres long and twenty-five metres wide, it's just about big enough to be a firing range, as well as a drill square. We ripped out most of the cranes and other machinery to make more space, dumping them before we jumped into warp space. With the help of the tech-priests we kept a couple rigged up for moving heavier objects around. They're useful for days like today.

'Get the tank ready,' I say, and the squad falls out to their assignments. A year in the warp, and drill every single day, they must have done this fifty times already. Still, no soldier is happy unless there's someone shouting at them, so the three sergeants, Blurse, Candlerick and Fiakir oblige, haranguing them for being slow and sloppy as they trot down to the far end of the chamber.

The 'tank' was devised by the Colonel. Made from welded-together packing crates and bits of old machinery, it's a blocky, square replica of a real tank, complete with turret and a gun made from old cable pipe. We moved a set of rails, which had previously run into one of the side chambers, so that they stretch for three-quarters the length of the training hall. Pulled along the rails by a loading winch, the tank can actually pick up a good speed for about twenty metres. We also have a dummy aeroplane, made of wood, thirty metres up in the overhanging gantries, which we can use to simulate an enemy strafing run.

The air in the chamber is sweaty and thick with grease as the platoon gets to work; hoisting the tank onto the rails and hitching up the winch. Almost half of the air filters on the ship have now broken down, and the air is becoming so stale it's difficult to breathe. Schaeffer, typically, sees it as part of the training. 'Good for working at altitude,' he says. I don't mind it at all; in fact it's almost welcoming. It reminds me of the rank atmosphere of the hive factories from my home on Olympas. I grew up breathing oil and stinking of sweat.

With the tank rigged up to go, the platoon falls in again. They stand to attention, to varying degrees, as I walk along the length of the lines.

'Squad one, fall out for tank operation,' I order, stepping out in front of them. 'Squad two, demolitions detail, escarpment setting.'

The two nominated squads run to their positions, while the third strolls over to the wall to watch the proceedings. On the mesh floor, we've painted outlines of different terrains – in red there is a three-way junction in an urban area, in green a clearing in a forest, and in yellow a defile through a mountain valley. All perfect sites for infantry to ambush a tank.

Sergeant Candlerick stands by the winch, looking at me for the command, while Sergeant Blurse details his squad for the mock attack, positioning them behind the outlines of rocks and in small crevasses in the 'valley' walls. I like Blurse, he's a barrel-chested man with a thick moustache, and very much a traditionalist. I cause him a few problems though, because in his experience the Imperial Guard is run by NCOs like himself, while the officers are just around to make sure everything looks nice. In his regiment, the 38th Cordorian Light Infantry, he was used to the officers just giving him the nod and expecting him to sort everything out. Then he had to go too far, and anticipate the orders of his captain one time too many, leading an attack against a traitor camp. It would have been good if the captain had not already ordered an artillery strike a few minutes later, so that half of Blurse's platoon was blown apart by their own gunners' shells. Blurse was thrown in the brig. He carries a shrapnel scar across his chin. Despite that, he still retains an ingrained respect for the officer class. I simply don't fit into that mould. I'm vicious, dirty, cunning and I know exactly what I'm talking about. I've been in the Last Chancers for five years now.

I'm perfect sergeant material as far as he's concerned, but the lieutenant's cap confuses him.

I give the signal and the winch grinds into life with a throaty growl, hauling the tank forward. Candlerick ups the gear and the tank lumbers forward quicker as it enters the 'defile' of the ambush site. Blurse gives a nod to his demo man, who rolls out in front of the tank with the dummy charge clasped against his chest. He waits for it to pass over. The magnetic charge clings to the underside of the tank as it continues, and I count for a five-second timer.

'Detonation!' I bellow and Candlerick kills the winch, bringing the tank to a halt. Within a second, the assault squad are out of their hiding places, leaping onto the immobilised tank. They tear open mock hatches and drop their fake grenades into the interior before jumping clear again.

'Emperor's teeth, what do you call that?' I shout at the squad as I stride down the hall towards them, stepping over the winch chain to march up to Blurse. 'Fall them in, sergeant!'

Blurse shouts them into line, and the ten of them stand there, looking straight ahead, avoiding my gaze. I can feel the smirks of the other two squads behind me. The bearable thing about being bawled out by an officer is watching it happen to someone else. Not me though. I turn to Fiakir's squad, lounging by the wall.

'Trooper Cardinal, what did squad two do wrong?' I ask. The man looks at me as if caught in a sniper scope; his thin smile turns to a look of horror, and sweat beads in his thinning hair.

'Sir?' he says, glancing left and right, seeking inspiration.

'Surely you realised that Trooper Dunmore exposed himself too early,' I say, referring to the Guardsman who had placed the charge.

'Yes, sir!' replies Cardinal, licking his lips nervously. 'The driver would have seen him and been able to take action, sir.'

'Don't lie to me, Cardinal!' I rage, storming back up the chamber towards him. 'Trooper Dunmore timed his attack perfectly. Suspended rations for you today, Trooper Cardinal. The rest of the squad piled in too soon. What did they forget, Fleschen?'

'I do not know, sir!' snaps the burly corporal, staring blankly ahead.

'Stupid, fat…' someone starts to mutter, but he or she falls silent as I pass my gaze along the line.

'That's a tank, in the Emperor's name, containing an engine and shells,' I say, and I see realisation dawn on the corporal.

'Secondary explosions, sir,' the corporal says. 'Squad two failed to wait and see if the charge set anything else off, sir.'

'That's right,' I say, turning and waving a finger to Blurse. 'Squad one on the winch, squad three ambushing in a town. Sergeant Fiakir, I want Trooper Cardinal on the demo charge, seeing as he's such an expert.'

AFTER FOUR MORE hours of training with the dummy tank, during which I suspend rations for another three of the platoon because they got into a fight with each other, we return the dummy charges and grenades and then retire back to the ablutions chamber to clean up for lunch. Responsibility for cooking is shared between the three squads, with Blurse's unit on food detail today. Not that it takes much, opening packets of dried rations, boiling them in water that's been reclaimed Emperor knows how many times in the last year.

I elbow my way into a space on the cramped bench with Candlerick's squad, who are tucking into the reconstituted slop with little vigour. I spoon the gruel in without ceremony, noting that it tastes of salt and not much else. The corporal, Festal Kin-Drugg, catches my eye and I give him the nod to speak.

'I can't see how this anti-tank training will be much use, sir,' he says, waving his spoon around.

'How so?' I ask.

'Infantry support,' Festal says, putting the spoon down. 'No tank commander's going to roll into a town or forest without infantry. We would never go in with just a tank.'

I look at him for a moment, and then at the rest of the squad.

'You were a drop trooper, right?' I say and he nods. He was one of the elite first company of the 33rd Kator Gravchute Regiment, in fact. He led an unauthorised landing to loot a town behind enemy lines, after it had been abandoned in advance of an ork attack. 'Used to operating behind the lines, then?'

'Yes, I'm trained as a pathfinder,' he says with a shrug. 'What of it?'

'So you're trained in sabotage, guerrilla activity and the like, then?' I ask, and he nods again. 'What do you think we're going to be doing?'

'I don't know,' Festal says with a shake of his head. 'The Colonel hasn't breathed a word about our mission.'

'That's right,' I say, finishing off the gruel and dropping the spoon into the bowl with a clatter. 'I don't know what we're up to either, but I'd bet my life it's something secretive. Not on the frontline, where tanks and infantry move together, but behind them, on tracks and roads, waylaying convoys and such.'

'You can't know that for sure,' says Gurter, another member of the squad. 'From what you've told us, we could be doing anything. For all we know, we could be on mine clearance or something.'

'Don't talk nonsense,' says Candlerick, slapping a meaty hand on the table. 'I'm not as sharp as some here, but I know that you don't ship thirty men across the stars like this just to clear a minefield! From what Lieutenant Kage has said, we'll be up to our necks in it, and no mistaking.'

'Have you not had anything from the Colonel, no hints at all, no mention of any particular type of training?' says Festal, leaning forward to talk quietly. I lean forward and whisper in his ear.

'Nothing,' I say, sitting back. He gives me a scowl and I smile at him. 'When the Colonel wants us to know where we're going, and why we're in such a hurry, he'll tell us. I've learned not to worry about it too much. It's all the same. One way or another, we're going to be up to out necks in cack and blood, and before it's over most of us'll be dead.'

They look at me for a long moment.

'What?' I say. 'Haven't you been listening to me? You're in the Last Chancers now, and when all's said and done, we don't have much of a chance.'

'There've been survivors,' says Gurter, glancing to the table to the left where Lorii is sitting with Blurse's squad. 'We might get through this. How long have you been following the Colonel, eh?'

I follow his gaze and then look back at him, resting my elbows on the table. I steeple my fingers against my chin.

'The difference being, Trooper Gurter, is that I'm invincible,' I say. 'What have you got going for you?'

He frowns and says nothing, turning his attention to the last few scraps of gruel in his bowl. The others glance at me as I stand up and step over the bench.

'Inspection in one hour,' I remind them. 'Full kit for the Colonel, right?'

They nod and mutter as I turn away. As I walk out into the central corridor, and turn left towards the wardroom where the Colonel's made his lair, I feel a twinge of pain in the back of my head. Knowing what's coming, I quickly make my way to the ablutions chambers, closing myself in one of the small cubicles there.

The pain extends forward, growing in intensity as it reaches my eyes. It feels like my brain is on fire. The off-white walls start to blur and dance in front of me, like pale flames. My ears are filled with the thunderous beating of my heart. I fall to my knees, my senses flaring with agony, and retch into the toilet bowl.

The roar of my heart turns into a drumbeat, before rising in volume to become like the deafening pounding of an artillery barrage in my ears. I go blind for a moment. Everything turns white. I find myself back on Typhus Prime, just outside Coritanorum. The ground is erupting around me from the orbital bombardment that paved our way into the rebel citadel. After a few seconds, I realise I'm no longer on the muddy fields of Typhus Prime, but in a grey desert, and the explosions are from bombs being dropped around me.

My whole body shudders. Part of me knows it isn't real, but my senses tell me that it's happening right now. The hallucination starts to fade, and I vomit the gruel over the floor and collapse sideways, slumping against the cubicle wall. A moment before my sight returns to normal, I see and hear something indescribable. It's a mess of confusing colours, clashing with each other amid a torrent of high-pitched screams.

I sit there for a few minutes, panting heavily. The pain subsides to a dull throb. It's happening more regularly, and it scares the hell out of me. In fact, I'm terrified of what the truth might be. The warp-dreams, Inquisitor Oriel's hints during the Brightsword assassination, the moments of instinct in combat when I seem to know what's going to happen a couple of seconds before it does. I have to face the awful fact.

I think I'm a psyker.

CHAPTER TWO
IRON DISCIPLINE

WHAT MAKES IT worse is that Oriel knows, and maybe the Colonel too. I can't understand why the Inquisitor has let me be, I always thought that rounding up untrained psykers like me was their reason for being. I don't know what worries me more: the thought that I might get turned in to the Inquisition for being a witch, or the idea that for some reason Oriel and Schaeffer are using me for something else. There's no way I can let the rest of the platoon find out. If they didn't kill me themselves, they'd be sure to make the Colonel take action. The problem is, with these seizures striking me more often, it's only a matter of time before the truth comes out.

Or perhaps I'm just going mad.

It's entirely possible, I suppose, given what I've been through. I instinctively touch the scar on the side of my head, a reminder of the operation I had. Some bastard drilled into my skull to release a dangerous build up of 'vapours', then dug around in my brain with a knife for good measure. I'm no medico, but surely messing around with someone's head like that can't be good for them? But the hallucinations had started before then, so who in hell knows what's happening up there.

Suitably calmed, I stand up and straighten my uniform. Opening the cubicle door, I glance around and find that the others are still in the mess. It's only been a minute, probably less, since the attack began. I open the storage cupboard and quickly mop up the floor before tidying everything away and leaving the ablutions chamber.

Just as I'm walking past the mess on my way to the Colonel's office to give my daily report, the others begin to file out on their way to the bunkroom. They've got an hour to prepare for the Colonel's inspection, and they're certainly good enough to be ready in half that, earning themselves a bit of leisure time. Lorii is one of the last to leave and looks at me questioningly.

'Are you alright, Kage?' she asks. 'You're looking pale.'

I laugh, perhaps slightly too hard. The thing is, Lorii is about as pale as you can get. Her skin is absolutely white, as is her short, cropped hair. Her pale blue eyes look into mine for a second, and I meet her stony gaze.

'Sorry,' I say glancing away for a heartbeat.

She doesn't say anything, but just stands there looking at me in that cool manner she has. Then she turns away and walks off without another word. I watch her. Any other man might have admired the swing of her hips, but I remember her gouging out the eye of a man who touched her, and so I can safely say I've got no interest in any kind of bunkroom tricks.

It was odd, meeting her again when I came on board. I thought she had been dead for the previous two years. The last time I had seen her before then, she had run off after her brother who had gotten his brains blown out while we were in Coritanorum. I'd heard gunfire and assumed she had died too. Turns out that Inquisitor Oriel, another person to have arisen like a ghost from the ashes of Coritanorum, had brought her out safely. She had worked for Oriel as a go-between for him and the Imperial Guard during the set-up for the Brightsword mission, and after talking to her, she confirmed that I really had seen her coming down the assault ramp of a lander after we'd killed the tau renegade.

Apparently, according to the Colonel, she requested to rejoin the Last Chancers. I think she has a death wish, perhaps because she lost Loron. Whatever it is, she's got a haunted look about her, and I haven't seen her smile once in the last year. She performs well in training, excellently in fact, but she's dead inside. I can tell from her eyes.

I felt a strange relief to find that another Last Chancer managed to get out of Coritanorum. It had been troubling me as to why I had survived when the rest of the team had ended up dead. I got over it of course, but, seeing her, I felt comforted that someone else was still alive who knew what we had done. Someone else knows about the three million men, women and children we killed. Someone else understands just what it is that the Last Chancers do, and why we have to do it.

I remember trying to explain it to the last squad, about how a soldier has to act, and learn to kill without thought or remorse. This time I haven't bothered to try. They'll either figure it out, or they'll die. Either way, I'm not thinking of them as my soldiers anymore. That was my mistake last time – thinking that the squad was mine. They never were; we're all the Colonel's meat for the grinder, and he doesn't think twice about any of us – not even me.

THE COLONEL LOOKS at me from behind his desk. His ice-shard eyes bore into me as I give my daily report. As usual, he's in his dress uniform, braids and everything. He sits erect in the high-backed chair, arms folded across his broad chest.

'And how about discipline, Kage?' he asks.

'Goran broke Topasz's nose last night for stealing his bootlaces,' I say, staring over the Colonel's left shoulder.

'His bootlaces?' asks the Colonel, leaning forward and resting his hands neatly on the desk.

'Topasz can't help herself,' I explain. 'Even when they've got nothing except their uniforms, she can't stop herself from taking something. And Goran is a bully, sir, through and through. He knows he's bigger than she is, all he had to do was ask for them back, but he asks with his fists.'

I meet Schaeffer's gaze. He's still staring at me intently.

'Nearly a year with them, and you cannot stop them stealing from each other, or fighting?' he says.

'Well, sir, if you had given me a stormtrooper regiment, I guess they'd be happy and smiling,' I say. 'As it is, they're the dregs of your gulag, and some of them won't be changed.'

'But every single day?' says the Colonel, showing his frustration. 'Five have been killed while they sleep; two in stand-up fights, and twice that number have spent a month or more in the apothecarium. It simply is not good enough, Kage.'

'They're stuck on the ship, in the middle of warp space, with absolutely nothing,' I say, trying to keep my voice even. 'Even if they weren't criminals, they would be slitting each other's throats or their own after all this time. There's nothing I can do about Topasz, short of cutting off her hands.'

'But you can deal with Goran,' says the Colonel, still staring straight at me.

His expression hasn't changed a bit, not outwardly, but his meaning is suddenly very clear.

'I've tried everything in the regulations detailed for the type of infractions committed, sir,' I say.

His stare doesn't waver for a second.

'Yes, sir,' I say with a vicious smile. 'Yes, I can deal with Goran, with your permission.'

'You have my full permission, Kage, to deal with the situation as you see fit,' the Colonel says, motioning me to leave with a flick of his head. 'I want to see a sharp improvement in discipline.'

I snap to attention and bring up the smartest salute I've done in a long time. I spin on my heel and march to the door.

'One thing, Kage,' says the Colonel, and I turn back. 'Bear in mind that the infirmary is not very well equipped, and the platoon is already at minimum strength after the incident with Morgan.'

'I'll bear that in mind, sir,' I say with a nod before opening the door and stepping out. As I turn and close the door, I catch a glimpse of the Colonel leaning the chair onto its back legs, a satisfied smile on his face.

IT'S TWO MORE days before Goran steps out of line again and gives me the opportunity to do what I've been wanting to do for the past six months. It's evening meal, and his squad, under Sergeant Candlerick, is up on dinner duty. He short-rations Brownie Dunmore's dish, and the heavy weapons man starts to complain. Although it's slush, it's the only thing we have, so I can see Brownie's point. Don't ask me why they call him Brownie, his real name is Brin. I should ask him sometime.

Anyway, things get a little heated over the counter, and Brownie ends up slapping his dish at Goran. Goran's a big guy, nearly a head taller than me. He looms over Brownie and takes a swing with his heavy ladle, smacking Brownie straight across the face. As Goran leaps over the counter, scattering pans and dishes everywhere, I make my move. I ghost up next to Dunmore, nobody noticing me.

Brownie's not seriously hurt, he's just smarting. Goran swings the ladle back for another attack. Goran, who once battered one of his squad mates to death over a game of cards, knows how to use his size well.

So do I.

Stepping forward, I drive the extended fingers of my right hand into Goran's windpipe, and he drops the ladle and clutches both hands to his throat. I drive my right boot into the side of his abdomen, low enough not to crack any ribs, winding him. My left hook catches him above the right eye. I don't break his jaw or nose, but the blow opens up a cut that bleeds down his face. Roaring, he takes a swing at me, which I duck. Then I turn the move into a leg sweep that crashes into the back of his right knee, sending him tumbling.

I let him get up and take a couple of swings at me. His face is contorted with anger. He's fast as well as big, and I have to stay on my toes, swaying back out of his long reach. Then I step inside his guard to hammer my right fist square onto his chin, driving his jawbone up into his face and stunning him. He swings another right at me, sluggishly this time, and I trap his wrist in my hands and twist. Pulling him towards me, I drive my left boot into his armpit and his shoulder pops like a cork.

A short strike to the back of his neck knocks him face down onto the metal decking. He lies there groaning, clutching his dislocated shoulder.

'Fix him up,' I say to Keiger, who's proved the most adept at blood work. 'Sergeant Candlerick, you will excuse Trooper Goran from heavy duties for the next two days.'

The platoon looks at me with a mixture of awe, shock and joy.

'It's time you all started acting like soldiers, not a pack of wild dogs,' I tell them, walking to the door. I pull out my small book of regs and tear it in half. I can't read it anyway; I always have to ask Lorii to find things for me. 'I'm the top dog, and anyone who steps out of line from now on answers to me. You were convicted under Imperial law, but now you're under Kage law, understand?'

They reply in murmurs, most of them are looking at the floor, avoiding my gaze.

'I'll think you'll find a sling in the infirmary,' I say to Keiger as I march smartly out of the room to the Colonel's office.

NEEDLESS TO SAY, the platoon is on its best behaviour for the next few days. Topasz manages not to steal anything, Goran gives me as wide a berth as possible, and I suspect that even Jueqna has stopped spitting in the gruel when he's on food detail.

Riding the mood, I give them solid drill for the next two days, marching them up and down the training chamber, and getting the sergeants to bellow out the orders. I never liked square-bashing myself when I was a trooper, but now I realise it's one of the best ways to show who's in charge. I say a word, a sergeant shouts a command, and they do whatever they've been told to do. In battle, unquestioning obedience is essential for survival. No pondering the rights and wrongs, no wondering whether I'm right. They do what they're told, because I'm in charge.

I exhaust them for the two days, drilling them until the sergeants are hoarse. I give them the next day as rest. Of course, with only half of them being able to bunk at any one time, they have to find their own diversions.

A lot of them sit in the mess, swapping stories. I remember doing that: telling the same old tales to the same people again and again, and listening to the same old tales from the same old people as if I'd never heard them. I listen to it all. I hear where they're from, what they did before joining up, their first love, their first battle, the wound that still gives them trouble whenever it's cold and wet. All of it is the same. I've met a lot of soldiers in my time, but underneath the skin, the uniform, they're all pretty much the same. Even these wretches.

In fact, I've come to believe that the Last Chancers are probably the ideal soldiers. I can understand why the Colonel finds us so useful. Every man or woman who joins the Imperial Guard knows that they can never go home. They are shipped for months to a war on a world they've probably never heard of. They might carry the memories of their home world and their family, but the reality is that they will never see either again. A regiment that serves well, does its time, fights its campaign, is often allowed to retire with honours. Some make their home where they have fought; others join an explorator fleet and conquer a new planet in the name of Holy Terra and the Emperor. Those are the ones that survive, of course.

Us Last Chancers get to live if we do well. It's as plain and simple as that. If we do poorly we'll die in battle, and that's the chance that every soldier takes. Our regiments aren't even our homes any more. I have no idea where the Olympas 24th Lifeguard is now. They might still be garrisoning that backwater hole called Stygies where I ran foul of my sergeant, causing me to be where I am now. Perhaps Stygies was invaded, perhaps not. Frankly, I don't give a damn.

All they have left is the Last Chancers, and the Colonel. No family, no friends, no home. Just comrades who would steal their teeth for a meal, or slice out their guts to look at the pretty colours. But they're the only comrades they've got, and so they tell stories.

The stories the Last Chancers tell always have a final chapter. It always ends with what they did wrong, and how they ended up with the Colonel. Take Brin Dunmore, for instance. His sin was pride. He's a top heavy weapons expert, trained as part of an engineer corps from Stralia. From heavy stubbers to lascannons and mortars, he can use them all. Problem is, he had to prove just how good he was. He took a bet that he couldn't use an anti-tank missile to shoot down an airplane. He proved he could, but unfortunately the plane he shot was an Imperial Interceptor returning from a sortie. They threw him in the lock house faster than the plane came down. I really should find out why he's called Brownie.

My musings are interrupted when klaxons begin to sound, reverberating off the metal walls. I leap to my feet and head out of the door towards the wardroom. The Colonel meets me halfway, his eyes dangerously narrowed.

'Send the platoon to the armoury,' he snaps. 'Meet me on the upper deck.'

I don't ask questions; I just turn and shout at the squad to move out to the armoury. I follow them down the spiral staircase to the deck below. Erasmus already has the doors open and is handing out lasguns and shotguns. I notice that the provosts are nowhere to be seen.

'Gear up, Last Chancers!' I shout, snatching a shotgun and a belt of shells from the back of the storeroom servitor. 'Time to die!'

I REACH THE upper deck at the head of the platoon and hear shots roaring out and ringing off the walls. We're halfway along the central access corridor that runs the length of the ship; it is about three hundred metres long. A few provosts stand at the far end, firing through the doors into the chamber beyond. There's a bright red flash and one of them comes flying backwards, trailing smoking innards. He crashes some twenty metres in front of us, screaming his head off.

'Keiger!' I snap, dashing past the stricken commissariat trooper.

The Colonel emerges from a side chamber just before I reach the double doors at the end. With him is Vandikar Kelth, one of the ship's Navigators. He's tall and thin, with the distinctive bulbous skull of a Navigator. He wears a silk scarf tied tightly across his forehead. He swishes past me in a skin-tight green suit under a white robe, and looks down the corridor.

'What's happening, sir?' I ask over the shouts of the provosts and the cannonade of their shotguns.

'It is Forlang,' says Kelth, turning back to me. He is referring to the other surviving Navigator. The third that started with us, Bujurn Adelph, went crazy and threw himself out of an airlock six months into the journey.

'Gone mad?' I ask, glancing at the Colonel.

'Worse,' Schaeffer replies.

Out of the corner of my eye, I catch a glimpse inside the far chamber, which is the landing that leads up to the tower where the Navigators stay, doing whatever it is that they do to steer a ship through warp space. There are two provosts on the ground, lying in a crumpled heap, blood leaking from their visored helmets. Three of the ship's crew are on the ground next to them, one of them a smouldering burnt husk, the other two missing limbs. I see Forlang standing at the foot of the steps. He's naked, except for a few tatters of bloodied white robes that hang from bony pro-trusions jutting from his flesh. His fingers have fused into long claws; there are scraps of flesh hanging from their tips.

A provost steps into the breech and fires his shotgun, obscuring my view. A moment later the sound of lots of bones snapping at the same time echoes down the hall and the provost collapses, crumpling in on himself.

'Possessed?' I say, horrified, turning to Kelth. 'How?'

'Take it down,' the Colonel says, ignoring my question.

'Squad one with me!' I shout, running down the corridor. 'Squad two, covering fire. Squad three, ready for reserve or rearguard.'

I hear Kelth shouting something after me, but I don't register what he says until I've burst into the room, the shotgun booming in my grasp.

'Don't look into his eye!' the Navigator warns.

'Don't what?' I ask, instinctively looking at the possessed Navigator's face.

His mouth is open in a grin; blood is streaming from toothless gums. His eyes are deep red, the colour of fresh blood. It's then I realised what Kelth had said. I always wondered what it was that navigators kept hidden under their scarves or bandanas. Now I know, and I wish I didn't. In the middle of Forlang's forehead is a swirling vortex, about the size of a normal eye, but it extends forever and into impossible depths.

To my right, Topasz screams. The sound echoes shrilly off the walls. There's the sound of a lasblast and parts of bloody matter spatter across my face and arm as she blows her own brains out. Just in front of me, Goran falls to his knees as Forlang turns towards him.

A blast of rippling energy leaps out of the possessed Navigator's third eye, enveloping Goran's chest. His ribs splay outwards, tearing through the skin and flinging ruptured organs across the floor.

Forlang turns his eye on me.

I look straight at it, into that swirling maelstrom. I feel a hot wind on my face, and hear the sound of crackling flames close by. The vortex turns red. Steam drifts out of the impossible orb.

I look away and bring up the shotgun. Forlang's face is twisted in a contortion of rage, which is replaced by a look of abject terror as I stare back at him.

'The fires await!' he screams at me, his voice unnaturally cracked and high-pitched. 'Damnation will burn your soul!'

I pull the shotgun trigger and the shell takes Forlang square in the chest, knocking him to the ground. He gets to one knee and looks up at me.

'It is not only the angel that ascends on wings!' he shrieks.

'Shut up!' I snarl, hoping that the others think he's raving.

I pump another round into the chamber and advance, shooting him in the chest again. Bone and muscle fly into the air, but still he's shouting at me. Three more shells, the last into his face, stop him moving. He's still not dead, though. I don't know how I can tell, perhaps just instinct, perhaps something more sinister.

The Colonel appears next to me, bolt pistol in hand, followed swiftly by Kelth, who sweeps past and runs up the steps into the Navigator's pilaster. He returns quickly with a black hood, which he pulls over the pulped remains of Forlang's head.

'He's not dead,' I say, and Forlang looks over his shoulder at me, his dark eyes glittering.

'Yes he is,' he says, standing up and taking a step towards us. 'But the thing still dwells in the carcass.'

'How do we destroy it?' the Colonel asks.

'We cannot, not here,' says the Navigator. 'I have a… a chamber, a special cell. I can keep it there until we jump back to the materium.'

'Do you need any assistance?' the Colonel asks, stepping towards the twitching corpse.

'No!' snaps Kelth, stepping in front of the Colonel and barring his way. 'I will deal with this, do not interfere.' The Colonel looks as if he's going to argue and then turns away.

'Notify me when you are done and I'll have the bodies cleared away,' Schaeffer says, looking at me as he walks out of the room.

'Clear out, platoon,' I say. 'Last squad ready for roll call is on gristle duty!'

CONVOY

CHAPTER THREE
UNHAPPY ARRIVAL

MORE THAN EVER, it's a blessed relief to jump out of warp space. Warp travel is the most dangerous thing a man can do, so I give an even longer prayer than usual to the Emperor for delivering me safe and sound into real space. We still have no idea where we are, and the Colonel's not forthcoming.

For another eight days we travel in-system, before the Colonel tells us to turn out for disembarking. We assemble in the docking bay, eager to find out where we are.

When the doors open, we walk across the threshold into a spacious airlock, and the ship's boarding gates close up behind us. The air that comes in is fresh and chill, a welcome relief for the others. After a long wait, the inner doors open and the Colonel leads us in. Waiting for us is a commissar, peaked cap low over his eyes, a data-slate in one hand. He talks quietly with the Colonel for a moment, before turning and walking down the corridor. We trail after him, exchanging questioning glances.

We're aboard an orbiting station of some sort, that's for certain. The corridors are of dull, unpolished metal, and here and there are signs of fighting, with blast and burn marks on the floor, walls and ceiling. There are old bloodstains in the grain of the floor, though everything else is polished clean. Some of the corridors are crudely barricaded, and the occasional blast door dropped across our path means that the commissar often has to take us on long loops around the blockages to get where we're going.

'Hull integrity breaches,' the commissar explains when he sees us looking at the blocked gangways.

I exchange knowing glances with the other members of the platoon, and we swap raised eyebrows and shrugs. It's no surprise really; we were expecting a war zone after all. Judging by the time it took us to get here after dropping from warp space, this is near the outer edge of the system – wherever that is.

I see jury-rigged generators attached to cabling that spills from broken ceiling tiles, and along one stretch, broken fans clank against internal ventilators through shattered grilles. After a few minutes, the commissar opens a large double door emblazoned with the Imperial eagle, and we step into a low auditorium.

The commissar makes his way to the pedestal at the front while the Colonel waves for us to sit down at the benches. When we're settled, Schaeffer joins the commissar.

'Armageddon,' the Colonel says, looking at each of us in turn. There are groans from some of the others. 'Even out on the Eastern Fringe, you have heard what is happening here. To bring us up-to-date with the facts, Commissar Greyt has compiled a briefing.'

The Colonel looks at Greyt and nods, before taking a seat on the front bench next to Candlerick's squad.

'Three Terran years ago, the orks returned to Armageddon,' the commissar says, glancing down at the data-slate. 'Led by the warlord Ghazghkull Mag Uruk Thraka, a large invasion force comprising hundreds of warbands entered the Armageddon system. Aboard hulks and smaller vessels, they swarmed in-system, and were engaged by Imperial Navy warships. However, we could not prevent a mass landing. Sporadic reinforcements have arrived over the years, some of them destroyed, but others get through. We do not know how, but orks from hundreds of days of journeying around Armageddon are being drawn to this world.'

The Colonel stands up at this point, and turns to face us.

'The surface of Armageddon is one large war zone,' he tells us, one hand resting on the hilt of his power sword. 'A hive world for several thousand years, Armageddon is a major manufacturing link in the sector, and its survival is paramount to neighbouring sectors. This is one of the largest military campaigns in recent history, and it is centred on this single system.'

He sits down again, and looks to Greyt to continue. The commissar pauses for a moment, to look at Schaeffer, before continuing.

'As well as this recent invasion, our forces on Armageddon must contend with indigenous feral ork populations that have remained since the first invasion fifty years ago,' he says, standing stock straight with his hands resting lightly on the lectern. 'Located in the equatorial jungles and the mountain ranges, these tribes have forayed forth in considerable numbers to engage our reserves, hamper logistics and generally stifle our efforts to destroy the ork landing sites. One hive has been destroyed, the others are heavily contested.'

He glances at the Colonel, who nods and stands up again.

'Armageddon is the most militarised planet you will have ever encountered,' Schaeffer says. 'The orks number in their millions, as do our own armies. In such an epic conflict, confusion and disorder are the norm, and we will be looking to our devices for the completion of our mission. The details of that mission will be related to you at an appropriate time, but I will tell you now that you are to minimise contact with the Imperial forces on Armageddon. Our presence is deemed secret, and any of you who divulge any information regarding our presence here will be executed immediately. The same applies to the contents of this briefing.'

Having given us this stern reminder of our duty, the Colonel sits down again and folds his arms. Greyt clears his throat, and continues.

'We thought Ghazghkull was dead after the first invasion, but we were wrong,' he says, his voice and gaze steady. 'We believe now that he retired to his stronghold in the Golgotha Sector, to recoup his losses and plot his return. As bold and huge as his first attack was, it was nothing compared to what was to come fifty-seven years later. There are some, myself and Colonel Schaeffer included, who think that his first invasion was merely to test our defences. It was nothing more than a reconnaissance, only performed on a planetary scale.'

He pauses to let this information sink in. Basically, this is no dumb ork we're dealing with here, but one who actually has the presence of mind to plan, to investigate and to scheme. I begin to wonder what we're here for, and I'm starting to get a good idea what it might be.

'Roughly thirty years ago, our base on Buca III was annihilated by missiles fired from an ork base hidden on an asteroid,' Greyt continues. 'The asteroid remained undetected before its attack, and we have now realised that this was the first test of what we now dub rock forts. They continue to play a pivotal role in this war, providing transport and fortification that can be landed on the surface.'

'I think we can skip to recent history,' says the Colonel. 'You only need understand that Ghazghkull, and a later warlord known as Nazdreg, systematically tested their weapons and tactics against a variety of targets over several decades. Would you like to continue the briefing with the start of the invasion itself?'

'Of course,' says Greyt with a nod. He is possibly the politest commissar I've ever met, but then again I've always been in the middle of a fight, one way or another, whenever I've met one before. 'After the near-loss of Armageddon during the first invasion, an investigation was launched to look at its defences, by all aspects of the Inquisition, the Departmento Munitorum, Imperial Guard, Imperial Navy and Adeptus Mechanicus. Given the importance of the system, it was recommended that they be seriously improved. Sector naval command was transferred to the Armageddon System and the naval facility of Saint Jowen's Dock was rebuilt and expanded to accommodate all classes of interstellar warship. We established three monitor stations on the edge of the system, this is Mannheim and there were two others, Dante and Yarrick. Other orbital and ground munitions, bases and forces were substantially bolstered. In addition, a ruling council representing many Imperial organisations was convened to govern the planet. The previous Imperial commander, Herman von Strab, had disappeared at the end of the war.'

'It was believed at the time that von Strab may have fled to avoid the attention of the Inquisition regarding his less than loyal conduct during the invasion,' says the Colonel, stroking his chin. 'As it turns out, that was true, but he had also actually sided with Ghazghkull. Although his knowledge of the details of the system's defences was outdated, there is little doubt that his intelligence regarding our general strategic and military methods aided Ghazghkull in his planning.'

Schaeffer waves Greyt to continue, and the commissar scowls. It's only for a moment, but I notice it. It is the first sign of irritation at the Colonel's interruptions. I'd bet that the commissar doesn't even know what we're here for, or why he needs to act as schoolteacher to a bunch of penal legionnaires.

'It began, perversely enough and I suspect not entirely by coincidence, on the day of the Feast of the Emperor's Ascension,' Greyt says, his expression sour. 'Monitor station Dante transmitted a hurried message warning that over fifty ork cruisers and several hundred escort vessels had entered the system, before the transmission was cut. We despatched several battleships and their attendant task forces, and a series of naval engagements took place. Against overwhelming numbers of the orks, Admiral Parol's forces were gradually forced back, in order to preserve ships for an extended campaign. It was immediately evident that this was no simple raid though we did not realise at first that the beast had returned.'

Greyt rubs a hand over his face. Then he pulls a handkerchief from the pocket of his greatcoat and wipes away his sweat. Even with his training and experience, it's hard for him to stay focused. He was obviously there when the attack occurred.

'It took the orks six weeks of battle as they orbited Armageddon, bombarding Saint Jowen's Dock into uselessness while they were advancing,'

Greyt continues. 'The landing itself happened after a three-day battle, but by then we were too late. It wasn't long before every hive was besieged. Our forces were battling merely to survive; there was no thought of any counter-offensive.'

'And so it has been for three years,' the Colonel concludes, standing up again, ignoring Greyt's irritated stare. 'The lines have moved back and forth, back and forth, but there has been little advance since the invasion was stifled in the first few weeks of fighting. We cannot afford to let up for a second, and the orks are never going to leave of their own accord. We are one of a number of strategies being employed to counter the orks or break the deadlock in the Imperium's favour. It is no exaggeration to say that our mission could decide the fate of Armageddon.'

AFTER GREYT IS dismissed and we're led back through Mannheim Station, we have a few hours in one of the bunkrooms before the Colonel pays us a visit. He tells us to get ready to embark. He leads down on to a different docking area, where we file on board an intrasystem transport, no roomier than our previous berths. But there is a bed apiece this time since there are no warp engines taking up half the length of the ship.

I bump into Erasmus Spooge as I head to the wardroom to see the Colonel.

'You're coming with us?' I say as the pudgy little man smiles up at me.

'Well, I'm responsible for your stores, aren't I?' he says. The servo-skull buzzes up from behind him, vibrating slightly. 'I have to stay with them until they're accounted for, don't I?'

'Is that alright?' I ask, looking at the quill-skull.

'Hmm?' says Spooge, glancing at the autoscribe with a look of concern. 'Oh yes, do you think I should have a tech-priest look at it before we leave?'

'Might be a good idea,' I say, stepping past him and continuing down the corridor.

I hear him tramp off as I knock on the door of the wardroom, hoping to get hold of the Colonel. Hearing a voice, I open the door to find the Colonel and the ship's captain inside.

'We have to wait for the escorts, Colonel,' the captain is saying. The Colonel looks up at me as I enter, a scowl on his face.

'Captain Hans Ligner, this is Lieutenant Kage,' Schaeffer says, nodding in my direction. I give them both a salute.

'All aboard and kit stowed, sir,' I say.

'Already?' says Captain Ligner.

'Lieutenant Kage has a way of motivating the troops,' says Schaeffer. 'As you have heard, we are now ready to depart, so what is the delay, captain?'

'The *Victorious* was having reactor trouble, Colonel,' Ligner explains. 'We will be departing at the end of the next watch.'

'Very well, captain,' says Schaeffer. 'Please inform me of any further news as soon as you can.'

'I will, Colonel Schaeffer,' the captain says before leaving. I turn to follow him but the Colonel calls me back.

'The system is still swarming with ork attack fleets,' he says to me. 'We're part of a ten-strong convoy that's gathered here to proceed to Armageddon, with a light cruiser, that is, the *Victorious*, and two frigates as escort. I want the platoon on standby status in case of trouble. I have authorised you to have direct access to a weapons locker. Familiarise yourself and the platoon with the ship's layout and drill for contingencies including boarding, counter-boarding, incendiary control and evacuation.'

He hands me a wad of schematics detailing the ship's decks, from engine rooms to bridge.

'Is it really that bad, sir?' I ask, taking the papers.

'It's about twenty days until we reach the fleet in Armageddon orbit,' the Colonel says. 'No harm in being prepared. Have the platoon ready for my inspection before we leave.'

'Yes, sir,' I reply, saluting and turning away. I stop and turn back to him again.

'Orks, sir,' I say. 'If they get aboard, I don't think we stand much chance at close quarters.'

'Then you best make sure they do not get aboard,' the Colonel replies.

I nod and leave, because there's nothing you can really say to that.

As I close the door behind me, I catch a glimpse of a green robe further down the corridor.

'Kelth?' I call out. The figure turns, confirming that it's the Navigator. He waits for me to approach. 'Why're you here? This isn't a warp-capable ship.'

'There have been heavy casualties amongst the families aboard the fleet,' says Kelth, turning and

walking down the corridor towards the steps leading to the bridge. 'There is an opportunity here for
my House to assist in this shortage.'

'Very honourable, stepping into the breach and all
that,' I say, falling into step beside him. He stops
and gives me a hard stare.

'Honour has nothing to do with it, Lieutenant
Kage,' he tells me. 'The standing of my House, and
the assurance of future prosperity, is my only concern.'

'You want to make a quick credit?' I laugh. 'Millions are dying in space, and on the planets of this
system, and you're concerned about profit.'

'Very laudable, lieutenant,' says Kelth with no
trace of sincerity. 'The Imperium is a fragile thing,
which does not bear too much scrutiny. It is nothing more than the sophisticated interplay of
political dynamics, mutual need and self-interest. It
survives because we need it, and we survive because
it is there. The Houses of the Navigators are essential to its existence, and thus our dedication is duly
rewarded.'

'But what is it you actually *do*?' I ask as Kelth starts
walking again.

'We steer the ships through the Immaterium,' he
says. 'You know this.'

'But how?' I ask, trying to keep up with his long
strides.

'Think of a crystal of ice in an ocean,' he says,
slowing his pace, his gaze drifting to the ceiling in
thought. 'It bobs on the surface, gets drawn down
by currents, and if it should melt, it would meld

and become one with that ocean. That is how it is to navigate warp space.'

'I don't understand,' I say, my eyes straying to the scarf wrapped across his third eye. 'What is it that you can see?'

'Imagine a ship as a grain of sand,' Kelth says. 'When it drops into warp space, it is flung on to a huge desert. It is part of the desert, just like the untold billions of other grains of sand. But as the winds shift and change, those grains of sand also move, forming valleys and drifts, hills and shallows. Imagine, if you will, how that grain of sand would travel if it had a mind to steer itself into the winds it wished to follow, and to avoid the swirls and gusts that would take it from its path.'

'I still don't see what you mean,' I admit.

'That is my point, lieutenant,' he says. 'To explain the warp to one who cannot see it, touch it, is like explaining light and sound to a deaf, blind man. I have senses you cannot comprehend. Some call it the third sight, but sight is such a basic sense in comparison. You cannot imagine the sensation of seeing into the warp, of reading motions born of desires, sensing the fragile flicker of souls. You cannot understand it, as much as I cannot understand why a man would be a soldier.'

We're about to enter the bridge and he stops and looks at me.

'I'm wasting my time here,' he says. 'You have the soul of a soldier, but you need the heart of a poet to understand the Immaterium. Describing colours to blind men is child's play in comparison.'

I let him walk into the bridge, and try to work out what he was telling me.

. 'Nope,' I mutter after some time. 'I still don't get it.'

THE CONVOY PROCEEDS as normal for eight more days, during which we practise anti-conflagration drill, close quarters boarding combat and all the other things that are essential to space combat. The Colonel tells us that we're just passing Chosin, the fifth planet out from the Armageddon star. We should reach Armageddon orbit in the next twenty days.

Unfortunately for us, despite the stretched patrols of the Imperial Navy, the orks are still very much active in the system, and a group of them comes out of hiding over Chosin and comes after us. I put the platoon on ready, and when I'm convinced, take a quick tour of the ship. The bridge doors are open, and the crew seem busy, so I figure nobody would mind if I slipped in to find out what's going on.

Captain Ligner and the Colonel are standing in the centre of the small chamber, deep in discussion. Arrayed like a horseshoe, the bridge is filled with panels and banks of screens and dials, attended by various uniformed officers and dribbling servitors. There's no other source of light, so the whole chamber is bathed in a multi-coloured glow, creating an eerie scene.

Everything seems busy but calm at the moment. A static-broken screen on the front wall displays the convoy's positions with blue circles. Projected courses are outlined in dots. I guess the series of dark red runes far to the left of the screen are the ork raiders.

'Have we got relay from the *Victorious* yet?' the captain asks an officer stationed at a panel to his left, a set of comms-gear at his ear.

'Not yet, sir,' the lieutenant replies. 'Trying to work out whether it's transmission or reception that's at fault.'

'Perhaps they could route through the *Saint Kayle*?' suggests the captain, the comms officer nodding in agreement.

'That's the closest ship to us, sir,' the lieutenant says. 'I'll hail Captain Mendez.'

'Good,' says Ligner, turning back to the Colonel.

I hear someone stand next to me and turn to see Kelth, noticing the holstered laspistol at his belt.

'Can't comprehend what it is to be a soldier?' I say, looking pointedly at the sidearm. He glances down.

'Purely for self-protection,' he says, looking directly at me.

'Ever fired it before?' I ask, avoiding his deep gaze by looking back at the main screen.

'In duels, not in combat,' he replies, his voice soft.

'What's happening?' I say to change the subject. Only nobility has the pleasure of duelling, a form of combat as different from the dirty knife-fights of my youth as the coming space battle.

'The data on the screen is almost half an hour old,' Kelth tells me, crossing his arms and leaning up against a dormant panel behind us. 'The strategic information from the *Victorious* has been interrupted.'

'Damage from enemy fire?' I say, casting a glance at the Colonel, who is bent over a chart with Ligner, pointing and talking in a low voice.

'No, the fighting hasn't started yet,' Kelth says. 'The orks are coming in fast and straight, but it'll still be another hour before first contact, unless the escorts turn to meet them.'

'Will that work?' I ask, noticing for the first time a servitor wired into the wall beneath the screen. It's chanting something in a monotonous tone, too low for me to make out above the humming of the bridge equipment and throb of the engines that are powering into full life. Kelth notices the direction of my stare.

'It's a comms-servitor,' explains the Navigator. 'It relays and records all traffic received and transmitted across the convoy frequencies. And no, in answer to your question, the frigates and *Victorious* are not capable alone of preventing a flotilla of six ork raiders breaking through into the convoy.'

'Could they buy us time to get away?' I ask.

'Unlikely,' the Navigator replies. 'This ship is a little faster than the others, but there are a few ships in the convoy that would get run down within a few hours.'

'So what do you reckon they'll do?' I say.

My brow furrows as I look at Schaeffer arguing quietly with the captain. Perhaps he's advocating that we make a run for it and leave the rest of the convoy to its fate.

'The *Victorious* can outgun any one or two of the enemy,' Kelth says, stroking his chin. 'The frigates will try to ensure that they stay in support of her. Ork ships are generally not very manoeuvrable at speed. They'll have to attack in a series of passes. The frigates will try to herd them onto the light cruiser's guns one or two at a time.'

'And how easy is that to do?' I ask, feeling that I already know the answer.

'Commodore Griffin is experienced at convoy duty, or so I hear from the command crew,' Kelth tells me with a thin smile. 'The Emperor wills.'

'Yes, he does, doesn't he,' I mutter, turning my attention to the quiet hubbub of the bridge. I just wish he didn't will it against me all the time.

AFTER ANOTHER FIFTEEN minutes, the comms problems are overcome with some ingenuity and, I suspect, a lot of shouting and swearing by some poor bastard elsewhere in the fleet. The updated positionals appear on the screen, but I can't really make sense of them. I hear a low series of groans and sighs from the various members of the bridge crew.

'A problem?' I ask, turning to Kelth, but he's gone. He must have slipped away while I was distracted.

'I have a fleet communication from Commodore Griffin,' announces the comms lieutenant.

'Well, let's hear it then,' snaps Captain Ligner.

'There's actually a Navy task force, with the cruisers *Holy Wrath* and *Torch of Retribution*, about two days away,' the lieutenant says. 'We're to proceed to the enclosed position and meet up with them.'

'Two days?' I blurt out, and all eyes turn to me. The Colonel raises an eyebrow having noticed me for the first time.

'Why are you here, Kage?' he asks.

'I wanted to keep the platoon informed of the ongoing situation, sir,' I reply, thinking quickly.

The eyebrow rises even higher.

'I will pass on information as I see fit, Kage,' he says. I just look at him with a pleading expression, unable to come up with any better reason than because I'm curious. He gives me a long hard look and then shakes his head in irritation.

'Very well, you can stay for the moment,' he says eventually. 'But do not interfere again.'

'No sir, I won't, sir,' I say with a shake of my head.

'It's a mobile delaying action, then,' says Ligner. 'I hope the orks don't have any reinforcements close by.'

'Is that likely?' asks the Colonel.

'Not really,' says the ship's captain. 'Ork communications are unreliable, they tend to stay in close packs otherwise they end up scattered all over the place. It's when their ships are mobbed up in that fashion that they're at their most dangerous.'

The crew bustle around for a few more minutes and I start to lose interest until the captain glances up at the screen.

'Hold on,' he says, catching the Colonel's attention. 'The orks are making their first move.'

The blinking icons representing the ork attack ships start to move around to the top of the screen, attempting to flank the convoy to port. The frigates and light cruiser move to intercept, turning inside the ork ships.

'Which ship is that?' the Colonel asks, pointing at a solitary blue circle split off from the main cluster of the convoy ships.

'The *Spirit of Gathalamor*, sir,' replies one of the lieutenants from a position to the forward and right.

'Oldest bucket in the merchant flotilla,' mutters Ligner. 'Emperor knows how Izander keeps her going, she must be at least seven hundred years old by now.'

Another few minutes pass as we watch the escorts cut off the ork attack, one of them detaching to shepherd the *Spirit of Gathalamor* back into the main fleet. The orks slow and allow the convoy to get ahead of them, before cutting back and trying to cross the stern of the flotilla. Again, the *Victorious* and her companions head off the attack, interposing themselves between the attacking ships and the transports.

Kelth appears again and glances at me.

'Are all battles in space this dull?' I ask him and he shrugs.

'This is my first, I wouldn't know,' he says. 'I would rather it was dull than exciting though. I expect excitement in a space battle is pretty dangerous.'

I nod and turn my attention back to the screen. The orks, despite Ligner's words, have split into pairs, one for each of three ships. One continues to harass the starboard flank while the other drives straight for the rear of the convoy.

I look at Ligner, but he doesn't seem concerned in the least. He stands leaning over the back of his chair, glancing now and then at his comms officer.

The flickering icon of the *Victorious* breaks away from the frigates and heads towards the flanking group, steering ahead of them. The frigates keep their distance from the attacking group, staying with their broadsides to bear but are out of range.

'Aren't they the biggest threat?' I blurt out, earning a scowl from the Colonel. Ligner turns to look at me.

'Just watch,' the captain says with a confident smile. My attention is fixed to the screen when I hear the comms officer.

'*Victorious* has announced torpedoes launched,' the lieutenant says and a new icon appears on the screen, its projected line intersecting the starboard ork ships a few minutes from now. Her payload launched, the *Victorious* slows suddenly and almost turns around completely, powering up her engines to cut through the heart of the convoy towards the other ork squadron.

The ork ships slow and turn away to avoid the torpedoes and several minutes later they're falling behind. The frigates close in on the ork squadron as the *Victorious* approaches them from the other side.

'Cunning bastard,' I mutter, seeing the orks are in a classic crossfire, the light cruiser and frigates are attacking at right angles to each other, and the *Victorious's* course takes her across their vulnerable sterns.

'Frigates have opened fire,' announces the comms lieutenant. 'Report light damage to one ship, no hits on the others.'

The frigates close their range as the orks desperately try to turn towards them.

'Ork ships have most of their guns to the fronts,' explains Ligner. 'They should have stayed on course and come for us, now they're in a turning race they can't win.'

'Sir, *Victorious* is sending details of a new contact!' snaps the comms officer, making adjustments to the screen controls. A solitary icon appears in the middle of the transport flotilla.

'A ship can't just appear!' I say, looking at the lieutenant, who ignores me; he is intent on the information being relayed down his earpiece and through the comms servitor.

'Space goes up and down, as well as forward, backward, left and right,' says Kelth, shaking his head in a condescending manner.

'You mean they're above us?' I ask.

'Or below us,' he says looking down towards the decking.

'Give me an intercept time,' says Captain Ligner, moving across the bridge to another station where a fresh-faced young ensign is analysing incoming data.

'Thirty to thirty-five minutes, given current velocities,' the ensign replies, pointing to something on his panel. Ligner looks over his shoulder to the main screen.

'Enemy destroyed,' announces the comms lieutenant. A red icon disappears from the screen to the starboard of the light cruiser. 'Full broadside from *Victorious*.'

The *Victorious* is still engaged with the other two of the squadron, while the group of three ships to the flank has managed to pull out of its course away from the torpedoes. It swings round to the front of the convoy.

'If they get ahead of us…' I mutter, and Kelth gives me a worried glance. 'How come you've never been in a battle before?'

'The Emperor wills,' he replies. 'He has seen fit to guide me along the brightest trail.'

I say nothing. The Emperor has seen fit to have the Colonel drag me through five lifetimes' worth of blood, mud and filth.

The Colonel walks over to me. 'How prepared are we for boarding?' he asks.

'As ready as we'll ever be, sir,' I tell him. 'A platoon that is under strength isn't going to be much use against a ship full of orks, though.'

'Better than just a ship's complement,' he says. 'This is the only troop transport in the convoy.'

'Sir, I don't think this is our fight,' I say, looking straight at him. 'You've haven't told us what we're going to do on Armageddon yet. But I'm sure that if it's important enough to drag us across the galaxy, then it's important that we don't sacrifice ourselves for a few grain and mineral transports.'

He gives me a long hard look.

'Our duty is always to the Emperor,' he says slowly.

'That's not what happened on Kragmeer,' I remind him. The Colonel risked his reputation pulling us out of the front line against orks on the ice world, so that we could continue on to Typhos Prime and the attack on Coritanorum.

'That was different,' he says, returning my gaze.

'How so?' I ask, not flinching.

'There were many other Imperial forces to hold the line,' he tells me. 'Our presence, or lack of it, would have had no impact on the campaign. There is no other line of defence for the convoy.'

'Did you ever hear what happened in the end?' I ask, the thought suddenly occurring to me. I've been in a dozen war zones on various missions with the Colonel, but we rarely hang around long enough to find out who's won.

'The campaign is still progressing,' he tells me. 'Besides, we are just as at risk from attack if we separate from the convoy.'

'Not if we head for the rendezvous with the task force,' I point out.

'The orks will pounce on us if we isolate ourselves,' the Colonel says. 'The *Victorious* and the frigates are the only protection we have, and they will not abandon the convoy for us.'

I look away from him, admitting the logic of his argument.

'How many orks are there on one of those ships?' I ask, looking at the main screen and the flashing red icon of the newly arrived ork vessel.

'The crew probably numbers in its hundreds,' he says quietly.

'And we've got less than thirty men,' I say.

'More if you conscript non-essential crew, and the four surviving provosts under my command,' he says.

'That's still not much against hundreds of orks,' I say. 'If they attack in force, we'll be overrun in minutes.'

Captain Ligner joins us.

'What are you two conspiring?' he asks, switching his gaze back and forth between the two of us.

'Please place your ship to intercept the attack on the fleet,' the Colonel tells him. He is answered by the captain's doubtful look.

'I don't see what good that will do,' he says. He points to the main display. 'Our only chance is to manoeuvre for time and wait for the escorts. The commodore has despatched one of the frigates in our direction.'

'How many vessels are armed?' the Colonel asks.

'Every ship has close defence turrets, the *Yarrick* and the *Boncephalis* have a few bigger guns,' he tells us. 'It doesn't matter though, just a few salvoes from that ork ship would be enough to destroy any one of us.'

The Colonel looks thoughtful for a moment and then turns to Ligner.

'Is there a council channel to the rest of the fleet?' he asks.

'I can have one arranged, including the warships,' says Ligner.

'Then please do so, and inform me when it is ready,' says Schaeffer. The captain looks dubious for a moment but soon melts under the Colonel's glare. 'Kage, come with me. Captain, if you could join me in the wardroom when you are able.'

He marches off the bridge, leaving me trailing in his wake. Ligner directs an enquiring look at me, but all I can do is shrug.

IN THE WARDROOM, the Colonel outlines his plan to Captain Ligner and me. I stand there, speechless with incredulity.

'Well, do you think you can manage that?' he asks.

'That's the best way of getting yourself killed I've heard in a long time,' says Ligner, shaking his head.

'Welcome to my life,' I mutter, earning myself a scowl from the Colonel.

'Is it possible?' the Colonel says.

'You're asking for good close quarter steering,' says Ligner. 'The only other military crew in the fleet is aboard the *Yarrick*, the other ships just have mercantile companies. I can't vouch for their abilities.'

'But you agree that it is possible?' insists Schaeffer. The captain sighs.

'Yes, Colonel,' he says. 'I can't see how the others will agree though.'

'They will agree because Commodore Griffin is going to invoke certain clauses of the naval articles of war,' says the Colonel. 'However afraid the other captains are of the orks, I am sure that they would rather face them than a military execution.'

'I see,' says Ligner. 'We have about twenty minutes to arrange matters. I shall transmit your intention to the fleet.'

Schaeffer watches the captain's back for a moment as he walks out, and then turns his attention to me.

'You will need to be ready in ten minutes,' he says and I nod. 'You understand your mission?'

'Of course, sir,' I say heavily. 'Everyday duties for a Last Chancer, sir. You want me to lead an attack on an ork ship with forty men, disable its engines and then return, sir. Not a problem at all, sir.'

'Your enthusiasm is noted, Kage,' the Colonel says, dismissing me with a wave of his hand.

Great, I think as I head down the corridor at a trot. Now all I have to do is explain this to the platoon.

WE'RE ASSEMBLED ON the docking platform when the provosts join us. Like us, they're geared up in vac-proof environment suits. Grey, bulky and hot, they'll be the only thing protecting us from the chill airlessness of space once we break through the hull of the ork ship.

'I have been ordered to report to you,' one of them says. I can hear the grudging tone in his voice, even through the visor.

'What's your name?' I ask, looking him up and down.

'Sergeant First Class Kayle,' he says.

'I think you'll find I'm a lieutenant, sergeant,' I say to him. 'Proper form of address and all that.'

He raises the visor on his helmet, revealing a craggy face with a long scar running from his left ear across his mouth to his chin. His dark eyes meet my gaze.

'I don't care if you're a trooper or a general,' he says between gritted teeth. 'You're penal legion scum to me, and that's the end of it. Don't push it.'

'I like a man with principles,' I say with a grin. 'I want you up front with me when we attack. I'm sure you'll watch my back, won't you sergeant?'

'I understand the objective, we'll do our part,' he says with a sneering smile.

'Just so that we understand each other, sergeant,' I say with a meaningful nod.

We eyeball each other for a few seconds until the Colonel strolls onto the deck. Sergeant Candlerick barks out the order and the platoon snaps to attention. I notice the holstered bolt pistol at the Colonel's belt, and his power sword hanging in its scabbard on the other side. Oh, and the fact that he's also wearing a vac-suit gives the game away.

'Joining us for this little jaunt, sir?' I ask.

'I will lead the attack,' he says, casting his eye over the platoon. Each is carrying a shotgun and a bandoler of ammo. Three men in each squad also have a sack of grenades, while the sergeants each have a demolition charge.

'So, we're still going do this, then?' I say with a sigh, stooping to pick up my vac-suit helmet.

'It is too late to alter the plan now,' the Colonel says. 'The *Yarrick* is moving into position as we speak.

'And how long before that frigate arrives?' I ask, knowing I won't like the answer.

'Twenty minutes at the earliest,' the Colonel says, still not looking at me. 'You seem unduly worried, Kage?'

'Unduly?' I laugh. 'We're about to use a ship as bait to lure an enemy ship in, then attack it with transports. Then you are going to lead a platoon to attack that same enemy ship in the hopes of disabling its engines. I think some worry is due, sir!'

'You expect us to fail?' the Colonel asks quietly.

'Not at all, sir,' I sigh. 'That's not the problem. We always succeed. The problem is, the more we push our luck, sooner it's going to run out. Perhaps we should be saving it for Armageddon.'

'You think some strange things, Kage,' the Colonel says. 'Luck has no part to play in your life. It is the will of the Emperor whether you live or die.'

I just wish He would make up His mind, I think.

A lieutenant appears. He walks up to Schaeffer and salutes.

'The captain reports that we are now simulating engine trouble, sir,' the Navy officer says. 'It appears the orks are taking the bait.'

'Thank you, lieutenant,' Schaeffer says before turning to me. 'Mount up the platoon, Kage.'

I shout the order and the sergeants hurry the men onto the shuttle. It's the only one the ship has, so I hope it stays in one piece otherwise this is going to be a one-way trip. A short one at that.

Once we're inside the shuttle, belted up and ready to go, the pilot appears at the door to the carriage compartment.

'We're ready to go in thirty seconds, Colonel,' he says and Schaeffer gives him the nod.

I watch the rest of the platoon as the engines power up. I can feel their apprehension, nervous excitement and fear. Dunmore is laughing with Cardinal, but I can hear the nervous edge to it. Candlerick has his head bowed in prayer, as do some of the others. Morin is checking the slide on his shotgun, for the tenth time I reckon. Radso is fidgeting with the bolt shell pendant he wears. Supposedly it's a good luck charm, since it hit him in the shoulder but failed to detonate. When it was extracted, he had an armourer disarm it for him, and now he wears it as a talisman.

Me, I sit there watching them, listening to the noise of the engines increasing in volume and pitch. With a lurch that pins me to the seat, we lift off, powering out of the open bay. The pilot then cuts the engines into reverse for a moment, and then off completely. We start to drift slowly away from the ship. The pilot's voice crackles out over the shuttle comms system.

'The captain's just told me that we're less than five minutes from contact,' he says.

I turn to the Colonel, who's sitting to my right.

'What if they just open fire?' I ask. 'Maybe they don't want to board.'

'They are raiders,' he replies. 'They want to capture the ship and its cargo, not destroy it. They will board.'

'But if they don't?' I insist.

'Then we can thank the Emperor that we are out here on a shuttle, rather than aboard the ship,' he says, and I laugh. He gives me a look and a chuckle dies in my throat when I realise he isn't joking. Of course he isn't, he never jokes.

It's a tense few minutes as we sit there in the shuttle, drifting through space as easy as a firing range target. If the orks spot us, which is unlikely I admit, we won't even survive long enough to know it.

I grab my helmet from under the seat and place it over my head. With a twist, I fit it into place and then turn to the Colonel, who's returned from the cockpit. I point to the sealing clamps. He fastens them for me, and then puts on his own helmet, and signals for me to fasten his clamps.

A thought crosses my mind briefly. If I just leave one of the clamps, just one of the four, a bit loose, it'll compromise the suit's integrity. Nobody would know what went wrong. Hell, these suits malfunction, break seals or just disintegrate one time in ten anyway.

I dismiss the thought and tighten all the clamps as far as I can. Killing the Colonel is just about the worst thing I could do at the moment. Oddly enough, he's the best chance I have of staying alive. Without him, there is no Last Chancers. And with no Last Chancers, I'm irredeemably corrupt and would be executed without hesitation. And there's that other bit, the one about me probably being a witch.

'Comms check,' the Colonel's voice echoes in my ear with a tinny note.

A series of affirmative replies come back from the platoon, and I add my own.

'Ready for disembarking,' the Colonel says and we all stand up and march clumsily to the rear doors. I'd cross my fingers but the suit won't let me.

Slipping the shotgun on its strap from my shoulder, I chamber a round and glance at the others. I see my face reflected in the black visor of one of Kayle's provosts, obscured by the condensation building up from my sweat inside the faceplate of my suit.

'Hey, provy, looking forward to your first real combat?' I ask. He swivels towards me, his shotgun levelled at my groin.

'I hope my finger doesn't slip with my inexperience,' he says, stepping forward. 'I'd hate to have a nasty accident on my first time out.'

He looks down and sees the tip of my gun angled up towards his chin.

'That would be terribly bad,' I say, easy as you like.

'Look, shit mouth, I fought on Danaa Secundus,' he says, swinging the shotgun away. 'I don't need to prove anything to you.'

I shut up. We never went to Danaa Secundus, but everything I've heard makes it sound like the Colonel would have loved it. More tyranids, a splinter of Hive Fleet Kraken after Ichar IV. Turned into a rout, only twenty thousand men out of a three million strong army got off alive. The number of non-combatants who escaped the three-month onslaught amounted to about a tenth of that. Three months is all it took for a world to die. Makes me glad that we won on Ichar IV.

'Hold on,' says the pilot over the internal speakers. 'Emperor's blood!'

I rush clumsily to the cockpit, heading through the door just a few steps behind the Colonel.

Looking out of the canopy, I see a slowly spinning field of stars. After a moment, the ork ship comes into view, its bulbous nose studded with cannons and jutting spars. A bright blue flare glows from its engines. It's several kilometres away, but I can see that, oddly enough, it seems to be painted red. What look like columns of flame are pouring from underneath the ship and as I watch, a series of detonations explode along its length. I look at the Colonel, and then the pilot.

'The *Yarrick* is reporting a previously unregistered energy spike,' the pilot informs us.

'What does that mean?' asks the Colonel, his voice in my comms-transmitter but distorting from the external speaker at the same time.

'Someone else was lying in wait, systems offline to avoid detection,' the pilot says. 'They were playing dead, basically.'

'Who?' I ask.

The pilot is listening to the fleet frequencies, his eyes widening with surprise.

'Space Marines,' he says, staring out of the shuttle canopy as another series of explosions tears the ork attack ship to pieces, its midsection breaking clean through. The two halves tumble away from each other, gouting gas and flames. 'Rapid strike vessel *Terminatum* of the Black Templars.'

The Colonel unbuckles his helmet and takes the comms-piece from the pilot, holding it up to his ear. He nods to himself as he absorbs what's going on, before turning to me.

'Stand the platoon down, Kage,' he says and I realise I've been holding my breath. I release it in a long sigh. Schaeffer looks at the pilot. 'Take us back to the ship.'

CHAPTER FOUR
WRATH OF GHAZGHKULL

IT TURNS OUT that the Black Templars had been hunting this particular band of orks for the last few days. They knew they were lurking near Chosin but were unable to locate them. Hearing that the convoy was passing their way, they decided to lie in wait, thinking the orks would be unable to resist the lure of the transports. As well as the *Terminatum*, there were two more rapid strike vessels and a strike cruiser all within an hour's travel of our position.

With the Space Marines as an additional escort, it's an uneventful journey to the inner system. We rendezvous with another fleet at Saint Jowen's Dock before we press on to Armageddon itself. The buzz around the fleet is that a new ork hulk has arrived in the system in the last week or so, but nobody's found it yet.

It's a cautious approach to Armageddon orbit.
Despite the fleet's victories, there are still hundreds
of ork vessels unaccounted for, some of them large
and dangerous. Added to that, it seems the orks
have captured one of the rocket factories on the surface and have been randomly launching warheads
into space, adding to the general fun.

We've just entered upper orbit and Captain Ligner
informs the Colonel that a small, previously
uncharted asteroid field lies across our line of
descent. Schaeffer agrees to navigate the asteroid
field, using it to cover our approach until we hit
lower orbit. The hope is that the orks won't be
aware of us until it's too late to launch any form of
attack.

Playing it safe, Ligner orders the ship to be
cleared and braced for combat, while he edges us
into the asteroid field. I'm on the lower deck with
Dunmore and Lorii, securing energy cells near the
engine room. The rest of the platoon is on various
other duties throughout the ship, under the supervision of the provosts. Lorii's just passing me a
fuel canister when the deck trembles under my
feet.

I look at the others and their bemused expressions confirm that they felt it too. We exchange
glances as I cautiously lower the fuel cell to the
deck. The ship shudders again, more violently this
time, sending the cell spinning out of my hand and
clattering across the deck. A second later, an alarm
klaxon rings out across the ship, deafening us as it
squalls from a speaker just overhead.

There's an explosion in the engine room behind us, a blast wave sweeps through the open doors along the corridor, hurling us from our feet. With the screeching twist of metal, part of the roof collapses and smoke starts to billow out of the ventilation system.

'The saviour pods!' I scream to the others, dragging myself to my feet. We're under attack, there's no mistake about that. I don't know how, and I don't care. It's obvious that we've already taken critical damage; we won't survive another five minutes. I race off up the corridor, with the other two following me. I vault up the stairs two at a time, until another impact causes me to lose my footing. I stumble, then fall backwards.

Brownie sticks out an arm and stops me. Flames in the ventilation ducts reflect off his bald head as he helps me to my feet, grinning.

'That one's for taking care of Goran,' he says, pushing me forward. I nod and start hauling myself up the steps again. Lorii's in front of me.

Reaching the mid deck, we're confronted by carnage and chaos. The walls are buckled, supporting rafters hang down from the ceiling, severed cables spewing sparks and oil, the air is filled with smoke. I can see at least half a dozen bodies crushed underneath the mess, pools of blood glinting as they spread across the decking. Their charred uniforms identify them as Last Chancers. I guess they won't be going any further, but there's no time to spare them a second thought. A smouldering pile of crates that has dropped from the storage bay above blocks our way forward.

'What now?' says Lorii, taking a step back as an oil hose ignites, sending a jet of flame scorching across the corridor just a few metres in front of her.

'Keep going up,' I say, pointing to the stairwell on the other side of the corridor.

Brownie forges ahead up the stairs, sweat dripping from him from the nearby flames. My shirt is sticking to my back as I feel the heat licking up the steps after us. Glancing over my shoulder, I see the flames spreading to the foot of the stairwell behind Lorii.

'Faster!' I yell, slapping Brownie on the back to urge him on.

The spiral staircase is littered with two more corpses, crew this time, which we have to jump over. Smoke is all around us as we burst onto the top deck.

The flashing red lights of the saviour pod doors stretch out in front of us. Most of them have already ejected. I see a green light a little further on, and lead the others to it, stepping over snaking wires and smouldering bodies. We're a couple of metres from the door when the Colonel appears, heading from the opposite direction. With him are Kelth, Kin-Drugg, Sergeant Candlerick and another Last Chancer called Oahebs, who joined the Last Chancers with Lorii.

The Colonel waves us into the saviour capsule with his bolt pistol, glancing over his shoulder. Two more figures appear out of the gloom, and as they emerge from the darkness and smoke I see that it's Corthrod, one of the Navy ratings. Behind him, cowering from the flames is Spooge, his servo-skull still obediently bobbing along behind him. The polished bone is tarnished with soot and oil now, and its anti-grav motors sputter and choke occasionally, causing it to dip alarmingly towards the floor.

I watch them all jump into the pod, and then duck inside just in front of the Colonel. We each slump down into one of the ten seats, laid out in a circle around the hull of the capsule. The main control panel juts down from the ceiling in the centre, while the retro rockets and parachute take up most of the floor space in between us.

It's cramped, but we manage to strap ourselves in as the Colonel cycles the door closed and sits down. Before pulling on his straps, he leans forward and activates the countdown launch sequence. He grunts and stares at the panel for the moment before looking up at me, and then Corthrod.

'There seems to be a problem with the electrics,' he says, prodding a few runes on the display.

Corthrod unbuckles himself and stands to have a look. He shakes his head a few times, muttering under his breath. My stomach starts to churn, I can see flickering hints of yellow through the small circular porthole in the pod door.

'The connection's broken,' Corthrod declares, spitting on the deck. 'There's a manual launch on the deck.'

'Kage, get to the manual launch and activate it,' says Schaeffer, not even looking at me.

'Why me?' I say, crossing my arms stubbornly. 'I always get this kind of shit. Send Corthrod, he knows what he's looking for.'

The Colonel doesn't even look up.

'Kage, get to the manual launch and activate it,' he says again. I notice the pistol in his hand is pointing straight at me from his lap. 'Before I shoot you.'

'For Emperor's sake, I always end up doing the hard work,' I say as I unstrap myself and cycle the door lock. 'Give me a fragging hand, Kage. Silence the fragging woman, Kage. Fragging eat the brains, Kage.'

I continue swearing as I step out onto the deck. The heat from the fire is nearly unbearable. I cough heartily from the smoke gathering in the corridor. I put my head back into the capsule.

'Where is it, then?' I ask Corthrod. He gestures back along the deck.

'It's about fifteen metres down. A red-trimmed panel, you can't miss it. Just pull the trip switch and get back here in thirty seconds. The door will close automatically and all the pods on this side will be fired off.'

'Right, thirty seconds,' I say, heading off at a trot.

Corthrod is right: the panel's easy to spot. Unfortunately, the piping that's collapsed from the ceiling ducts is in the way and takes some shifting, but after a few seconds of pushing and grunting, I clear the panel. I wrench it open and pull down on the lever. There's a warning siren, and a red light begins to blink just below the lever.

Just as I'm about to turn back to the capsule, a dark figure appears out of the smoke. I recognise

Kayle, the provost sergeant. He's without his helmet, and his face is half-burned, his hair smouldering. He has his shotgun in his hands.

'What are you doing?' he demands, grabbing hold of me.

'Emergency launch!' I snap at him, throwing off his hand. 'You've got about twenty seconds to get in a capsule.'

He nods and shoulders his way past me, pushing me up against the wall. The metal is hot, and it sears my hands as I push myself upright. It's then that I realise he's heading to the open pod.

There's only one seat left, and it's mine.

A swift kick between the legs from behind connects with Kayle's prized possessions, toppling him forwards into a crumpled heap. I snatch the shotgun from his hands and ram the butt into his face, driving him to the deck. He makes a half-hearted grab for my ankle but I skip past, heading for the capsule door.

'Bastard!' he shouts after me and I give him a grin as I duck back through the door.

The Colonel looks at the shotgun in my hands, eyebrow raised.

Ignoring him, I hurl myself into the remaining seat and drag the harness over my shoulders, ramming the lock down into the seat socket between my legs. The door grinds shut and locks itself, while the ejection motors grumble into life below our feet. I see Kayle's twisted, shouting face appear at the door window for a second before the pod is launched upwards, punching out of its ejection tube into space. The force rams us all down into our seats and I grit my teeth against the pressure. The blood rushes to my legs, making me dizzy. Out of the corner of my eye I see Spooge collapsing inside his harness. He's blacked out. As the retro fires, we begin to circle slowly.

Free of the artificial grav of the ship, we tumble in weightlessness, straining the safety straps. After a few minutes I heave a massive sigh of relief.

'What the frag?' I finally say, looking at the Colonel. He doesn't reply for a while.

'The asteroid field was not safe,' he says eventually. 'Most of them were the rock forts that Commissar Greyt warned us of. They opened fire as soon as we were in range.'

Corthrod is busying himself with the short-range comms unit fitted to the saviour pod's control panel. I unharness myself and guide myself over to the viewing portal in the door. I can see the burning remnants of the ship, and it suddenly occurs to me that I never knew its name. There are other explosions and trails of fire as the orks launch attack craft to hunt down the saviour pods and open fire at random. Not so far away, I see the glinting reflection of another capsule, a moment before a missile detonation engulfs it.

All around us, missile trails zoom past, probably kilometres away but too close for comfort. Amongst the debris, I see charred bodies, clumped in groups as they are blown out of the ship by hull breaches. They slowly freeze together. Everything dwindles away as we drift away from the battle, and soon all

I can see are the distant sparks of engines and the ominous shadows of the rock forts blotting out the views of the stars beyond. Minutes later, I can't even see them.

'We're going to die,' Corthrod says, his voice shrill. 'There are only two other capsules left. The orks are going to hunt us down!'

'Shut up,' snaps Lorii. She turns to her right, where Erasmus is unconscious, and tries to revive him. With no gravity field to support it, the quill-skull is nestled in the scribe's lap, buzzing erratically.

'Shut up?' says Corthrod. 'The beacon isn't working because the transmitter was fragged on launch. We're also getting pulled down into the gravity well. Even if the orks don't get us, and we manage to avoid burning up on entry to the atmosphere, we're going to crash Emperor-knows-where.'

'Stop whining,' I say, still staring out of the window. I can't see any fire that's directed in our area, or telltale flickers that might be closing attack craft. 'We'll be fine.'

'We are not going to be fine!' says Corthrod and I turn to see him sneering at us all. 'You don't understand. It's not a war zone down there. It's hell. We might get lucky and actually land on solid ground. Then all we have to worry about is perhaps freezing to death if we land near the poles. Or dehydration. Maybe we'll land in a radzone, or a chem-pit. Or we might get fortunate and just be killed by orks. We have no weapons, no survival gear, and no comms. Even if we landed near Imperial forces, there's no way of us knowing it, or of them finding us. We're as good as dead.'

'Kage, silence him,' snaps the Colonel.

The boom of the shotgun is unbearably loud in the confines of the pod. The recoil sends me crashing into the door and bouncing back. The remnants of Corthrod drift around in the air, globules of blood and brains spattering against my face and chest as I glide through the cloud of gore. Everyone's looking at me aghast, except the Colonel and Lorii.

'That's out of order!' roars Candlerick, but he falls silent as I steady myself and the muzzle of the shotgun swings in his direction. He glances at Schaeffer for a reaction.

'Our first priority is survival,' the Colonel says slowly. 'Doubt and fear compromise our chances of success. Everyone here is subject to summary execution for cowardice under military law. Once our immediate survival is no longer an issue, we will proceed with our mission to the best of our abilities.'

That's no surprise. Losing three quarters of our force is just a minor setback when you're with the Last Chancers.

ARMAGEDDON

CHAPTER FIVE
MORE BAD LANDINGS

THE NEXT HOUR was probably the most terrifying of my life. Though I've been through some of the most Emperor-awful stuff you can imagine – battlefields choked with the dead, and personal moments like the time a tyranid warrior sawed halfway through my leg at Deliverance – the utter helplessness of our predicament sets my nerves jangling.

Aided by Kelth, the Colonel manages to at least get the automated telemetry working so that the capsule will take us into the atmosphere at the correct angle, rather than bouncing off or burning us up. Well, in theory. The only way we'll know if they've really got it right is when we hit the upper atmosphere in about fifteen minutes.

I'm not the only one getting stressed out by the situation. Erasmus is quiet now, though he was

gabbling nervously to himself a little while ago.
He's just sitting there, cradling the servo-skull in his
hands, and stroking it carefully, reverentially. Lorii
is alert, her eyes continuously flicking from one of
us to another, her jaw clenched tight. Candlerick
fidgets with his buttons on his cuffs all the time,
drawing little circles with his index finger on the
dull brass hemispheres.

Kin-Drugg is pretending to be cool. He is sitting
with his hands behind his head, eyes closed, but I
see them half open occasionally, checking everything before closing again. He's a drop trooper, so I
guess this situation isn't as alien to him as it is to
the rest of us. But then again, there's a world of difference between plummeting into a savage war
zone in an out-of-control saviour pod, and grav-
chuting into a prepared DZ with a platoon of your
comrades.

Brownie's humming to himself, and tapping out
the beat of some regimental march on his knees.
His eyes stare at the floor between his legs. As I
watch him, he stops his little tune and pulls his
combat knife from his belt. Immediately I'm tense
and ready, and I see Lorii shift slightly in her seat,
ready to act if he does anything stupid. Instead, he
spits in his left hand and rubs it over his scalp and
then, carefully and slowly, he scrapes the blade over
his head, removing the tiny protrusions of stubble
that have appeared since he shaved his head this
morning.

He looks up at us, feeling our gazes on him. He
lifts the blade away a little and shrugs, then turns

his attention back to the floor as he continues to scrape the knife across his scalp.

Gideon Oahebs is directly opposite me but it's only by leaning slightly to one side that I can see him. I'm glad of that, because he absolutely freaks me out when I'm near him. I don't know why it is, but whenever I'm in close proximity to him, I feel kind of giddy. It's hard to describe, it's like someone you dislike on first sight, even though you have no idea what kind of person they are.

I've spent most of the last year avoiding being in the same room as him as much as possible. There's nothing physically wrong with the guy, and he's certainly one of the more quiet and obedient of the platoon. I correct myself as I think this – there is no platoon, it's just us now. I feel a bit better about that, in an odd sort of way. The Last Chancers, the *real* Last Chancers, are only ever a handful of soldiers. Maybe the Colonel started out with a four thousand-strong legion a couple of years ago, but the rest were just baggage really. They were being tested and only a few of us survived long enough to get to Coritanorum.

Oahebs is sitting comfortably, hands clasped in his lap, gnawing at his bottom lip. I can see that his fingernails are worn and ragged too, so it's easy to see how he deals with his nerves. Beside him, Kelth squirms uncomfortably, casting looks at Oahebs every couple of minutes, brow knitted. So it isn't just me that finds him awkward to be around.

And finally, there's the Colonel. Unflappable, unlovable and unkillable, I can feel him on my right like a rock. With parade ground stiffness, he just sits there, a hand on each knee, staring straight ahead. He doesn't even glance at the panel to check our progress. It's like he's deactivated on something, like a lasgun with the safety on, just waiting for someone, or something, to flick the switch and put him into action again. That said, I can see the subtle tic of his jaw muscles, the only sign I've ever noticed of stress or anger.

Sensing my gaze, he turns his head slowly towards me, his icy eyes boring into me. He doesn't say anything, he just stares at me.

'How long before entry, sir?' I ask, eager to break the crushing silence.

'Two and a half minutes,' he replies without even needing to check the display.

'Any idea where we'll crash-land?' I say, leaning forward to look at the meaningless scrolling runes and numbers of the telemetry panel.

He finally breaks his stare to look at the display, and then reaches inside his coat to pull out a battered-looking map. He unfolds it and then refolds it, glancing up at the co-ordinates glowing from the screen, until he's found the area he wants.

'The good news is that we are not likely to land in water,' he says, putting the map away.

'The bad news?' I say.

'There is a good chance that we will make planet-fall somewhere in the jungles,' he says.

He doesn't have to add anything. From Greyt's briefing, we know that the jungle is teeming with ork activity, despite several fire missions to clear it out. Our only hope is that someone at Cerberus base notices us crash and sends out a search and rescue party.

There's little chance of that, I reckon. With all the problems they have, I figure that a saviour pod coming down is going to be the last thing they're worried about. They're virtually under siege from the orks and have got much better things to do with their time.

'That is assuming we do not get caught in an electrical storm and go off our current projected trajectory,' the Colonel adds.

There are a few groans around the pod, one of them my own. Not for the first time, and probably not the last, I ask myself whether this was worth the satisfaction of killing my sergeant. In the great balance of things, I should've just let him have the girl. Still, regret's for the weak. I cast my own die and the Emperor took the bet and left me here, so all that I can do now is deal with it. I've long since stopped blaming anyone else for my predicament; it makes it so much easier to deal with. Once you stop looking elsewhere for the reasons why crap happens to you, you realise it's all your own doing, one way or another. Unfortunately, I guess that's one of life's little wisdoms that are denied to us until after we've made an important mistake. We don't normally get the chance to learn from it.

THE INTERIOR OF the pod begins to heat up considerably, to the point where it starts getting difficult to breathe. We look at each other with consternation, wondering if this is a prelude to exploding into a ball of fire, the heat shielding tearing away, the metal casing melting and our bodies vaporising into nothing. The capsule begins to shake, jarring us from side to side and we can really start to feel the pull of the gravity well and our own velocity. Candlerick starts swearing, under his breath. Kin-Drugg laughs and we all stare at him.

'If the atmosphere's thickened enough to make things turbulent, then we've entered okay,' he says with a grin. 'Just the landing to worry about. Or maybe I should say impact.'

'Thanks for pointing that out,' mutters Dunmore, shaking his head. 'You really are a bonehead, aren't you?'

Kin-Drugg laughs and shrugs, and then seeing that we're not sharing the joke, points to Brownie's shining scalp.

'He's calling me a bonehead?' Kin-Drugg says.

'You want me to slap that smirk off your face?' says Dunmore, bringing his hand back across his chest to emphasise the point.

The vibrations become more and more violent as we dive down through the sky of Armageddon, and then stop suddenly. For a couple of minutes it feels like we're just floating, but then we hit the solid fume cover that fills the Armageddon air with thick clouds, and the turbulence starts again.

'Not long now,' says Kin-Drugg, checking the bindings on his harness.

'Let's just hope the retros didn't get fragged with the other systems,' I say, earning myself scowls from the others. 'I'm just saying what we're all thinking, so don't give me that.'

THERE'S A TANGIBLE release of tension when the pod shudders and a dull roar emanates from beneath us as the retrorocket fires. I can feel us slowing, the weightlessness of our descent disappearing. As the retro grows to full power the deceleration pushes us down into our seats and I feel blood rushing to my head, making me dizzy. There's another jolt as the chutes open and the retro burns off, leaving us, with any luck, drifting down to a not-too-speedy landing.

A few minutes later and the capsule tilts slightly to one side, accompanied by the metallic clang of branches slapping and snapping against the hull. We shudder to a stop, and I'm slightly hanging to my left in the seat strap. There are a few creaks and groans and I feel us settling little more. Candlerick slaps the release on his buckle and pushes himself up.

'Wait!' says the Colonel, just as I'm opening my mouth.

We're both too late.

As Candlerick steps forward, the weight in the capsule shifts. There's more snapping of branches and we drop. I'm spinning to my left and pitching forward, and Candlerick is thrown clear across the pod, ricocheting off the central control column and smashing headfirst into the hull just to my right. His face explodes on impact and his head snaps back. I don't hear anything over the crashing through the branches, but his body lolls across me and then falls away, his dangling neck all the evidence I need. His neck snapped as easily as the branches outside.

With an impact that sends a shudder up my legs and along my spine, and jars my head back against the pod wall, we slam down to the ground. The pod rolls back and forth a little as it settles.

We sit there, waiting for further movement. I can hear Spooge whimpering, and out of the corner of my eye see Brownie clenching and unclenching his fists, muttering under his breath. Kin-Drugg is gripping tightly to his harness, head back against the wall. Gideon is staring at Candlerick's corpse lying bunched up against his feet. He nervously kicks it away, but at the angle we've landed it rolls straight back against his shins.

'I think we're done,' says Lorii, looking at me, and then the Colonel, who nods and undoes his straps. I notice him pulling out his pistol as he hauls himself up using the display column. Undoing my own restraint harness, I fish the shotgun out from where I stowed it beneath the seat, tucked behind one of the chair supports. I'm glad I did, because the last thing we needed was a loaded firearm tumbling about the pod as we fell.

As the rest of them free themselves, the Colonel pulls himself across to the door, which is slightly higher up than the ground, and at a shallow angle. He peers through the condensation-covered porthole, looking outside.

'It appears clear to this side,' he says. 'No immediate threat, at least.'

'What's the plan?' asks Brownie, steadying himself with a hand on his seat and wringing a kink out of his neck. The Colonel turns and looks at each of us in turn as he speaks.

'We secure a perimeter around the pod, and then make a further appraisal,' he says.

'What are we going to secure a perimeter with, sir?' asks Kin-Drugg. 'Apart from Kage's shotgun and your pistol, all we've got are knives.'

The Colonel tosses his bolt pistol to Kin-Drugg, who catches the heavy sidearm awkwardly.

'I want you twenty metres out from doorward. Kage, you are to position yourself on the opposite side,' Schaeffer says, gripping the door lock. 'Understood?'

I give him the nod, and Kin-Drugg follows suit after a dubious look.

The Colonel spins the lock and thrusts the door outwards. As it clangs against the hull, I let Kin-Drugg out first, even though I'm closest to the opening. If there is something out there waiting for us, there is no reason to be in a rush to meet it, I figure.

The drop trooper clambers through, and I follow him a few seconds later. Pulling myself out of the opening, I see that we're definitely in the jungle, as if there was any doubt. The burned shell of the pod is resting on a litter of dried leaves and freshly broken branches. Leaping down to the jungle floor, shotgun in hand, I peel right and work my way around to the other side of the pod. The two white chutes lie in tatters a few metres above us, hanging like signal flags from the trees.

It's damn hot, and the air is thick with moisture. I'm already sweating buckets and it's difficult to breathe properly. There's an edge to the air that catches in the throat, making me feel as if I'm choking. It's pretty dark too: most of the light is coming through the hole in the canopy made by the crashing pod. Beyond that circle, the jungle looms dark, and other than the vague shapes of twisting trunks, I can't see anything beyond twenty metres or so. Gigantic fungi erupt out of warped roots and branches, and thin, thorny bushes somehow leech an existence from the dry ground. It's deadly quiet; any birds or beasts in the vicinity were obviously put to flight by our dramatic entrance. Seeing nothing, I bang on the pod with the butt of the shotgun.

'All clear,' I say, not too loudly because I don't want my voice to carry too far.

I drop to a crouch and work my way forwards away from the capsule, scanning left and right as I move. I'm moving slowly but surely, controlling the urge to just get in place and then burrow down. There're two things that are bound to attract notice. One of them is something absolutely still when everything else is moving. The other is quick movement, which will attract the eye faster than anything. Ever been jumpy? Ever been looking left and right constantly, thinking you saw something moving? That's pure survival instinct, and that's what I'm relying on right now.

There's scattered undergrowth, clawing for life in the little light that gets through the mass of foliage above us. Dark, prickly bushes and trailing vines criss-cross the jungle floor. As I settle down between two trees, shotgun laid in front of me, I do another quick scan ahead but see nothing. But once I'm in place an uneasy feeling starts to creep up my spine. Not a feeling, more of a memory. I recall a planet called False Hope that I visited with the Colonel. It was a jungle death-world, and contact had been lost with the station there. What we found was one of the most fragged up, strangest things I've ever encountered, but you wouldn't believe it unless you'd been there yourself.

The memories of that jungle fight, the smell of burning vegetation from the flamers and the screaming of men being torn apart, rush back to me. I keep my finger over the trigger of the shotgun, ready to pull it into position.

I hear the sound of footsteps behind me, but resist the temptation to turn around. I've been told to keep watch and, whatever else you think of me, I'm a bloody good soldier these days and I do what I'm told. Whatever I'm told.

'The Colonel says we're setting off,' says Lorii. I push myself to my feet and look back at her.

'Which way?' I ask, and she nods to the right. 'What's that way?'

'Doesn't matter,' she says with a shrug. She turns and starts to walk off. 'We haven't got a clue where we are anyway, so the Colonel just picked a direction. Keep walking long enough, we'll find something to orientate ourselves.'

'Fair enough,' I say, slinging the strap of the shotgun over my shoulder and heading after her.

THE GOING IS tough, and I'm seriously short of breath after just a few hundred metres. The Colonel says that Armageddon's air is so full of pollutants that it can kill a man in three days. We're lucky we landed in the jungle, where the trees make it a little more bearable. Out in the desert, we'd have been coughing and choking the moment we were out of the pod. What with the thick air and the exhausting effort of wading through dead leaves, uniform-snagging bushes and sometimes having to saw our way through vines with our knives, it's an arduous march.

Things scuttle away through the brush at our approach. Beetles the size of my fist with glowing wings buzz to and fro in the gloom. The shrieking and cackling of birds and branch-dwellers hidden in the treetops announce our advance, and destroy any chance of our going undetected.

Brownie's up ahead on point, and I'm the man at the back. We're spaced out at ten metre intervals. Well, most of us are. Kelth and Erasmus are walking as a pair in the middle of the group. The scribe's been well behaved since we came down. The motor's gone in his servo-skull, but he insists on carrying it with him. So far they don't seem to be slowing us up, but we'll see how long that lasts.

We're not quite sure how long until last light, but we'll have to allow plenty of time to find a good lying up point to make camp. I reckon we've still got a good couple of hours marching ahead of us. Although the going isn't great, there's no reason why we can't cover at least ten kilometres before finding ourselves a bolt hole.

As we go further, the jungle seems to take on a little more character. There are a few shallow streams and pools across our line of advance, and we're steadily working uphill. Although we've scrambled in and out of gullies and depressions, I know it isn't my imagination that the climbs out have been higher than the routes in.

The Colonel advises us not to drink any of the water. Thousands of years of industry have contaminated pretty much everything on Armageddon. It's a wonder the jungle flourishes as it does. I guess sometimes plants know how to hang on to life just as much as a Last Chancer.

Every now and then, Brownie indicates a particular feature, like a large exposed boulder, a small cave under a tree's roots, a particularly splendid splay of red fungus, or a fallen trunk. As he passes between two gargantuan trees whose roots form an archway above him, Dunmore points to the ground again. Kelth drops back from Erasmus and falls in beside me.

'Why does he keep doing that?' the Navigator asks.

'Meeting points,' I tell him. 'If we run into some kind of trouble, and the Colonel tells us to bug out, that's where we meet up. Just remember where the last rendezvous is, and if there's any kind of a crisis, just head for it as best you can. Better tell Spooge too, in case he doesn't know.'

'I will,' he says, glancing over his shoulder behind me.

'Look,' I say, giving him a shove. 'Get out of my fraggin' way, you're right in my line of sight.'

'Sorry,' he says, stumbling ahead. I shake my head as he catches up with Erasmus.

'Bloody amateurs,' I mutter to myself, checking to the left and right as we continue on.

WE FIND AN area of high ground just as the twilight is making it difficult to see more than ten or twenty metres. The trees are sparser here, and so the under-growth is a lot thicker, providing perfect cover to hide us from view. There's nothing to eat or drink, and despite the humidity my throat is parched. I feel my stomach growling empty as well. I hand the shotgun to Kin-Drugg, who's drawn first watch with Lorii.

The Colonel's already sitting with his back against a tree root, his eyes are closed, and he is breathing shallowly. I help Kin-Drugg scout out a good van-tage point, nestled under the root of a tree a little further down the bank but with a view of the sur-rounding area.

'The Colonel will give me the tap when it's time to relieve you,' I say, and Kin-Drugg nods and crawls into the lookout position, shotgun across his knees. I walk over to the other side of the hill and find Lorii lying under the spreading thorns of a dark blue bush. The bolt pistol is under her right hand, just to her side, a few leaves scattered on top of it to hide it from view.

'You're being cautious,' I say, nodding to the pistol. 'There's going to be barely enough light to see your hand in front of your face, never mind enough to glint off metal.'

'And thinking you can relax is one of the best ways I know of getting yourself killed,' she replies, not turning around.

'You have to wind down some time,' I say, sitting down next to her.

'Piss off, Kage,' she says, not harshly, but with enough edge to her voice that I know she means it. She sounds more resigned than angry. 'Don't start pretending now that you cared.'

I open my mouth to answer, but think better of it. With a shrug, I push myself to my feet and walk back through the ferns and bushes to our camp. Spooge is near the Colonel, sitting cross-legged in the dead leaves, the hatch in the bottom of his servo-skull open. He's prodding around with his finger, a despondent look on his face.

Spooge's skull is cracked wide open, split asunder, his brains bulging out of the wound. I prod it with my fingers, exploring its depths, pulling it apart. I lick the fluids off my fingers, enjoying the sensation of the taste. The feel is rubbery in my hands, and I run my palm along the jagged edge of the broken skull to compare the harsher sensation. My sense of touch sends an ecstatic thrill through me; it is one of immense pleasure. I giggle as a shard nicks the flesh and my own blood bubbles out to mix with the scribe's life fluid.

I stumble, momentarily dizzy. Spooge looks up at me with his watery eyes and smiles. There's a flicker of memory for an instant, something to do with Erasmus. I can remember the taste of blood, but can't place it. There's a rippling at the back of my head, and it moves forward. But this isn't the crushing pain of a vision; it's just a pleasant little tremor that sets my skin tingling.

'Could you have a look at my skull, please?' says Erasmus and I stand there looking at him for a moment, feeling the urge to laugh, though I don't know why.

I suppress the notion, and sit down next to Erasmus. He proffers me the servo-skull and I take it from him. It weighs more than I thought, and I'm amazed he's carried it with him this far. I look at him out of the corner of my eye, so that he won't see me looking at him. I turn the skull over in my hands, pretending to examine it. He looks at me with eager expectation.

'I'm no tech,' I say, handing him back the lump of inert machinery.

'No, you're a soldier, aren't you?' says Erasmus, placing the quill-skull on the ground beside him.

'Yes, I'm a soldier,' I say, looking straight at him, trying to detect some kind of insult or criticism. 'What of it?'

'Do you know that I used to want to be a soldier?' he says. I shake my head. He could've wanted to be a glow-globe for all I care.

'I had to follow my father though, did you know that?' he says, with a quick glance towards the servo-skull. 'Did you know that the Departmento Munitorum gives an extra surrogacy allowance if you father a son to assume your position when you've passed on to the Emperor?'

'No, I never knew that,' I say.

'I was a scribe-apparent for thirty-five years. Don't you think that's a long time to wait for your calling in life?' he says.

'I have no idea,' I tell him. 'I'm not sure, but I don't think I'm even thirty-five years old. It's never been much of an issue. I was a kid, then I was a factory worker and then I was in the Guard.'

'You don't know how old you are?' he asks, incredulous. I shouldn't be surprised by his reaction; after all, he does surround himself with numbers and figures every day. I think statistics and records are his lifeblood. 'Give or take a couple of years for transit deviation, mistranslation and primary reference error, you're not even thirty Terran standard.'

I'm about to reply when I stop myself. I notice something about what he just said.

'That wasn't a question,' I say to him, turning full on to face him.

'What wasn't a question?' he says. 'Is that important?'

'Not important,' I guess,' I say to him, brow furrowed. 'It's just that… Well, you always…'

'Just what?' he says, concern on his face. 'I always what?'

'Have you always talked by asking questions?' I say, smirking to myself to see what his reaction is. I know he probably isn't even aware of it, but it's about bloody time he stopped.

'Have I always talked by asking questions?' he asks, staring up at me with his wide, honest eyes. 'Do you think it would be strange if I didn't?'

'Never mind,' I say, standing up. 'Get some shut-eye, we'll be heading off before first light.'

'How do you sleep in these conditions?' he says as I turn away. I stop and think for a moment, before replying. I don't look at him when I speak.

'Close your eyes,' I say. 'Then try not to remember all of the shit that's happened to you. That usually does the trick for me.'

DAWN IS JUST a glimmer above the treetops when we set out. I did my stint on watch around midnight, near as I could tell in this lightless, starless dump. Nothing happened. Brownie snored until the Colonel gave him a kick. There were a few bats, or possibly night birds, flapping about in the trees. I was sitting on a nest of ants for half the time, and I count myself lucky that the worst I got was that creepy sensation of having the little bastards in my clothes for a while. I've heard tales, one of them from False Hope, of insects that could poison or devour a man in a few minutes. I'll pay more attention in the future.

It's a monotonous, grinding leg for most of the morning. Dehydration is becoming a serious problem. All the moisture in the air counts for bugger all if none of it's inside. Combined with the acrid tang of the atmosphere, my throat's harsh and ragged by the time the Colonel calls a stop after four hours of marching. Kelth and Erasmus, who's still carrying that bloody skull, look completely done in. The rest of us aren't looking too great either.

Wheezing, coughing up gobbets of phlegm, drenched in sweat, we take a short break in the overhang of a long, shallow ridge. The Colonel uses a tree root to pull himself up the bank, and though I'm loth to miss any second of rest, I push myself to my feet and follow him.

'We can't keep pushing on like this, not without something to eat, or at least a drink,' I say. 'Sir,' I add as he glances at me with that icy look of his.

'There is no telling how long we must survive on our own resources before we reach new supplies,' he says. 'We must conserve what we have and not waste it at the outset.'

'We'll make better time with a little something in our bellies and a drink,' I say. 'There were enough rations in the pod for two days, I reckon. There's no harm in having some now before we set off.'

'Very well, but we eat and drink on the march,' he replies. He looks about to say something else, but is distracted by something off through the trees.

'What is it, sir?' I ask. He doesn't reply, so I follow his gaze. There's a darkness out there, but oddly better lit. It's about two hundred metres away. 'A clearing, do you think, sir?'

He grunts and looks back at me.

'Bring me my bolt pistol, and get Lorii to bring the shotgun,' he says. 'Tell the others to stay here while we have a look.'

I nod and jump back down the bank, passing on his orders to the squad. They ask what the fuss is about, but I don't tell them anything. I don't really know myself. It's just a clearing. Armed, we set off for the strange patch of sunlight, the Colonel waving us down to a crawl, as we get close. Through the trees, I can see that it is indeed an opening, with bright yellow light pouring in from above. The clearing is actually the edge of the jungle.

As we cautiously move forwards, we find the jungle filled with blackened, charred tree stumps and shattered trunks. Ash covers the ground, ankle deep. Wandering through this blasted maze, the destruction gets worse, and after about another kilometre we come out into the direct sunlight.

A massive open space is laid out in front of us, burned to the ground as far as I can see. In the distance, at the top of a rise, the light glints off metal, but it's too far too see what it is. Perhaps it's some kind of structure, but there's no way to be sure.

We do a quick circuit, checking for any sign of tracks, but draw a blank. The Colonel sends Lorii back to fetch the others while we head out into the open, keeping low all the same. Ash and charred wood crumbles underfoot as we make our way down the rim of the crater. Under the unfiltered sunlight, the heat is almost unbearably hot. I can feel it burning on my forehead and hands. The shotgun, which I took from Lorii before she left, gets very warm in my hands, and is rapidly becoming uncomfortable to hold. I see that the Colonel has holstered his pistol.

'Some kind of incendiary, sir?' I venture.

'It found it's mark, whatever it was,' the Colonel says, kicking over a lump of charred branch. Underneath, gleaming in the bright light is a piece of shattered bone.

'Looks old,' I say, crouching down and pulling it free. It's part of a skull, much thicker than a man's. 'It's ork.'

As I toss the fragment back into the ash and begin to pace around, I find other bits and pieces that survived the attack. A long knife with a crudely serrated edge lies next to the finger bones of the hand that was holding it. I see the muzzle of a gun protruding from underneath a shattered half-log and eagerly dig it up. I let it drop from my fingers, disappointed to see that the rest of the pistol has fused into an unusable lump. I look over at the Colonel, who's glaring up into the sky, one hand shielding his eyes from the sun.

'We will be too exposed if we make for that,' the Colonel says, looking towards the glint in the distance. 'It will be best if we keep to the cover of the jungle.'

'I don't think there's anything to help us here, sir,' I say, eager to get out of the sun that is beating on my head like a jackhammer on a plate-press. 'We should move on.'

He gives the crater another quick sweep with his gaze and then nods, heading off towards the edge of the jungle to our right. I glance back and see the others have caught up with us. They are looking around the massive crater with the same curiosity that we had.

'We're moving out,' I call to them, waving them onwards. As Brownie comes up to me, I toss him the shotgun. 'You can be on point, get going.'

His bald head prickling with sweat, he stares dumbly at the shotgun for a second, and then sees my impatient look. He hawks and spits before heading off at a jog to get ahead of the Colonel.

The inferno engulfs Dunmore, lighting him up like a candle. The stench, like burning swine, drifts on the smoke that fills my nostrils. His screams, choked and hoarse, are a symphony in my ears. They are accompanied by the crackling of the flames. His skin blisters and tears, creating circular patterns pleasing to the eye, before the blood boils away. The fireball strips him down to muscle, the fat hissing and spitting off him like a delicious roasted haunch. Shrivelling to ash, the muscles turn to powdery cinders that blow up in the thermal of the fire, dancing motes of greyness that look like dark snow. His organs rupture as his bones crack and wither, each popping noise is like a lover's kiss on my soul. His suffering emanates in a palpable wave that sends a shiver down my spine, arousing and satisfying. The last thing to go is his shining scalp: the last beads of moisture from his burning brain sizzle away into nothing.

With a start, I open my eyes and see Oahebs staring at me, his face full of concern. I don't remember closing my eyes. The light from the sun hurts and the heat makes me dizzy. Despite that, I feel a chill shiver run along my spine. I'd swear it was a cold sweat if it hadn't started at the bottom of my spine and worked its way up to the base of my skull.

'I think the heat's getting to me,' I admit, waving away Gideon's frowning face. He lingers for a moment longer, his eyes seeming to be looking at a point somewhere inside my skull. Then he slowly turns away. A few steps on, he glances over his shoulder at me, before pressing on after Brownie and the Colonel.

CHAPTER SIX
JUNGLE GHOSTS

DARKNESS FINDS US with no sign of Cerberus Base, so we set up another laying up point, this time in the hollow between the root systems of two immense trees. It is deep enough for a man to stand and not be seen from a couple of metres away. Following the routine of the night before, we set up the sentry points and allocate watches.

I feel ever so weak now, as do the rest of us. Even the Colonel is showing early signs of dehydration. We have only had a few sips of water every couple of hours to keep us going. I actually saw the Colonel stop once and lean against a tree to get his breath back briefly. It doesn't sound like much, but when you've been with him as long as I have, you know it must be getting bad for him just doing that. The Colonel's the most stubborn, unstoppable son-of-an-ork you'll ever meet. I saw him with his arm blown off once, and it barely even slowed him down. Emperor knows how the hell he got a new one. I suspect the tech-priests did something for him, but just what it was, I haven't got a clue.

I've only just closed my eyes after bedding down after first watch when there's an urgent whisper in my ear. Moving slowly, I sit up, to see the face of Oahebs right in front of me in the darkness. As I look at him, I feel a churning in my stomach. I tell myself it's just the dehydration, but I know it's him really.

'Movement,' he says, gesturing over his shoulder with a thumb. I crawl across the floor of the dell after him, and pull myself up the side to lie next to the Colonel. He has his pistol in hand and is peering through the ferns along the edge of the hollow. I glance at Oahebs and he hands me the shotgun without hesitation. The others are crouched under the overhanging roots, white eyes staring at me out of the darkness.

Not far away, perhaps twenty metres, I can see shadowy figure in the gloom. I can't make much out, just shifting shapes between the trees. Listening, I hear the soft crunching of the dead leaves under foot.

'Not orks,' I say and the Colonel grunts in agreement.

'Not moving that quietly,' he says.

He thumbs the safety catch of the bolter as the group, perhaps no more than a dozen strong, passes about fifteen metres in front of us. Behind me I hear the scrape of a boot searching for a footing. I resist the urge to glance back, knowing that a sudden movement might attract attention.

'Ours?' I say, my voice so low, it's little more than a breath. The Colonel nods slowly. I can't understand why he's so damned paranoid if he reckons they're on our side.

'I do not want to be shot in the dark,' he whispers, as if reading my thoughts. I understand immediately. I know that if I was one of the guys up there, and we suddenly sprang up, my trigger finger would work quicker than my eyes.

The Colonel slowly reaches up his hand and lifts up an old twig from the jungle floor just in front of us. With deliberate care, he snaps it between his fingers, the noise as loud as a gunshot in the still night.

The troops out there are good; I'll give them that. There's no sudden rushing for cover, no hectic movement. Over the next few seconds, they simply melt from view. The vague silhouettes just vanish into the bushes and trees. I know they're still out there, and they're probably just as worried about what's going to happen in the next few minutes as we are.

I wait, heart hammering on my chest, peering intently into the darkness. I can't see anything except the faint swishing of the wind through the ferns and long grasses. It's then that I feel something cold and round press against the side of my neck. I let go of the shotgun, easing my hands away, and slowly turn my head to the left.

There, just a metre away from me, autogun still at
my throat, is a jungle-fighter. His eyes stare at me
from out of the camouflage across his face. He's
sprawled headfirst down the bole of one of the trees
we were sheltering under. His free hand and toes are
rammed into the thick cracks in the bark to hold
himself in place.

With measured precision, the gun muzzle not
wavering more than a centimetre, he spins himself
around until his feet are on the floor. He winks at
me and then makes a purposeful glance over my
shoulder. I turn and look back into the hollow to
see the others with their hands up. There're three
more troopers on the far bank, guns levelled at the
rest of the squad. They notice my stare and one of
them points up. I follow the gesture with my gaze.
As my eyes focus, I see the faintest of glimmers from
a scope right above us, and then a movement that
my brain only recognises after a moment.

It's a sniper waving at us.

'WELL, YOU'RE BLOODY well up a vagrin tree without
a knife, aren't you?' says the lieutenant of the
Armageddon Ork Hunter platoon after the Colonel
has explained how we ended up on their patrol
route. He says a few words to his platoon sergeant,
and a few minutes later we're passing around their
spare water canteens and scoffing down the rations
offered.

We're sitting about a kilometre from where they
met us, with the platoon's first squad spread out in
a defensive cordon around us. The lieutenant,

Golder Fenn, is the one who climbed down the tree to get the jump on me. He's a big guy, a little taller than me, and muscled like an ogryn. He's handsome, in a rugged, scarred sort of way, and seems always ready to use his smile.

'You did bloody well to get this far, I'll give you that,' he says with an appreciative nod. 'You were right, Colonel, to head this way. It's another hundred and twenty kilometres further than you thought it was though. And this sector is teeming with bloody orks. Hundreds of them, in fact. Nice lair you had there, as well.'

'It didn't stop you finding us easily,' says Brownie, tearing off a chunk of salted meat and chewing heavily. 'We might as well have stood in the open with signs on our heads, shouting at the top of our lungs.'

'That's just your bad luck, actually,' says the platoon sergeant, an older, heavy-set man named Thorn. 'That's one of our regular observation posts. Fenn's right, if we hadn't been heading for it anyway, we might have walked straight past. Our poor sniper Daffer, had to sit there all night watching you!'

'We're on our way back to Cerberus, as it happens,' says Fenn. 'We have to finish our sweep first, but we'll be back there by dawn the day after next. You're welcome of the company.'

The Colonel looks dubious.

'We need proper supplies as soon as we can get them,' he says. 'I think we might be more of a hindrance in our current state.'

'Well, we'll be stopping by one of our caches anyway,' says Thorn with a glance at his lieutenant. 'You can arm up there for the duration. It's only about three kilometres from here. We'll be there by first light.'

'You patrol by night?' asks Kin-Drugg. 'Isn't that dangerous?'

'It is for the orks,' laughs Fenn. 'They still haven't learned not to light fires. We can see them kilometres off. Anyway, I do strongly suggest you come with us tomorrow.'

'Strongly suggest?' says the Colonel, turning the full force of his stare on the Armageddon officer. Fenn shrugs it off without batting an eyelid.

'Well, actually, I insist,' he says. 'There's all kinds of traps and tripwires as you get near Cerberus and I can't spare one of my men as a guide. Plus, I wouldn't have it on my conscience if you didn't make it. Think of it as welcome hospitality.'

We sit in silence for a while as the Colonel chews this over. It's Oahebs who speaks up, his voice the barest whisper.

'I notice your platoon doesn't have a commissar,' he says, looking around.

'They tend to have accidents in the jungle,' says Thorn, glancing round at the rest of the command squad, who give knowing nods.

'Their greatcoats aren't good for jungle work,' says one of them, a comm-set strapped to his back.

'Too ready to rush in when you should be falling back,' adds another, slowly sharpening his long hunting knife on a whetstone. 'Gotta be nice and careful out here, nice and quiet, like. No good running about bellowing orders when you've got an ambush set up, is it?'

'Most of them stay back at Cerberus,' explains Fenn. 'Those that venture out tend not to come back, I'm afraid.'

'Sometimes they're even got by the orks,' mutters one of the men, to the stifled laughs of the others. Fenn scowls.

The lieutenant glances at the Colonel.

'Don't listen to them,' he says with a dismissive wave of his hand.

'I'm well aware of the reputation of jungle fighters like yourselves,' says the Colonel heavily. 'When do we move out?'

Fenn checks a chronometer from his webbing.

'Oh, about another hour or so,' he says. 'I'll send out the first patrol in a few minutes and we'll see what they have to say.'

'Good,' I say, and Fenn looks at me with a puzzled expression. 'Time to grab a bit of sleep. It's good not having to be on watch. Wake me when you're ready.'

I shuffle off and find a boulder to use as a pillow, folding my fatigue jacket over it and curling up. There are thirty-five Guardsmen who grew up in these jungles out there, and they've been fighting the orks for over fifty years – ever since Ghazghkull's first invasion. Sleep comes easily when you feel safer than you've done in years.

FIRST LIGHT GIVES us a better look out our new companions. Like Fenn and Thorn, they're all well built, raised from the hardy stock of many generations that have lived in these savage conditions. They're almost as barbaric as the aliens they're fighting. Dawn reveals necklaces and ear-piercings of ork fangs and heavy green tattoos beneath the camouflage. Fenn himself has the lower jawbone of an ork strapped beneath his helmet along the chinstrap. I didn't see it last night because he'd left it in his pack.

They certainly seem raring to go, which is more than can be said for the Last Chancers. I kick Kin-Drugg awake and send him to rouse the others. Moaning and stretching, they assemble around the Colonel as he waits for the signal from Fenn.

It's then that I notice someone is missing.

'Where's Spooge?' I say, looking around the encampment.

'I think he's talking with one of the squads,' says Kelth, picking at the tattered threads of his robe. 'Something about his skull.'

'For Emperor's sake,' I say, and I'm about to send Brownie to look for him when I notice him clawing his way up the bank towards us, servo-skull under one arm.

'No fixers?' says Lorii, seeing the little man cradling the quill-skull. He just shakes his head sadly and then looks at Fenn.

'Do you have tech-priests at Cerberus?' Erasmus asks, hope suddenly returning to his face.

'A few,' the lieutenant replies. Spooge nods happily to himself. 'Let's move out.'

After only a short while, we're at their supply cache, hidden in a cave between two tumbled boulders, a fallen log concealing the entrance. Inside are several packs full of water and rations, as well as ammo crates, spare autoguns, heavy stubber barrels and power packs.

The platoon begins to gear up properly and Fenn invites us to join in. I snatch myself an autogun and five mags of ammo, and while I'm at it I snaffle a couple of frag grenades. Lorii passes out full water bottles, which we thirstily drink from, having had only a few mouthfuls since we crashed down. We spend the next few minutes checking magazines, finishing off part-full water bottles to avoid them making noise, all that kind of stuff. After a few minutes, Fenn gives us the nod, and we move out again.

With one squad out ahead, and one out to each flank, we march off, keeping a steady pace. The Colonel splits us into two groups, Kelth and Spooge under the watchful eye of Kin-Drugg and Oahebs, while the rest of us accompany Fenn's command squad.

A COUPLE OF hours in, Fenn signals a halt. From up ahead, one of the scouts emerges from the jungle, moving at a fast jog.

'We've got ork sign, about three kilometres ahead,' the ork hunter reports. 'A large group, perhaps forty or fifty of them.'

'Headed west like the last ones?' asks Thorn, kneeling down beside Fenn. The scout nods.

'Alright, assemble the platoon,' says Fenn. 'Squad one to stay on scout and follow the trail. Squad two move ahead, and set up an ambush a couple of kilometres ahead of them. Squad three is reserve. I'll provide regroup back-up and second reserve.'

I like the way Fenn includes himself with the platoon, not at all like a lot of lieutenants I've known. There's very little ceremony, something I've noticed with a lot of the wilderness-based regiments. I guess they realise that getting it right out on the battlefield is more important than shining buttons and sharp salutes. On top of that, these guys have been fighting together for years now. I can vaguely remember that kind of bond, when you know you can't trust the guy next to you not to spit in your coffee, but when the bullets and lasbolts start flying he'll be watching your back, because he knows you're the one watching his.

As the squad sergeants begin to filter back through the brush, Fenn briefs each of them in turn, giving them precise instructions and checking they understand. A few ask questions about positioning and timing. It's all very relaxed, but without being careless or casual. Thorn stands up and walks over to us, where we're sitting on the edge of a narrow stream having a quick break.

'You'll be staying with us, secondary line,' he says, looking at the Colonel to see if he has any objection. Schaeffer just nods in agreement. 'When Fenn gives the signal, we'll close up with the front squads and provide support.'

He nods over to the other members of the command squad. One of them has a 25mm heavy stubber across his shoulders, and the other two are stripping down and oiling their heavy bolters.

'How come you use autoguns instead of lasguns?' asks Lorii. 'Surely lasguns are more practical for extended patrols, what with being able to recharge the packs?'

Thorn smiles. The black and green camouflage twists across his face, his bright teeth showing.

'It's a platoon-by-platoon thing,' he says, pulling his autogun off his shoulder and patting it. 'Carrying ammo can be a bitch, you're right, but we don't mind trading that hardship for the added psychological effect.'

'What psychological effect?' asks Brownie. I notice with a smile that he managed to find a heavy stubber for himself. He has ammo belts looped over his shoulder, and spare shells thrust into pouches in his belt.

'You have to understand how an ork thinks to fight him properly,' says Thorn, getting serious. 'Autoguns make a lot of noise and bright muzzle flare, and that's something they can respect. There are not many things orks are scared of, but you can be sure we're one of them. When a platoon lets rip with these beauties from hiding, the air's filled with hot metal and it's an almighty din. Especially at night, when we usually operate. Orks just don't care about the pissy little zip-zip-zip of lasguns, it just doesn't register as proper weapons fire for them.'

'Weight of fire counts for a lot, too,' adds Fenn, and we glance up, not noticing that the sergeants have dispersed and he's joined us. He moves so damn quietly all the time, despite his bulk. 'When you're laying down fire into the bush, you're not looking for precision, aimed shots. Hell, that's why we got snipers in each platoon. And when one of them big green uglies is legging straight at you, you want to put as much fire into him as possible, 'cos it don't matter whether you shoot him in the leg, the head or the chest most of the time.'

Makes sense to me. Fenn makes it clear that it's time to head out, so we grab our gear and file off behind him. About thirty minutes later, and even I can see where the orks have been. The undergrowth is trampled flat, and there are hundreds of boot marks in the mud, overlapping each other. Fenn falls back to walk beside us.

'These are from seconders,' he says, and, seeing our perplexed expressions at the term, explains: 'Firsters are the orks that came down or are descended from the first invasion, fifty years ago. They've gone very feral, but they're heaps more jungle-wise than the ones we're following. Their weapons might be cruder, but they're cunning as a foxrat and it's almost impossible to find their camps.'

'So these orks are newly arrived?' says the Colonel, looking ahead through the trees as if he could see them.

'Yeah, it's a worry really,' says Fenn. 'We've come across more and more of them in the patrol, at least four groups. All heading west or north. This is the only one we've been close enough to follow.'

There's the distant crackle of fire from up ahead. Fenn doesn't seem the least bit concerned. He is marching along and chatting quietly with the

Colonel. The rest of his squad are similarly relaxed. I can feel my heart beating faster in my chest. I tighten my grip in the autogun, checking once again to make sure that the safety's off.

'Erasmus?' I call out to the scribe, who's just ahead of me. He turns and stops, waiting for me to catch up. I nod towards Brownie. 'Go and act as loader for Dunmore.'

'You w-want me to help him?' he says, staring at me in disbelief. 'In combat?'

'You're an armourer, you know how that twenty-five mil works, don't you?' I tell him. He nods. 'Well, go and tell Brownie that I've assigned you as loader.'

Spooge jogs off, casting another worried glance back at me, then he joins Brownie. They exchange a few words and Brownie looks over in my direction and then heads towards me.

'What's your game, mate?' he says through clenched teeth. 'Why you dumping that useless fat-ball on me?'

'Because he's better off doing that than firing a gun,' I say, not looking at Dunmore. 'Better to have him loading for you than a soldier who should be putting down fire.'

I can almost hear gears in his brain trying to work out a flaw in my logic, but he doesn't come up with anything, so he simply scowls and stalks off. I check the safety is off on the autogun again, and out of the corner of my eye see the trooper with the comms-set holding the headpiece to his ear, listening. He gestures to Fenn, who jogs over and listens to the relayed message. The lieutenant looks in our direction and then walks over to us. He points to a fallen tree alongside the ork trails, about twenty metres away.

'Set up a position around there,' he says, looking at the Colonel. He gives Schaeffer the order as if he was one of the platoon. He turns around and points behind us, opposite the fallen tree. 'That's the area of engagement, no firing anywhere else. Orks have pulled back from the ambush, squad one will be following them up and we'll be on the diagonals to catch them. I don't want any stray shots catching our own guys.'

He turns to walk away and then changes his mind.

'I'm sure I don't have to tell you this, but I will anyway,' Fenn says, looking at each of us, his normally smiling face deadly serious. 'Nobody opens fire until we spring the trap. You mess this one up, and you're walking to Cerberus on your own.'

I expect the Colonel to reply, but he just stands there, unclipping the cover on his holster and then looks at me.

'You have your orders, Kage,' Schaeffer says, turning his back on Fenn as the Armageddon officer walks away. 'Detail fire teams to cover our position, and make sure you have someone covering our rear.'

I nod and start snapping out orders to the Last Chancers, pointing to various hiding places and vantage points in the area assigned to us. They break apart, heading to their individual places, leaving me with the Colonel and Kelth. I look at the Navigator.

'What am I going to do with you?' I say.

'I will find myself a safe refuge,' he says, looking around. 'Perhaps with Lieutenant Fenn.'

'Everyone fights,' says the Colonel, pointing to the laspistol hung at his belt, taken from the ork hunters' cache earlier that morning.

'Not me,' Kelth says, shaking his head slightly, eyes meeting the Colonel's stare. 'My abilities are far too rare to risk in some pointless skirmish.'

The click of the bolt pistol in Schaeffer's hands sounds ridiculously loud, and his brings his arm up, aiming straight at Kelth.

'Are your abilities too rare to waste getting shot *avoiding* a pointless skirmish?' the Colonel asks, his arm as steady as a rock, his icy glare burning into Kelth. The Navigator glances at me, looking for some sign that Schaeffer's bluffing, and then looks away, seeking Fenn or one of his men. They're all out of sight, there's nobody but him and the Colonel.

'This is ridiculous,' says Kelth. 'And it is also in contravention of my charter as Navigator. You are supposed to uphold the law, Colonel, not break it.'

The Colonel's finger curls inside the trigger guard.

'Under regulations, our escape qualifies as a military crisis,' the Colonel says. 'All present are therefore subject to military law. As I said in the saviour capsule, anyone guilty of cowardice will be executed.'

Kelth's look of disbelief turns to resignation and he pulls the laspistol from his belt. There's a barely audible whine as he presses the charge button. The Navigator looks at me.

'Where would I be most useful, lieutenant?' he asks, eyes narrowed.

'Stick with me, you'll be fine,' I say, leading him away from the Colonel to a narrow depression a few metres in front of the fallen log.

Brownie and Erasmus have set up the heavy stubber at one end of the log, facing the trail. They are hidden behind a clump of ferns and the log itself. There's a loud clank as Dunmore cocks the slide and moves the first round into place. He gives me a thumbs-up signal as I settle down.

It's not long before I can hear the orks approaching, the snapping of twigs and rustling of dead leaves underfoot. I can see them moving straight back down the trail, dumb green bastards that they are. I can't tell how many there are, not yet, but my guess would be two dozen or so. Glancing to my left, I can't see a trace of Fenn and his squad, so well hidden are they behind rocks, bushes and in depressions. Not even a single muzzle is in view. There are no sounds from them either, just the gentle wind in the trees above. In contrast, I can hear feet scraping behind me, the click of a safety being released, and a stifled snort.

The orks are coming forward in small groups of threes and fours, hurrying but not rushing headlong towards our position. They stumble along with their characteristic stooped gait, long arms swinging beside their short legs. Their green skin blends in with the colour of the jungle, but their dark clothes, rusting belts and chains, show up easily enough. A few of them stop to fire off shots behind them, at the pursuing squad I guess, or perhaps just at shadows. I don't know how closely they're being followed, and I suspect they don't either.

The front group is about fifty metres away now and I can make out their features more clearly. Their leader is at the front; it is larger and more heavier set than the others, with crude metal plates of armour riveted to its jerkin, a tight helmet on its bucket-jawed head. It's snarling something to the others, exposing a ragged row of long fangs, in a jaw powerful enough to crush a man's skull. I know, I've seen them do it, almost had my faced gouged off by one of them in the past.

At thirty metres, all hell breaks loose.

The bushes to our left erupt with muzzle flare and the chatter of autoguns. This is swiftly accompanied by the roar of the 25mm opening up. The front orks go down in the first concentrated hail of fire, bloody eruptions stitching across stomachs and chests, heads blown apart by heavy stubber fire. The heavy bolter opens up with a distinctive rapid booming, each shot hurling a rocket a little bit bigger than my thumb. The first shot explodes against a tree trunk, hurling bark and sap into the air. The gunner adjusts his aim quickly, the second bolt smacks cleanly into the chest of the leader and explodes, tearing the ork boss apart from inside, scattering ripped entrails.

It's all happened in just a few seconds and I realise that Brownie's been firing from behind me, the zip of heavy stubber bullets zinging past a few metres to my right. I pull the autogun round and squeeze the trigger, letting off a four shot burst to get the feel of the gun. It's got a bit of a kick to it and with my next burst I aim low at an orks that's raising its crude gun towards Fenn's position. Three shots rip out, the first missing, but the next two stick it in the abdomen. It swings back from the shots, its own gun roaring wildly into the trees. I down it with my third burst, putting a few rounds into its chest and neck.

The orks are running towards Fenn's position, not realising where we are, and I open fire again. A longer burst shatters the kneecaps of another ork, sending it tumbling into the leaves and dirt. It howls and then swings towards us on its belly, its bulky pistol erupting, sending bullets chewing into the dirt a little to my left. Before I can finish it off, Dunmore's heavy stubber chatters again, a line of impacts bursting in front of the ork until the fire intersects with it, gouging lumps out of its face and tearing into its shoulders. It slumps down, dead this time, and I pick another target.

The trail is littered with ork bodies, half of them dead already, and I realise with a shock it's only been about ten seconds since Fenn's group opened fire. Some of the orks are scattering into the jungle, while a five-strong group, much braver then the rest, charge towards us, brutal cleaver-like knives raised, pistols and guns hurling metal in all directions, chewing lumps out of the fallen tree just behind me.

They're about ten metres from us, and I'm about to stand up ready to flee when there's a burst of fire from behind them. The pursuing squad opens fire, adding to the din of autofire, and three of the orks go down in the surprise salvo, their backs ruptured and bloody. One of the orks falters and turns, only to get a heavy bolter shell in the ribs under its half-raised arm, its chest exploding outwards from the detonation.

The last hurls itself towards me, bringing its wicked cleaver down in a long arc. I roll to my right, finger on the trigger of the autogun as I throw myself clear. The point-blank fire tears into its left arm and stomach. It grunts and sways, and then steps forward again. Out of the corner of my eye, I see the Colonel rise up from the undergrowth to my right, bolt pistol in both hands.

He plants the shot straight into the side of the ork's low forehead; its head disintegrates a moment later. The steaming remnants of an eyeball plop onto my leg as the ork's headless corpse falls across me. Kicking it free, I leap to my feet, searching for another target, but the orks have scattered. I can hear bursts of autogun fire out in the jungle, and see occasional muzzle flashes in the gloom, as the other two ork hunter squads stalk through the murk, earning their title.

Fenn stands up from the tangled roots of a tree about twenty metres to my right, slapping another magazine into his autogun and waving for his squad to emerge. He sees the blood and shit all over me and grins. Striding over to me, he slings his firearm over one shoulder on its strap, and drags free a combat knife about as long as my forearm.

'Got yourself a couple there, eh, Kage?' he says, stooping down and rolling the ork over.

He digs into the remnants of its face with the knife and his bloodied hand emerges a few seconds later, proffering me four large tusks. He nods for me to take them and I hold out my hand. He tips the fangs into my palm and steps back. I look at them for moment and then he laughs, a deep noise, and steps forward to slap me on the shoulder, leaving a bloody handprint.

'Keep them safe,' he says with a smile. 'You've just killed your first ork on Armageddon. There's millions of the ugly green bastards out there for you to get, but always remember that first one!'

I look around to see the other Last Chancers being given similar prizes by the rest of Fenn's command squad. Erasmus staggers up to me, servo-skull under one arm, outstretched hand with a bloody ork tooth thrust towards me.

'Did I do alright?' he says, his stare slightly vacant. I take his fingers and close them over the fang, and give him a wink.

'Welcome to Armageddon, Erasmus,' I say. 'Welcome to the green hell.'

He smiles, nods slightly, and then faints.

CERBERUS BASE
AND BEYOND

CHAPTER SEVEN
ALONG THE CHAERON

I'm not sure what I was expecting Cerberus Base to look like, but it's nothing like what I would have said if you'd asked me. I was thinking of some huge armoured bastion, with towers and ramparts and everything. What I find out, as Fenn leads us through the gap in the fourth concentric ring of razor wire surrounding the Imperial station, is that it's a huge camp. And it looks a complete mess.

The jungle is scorched and ripped up for about a kilometre in every direction, craters dotting the landscape. There are wooden watchtowers placed along the razor wire and minefield defences, and I can see mortar and artillery emplacements dug down into the earth behind wood-reinforced revetments. Here and there I spy a bunker roof, buried under sod and leaves, heavy stubber and lascannon muzzles protruding menacingly from their dark interiors. Trench works criss-cross the whole hill as it rises up from the jungle, overlooking the surrounding wilderness for kilometres on all sides.

As we pick our way through the traps, receiving waves from hidden snipers and gun post officers, I see a huge bonfire about half a kilometre to our left, a thick column of black smoke rising into the yellow sky. Out in the open, we're subjected to the full force of the sun, as it beats its way through the permanent low cloud, heating the air like an oven. I'm drowning in sweat after the first few metres, and I can already feel my face burning.

Fenn looks over at the bonfire, a concerned look on his face. He urges us to hurry on, without giving us a reason, but I collar Thorn and ask him what the blaze is all about.

'Ork bodies have to be burned,' the platoon sergeant says, glancing at the bonfire. 'Standard practice.'

'Yeah, so what's strange about that?' I ask. I've heard that advice given many times before, something to do with orks reproducing with spores or some other stupid theory the tech-priests have.

'A fire that size means there must have been a pretty serious attack,' Thorn says. 'We received a recall for defence when we were out on patrol, but Fenn figured it wasn't anything too major. I guess we know where all those seconders were going to or coming from now.'

Set just below the crest of the long low hill at the centre of the base is an armoured portal, its steel gates open. I can see rows of figures coming and going. Just above it, comms aerials sprout out of the ground like metal ferns, spreading high into the air, relaying and sending signals to all the patrols across the jungle, and to the high command out past the edges of the tree and in orbit.

Negotiating another kink in the trail through the razor wire, we start heading further uphill, towards the command bunker. As we move on, the other squads peel off to the right, heading for their own digs in a trench further around the hill. Only Fenn and his command squad are left with us.

IT'S A BLESSED relief to walk in through the open gates of the command complex, into the shade. Although it's still hot and humid as hell, it's good to be out of the direct heat, and with the change my sweat suddenly feels icy cold.

Suppressing a shiver, I stop for a moment, allowing my eyes to adjust to the gloom. The interior is carved out of the hill itself, and is reinforced in places with metal plates and spares. Corridors and rooms lead up, down, left and right. It's a total rats' nest, and my experienced eye notices some of the little details, such as loopholes in the walls covering the entrance so that any attacker can be fired on through the walls. Looking up, I see that as well as the main gates themselves, there are two more blast doors ready to be dropped down across the accessway. It'd be hard to imagine any enemy getting that far.

More ork hunter squads are heading out, giving nods and waves to Fenn and his men, and casting interested glances at us. A few tech-priests scurry about, and Erasmus tries to attract the attention of one but is ignored as the red-robed adept of the Machine God drifts past. There are a few officers floating around, chatting to each other, looking at maps as they walk, or carrying steaming mugs. It's all quite civilised really, considering there are thousands of orks out in the jungle, all of them intent on wiping this place from existence.

'There are a few secondary camps further north and south,' says Fen. It is the first thing he's said since we came in sight of Cerberus. 'They used to be training bases, but of course you can get all the training you need these days, just a day's march out into the jungle! We also used to have another major base to the northeast, Wolf Outpost. The orks almost overran it until the commander blew the self-destruct. You might have seen the remains, actually, made a hell of a mess for twenty kilometres in every direction.'

Well, that explains a lot. As we walk down the tunnels, turning left and right, seemingly doubling back on occasion, Fenn gives us a running commentary. The main comms room, buzzing with equipment, low chattering voices and radio static, opens up on our left. The hall down to the main armoury leads away a little further on. Steps that wind up to the artillery and observation posts are dotted at regular intervals along our route, along with officers' mess rooms, kitchens, cells, storerooms and all the other assorted junk you'd find in any Imperial military base. We've been walking about ten minutes when I realise how far down we've gone.

'Just how big is this place?' I ask Fenn, my voice loud in the confined space.

'It goes through the entire hill, with a few tertiary corridors out into the jungle itself,' he says. 'They've been sealed; the only way in or out now is through the main gates. It's too hard to defend that many entrances. We learned that in the first few days after the second invasion began.'

By the expression on Fenn's face, I know not to ask more. I can imagine what brutal fighting must have occurred when the orks got inside; fighting at close quarters where they're at their best.

'Here we are,' says Fenn, leading us through an open doorway to the right.

Inside is the command hub: an open room with a large table emblazoned with the Imperial eagle at the centre and a huge map hung on the wall. There are red and blue scrawls all over the chart, and there's a handful of officers moving back and forth in front of it, updating the annotations and making cryptic marks as they refer to scribbled notes on the pads they carry.

Through another doorway we walk into the real nerve centre, with comms panels all around the walls, linked to the various other stations in the hill I guess. Monitor servitors and lexmechanics churn out data from the incoming flow, scribbling the intelligence on long reams of parchment that spill onto the floor. Every now and then a map officer walks back in, tears free a strip and then goes back to update the map again.

At the far end, sitting in what can only be described as a metal throne hooked up with monitors, is a broad man, leaning over talking to a huddle of tech-priests and a man with the markings of a major on his cap. He looks up as we approach, smoothes his thick moustache with a gloved hand, and then slicks back his short greying hair.

'Ah, you've decided to come back after all, Lieutenant Fenn,' he says, his voice a cracked wheeze. I notice the scars of two puncture marks in the side of his throat. I guess that he's had his fair share of run-ins with orks before being cocooned in this command centre.

I then notice that he's not actually sitting in the throne, he is wired into it. He has no legs, the stumps sitting in metallic cups. Out of the corner of my eye, I see the Colonel do his best to straighten his dress coat and brush off the worst of the burrs and scratches inflicted by the jungle trek.

'Marshal Vine?' says the Colonel, stepping forward and saluting sharply. 'Colonel Schaeffer, commanding officer of the 13th Legion, sir.'

'Ah, you're the Last Chancers man, are you?' says Vine. 'I'm afraid you'll have to come to me so I can shake your hand, since my bloody chair isn't working!'

These last words are shouted at a thunderous bellow, directed towards the major and the tech-priests who visibly flinch. The Colonel takes a couple of steps forward and takes the proffered hand, giving it a short shake, and then steps back.

'Ah, I heard you ran into a spot of trouble,' says Vine, wheezing, folding his hands in his laps. 'Sorry about the welcome, but our intelligence is out of date all the bloody time!'

Again this damning criticism is delivered as a deafening roar, aimed this time at the map officers scurrying back and forth from the other chamber. I see Fenn suppressing a smirk, but not soon enough for the hawk-eyed marshal to miss it.

'Ah, you can stand there and smile all you bloody well like, Fenn, you piece of tree rat shit!' Vine shouts, pointing an accusing finger at the lieutenant. His hoarse voice turns shrill. 'Ignore my orders? Ignore my orders? I'll have you strung up as ork bait, you insubordinate little arse.'

'To return would have compromised our patrol security,' says Fenn, calmly taking in the commander's enraged glare.

'Ah, I don't care if you had to wade through a sea of bloody greenskins,' says Vine. 'When I tell you to get your smug arse back here, you do as you're told! How the hell am I supposed to run this bloody war, surrounded by incompetents and know-it-all arrogant ork fondlers like you?'

He breaks down into a hissing, wheezing fit, and the major steps forwards and proffers a handkerchief. Vine snatches it from him and uses to dab at the spittle dribbling down his chin.

'Ah, you're a good man, but I'm not having this, not having this at all,' he says after he composed himself again. He flings the sodden piece of cloth back at the major, who hurriedly tries to catch it before it hits him in the face. 'An order's an order, and if you disobey, that's insubordination. Am I right, Colonel?'

It takes Schaeffer a moment to realise that the marshal is now looking at him. He clears his throat purposefully. I guess he's buying time to work out what he's going to say.

'Failure to comply with a direct order is a charge of gross misconduct,' says the Colonel evenly, not looking at Fenn, but directing all his attention to Vine instead. 'It is punishable by flogging or other physical chastisement, incarceration not exceeding twenty years, or death.'

'Ah, hear that, Lieutenant Fenn?' says Vine, leaning forward as far as the bindings holding him to the chair allow. 'Do you deny that you did not comply with my orders? My bloody direct orders?'

'Is this a court-martial, sir?' says Fenn, stiffening to attention. 'If so, I think there are procedures to follow, and such.'

The Colonel looks at Fenn and then studies his glittering eyes. I can see something in them, something he's thinking quickly about.

'In a military crisis, jurisdiction and enforcement of Imperial law resides solely with the commanding officer in charge,' says Schaeffer.

'Ah, hear that too, Fenn?' wheezes Vine. 'Bloody well judge and executioner, that's what you're looking at here. So, did you receive my orders or not? I can check your signals record, so don't give me any ratshit about crossed wires or anything.'

'I received your signals, sir,' says Fenn, sighing heavily. He looks at the Colonel, eyes narrowing.

'Ah, and did you drag your sorry arse back here to protect Cerberus against attack, given that I'd issued the recall order to your platoon?' says Vine, his dark eyes glowering at the lieutenant.

'I did not, sir,' says Fenn.

'Ah, then what am I supposed to do, you daft bastard?' roars Vine, his anger reducing him to a coughing wreck again for a few seconds. His voice is a low hiss when he speaks again. 'Everybody knows you could make captain as quick as piss runs downhill, but I can't play favourites, can I?'

'No, sir, you cannot,' Fenn says, his voice quiet. I see him take a deep gulp. He really is taking this seriously, but it's just a bawling out, I'm pretty sure of that.

'Ah, discipline has to be maintained,' the marshal continues, scratching at one ear. 'So, do you want to be flogged, jailed or shot, you disobedient monkey-rat?'

'If I might offer an alternative, Marshal Vine,' says the Colonel before Fenn can reply. 'There is an alternative.'

I look at Fenn, who notices my glance. You poor bastard, I think. I've just realised what the Colonel's going to suggest. With just the look in my eyes and a slight shake of the head, I try to communicate to Fenn that he should go for the flogging, but he has to look back at Marshal Vine when the commander clears his throat.

'Ah, what have you got in mind, Colonel Schaeffer?' he says, sitting back heavily, causing his support chair to wobble slightly. I glance down at the floor and see that it's on narrow tracks, but one of the drive wheels is hanging off at an odd angle. No wonder he's annoyed with the tech-priests if they can't fix something that simple.

'It is within my power, under special considerations of the Imperial Commissariat as a penal legion commander, to commute any sentence, sir,' says the Colonel.

'Ah, so I don't have to flog this worthless idiot then?' says Vine.

'You have to sentence him first, sir, for the powers to be active,' prompts the Colonel.

'Ah, alright then,' says the marshal, leaning forward again. 'Golder Fenn, Lieutenant First Class, commanding officer of the third platoon, first company, fourth Armageddon Jungle Fighters Regiment. I hereby find you guilty of gross misconduct by order of insubordination, through deliberate failure to obey a direct order.'

Vine and Fenn look expectantly at Schaeffer. He blinks a couple of times, his ice blue eyes regarding them both. He then looks up at Vine.

'You have to pass sentence, sir,' he says.

'Ah, right, I sentence you to…' Vine's hand flaps for a moment, in mock indecision. 'Death by firing squad. Yes, I sentence you to the full penalty of Imperial Law.'

Oh frag. If only he'd stuck with the flogging. Now Fenn's up to his ears in the brown stuff and sinking quick. The Colonel turns smartly towards Fenn, eying him up and down.

'Golder Fenn,' he says, and I know the exact words that are coming next. 'You are sentenced to death for insubordination bringing about gross misconduct. Sentence commuted to penal servitude under the special supervision of Colonel Schaeffer, commanding officer of the 13th Penal Legion. Do you accept this new sentence?'

'What?' says Fenn, his brain catching up with the Colonel's words. I hear a spluttering cough from Vine as he also realises what's happened. 'Penal servitude?'

'What the hell are you doing, Schaeffer?' spits Vine.

'I need good soldiers,' the Colonel says, eyeing Fenn.

'Well, you can't have him, he's one of mine,' says the marshal. 'I can't have such a thing.'

'By the laws that you yourself invoked, Fenn can come with me or he can be put to death,' says the Colonel. 'It is the choice you gave him. My credentials with the Commissariat are of the highest authority, and I do have the power to remove you from command.'

'You wouldn't dare!' says Vine, shaking with anger. 'We're at bloody war, or didn't you notice?'

'It is for the successful conclusion of this war that I do this,' says Schaeffer. 'He will be mine with or without your approval. The association with countermanding an officer of the Commissariat will be enough to ruin you.'

'I'm sorry,' Vine says, looking at Fenn, and then looking away. 'I'm sorry.'

I take a couple of steps and lean forward to whisper in Fenn's ear.

'Gotcha!'

THE CHUGGING OF the barge's engine mixes with the slapping ripples of the water as we inch our way along the Chaeron River. Unsurprisingly, Marshal Vine was less than happy after the Colonel's little coup to snatch Golder Fenn, and Fenn himself hasn't spoken a word to any of us since. The marshal had us geared up and shipped out to the Chaeron docks within six hours, not even giving us time to get some sleep before we departed on a rescheduled supply hopper. Two bumpy, turbulent hours eastwards in the air and we were out of the jungle. Then we were dropped down at the docks where the Chaeron River comes down from the Diablo Mounts far to the east and enters the jungle. I managed to snatch a couple of hours at the wharfs while we waited for the barge to be readied, and then the Colonel took us aboard and we were off.

That was two days ago. Two days of dull, monotonous routine. There's barely room to swing a rat on board, and so we have to spend most of our time up on the deck or the roof, in the fume-filled air. The barge is low and wide, with a reinforced hull rusted and stained by the polluted waters. The roof is coated in layer after layer of peeling protective paint, eaten away by the air itself. Luckily, Schaeffer managed to commandeer us some rebreathers from Cerberus, but that still doesn't stop the stinging in your eyes, or the feeling of your skin being constantly etched away.

The Chaeron itself is a sluggish, bubbling tar-flow of chemical residues, thick with streaks of green and red. I would have thought it was impossible for anything to survive in that toxic soup, but telltale bubbles betray the creatures beneath the surface. Now and then I see vicious-looking, fin-backed lizards slipping into the murk from the banks, trailing after us for a few kilometres before deciding that none of us are going to fall overboard and provide them with a meal.

The barge is captained by Hauen Raqir. He is a wizened old man, his face shrivelled to a husk by the elements, his skin almost black with ingrained grit and dust. With his two sons, he keeps the engine coaxed into life, shovelling raw, solidified sewage into the burner to keep it ticking over just enough to propel us along. There's little other traffic on the river that we've seen, although I've seen abandoned Imperial gun emplacements along the banks in places, and the corroding shells of tanks, APCs, and a few ork vehicles too. Now and then, there are contrails in the sky high above us, left by Imperial Interceptors or bombers, or maybe ork aircraft.

It's pretty lazy-going in comparison to the jungle, but we still have to keep a tight ration on food and water. Apparently both are valuable commodities everywhere. The orks have continually attacked the water pumping stations far to the south and according to Raqir, millions have died from dehydration in the hives and whole regiments have deserted their positions looking for water.

It's mid-afternoon and I'm sitting up on the roof of the barge as normal, near the front, playing cards with Brownie, Kin-Drugg and the captain's eldest, Yaidh. The rounded prow bobs up and down through the water ahead of us, the wind blowing smoke from the exposed engines back along the length, covering us in fumes, but the rebreathers keep the worst out of our lungs. There's frag all to actually bet with, but we make do with spent casings taken from the hold.

Raqir spends his time sifting through the desert looking for anything that can be taken back to the forges and smelted down again. Apparently metal is in pretty scarce supply too these days. It reminds me of the care taken to protect the transports in the convoy that brought us here.

'I'm sure you cheat, but can't see how,' says Yaidh, throwing up his hand with a grin. I scoop my winnings into a pile in front of me.

I pick up one of the spent cartridges while Brownie shuffles the deck.

'So how many of these have you got on board?' I ask.

'Nearly two thousand,' says Yaidh. 'Fifty of them worth a ration pack, hundred will get you a half-charged power pack.'

'Fifty for a rations tab?' says Kin-Drugg, looking at my stash. 'You've got my breakfast and lunch there, Kage.'

'Wish I'd kept all those we fired off in the jungle,' says Brownie, passing the deck to Yaidh to cut. With a deft flip of his fingers, Dunmore brings the two halves back together and starts to deal.

'So how many shells for the love of a good woman?' he asks with a grin. Yaidh smiles and taps the side of his nose.

'I know good place, but take more than empty casings to buy affection,' he says.

'Brownie's got nothing but empty casings anyway,' laughs Kin-Drugg, earning himself a punch on the arm. 'Why do you think he likes the biggest guns. He has to compensate somehow.'

I pick up my cards, keeping my face blank as I look at my abysmal hand. Brownie fidgets with his stake, toying with the casings with his left hand. He's got a good one, because every time he's bluffed so far, he's occupied himself with his right hand. Yaidh scratches his chin and takes a snort through his rebreather. He's gonna fold.

Kin-Drugg I haven't been able to read yet, but he's such a bad player he hasn't got any consistency to base my observations on. Hey, I spent two years on garrison duty on Stygies, I had to learn something while I was there, and cards was the main attraction. Thinking about it, it was the gambling that got me in trouble eventually. A bet with a woman as a stake, and a bad loser for a sergeant. Funny how things repeat themselves.

I fold.

As the others throw in their stakes and start the betting, I glance over to the bank, a couple of hundred metres to starboard. The ash wastes of Armageddon stretch out to the horizon, bleak and virtually featureless. Around here, the ground's not even proper ash dunes, just tiny rocks and pebbles, kilometre after kilometre of flatness. I'd hate to get lost out there, because except for an hour each way at dusk and dawn, you can't even tell where the sun is, and I haven't seen a star in the night sky since I got here. High-level smog covers the whole desolate planet. Doesn't stop it getting damn hot though, I think, pulling at my collar as if to let some of the heat out. A trickle of warm sweat runs down my chest.

'Do you think Fenn will ever come round?' says Kin-Drugg, tossing in his hand. He's obviously smarter than Yaidh, who doubles his bet.

'We'll have to see,' is all I say.

'How come he stays down below all the time?' asks Brownie, matching Yaidh and raising him again. The bargeman grins victoriously and then immediately matches the bet.

'Yeah, an outdoor man like him should enjoy all this fresh air,' says Kin-Drugg with a snort.

'He likes his open spaces to be not so open,' I tell them quietly. 'He's never been out of the jungle before, it's kind of creeping him out. He's not used to so much sky.'

'Oh great. Good one, Colonel,' says Kin-Drugg, pulling the stopper from his water bottle and taking a swig. Brownie lays down his cards and Yaidh starts muttering in some local dialect we can't understand. I'm pretty certain he's swearing his head off.

'I was sort of the same for a little while,' I say, pointing at Kin-Drugg to shuffle and deal. 'I grew up in a hive, so I never really knew you could get distances more than a hundred metres. Imagine how I felt when I was on the shuttle going up to orbit. I saw this massive hive that I only knew a tiny bit of, dwindle to a little blob. Damn near pissed my pants. And I really had never seen the sky before, although my grandpa used to tell us what lay outside the hive.'

'Well, Stralia's kind of average really,' says Brownie. 'Lot of islands, so I pretty much everyone grows up on the coast. I couldn't sleep for two weeks, not hearing waves nearby, or smelling salt.'

'Well, Kator's renowned for its grav-chute regiments because we pretty much live in the sky,' says Kin-Drugg. 'Gas harvesters mostly, a few sub-orbital cities. I'm the opposite from you, Kage. I never set foot on proper ground 'til I joined the guard.'

'And I was born on a boat that runs on shit,' says Yaidh. 'Less talk, more cards. Deal the cards. I win this time.'

SEVERAL MORE DAYS' travel brings us to the intersection with the Krynnan canal. A series of huge locks, fifteen in total over two kilometres, bring ships up seven hundred metres from the lowlands to the south. It's here that we part company with the Raqirs. We're due to meet with some kind of military transport heading up the canal, which will take us on to Infernus Quay. After that, I've got no idea, the Colonel didn't tell us any more. He obviously knows exactly where we're heading but for some reason is reluctant to tell us. That worries me, because last time he was so cagey about a mission, it was because nobody would have believed it.

I'm expecting something a bit like Raqir's barge, perhaps with a bit more accommodation, but when dawn reveals the transport pulling in to dock the next morning, I have to admit I'm a little bit more impressed.

Over two hundred metres long, the heavily-armoured barge cruises through the murky river waters at speed, a bow wave foaming ahead. It leaves smaller vessels bobbing madly in its wake. Smoke billows from three exhaust stacks, the clanking of powerful engines clearly audible over the noise of the dock. Two gun turrets jut out of her prow deck, each housing two large-bore cannon, and a third smaller gun is mounted on her rear. As she slows and pulls up at the wharf, a long metal gangplank hisses out on hydraulics, clanging down onto the ferrocrete. The Colonel walks up and talks to one of the officers by the boarding ramp, signing something and then waving us on. We grab our kit bags, scrounged from the ork hunters before we left Cerberus, and jog on board.

At the top, a corporal gives us a surly look and directs us to the lower deck. Heading down the stairwell, we find ourselves in a bunkroom, large enough for a hundred men, with kit lockers down the length of the ship. The hull vibrates even with the engines just ticking over, rattling bolts in their holes and causing tremors to run up my leg.

'This is a bit more like it,' says Kin-Drugg, dumping his bag on one of the upper bunks.

'Nice to have a bit of space,' says Brownie, wandering to the far end.

We stop as we hear the thumping of boots on the deck above. Lots of boots.

'Bugger,' says Brownie as a sergeant leads his squad down the steps, barking orders for them to sort themselves out. We drift down to the far end as two whole platoons file in. The last to arrive stand looking confused, looking for non-existent empty bunks. Then the Colonel strides in and the Guardsmen all leap up from their lounging, jump into line and snap off salutes. He marches over to us.

'I hope you are not occupying bunks needed by proper soldiers,' he says, nodding to the door through the next bulkhead.

With a sinking feeling, I lead the Last Chancers through. Sure enough, it's an empty storeroom, or more likely an ammo magazine. There's even shelving around the walls. Not a bed in sight, not even a scrap of mattress or blanket. A single yellow glowglobe illuminates the cramped chamber. It's dark, and below the waterline, and the throbbing of the engines is even more powerful. It makes my teeth rattle. There's a constant sloshing of backwash against the hull as the barge rides the river swells.

'Come on Last Chancers, make yourselves comfortable,' I snap, directing a venomous look at the Colonel's back as he steps out. The door swings shut behind him, and we hear the sound of a lockwheel squealing into place. I notice there's no wheel on the inside. Why would there be? It's a storeroom after all, it's not like cargo needs to let itself out. And that's all we are, human cargo.

INTO THE DIABOLUS

CHAPTER EIGHT
DEATH IN THE RUINS

ANOTHER DAY AND a half, getting only brief exercise
and five meal periods. Then the door opens again.

'Full kit, combat readiness,' says the corporal who
welcomed us aboard. 'Muster aft.'

As he turns sharply on his heel and marches away,
we look at each other.

Once we're up on deck, rebreathers in place, lasguns charged and ready to go, we find out what all
the fuss is about. About half a kilometre down the
river is Infernus Quay, a sprawling maze of ruined
warehouses, docks and factories. Smoke fills the
sky, and the steady pounding of artillery can be
heard from the southern shore, about three hundred metres to our starboard.

With a roar of jets, a flight of three attack planes
scream over, rockets rippling out from pods slung

169

under their wings. Detonations erupt a few hundred metres inside the quay buildings. There are the constant sounds of small arms fire and grenades. Shells from the ork guns explode along the quay and send up massive plumes of water from the river. Another transport barge, slightly smaller than the one we're on, takes a direct hit. Its stern is flung into the air, and propellers splinter and fly off. The men on board are plunged into the murky water; they struggle briefly before the corrosive soup eats through their uniforms and sucks them below.

Half-ruined wharfs and piers jut into the Chaeron, swarming with Guardsmen pouring off barges, lighters and rickety old steamers. They surge forward into the ruins. As we close, I can see the black coats of commissars, chainswords waving the troops on, and I can just hear their shouts blended in with the cacophony of battle, exhorting their men to their greatest efforts.

The Colonel appears, bolt pistol in hand, a newly acquired power sword hanging in a scabbard at his coat belt. He doesn't look at us, instead he fixes his attention on the mangled remnants of a pier about two hundred metres away, evidently our destination.

The other troops on board clump up the stairs onto deck, and it's then that I realise how young and old most of them are: some of them are barely old enough to shave, while others have thinning and greying hair. Their officer, a gangling lieutenant, moves along the line, checking weapons and packs. Behind the visor of his gasmask I can see wide, scared eyes.

The barge shudders as the engines are put in reverse, slowing us down for the approach to the pier. Looking out over Infernus Quay, I can see that there are very few buildings more than two storys high. A half ruined steeple of a shrine rears up near the centre of the complex, the wing of a massive golden eagle hanging forlornly from its twisted brackets. The whole place is littered with rubble, burnt out tanks and transports and piles of bodies.

'This doesn't look fun,' mutters Brownie, standing just behind me. I ignore him, focussing my attention on the landing place as the metal gangway soars down, clanging against the twisted platform. The Colonel turns and points at us, then heads off down the ramp.

'Come on Last Chancers, time to die!' I shout, breaking into a run.

With my boots thudding on the metal walkway, I hurl myself down the boarding ramp at full tilt, following the Colonel into a shattered office building just to our left. Glancing over my shoulder I see Brownie following, the heavy stubber slung over one shoulder, and Erasmus running behind him with loops of ammo belt.

Lorii leaps across a pile of bricks and slams into the wall next to me, breathing hard. She glances out of the jagged frame of a window just behind me, lasgun held ready. The others follow quickly, taking up covered positions in this room and the one next door.

I glance down at the rubble we're crouched on, and notice skeletal fingers protruding from underneath a twisted metal roofing beam. Putting it to the back of my mind, I scoot forward to kneel beside the Colonel, who's peering out of a doorway to the front.

'The orks hold the west quarter,' he says, pointing off to the left. 'This is a counter-attack to push them back. I want the heavy stubber up in that roof two hundred metres down the road, half the squad to its right, the other with you circling left.'

I nod and point to Brownie, Erasmus, Kelth, and Oahebs.

'You're with the Colonel, straight ahead, don't slow down,' I say. 'The rest of you, follow me.'

Without waiting for an acknowledgement, I put my head down and slide out of the door, keeping close to the wall. A squad of Armageddon guard, gas masks on, trench coats flapping, crosses the street about seventy metres further on and I head after them, running across the road into the building opposite. Finding myself in a large, corrugated-metal warehouse choked with smashed crates and splintered pallets; I head across, scrambling over the debris.

Scuttling from building to building, we cover about two hundred metres in the next few minutes. I'm breathing hard; my heart is hammering in my chest as I crouch at a corner, peering left and right, my whole body tense. Taking a deep breath, I force myself to relax and focus. There's sporadic firing from our right, and the crump of mortar shells falling not far ahead. To our left, past a fallen archway, a Leman Russ tank smokes fitfully, its tracks thrown, the turret dislodged from its ring. Ahead, a multi-storey building has collapsed across the road, filling it with rubble and chunks of masonry. I duck back when I see a flitting movement just beyond the mound.

Easing my head back around the corner, I look over the rubble, scanning to the left and right. I hear a barked order; it's obviously one of our squads.

'Come on, the Colonel will be waiting,' I say, heading forward at a jog, lasgun held in both hands.

Reaching the pile of rubble, I drop to my stomach and pull myself forward, ignoring the scrapes and scratches from the jagged debris cutting through my fatigues. Reaching the crest, I see three mortar teams huddled behind a sandbag wall, inside a large shell crater. Looking further ahead, I can see more movement, orks massing in a couple of half-demolished storehouses about three hundred metres away. The mortars are laying down constant fire on their position, but it'll only be a matter of time before the orks take their chances and head forwards.

Scrambling over the rubble, bricks and crumbling mortar cascading down over my boots, I make my way over to the mortar squad. Their sergeant glances around at the noise, laspistol ready, and then relaxes when he sees us. It's at that moment that I dearly wish we had a comms-set to communicate with the Colonel, or somehow find out what's going on. Looking down the side street to the right, I can see the position of the others, the nose of the heavy stubber poking out from a large crack in the wall on the third floor, the position covered from above by a slope of cracked roof.

'Wait here,' I tell the others, and they fan out into cover on either side of the road. I run down the street towards the Colonel, ducking instinctively as a shell screams overhead; it explodes on the far side of the block. Running into the ground floor, I see Oahebs by the door, lasgun resting against the frame.

'Where's the Colonel?' I ask, and he jabs a thumb over his shoulder towards the next room on.

I walk through and the Colonel's there, talking to Kelth. He looks over at me.

'We're down the street near the mortar battery,' I tell him. 'There's a good number of orks ahead, getting ready to attack. We'll be better off in front of the mortars to give them some protection.'

'Very well,' he says with a nod. 'This will be our fallback position if we need to retreat. Have your team secure the left side of the approach, we will be up shortly.'

I turn and start running back to Lorii and the others, hoping that the Colonel gets a move on. It'll be over very quickly if the orks advance on us before we have any support. Jumping down into the cracked plaster behind a wall, I glance around at the others. I point to a building across the junction and gesture for them to move up. As I do so, I see a couple of squads of Guardsmen coming up to our position from the rear. I recognise their lieutenant from the barge. Not wanting to exchange pleasantries, I head after the rest of the team before they get within talking distance, running at a crouch across the ruptured ferrocrete.

'What are they waiting for?' asks Kin-Drugg, looking at the orks. There's a fair few of them now, under bombardment from the mortars, splinters and shrapnel scything through the buildings and across the road. 'They're getting a pasting just sitting there.'

I shrug, not knowing the answer. I don't really care, as long as they hang back for a few more minutes. Ahead and to the left is a stairwell, leading up to the remnants of the floor above. I lead the others up, directing them to move along the level which seems to stretch for about fifty metres up the street. I poke my head out of a window, the glass crunching underfoot, to see what's going on. The sound of orkish chanting carries to me over the distant explosions and rattle of fire. They're definitely working themselves up for something.

'Any way up at the far end?' I ask Fenn. He turns to me, face as white as snow, blinking slowly. He opens his mouth and then shuts it again without saying a word. 'Come on, this is the urban jungle. It's just the same, only you've got rubble for undergrowth and walls for trees. Pull it together!'

He stares blankly at me for a second and then recognition lights up his eyes. He blinks a couple more times.

'No,' he says finally. 'There is no way up at the far end, unless they climb on each other's backs.'

'I want you down there, with grenades ready in case they try to get underneath us,' I tell him. 'Have you got that?'

He nods and turns away, to be replaced by Lorii.

'You'd better see this,' she says, and her expression makes my stomach knot.

I follow her along a ledge that leads out to the remnants of a bridge that once crossed from this building to the opposite side of the road, some ten metres away. The tangled wreckage of metal lies on the street below us. I can hear a loud rumbling, and creeping forward on my belly, stick my head out to look at the ork position. I can see them swarming through the buildings now, but it isn't that which is causing my heart to skip a beat.

Grinding along the road is a huge armoured vehicle, larger than a Leman Russ, three turrets pointed at the mortar section down the road. Its iron-rimmed wheels crush masonry and corpses under its weight as it rolls forward, oily smoke fuming from a cluster of exhaust stacks at its rear, filling the street with a reeking stench. Crude banners flap from flagpoles attached to its main turret.

'Battle fortress!' I turn and shout to the others. Glancing back, I see the orks pressing in behind it, using its bulk for cover. A mortar shell lands just in front of it, kicking up chunks of ferrocrete that bound harmlessly off its thick hull. The stutter of heavy stubber fire echoes down the street as Brownie opens up, bullets zinging of the metallic beast and cutting through the orks to either side.

'Hold your fire,' I say, making myself relax my grip on my lasgun, massaging some life back into my hand. 'Fenn, Kin-Drugg, I want covering fire against the infantry when we attack. Lorii, ready with grenades.'

She nods, pulling two from the pouches at her belt.

'Wait for my signal,' I say, my voice an urgent hiss, as I see Fenn crouching down, bringing his lasgun up to his shoulder.

With a great belch of flame and smoke, the battle fortress's main gun opens fire. A split second later the wall of a building across the street explodes outward in a shower of steel splinters and ferrocrete shards. The two secondary guns open up, raking the ground line with large calibre shells, tearing more pockmarks into the road and surrounding buildings. Sitting in hatches thrown back, two orks man heavy autoguns, their staccato firing interrupted frequently as the crude guns jam.

The battle fortress rumbles to a stop just beneath us. Orks move forward around it like a green wave breaking across a rock. The main gun fires again and I can feel the pressure wave slapping across my face, only a couple of metres above it. The sound makes my ears ring, as it echoes off the inside of the half-ruined room.

'Let's do it!' I shout over the din, bringing up my lasgun and firing off shots at the nearest cupola. It swings the gun around towards me and bullets rattle along the brickwork just below me, causing me to duck back. After the expected pause when the weapon jams again, I lean back out, this time putting two shots into the ork's head as it bends down, examining the breach of the gun. It slumps forward. All around me the others are opening fire, a torrent of lasbolts tearing into the orks that clamber around the immense vehicle.

Fire from the others and another mortar salvo join the attack, heavy stubber and lasfire cutting down half a dozen orks. Their bodies are flung into the air by the detonation of the mortar bombs; dirt and limbs scatter across the road and the hull of the battle fortress. Firing off another few shots in rapid succession, I lean back out of harm's way and check on the others.

Fenn is throwing a grenade underarm into the room below us; it bounces off the twisted remnants of a metal stairway. The growling cries of wounded orks follow the bang of the grenade's detonation. Kin-Drugg is snapping off shots left, right and centre, and I can already see a discarded power pack next to him. Each of those is good for forty shots, so he's been busy. Lorii's close by, crouched a couple of metres behind me, waiting for my signal.

A series of explosions ripples along the wall in front of me, and shards of ferrocrete fly inwards, grazing my face and tearing at my uniform. I look at Lorii and give her the nod. Leaning back out, I rake the second cupola with fire, only to discover that the ork's already dead, its finger tightened on the trigger, spraying bullets wildly into the air as the turret turns and it flops to one side. Lorii jumps past me, dropping down the metre and a half to the top of the battle fortress's roof. I sling my lasgun over my shoulder and follow.

Keeping low, we scuttle to the two hatches, ready-ing our grenades. Lasbolts skip off the armour in bright flashes, and bullets scream past within cen-timetres of my face. With another glance at each other, we each toss two frag grenades in. With a run-ning jump, I leap back, grabbing hold of a twisted bridge support jutting from the wall. Wrapping my legs around it I reach up a hand, which Lorii grabs, and I swing her up.

Below us, as we hurl ourselves behind the shattered wall, the grenades detonate. Shrapnel scythes through the interior of the battle fortress. The secondary guns fall silent and the huge tank begins to lurch forwards again. I guess the driver has either died at the controls or has decided it's better to keep moving. The main gun booms out again, the shot sailing high into the distance, the gunner's aim spoiled by the sudden movement. If it gets away, it'll roll over the position at the end of the road with no trouble.

'Again?' says Lorii and I nod, pulling another grenade from my belt.

'Kin-Drugg, get your arse over here, and give me your grenades!' The ex-grav chuter pulls back from the edge of the floor where he's been firing down into the orks, and legs it towards me, keeping his head down. I see that he's limping, blood streaming from his right leg.

'It's no bother,' he says between gritted teeth, noticing the line of my gaze. He hands me a grenade and shrugs. 'It's the only one I've got left.'

He makes his way back to his firing post and pulls his lasgun round. A second later, the ferrocrete explodes underneath him, and a whole section of the floor gives way with a crash and the screech of torn reinforcing rods. He's alright though, I can hear him shouting and shooting. Fenn glances down and then jumps over the edge after him.

'Looks like we're going downstairs then,' I say to Lorii, scuttling out onto the remnants of the bridge and then leaping down onto the top of the battle fortress as it crawls forwards. An ork sticks its head up through the nearest cupola and I ram my boot into its face as Lorii moves past, headed for the front of the tank. I slam the hatch shut, and then drop to my stomach as a bullet grazes my left shoulder. Crawling forwards, I hang over the edge of the track guards.

The clanking of wheels deafens me, but I see an air grille just to my left and smash it in with the butt of my lasgun. Throwing the grenade inside, I leap away, flattening myself against the hull as the orks around the tank fire up at us. Flames billow out of the exhausts and my ears are suddenly torn apart by the shrieking of metal grinding on metal as gears topple off, and the engine is torn to shreds.

The battle fortress slews to the left for a few seconds, crushing orks beneath it, before crashing into a building and coming to a stop. Debris showers down around me, but I can't stop myself grinning. It makes all those days spent on the ship with our mock tank worthwhile.

The sound of a shell, much heavier than a mortar bomb, whines overhead and a moment later the road just behind the battle fortress erupts, tossing orks into the air and causing the immobilised tank to shudder. As the smoke clears, it reveals a deep crater. I can just imagine the forward observation officer's next words. Concealed somewhere around here, he'll be saying, 'Fire for effect.'

It's time to get the hell out of here.

Lorii has the same idea, leaping clear and disappearing into the building where Kin-Drugg and Fenn are. I imagine I hear the distant boom of massive artillery pieces, though I doubt it's true, and I jump down, stumbling over the ork bodies littering the road.

'Run!' I scream at them, slapping Lorii on the back to get her moving.

Kin-Drugg has one arm around Fenn's shoulder. His trousers are soaked with blood from his injured leg. I grab his other arm, and between the two of us, we race towards the Colonel's position. Bullets skip off the walls and whistle around us as we put our heads down and sprint as best we can over the uneven surface.

Hurling ourselves through a shattered window into the street, we pick ourselves up and start across the roadway. A second later, there's an immense series of detonations. The building explodes into dust under the artillery bombardment, and the shockwave hurls us from our feet again. For several seconds the salvo continues, the floor shaking under the impacts, the air filled with choking smoke and dust. After the tumult dies down, it starts raining body parts. Green-skinned gobbets of flesh and dark blood spatter down onto the street around us, ash sticking to the gore as it settles slowly.

Kin-Drugg pulls himself up to a sitting position and looks back across to where the street had stood. The buildings are now nothing more than a crater-pocked wasteland about two hundred metres across.

'Why couldn't have they done that ten minutes ago?' he moans, grasping his leg tightly, spitting in pain. 'Bloody artillery crews.'

'What, and have the infantry complain they don't get any fun?' I say, mopping crap from my face with a dusty sleeve.

I hear a trumpet in the distance, signalling a general advance, and within a minute, squad after squad of troops are pounding down the street to reoccupy the position the orks were in. We sit there as the platoons march past us at the double, gazing around in astonishment. A shadow falls over me and I look up to see the Colonel silhouetted against the yellow sky.

'Where did all these late fraggers come from?' I say, pushing myself to my feet and picking up my lasgun.

'It was good that we stalled the ork advance,' he assures me, looking across now at the hundreds of men moving into place.

I wonder. There are at least two companies here, I suspect less than a dozen Last Chancers would not have made much of a difference. Still, better to be busy than bored, I suppose.

* * *

HEADING EAST ACROSS Infernus Quay, we pass hastily rebuilt barricades and emplacements, and thousands of Guardsmen digging in for the next ork assault. We take it in turns to help Kin-Drugg. We steadily make our way up through the centre of the complex and to the higher ground to the east. There's a medical station about halfway up the slope of one of the hills and we stop there to get treatment for Kin-Drugg. Sitting him down, we all turn and gaze east and north towards the ork lines.

You can easily see them out in the ash wastes, even a few kilometres away. The ground is swarming with them: huge mobs camped out in the harsh dunes, buggies and bikes roaring back and forth. The smoke from the fires and engines casts a pall for kilometres in every direction.

As we watch, something draws our attention to the horizon. They start out as specks, and at first I think I'm imagining it, but as the orderlies come and take Kin-Drugg, I stand there watching the distant shapes. As the minutes pass they grow larger, changing from specks to blobs. To be able to see them at this distance, they must be immense.

'Gargants,' says Fenn, shielding his eyes against the glare. 'Massive war engines, larger than a Warlord Titan. Three of them by the looks of it, plus a load of battle fortresses.'

The orks on the plains seem to be content to wait for their reinforcements to arrive. There's a cry of pain from Kin-Drugg inside the makeshift blood-station. Nobody turns round.

I look over the defences arrayed against the orks, from the batteries of cannons and howitzers on the far bank of the Chaeron, to the legion of troopers in and around the buildings themselves.

All around on the hillside are the wounded, lying in lines along the sides of the road. The lucky ones have blankets to cover themselves from the burning sun, but most of them don't. A little way to our right, amongst the ruins of an old pumping station, dozens of men wearing the white armbands signifying punishment duty are digging a massive hole for the pile of bodies behind them. There must be at least two hundred corpses there, swarming with flies and rats. Luckily the breeze is blowing the other way, so the stench isn't too bad.

One of the orderlies comes out and stretches, his dark uniform crusted with dried blood. He notices us looking at the mass grave.

'That's just the ones that we've sent out this morning,' he says, rubbing a bloodied finger along his nose at an itch. 'There are fourteen more medic stations around here. Well, there were, a couple of them got bombed out by fighter-bombers this morning. On average, we're losing about fifteen hundred men a day. When the orks attack, that doubles, but on quiet days we just have to worry about lung poisoning, infected rat bites, the usual stuff.'

We look down at the dockside and see more troop transports unloading their cargoes of new soldiers. There are so many of them, marching up the piers and disappearing into the ruins.

'A real meatgrinder, eh?' says Brownie.

'It has been,' says the orderly. He proffers a hand to each of us, which we shake. All except that Colonel that is, because he's disappeared off somewhere in the last few minutes. 'The name's Syzbra, I'm with, well was with, the 14th Vastan Armoured Infantry.'

'We're Last Chancers,' I tell him. He gives me a puzzled look. 'Penal troopers. Anyway, it doesn't matter. What do you mean "was with"? Where's your unit now?'

'Well, with all the attacks and counter-attacks, we're pretty much scattered all along the north bank of the Chaeron as far as I can tell. I sort of ended up here, and it seemed there was plenty to do.'

'And what did you mean, it has been a real meat-grinder?' asks Lorii, picking up on his earlier choice of words. 'Are you expecting it to stop soon?'

Syzbra points to the ork horde stretching around Infernus Quay.

'Last time they came in with just one gargant, they almost overran us in a few hours,' he says. 'Luckily we had orbital support back then. I hear it's needed elsewhere at the moment, somewhere near Tartarus I think. They've got three of them this time. I figure you guys turned up at a really bad time. Things are going to go from meatgrinder to slaughterhouse tomorrow.'

I hear Brownie swearing under his breath and Lorii's shaking her head. Kelth slumps to the ground, burying his head in his hands between his knees. I turn to face Syzbra.

'So what are you going to do?' I ask him.

'Keep patching up the bits they throw me, then start using this,' he says, pulling a bolt pistol out from the waistband of his fatigues. 'I figured the commissar who coughed up his lungs all over me the other day wouldn't need it.'

Kin-Drugg comes out, hobbling badly, his face ashen.

'Your friend lost a lot of blood. Lucky you got him here in time,' says Syzbra. 'Any other time, I'd recommend keeping the weight off it for a few days, but that just ain't going to happen is it?'

The Colonel reappears, a quartermaster sergeant trailing behind him. He glances at Kin-Drugg's leg and then looks at the rest of us.

'Grab your gear and move out,' he says. 'There is a supply train back into the Diablo Mounts, and we are going to be on board. Kin-Drugg, you will be staying here. Congratulations, you've survived the 13th Penal Legion.'

The drop trooper smiles for a moment, and then the expression turns to one of anger.

'Hold on, I'm not staying anywhere,' he says, limping forward. 'I heard what you guys were talking about. I'll be dead within the day I reckon. I'm sticking with you, Colonel.'

'Nonsense,' says Schaeffer with a snort. 'We cannot possibly accommodate walking wounded on this mission. You will slow us down.'

'I'll bloody well sprint if I have to,' says Kin-Drugg, lifting up his good leg and standing on the injured one to try and prove how strong he is.

'I said no, you are staying here,' the Colonel says, turning and walking away.

'I demand my redemption!' Kin-Drugg calls after him, and when the Colonel turns around he continues. 'Die or succeed, you said! They're the only two ways I got of redeeming myself in the eye of the Emperor, you said. Well, the mission's not over, and I'm pretty damn sure that if I was dead I wouldn't be looking at this bunch of ugly wasters. So I demand you take me with you.'

Colonel stares at him for a long while, and I expect him to reach for his pistol and blow his brains out. He'd be dead and redeemed then. It's just the sort of thing the Colonel would do. He gives a depressed shake of the head and then looks at me.

'Kage, if this man falls behind, no one goes back for him,' he says before stalking off.

'Too bloody right,' mutters Brownie, stomping after the Colonel. The others follow, leaving Kin-Drugg standing there, watching them go.

'What you waiting for?' I snap at him and he flinches. 'On the double, move out!'

He hobbles off as fast as he can, my laughter following him every painful step.

CHAPTER NINE
THROUGH THE MOUNTAINS

WHEN THE COLONEL had said we were travelling on a supply locomotive, I had been expecting some rickety old steam engine. The reality is very different. The glistening black armour is scuffed and dented in places and covered in ash, but the six carriages and engine look pretty impregnable at first glance. About three times higher than I am tall, the ten-metre long armoured compartments are each protected by anti-aircraft cupolas with twin multi-lasers, while the carriage behind the engine boasts a modified tank turret.

Climbing up the ladder into the central wagon, I note the thick armour plating spaced a little way off from the carriage sides. Inside it's sparse though, it is still a supply train after all. There are no windows, and as the crew slam the door shut we're plunged

into darkness. We sit ourselves down on the reinforced steel floor, feeling something gritty
underfoot. I don't know what it was delivering, but
there's still some of its previous cargo scattered
across the floor.

The train shudders as the engines growl into life
and a fitful light emanates from the glow-globe set
into the ceiling. At each end, hand and foot holds
are set into the wall to allow access to the cupolas
above. I pull myself up and open the hatch, allowing more light to spill in. Dragging myself up to
look out of the roof, I see the track stretching ahead
of us and up into the mountains.

'Check the other gun, Dunmore,' I call down,
pulling the securing catch free on the multilasers in
front of me.

Settling myself against the edge of the hatch, I
swing the guns left and right along the rail. They've
got a good traverse, moving around three-quarters
of a circle to the front and sides. The elevation is
good, almost going up to the vertical, although the
size of the wagons themselves means that they're
little use for clearing the ground unless the target's
a few hundred metres away. Hearing the other
hatch clang open, I glance over my shoulder to see
Brownie pulling himself up. Turning my attention
back to the guns, I press the power up switch and
read the charge meter. Both power packs are almost
full, which is good. Overall, everything seems to be
in good order. Stowing the multilasers back into
their locked position, I take the opportunity to have
a look around.

We're already travelling at some speed, rocking gently side-to-side along the track accompanied by the rhythmic clattering of the wheels. To the right, the Chaeron is disappearing behind the ash dunes, and turning around I see the smoke-shrouded buildings of Infernus Quay are already a few kilometres behind us. To my left, the ash wastes of Armageddon stretch out: kilometre after kilometre of barren wasteland as far as I can see. All in all, it could be worse. I'm glad I'm not marching across those lifeless tracts.

As NIGHT CLOSES in, I give the word to break out our rations. I realise that we left most of the kit on the barge in the Colonel's eagerness to get into the fighting. It's just what we've got in the pouches on our belts, probably enough food and water for three days. I hope that it's either a short journey, or the Colonel has made other plans. I've already had enough of being hungry and thirsty.

Gnawing on a piece of bland dried meat substitute, I take a swig from my canteen to soften the rations.

'So what's the deal with you, then?' I say, looking at Gideon Oahebs. His face looks even more thin and pinched than normal in the dim yellow glow of the compartment, the shadows dark in his sunken cheeks.

'Nothing special,' he says, tearing a chunk out of his ration bar and stuffing it in his mouth.

'Come on,' says Brownie. 'It's been a year now, and we hardly know anything about you. So come on, Gideon, what got you into the Last Chancers?'

'I'd rather not talk about it,' he says, gazing down at the floor, and fiddling with the rations wrapper.

'Alright then, we'll ask Lorii,' I say.

'Don't drag me into this,' she says. 'I'm not going to talk as if he isn't here.'

'It can't be anything as bad as we're imagining,' I say, focussing on Oahebs again. I walk over and sit next to him.

'Just leave the guy alone,' says Fenn. 'If he doesn't want to talk, he doesn't have to.'

'You're just pissed because the Colonel got you good and proper,' says Kin-Drugg.

'Like any of you volunteered,' replies the ork hunter, tossing his crumpled-up wrapper at Kin-Drugg. 'I'm sure you were all queuing up for the penal legions.'

'Some of us had a choice,' says Brownie, looking at Lorii. 'So what's with that, eh? Did you miss your old mate Kage too much?'

She gives him a venomous stare.

'Who's got the cards?' I say, trying to break the uneasy silence.

'Don't change the subject,' says Kin-Drugg between slurping chews of his rations. 'Tell us, Lorii. Tell us what the hell you were thinking when you signed back on with Schaeffer?'

'It's none of your Emperor-damned business,' she says, giving them each a glare. 'I have my reasons, that's all you need to know.'

'I think we deserve more than that,' says Brownie. 'You too, Gideon. If I'm putting my arse on the line for you in a firefight, I want to know who I'm with.

The rest of these meatheads I know, but you two are a mystery. How do we know you're not going to bug out in the middle of a scrap?'

Lorii pushes herself to her feet and walks towards Brownie, who hurriedly stands up, his arms raised to defend himself. She stands right in front of him, eyeballing him.

'I can look after myself, no need to make sacrifices on my account,' she says, and I can't help noticing the emphasis on the word "sacrifices". 'In fact, I'd feel safer knowing that I wasn't relying on you.'

'Is that so?' says Brownie, bristling with anger. 'And why would that be?'

'You're a show-off,' says Lorii, crossing her arms and leaning back on her heels. She glances over at the heavy stubber stowed in the corner. 'Without your big guns, you're nothing, are you?'

Kin-Drugg stands up next to Brownie, sneering.

'And what's so special about you?' says the drop trooper. 'Apart from being a white-skinned freak, obviously.'

Oh frag. He had to go and say something like that, didn't he? I launch myself to my feet in an instant, throwing myself in front of Lorii. My right fist cracks straight into Kin-Drugg's jaw, the sudden blow knocking him to the floor.

'Back off, everyone!' I snap, shoving Brownie back a step. 'Anyone here want to pick a fight with me?'

Kin-Drugg scrambles to his feet, hands balled into fists, but I dart him a look that stops him in his tracks.

'Back down,' I say to him, my voice quiet. Behind me, I hear Lorii snort and walk to the far end of the compartment. Glancing over my shoulder, I see her slump down against the wall, eyes closed.

'What the hell did you do that for?' hisses Kin-Drugg, rubbing his jaw.

'You'll have a bruise, nothing more,' I tell him. 'Count yourself lucky I didn't let Lorii have a go at you.'

'She's not that tough,' he says, puffing up his chest.

'Yes she is,' I tell him. 'I don't need any more corpses at the moment, so don't start throwing around words like "freak", okay?'

He sees the sincerity in my eyes, and opens his mouth to say something but then shuts up. It's the first sensible thing he's done in the last five minutes. With an exaggerated shrug, he steps back and sits down, his gaze avoiding everyone else.

'And you,' I say, turning on Brownie. 'You just keep your mouth shut before someone here puts their fist into it.'

He nods and looks down at his feet. I take a few steps back so that I can look at them all. Kelth is sitting in the corner, eyes closed, apparently meditating or something. Oahebs is just sitting quietly toying with a rations wrapper, folding int and unfolding it. Next to him, Fenn has knife and whetstone out; slowly sharpening the blade with smooth, gentle motions. The others are looking at me, trying to guess what I'll do next.

'Listen up,' I say, raising my voice. 'I don't know what the Colonel has in store for us, but you can believe me that it won't be pretty and it certainly won't be easy. There will be enough fighting and dying to be done before we see this thing out; we haven't got the luxury of doing the orks' job for them. I don't give a rat's arse if you hate each other's guts. Hell, I despise most of you myself. That isn't the point. You're still fraggin' soldiers, and you're still damn well fighting for the Emperor. The next one of you to step out of line will have more than a sore jaw to worry about. You're damn lucky the Colonel isn't here to see you squabbling like kids. He'd probably shoot one of you, just to show he's not to be messed with, and I wouldn't blame him. We are going to be in the cack again pretty damn soon, so stay sharp, because the moment one of you misses a trick, we could all be dead.'

Lecture over, I pick a spot along one of the walls, pull off my jacket and ball it up into a pillow. I lie down, closing my eyes. Soldiers always need to let off steam now and then, and particular after they've been in action. It won't be the last time, I reckon. With any luck, they'll soon be too busy fighting for their lives to worry about their petty personal problems. Whatever happens next, I figure there's no sense in losing sleep over it.

THE SCREECHING OF brakes wakes me instantly, and I can feel us slowing rapidly. Pushing myself to my feet, I throw on my jacket, grab my lasgun off the floor and step over to the compartment doors. The others are stirring too. Fenn's on his feet already, Lorii's reaching out for her weapon. Feeling us shudder to a halt, and the jolt unbalancing me for a moment, I grab the door lock lever and pull, sliding the door open.

Bright light from lamps all along the side of the train floods in, painful after the gloom of the wagon. Shielding my eyes against the glare, I jump down to the ground, feeling rocky scree underfoot. Looking around, I see that we're heading up some kind of wide defile, ten to fifteen metre high cliffs punctuated by gullies and caves on either side. Silhouetted against the lights, I see other figures emerging from up near the engine.

Lorii's next out, instantly alert, scanning the top of the nearest cliff for signs of movement. Fenn and Brownie follow soon after, Brownie turning to take his heavy stubber from Kin-Drugg who lowers it out of the compartment. The drop trooper then helps Erasmus down, coils of belt feed in his arms.

Fenn ducks between the large wheels and heads under the train, and I motion for Lorii to go with him. As the others scramble out, Kelth brings up the rear with his laspistol drawn. I head off towards the front of the train.

The Colonel meets me a couple of carriages along, bolt pistol drawn, power sword glowing in his hand. His face betrays nothing of what's happening.

'There is a blockage on the rail ahead,' he says. 'Boulders across the track. It could be some type of ambush. Sergeant Manners and his squad will protect the crew clearing the rocks. I want you to lead the team up onto the cliffs to give them covering support. I will take Dunmore, Kin-Drugg, Oahebs and Spooge up the left, the others go with you.'

'How long do you reckon it'll be, sir?' I ask, and he replies with a shake of his head.

'I am not sure,' he says, glancing over his shoulder as a work crew with picks and shovels jump of the wagon behind the engine and head along the track. 'An hour at least, I think.'

Calling out orders, I head back to the others. The Colonel's team hurries past me to join Schaeffer.

'Two man teams, one defile each,' I say. 'Kelth and Fenn, Lorii and me. You two, take that gully on the left, we'll go further up the track.'

Watching them head across the rocky ground to the defile, I head forwards, Lorii just behind me. Getting to the front of the train, I see that the track is well and truly blocked. Starkly lit by the searchlights on top of the engine, a pile of boulders as tall as me lies across the tracks and spills out several metres either side. Workmen are already crawling over the heap, pulling free the smaller rocks and tossing them clear. Just ahead and fanned out to the left and right are the men of Sergeant Manner's contingent, taking up positions along the foot of the cliffs and behind boulders.

'That's deliberate,' says Lorii, looking at the obstruction. 'If it was a natural rock fall, surely it would have spilled down from one side of the gorge.'

'All the more reason to get into position quick, then,' I say, searching for some way up the cliff.

About twenty metres ahead of the train, the canyon wall shallows, and I can see what looks like a natural trench running back up the slope. I head for it, my eyes adjusting slowly when we're out of the lights and into the pre-dawn gloom. Just before sunrise is a perfect time to attack.

I check the safety on my lasgun is on before slinging it across my shoulder. It's not too difficult to climb up to the crack in the rock face, there are plenty of handholds, and it's only a matter of minutes until I'm wedged into the crevice. Pulling my lasgun free, I crawl forwards, ducking under a natural arch of rock into a short tunnel and then out into a low gully. I guess this used to be the bed of a stream, carved through the rock thousands of years ago before the industrialisation of Armageddon and the exhaustion of all the water supplies except for the polar ice caps.

Remarkably, there's even a few scrubby, thorny bushes along the gully's edge, and it's then that I notice that the air's a little easier to breathe, although it gets thin at this altitude. I guess the crap that's in the air either rises up to form the permanent cloud layer or settles as smog near the ground. There's quite a strong wind, blowing straight into my face, dust gets in my eyes and down the front of my jacket.

The night is cool and crisp, and there's not a shred of moonlight. The glow from the train's lights doesn't extend very far past the cliff edge, and in front of us is a huge expanse of darkness. I crawl forward on my belly, eyes scanning for any sign of an enemy.

Looking over my shoulder, I see Lorii emerging from the crevice and with a wave of my hand, send her a little way off to the right.

Trying to make as little noise as possible, I crawl to my left, lasgun held out in front of me, until I see a large boulder sticking up out of the ground.

A stubby little tree clings to existence in the lee of the rock. I rise to my feet and scuttle over, taking cover in the shadow of the boulder, looking out from the canyon wall. Now that my eyes have adjusted, I can see that we're in the valley between two peaks, a pass up into the heart of the Diablo Mounts. There's cover everywhere, the valley is cut into by meandering gullies and dotted with boulders. Too much cover for my liking, any enemy could be right on top of us before we noticed.

WE DON'T WAIT long before the orks make their move. A hundred metres to our right, there's a bright flash as Fenn opens fire with his lasgun, the bolt flaring off the rocks ahead of us. He fires again, and now Kelth joins in with his laspistol, and in that brief moment of illumination I can see shapes moving through the rocks, running from shadow to shadow. There's no return fire, which is puzzling, and I bring my lasgun up to my shoulder and scan along the ground ahead of me. There are fuzzy after-images flashing across my eyes, and I can't see a damned thing.

Thinking it's better to do something that nothing, I swivel round on my belly until I can see where Fenn and Kelth are firing. The orks are in amongst a rocky area of scrub, ducking down behind the boulders, running from one to the next. I pick a likely looking patch of shadow and fire. The flash of the lasbolts illuminates something just to my left, about ten metres away. It's an ork face emerging from a hole in the ground.

'Enemy to the left!' I roar, bringing my lasgun round, but the ork is up and running at me.

It lopes towards me and I pull the trigger, but my reflex shot goes wide. Everything slows down as it charges towards me, just a few strides away. It seems like an age has passed as I hear the recharging power cell whining in my ear. The beast is skinnier than other orks I've seen, dressed in a ragged loincloth, a long hatchet in one hand, and a jagged knife in the other. Human scalps hang from a rope belt around its waist. I can see other shadows emerging from the ground behind it. I can feel my blood rushing in my ears, and my heart pounding in my chest as the ork raises the axe over its head.

A bolt from Lorii takes it square in the chest, scorching flesh and knocking it sideways. Its faltering step is all the time I need as the firing light on my lasgun flicks on and I pull the trigger again. Everything is suddenly happening at once. I put three more shots into it as it crumples to the ground, and then turn my fire on the aliens storming forward from the cave entrance. I can't believe I missed it, but I can see it clearly now: a narrow hole about ten metres to my left, slightly obscured by a bush. Luckily it's only wide enough for them to come out one at a time, and between Lorii's fire and mine, we down four out of the next six to emerge.

'Fall back,' I yell, leaping to my feet and starting backwards, firing from the hip. The nearest ork, by some dint of lucky or divine intervention, seems to skip through the salvo without being touched and is barely metres from me. My next shot scorches across its left shoulder but it doesn't even notice; it continues charging towards me, fangs bared.

'Frag,' I mutter, snatching my lasgun by the barrel in both hands.

I step forwards and swing upwards; the attack catches the ork by surprise. The butt of the lasgun smashes into its jaw, shattering a tooth, and it stumbles, falling to one knee. Swinging the lasgun from overhead, I slam my weapon into the side of its head, flattening it. I'm about to swing again when I see that there are more of them just behind. I don't have time to finish the green bastard off.

I turn and run, realising that none of the orks have guns, and as I pass the position, Lorii stands up, still firing, and then turns and joins me.

'Back to the gully, we'll hold them off there,' I shout in her ear, though there's no need to yell because she's right next to me. My blood is rushing through my veins after the close encounter with the ork, and I can feel myself slipping out of control.

Leaping down into the gully, I turn and fire off a few shots without even aiming. I am gasping heavily. My random volley is rewarded with another ork tumbling to the ground. Lorii shoves me aside and down, a grenade in her other hand. She tosses it just in front of the charging orks, and we throw ourselves flat.

The grenade explodes, raining dirt down onto us, and I'm back up and firing again in a split second, spitting grit from my lips. Three orks lie writhing in the smoke of the grenade detonation, grasping onto shredded limbs and guts, their howls echoing off the mountainsides.

I risk a glance over towards Kelth and Fenn, and see that it's fallen quiet where they are. Are they dead? Have they staved off the orks? There's no obvious answer, so I have to assume the worst.

Leaning on the edge of the natural culvert next to me, Lorii keeps up a steady rate of fire, and I notice that orks aren't charging forwards any more. I can see them keeping to cover, spreading out to the left, trying to surround us. Perhaps they're scared of more grenades. I hope so.

I notice the shot counter on my gun is down to the last few, so I use the lull to rip out the power pack and stow it in my belt, drawing out a fresh one and slamming it home. I wait for the gun to recharge and then bring it up to my shoulder, sighting along the barrel.

'Save your ammo for clear targets,' I say to Lorii, without looking. I keep my eyes focussed on a small ridgeline about twenty metres ahead of me. I'm sure there are some orks behind there.

I pray the orks don't realise that one concerted charge and they'll be all over us. There are too many for two soldiers with lasguns to stop. I'm pretty sure it's only the threat of more grenades that's keeping them back, but then again maybe none of them wants to be the first one to make the charge. Even if they work out that they can storm us, they'll know that we'll take a few of them down.

'Keep your head down,' I tell Lorii, scrambling out of the trench and sprinting to a shallow depression to my left.

Throwing myself down, I pull a grenade from my belt. From here I can see along the ridgeline. Pulling the pin, I get up to a crouch and then throw, placing the grenade right where I wanted it. As it goes off, I run back to Lorii, and leap back down.

'What do you think?' I say, bringing my lasgun up to the firing position.

'I've got one grenade and one power cell left,' she says, looking at me out of the corner of her eye. 'We can hold them for a little while longer I reckon.'

I nod, squeezing off a shot as a shadow moves to my right. I see that both Kelth and Fenn are alive and well as more lasbolts flicker off to our right.

'Okay, we'll hold here for the moment,' I say. 'Save the grenade in case we need to cover a retreat.'

FOR THE NEXT half hour or so, we stay there, firing the occasional shot as an ork head appears out of the gloom. I can hear lasfire echoing along the canyon, so I know that we're not the only ones under attack. It's a tense time, because I haven't got a clue whether the orks have another way down into the canyon, or whether they're about to work their way up behind us and chop us into a bloody pulp. I don't know if Schaeffer's still alive, though I suspect he is, or if anyone else is dead or wounded. Most of all, I don't know how long I'm going to have to stand in this fragging gully, the chill biting through my fatigues.

The first glowing touch of dawn starts to spread across the clouds ahead, but too little to improve visibility. I figure the orks know that they've got to push ahead now, or they'll stand no chance in the light. I tighten my grip, blink a couple of times to clear the dust from my eyes, and get ready.

In the sudden quiet, I can hear the shouting of the train crew, the wind stirring up dust devils and rustling through the scattered thorn bushes. I can hear Lorii's shallow, steady breathing next to me, and feel the body heat in the pre-dawn chill.

Waves of heat emanate from the open wounds across Lorii's chest, as bright red blood spills across her white skin. The blood is as hot as lava flows as it settles under her breasts and leaks down the sides of her gashed stomach. Like the heart of a volcano, her heart continues to throb inside her, spilling the crimson heat from within shattered ribs. Her pale flesh is like ice, steaming and hissing as the blood flows across it, a heat haze shimmering into the air.

Lorii's looking at me funny, and it's only then that I realise that I'm holding my knife, and my lasgun is on the ground. I don't remember turning around.

'What are you doing?' she says, staring at me with suspicion. I look at her dumbly, and then sheath the knife without answering.

Picking up my lasgun, I hear an echoing cry from the canyon, calling us back to the train.

'You go first, I'll go rearguard,' I say. She hesitates, still looking at me in an odd way, before turning and worming her way back down the gully.

Hearing the echo of her passing through the archway, and seeing nothing of the orks ahead, I turn and follow her, squeezing back down into the defile and out onto the cliff face. As I climb down the rocks, I keep glancing up, expecting to see ork faces leering at me from out of the gully, ready to leap down on top of me. No such thing happens, and I reach the ground safely.

The track's cleared – the rocks are now in a couple of piles to the side of the track. I see the Colonel and his team working their way down the cliff on the opposite side and I walk back to our carriage, a few metres behind Lorii. I stop as something occurs to me. I turn to look at the piles of rocks again. I grin to myself as I come up with something special for the orks the next time they try blocking the rail.

'Hey Lorii,' I call out and she stops and turns. 'Give me your grenade.'

She walks back and hands it over, a questioning look on her face. I give her a nod to follow me as I walk over to the nearest rock pile. I hand her my lasgun so that both my hands are free. Pulling the pin on the grenade, but without letting the spring clip come free, I lift up one of the rocks and wedge the grenade into the gap underneath, using the weight of the rock to hold the clip in place. I repeat this with the other pile and the last grenade from my belt, and turn around smiling.

'Let's see how much they like grenades after today, shall we?' I say, dusting my hands off with satisfaction.

As THE TRAIN starts moving off again and the wagon begins to sway side-to-side under the motion, I notice that Fenn has a particularly smug look.

'What are you so happy about?' I ask him, sitting down with my back to the wall. The others have done likewise around me.

'Nothing special,' he says, still smiling. 'Just always happy to be killing orks.'

'How come these had no guns then?' asks Brownie. 'It was like being back on a firing range, them running about, taking them down without a shot in return.'

'Well, the orks up here are firsters,' explains Fenn, pulling out his knife and running his whetstone along the edge. 'They've gone really feral. There's nothing up here for them to scavenge except what we bring up ourselves, and there's few enough people up here anyway. Knives, cleavers and their fangs, that's what they rely on. Doesn't make them any less dangerous though. Like them back in the jungle, they've got natural cunning to make up for it. Doesn't surprise me, them springing a trap like that. You see, most folks think that orks are just plain stupid, but not in my experience. They can't think things out like you and me, that's for sure, but it doesn't make them dumb.'

'You seem to know a lot about orks,' says Kin-Drugg, nursing his injured leg.

'Been fighting them all my life,' says Fenn. 'You learn a thing or two about your enemy after thirty years, that's for sure. And my father fought in the first invasion before me, and passed on a thing or two he'd learnt.'

'You're still fighting the remnants and descendants of the attack fifty years ago,' says Lorii. She pulls a rag out of her pocket and starts cleaning the dust from her lasgun. 'What makes you think you'll ever drive them out, or get rid of them completely?'

'Never said we would, did I?' says Fenn with a grim smile. 'Once you've got that many orks planet side, I reckon you'll never get rid of them completely. You can hunt them down, burn the bodies from here to world's end but there'll always be a few left. And all it takes is a few to start breeding, and than you've got a problem again before your sons are grown up.'

'So what do they want here, anyway?' asks Kelth. He looks drawn and tired, his robes tattered, stained and dusty.

'Who cares?' says Kin-Drugg. 'What do they ever want? They're interplanetary vermin, that's all. It's like going to a cheap whore, once you've been you might never cure the consequences.'

'I reckon I know why Ghazghkull's back,' says Oahebs, and we all turn and look at him. He hardly ever speaks. I think this is the first time he's ever volunteered information. We gaze at him expectantly, and suddenly self-conscious, he looks down, occupying himself with his bootlaces.

'Well then?' I say, when it becomes obvious that he's not going to say anything else. He looks up at me, and then at the others, uncertainty in his eyes.

'It's just a theory,' he says, his voice subdued. He pauses, obviously gearing himself up for the explanation. 'Orks never know when to give up, do they? You shoot them, they retreat, regroup and come back again. The last time Ghazghkull came, Commissar Yarrick kicked his arse good and proper, with the help of Commander Dante of course. What was one of the first things that happened, Fenn?'

The ork hunter thinks about it for a moment before replying.

'Well, obviously there was the space battles, but in terms of the ground assault, I guess that was when the rocks forts came down,' he says. 'Big asteroids hollowed out and protected with force fields, like mobile bases with engines fitted.'

'Yeah, we know what they are,' says Kin-Drugg, shaking his head with bitterness. 'Why the hell do you think we decided to drop in to the jungle and say hello?'

'And when the fortresses were coming down, the orks dropped a huge great big asteroid on Hades Hive, yes?' says Oahebs. He doesn't wait for confirmation, having got up a head of steam now. 'Hades is where Yarrick held out last time, giving the Spaces Marines enough time for their counter-attack. So what does Ghazghkull do this time? Flattens it completely, wiping it out in one go to make sure that doesn't happen again.'

We all sit digesting this idea for a while.

'So you mean that we got dragged across the galaxy for Emperor-knows-what because some ork warlord's pissed off and wants to get his own back?' says Brownie.

'Could be,' says Oahebs.

'Just why the hell are we here anyway?' says Kin-Drugg. 'There are millions, tens of millions, of Guard and Space Marines on Armageddon, what the hell is Schaeffer expecting us to achieve?'

'Something none of the rest can do,' I say, scratching at my belly. Sand and dust got in under my clothes while I was crawling about outside and now I've got itches in dozens of places.

'Something Space Marines can't do?' asks Fenn, his disbelief obvious from his tone. 'I can't imagine that.'

'Perhaps it's something the Space Marines won't do,' says Lorii. She looks at me with a pointed expression. 'Remember Coritanorum, Kage?'

'Course I do,' I say. What a stupid question.

'A handful of Last Chancers, and a city to destroy,' she says. 'Four people got out alive, two of them are in this wagon. Nobody else could have done it.'

'So, we're heading east, right,' says Brownie. 'What's so important to the east?'

'For all I know it could be something in the mountains, or on the other side of the planet,' I say. 'Look, the Colonel will tell us in good time, when he's ready. It's not going to be anything we can think of, I'm sure of that. Better off not wasting time dwelling on it.'

'So, where's this Coritanorum place?' asks Kin-Drugg.

'Nowhere,' Lorii says quietly. 'It isn't anywhere any more. Not even a pile of ash to remember, to mark the spot.'

She has a far away look in her eye and I know exactly what she's thinking about. She's thinking about her twin brother's blood splashing across her face; his head blown apart.

I wonder again just why it is she decided to come back. Surely she'd be better off burying the memories as far away from the Colonel as possible. Or perhaps not. It's been over two years since that mission, and in that time I've seen more blood, more killing, and suddenly Coritanorum doesn't seem that bad after all. Perhaps if she dives into a sea of blood, she'll no longer be able to tell if it's Loron's or not.

Whatever it is she's after, I'm glad she's here all the same. It's good to know that at least one other person, other than the Colonel, has some idea what might be in store. I don't think about it any more. I just take each day as it comes, each battle, each firefight's just the latest in a long line that stretches out until the end of my life. Nothing's going to change that now, so there's no point fretting about it.

In a week, in a day, in an hour, I could be dead. It doesn't matter, even high lords die eventually I guess. If I get another hour, another day or another week, then that's fine with me. When you're in my position, it doesn't matter what you can or can't do with your life. It's just enough to still be alive.

CHAPTER TEN
AMBUSH

WE SPEND ANOTHER two days rattling around in that wagon before we finally come to a stop. Stiff and tired, we jump down out of the train to find ourselves in a marshalling yard on the slopes of a mountain. Rickety, temporary-looking sheds and storehouses line the track, watched over by a high tower with skyward pointing. Beyond is a mass of shattered buildings, their skeletal ruins rising up against the dark, tar and dust covered slopes beyond.

Not far on, the rail track comes to an abrupt end as it disappears into a crater several hundred metres across. The rock has fused in strange organic shapes from some immensely hot detonation. The mountains are obscured just a few hundred metres higher up the slopes by a thick layer of cloud. It has a dirty,

Gav Thorpe

reddish tint to it, clinging to the mountainsides. I make a silent plea to the Emperor that we don't have to go up into the deadly-looking smog.

The place is half-deserted; a few men are hurrying around swathed in robes and scarves to ward away the chill mountain air. Without a word, the Colonel leads us between the buildings, heading uphill.

'Where the hell are we now?' asks Brownie, gazing around at the empty buildings.

'I think it's Diabolus forge,' says Erasmus, staggering along with heavy stubber ammo under one arm and his servo-skull under the other.

'And what's Diabolus?' says Kin-Drugg. 'Looks like the arse-end of nowhere to me.'

'It's where I was due to be stationed on my arrival,' Erasmus says quietly. 'It's a Departmento Munitorum outpost, set up during the second Armageddon War. As you can see, it's very low priority now. The mine has been abandoned since the latest invasion, so there's not much to protect any more.'

'You knew we were coming here and you didn't say anything,' I ask, rounding on Spooge. 'Why didn't you tell us?'

'Was I supposed to have told you?' he says, cringing back from me. 'When did anyone ask me? And how was I supposed to know you were all coming here too?'

'Just ignore him,' says Brownie, wrapping an arm around Erasmus's shoulders, his skin seeming even darker against the pallid neck of the scribe.

'Since when have you two been friends?' I say, taken aback by this show of support. It's not like

Spooge is really one of us, he's just been tagging along because there's been nowhere else for him to go.

'Razzy here's the best damn loader I've ever had,' says Brownie, patting the scribe on the head. 'Not had a belt jam yet, have we, mate?'

'Razzy?' I say, trying not to laugh.

'Well, Erasmus such a mouthful, isn't it?' says Brownie. 'And so's Spooge. I like Razzy.'

'Well, you better start saying your fond farewells,' I say with a snarl. 'It's the end of the line for Razzy, and I bet that we're not going to be hanging around any longer than necessary.'

I quicken my stride and walk ahead. Brownie's gone soft in the head, worrying about a damn scribe. He'll be glad to be rid of him once the serious fighting starts. I've had some pretty desperate company in the past, but this group are really starting to wind me up. Kelth's a stuck up Navigator who's just as keen to crawl into a hole as fire a gun. Emperor knows what's going on in Lorii's head and I've got a gut feeling that something's going to crack before the mission's over. I can't stand to be within five metres of Oahebs, he makes me feel physically nauseous. Fenn's scared of the bloody sky, and Kin-Drugg is a loudmouth with a quick temper. I'd happily trade them in for the team we had on Typhos Prime, even for Kronin who was utterly insane and could only speak in litanies and Ecclesiarchy teachings.

* * *

THE COLONEL TAKES us a to a large, low building just outside the railhead itself, and we follow him inside into a small, bare chamber. There are no windows, and other than the door leading in, the only feature is another scuffed steel door at the other end.

'Make yourselves comfortable,' he says, and we slump down against the wall.

'We have recently suffered some setbacks,' says the Colonel, slowly pacing back and forth in front of us. 'However, we have overcome these, and now the mission is ready to proceed as originally planned. It was expected that there would be losses, but now the success or failure of our mission depends solely upon your abilities and determination. You have fought well so far, but it is not your fighting skills that have ever been in doubt. The road ahead will test your resolve and your discipline, and many of you will fail. The reward is the same as it always has been, the chance for absolution through success or death. There are no other alternatives.'

He stops and looks at us, eyeing each of us in turn, and weighing us up. It might be my imagination, but it seems his gaze lingers on me for longer than the others.

'You are all wondering just what it is that we few can do in a war that has killed millions,' he says, resuming his pacing, hands clasped behind his back. 'The status of Armageddon is finely poised. A shift in power either way may yet decide the fate of the planet. Victory on Armageddon is more than just a strategic necessity; it is also a spiritual and moral test. If the forces of the

Emperor cannot prevail here, where we are in such strength, then what hope is there for those worlds far from Terra, out on the Eastern Fringe, in the far-flung stars? The Imperium needs hope now more than ever, because enemies surround us on all sides. This is a test of our fortitude that we have not seen the likes of for hundreds of years. If Armageddon can endure, then the realm of the Immortal Emperor can also endure.'

His eyes shine as he speaks. He gazes over our heads, through the wall and into the galaxy beyond. His voice rings with faith, assurance, and authority. Once again I'm struck by how strongly he believes. His faith in the Emperor, in the Imperium and in himself provides him with his invulnerability, like a physical shield. Despite what he's done to us, and to me in particular, I have to admire his conviction. He's never failed. Never. The reason for that is simple – he's never even considered it a possibility. Whatever he sets out to do, he does, with never a moment of doubt.

'Our mission here is simple, and yet the consequences of what we do will reach out beyond this world, out beyond this system into the farthest reaches of the glorious Imperium,' he pauses for a moment, head bowed, before continuing. 'Armageddon, and our victory here, will shine like a beacon, reminding those who doubt that the Imperium still fights on that mankind has not yet laid rest to its claim to the galaxy. Such a victory could well depend upon one man. One man could hold the key to winning the Third Armageddon War.'

He walks. close, passing along the line just out of arm's reach, gauging us again.

'That man is Imperial Commander Herman von Strab,' he says. 'And we are here to either rescue him or kill him.'

WE TAKE THIS news in silence for the moment, until Brownie raises his hand.

'Yes, Dunmore?' says the Colonel striding over to stand in front of him.

'Rescue or kill?' says Brownie. 'Kind of opposite ends of a piece of string, aren't they? Which is it?'

The Colonel coughs, clearing his throat, and then walks back to the other side of the room. He pulls his map from his pocket and opens it up, spreading it across the bare floor. He motions for us to gather round.

'We are here, in the Diablo Mounts,' he says, drawing a circle on the map with his finger. His finger moves quite a distance. 'Von Strab is here, in Acheron Hive.'

'But I thought Acheron was declared purgatus?' says Lorii, kneeling down beside the Colonel. 'Hasn't it fallen to the orks?'

'That is the first part of our mission,' says Schaeffer. 'We must determine if Acheron is irretrievably lost to the enemy. Part of that task will be to determine the loyalties of von Strab.'

'He's turned traitor,' says Fenn with a growl. 'He disappeared after the last war and led Ghazghkull back three years ago. Acheron's his now, from what I hear. He even has orks fighting for him.'

'The reality may not be so simple,' says the Colonel, sitting back. 'It is suspected that those orks are just as likely to be enforcing Ghazghkull's will on von Strab as the other way round. Acheron Hive is being held hostage, in effect, forcing von Strab to comply. There is evidence that the former overlord has indeed provided intelligence information to Ghazghkull and his warlords. However, the latest news from our agents inside Acheron say that von Strab has begun to recruit what he has called the "Army for the Liberation of Armageddon". It is unsure what he intends to do with this army. It may be that he intends to use it to overthrow ork domination of Acheron, in which case we will assist him in whatever way we can before extracting him to safety.'

'And if it's not for that?' I ask.

'If the Army for the Liberation of Armageddon is a counter-Imperial militia, then we must kill von Strab,' says the Colonel. 'The military importance of such a traitor army, and the moral damage it would do to our resistance against the orks, could swing the balance of power on Armageddon. Von Strab still commands great respect and loyalty amongst the local nobility, some of the hive rulers and even senior military officers. If we discover that he is not acting under duress, then we have orders to remove him by any means necessary. He cannot be allowed to stand as a figurehead for anti-Imperial sentiment.'

'So what was the original plan?' I ask. 'You obviously didn't mean for us to crash in the jungle. How do we get to Acheron?'

'We walk,' says the Colonel. 'There's a disused pipeline from this mine that leads across the ash wastes and down into the Acheron underhive. The wastes are devoid of any major activity, and any kind of transportation would soon be noticed and reported. In particular, the wastes nomads are thought to be working for von Strab. As it is, a small group of us can masquerade as deserters to gain entry to the hive if we are discovered.'

'That's hundreds of kilometres across barren wasteland,' says Fenn. 'We're never going to survive that on foot. We've got no food or water, no environmental protection gear or camping equipment. We wouldn't survive to the first dusk.'

'That has already been considered,' says the Colonel. He turns to Erasmus. 'You were given something when sent your orders to report here, I believe.'

Standing, Erasmus reaches inside his jacket and pulls free a thick neck chain, with three large brass keys hanging from it. He steps forward to hand them to the Colonel, but Schaeffer backs away and waves a hand to the door leading out of the room.

'It is time to assume your new office,' says the Colonel.

Erasmus walks over to the door. Glancing at the lock, he picks a key and inserts it. It turns with a heavy click, and with a short push, Erasmus opens the door. A dark void lies beyond. As he steps through, lights begin to flicker into life from a high ceiling and we stand and crowd through the door after him.

As glowstrips illuminate the chamber, they reveal row after row of high shelf units, stretching across the large warehouse. The storeroom is full of supplies. Just from the door I can see ammo boxes, stacks of blankets, power pack chargers, and thousands of rations cartons.

'What is this?' I ask the Colonel, walking right into the warehouse, and gazing in wonder at the stacked shelves receding fifty metres to the left and right.

'When the Departmento Munitorum withdrew from the Diablo Mounts, there was a certain oversight in its stock records,' says the Colonel, prompting a gasp from Erasmus.

'An oversight?' the scribe says. 'But... but that's impossible, isn't it?'

'No, not impossible,' says Schaeffer. 'And especially possible if certain documents are requisitioned and classified by the Inquisition.'

'The Inquisition?' I say, instantly suspicious. I knew it had to be too good to be true. Nothing's ever straightforward when the Inquisition is involved.

'The Inquisition has had a strong presence on Armageddon,' says the Colonel, as we walk between the shelves of stores. 'Given the nature of most of its activities, it is only prudent for them to maintain facilities and resources overlooked by normal channels.'

'Lucky for us,' I mutter, picking up an empty autogun magazine and pretending to examine it.

Erasmus is pacing back and forth with small steps, looking around with wide eyes.

'The Inquisition?' he says, his voice quiet with awed reverence. 'This all belongs to the Inquisition?'

I notice that most of the others are also walking around with the same sort of expression. I'd forgotten that for all but a few, the Inquisition is little more than a myth. Sometimes it's a shadowy threat used to elicit obedience from children and adults alike, other times it is composed of secretive heroes who hold the power of the Imperium in the palms of their hands.

My experience has been slightly different. My dealings with them on the last two missions has led me to believe that they are overly paranoid, political, and quite possibly power-hungry. Their open mandate, to protect the Emperor and Imperium from any threat by whatever means deemed necessary, is so vulnerable to abuse, I have to wonder who it is who watches the protectors of humanity.

I then realise that Lorii is watching the Colonel carefully, and Oahebs too is paying him a lot of attention. I remember that they were working closely with Inquisitor Oriel before they joined the Colonel, and they both look slightly nervous with this talk about the Inquisition. I suspect they have seen things and done things that most people would never want to know about.

'It does not belong to anyone,' says the Colonel. 'Officially, this place does not exist. That is the point.'

'But, doesn't that mean that if we take anything, we will be looting?' says Spooge, taking the magazine from my hands and carefully placing it on the shelf. 'I can't be party to looting, can I? I mean, if everybody thought they could just help themselves to stores, where would we end up?'

I stroll along to the next set of shelves, which are stacked far above my head with ammunition cases. Bolter ammunition by the look of it.

'I can just about understand the Inquisition's motives here,' I say. 'A potentially renegade Imperial commander has thrown in his lot with alien invaders. Yes, that's very much their bag. What I can't understand is you, I mean us, being here.'

The Colonel gives me a quizzical look and I continue.

'Why the Last Chancers?' I say. 'It took a lot of resource and clout to get us all the way over here from the Eastern Fringe. Now, I know you've got a good record of success, but I can't believe that we're the only ones who could do this.'

The Colonel looks thoughtful for a moment, probably trying to work out if he should answer, and how much he can tell us, or whether he even wants to tell us.

'Several attempts have already been made to ascertain the loyalty of von Strab,' he says slowly. 'They have proved unsuccessful. Other agents and organisations have also made attempts on the Imperial commander's life, and except for news of their failure, they have been unable to provide any accurate intelligence.'

'But why us?' I say insistently. 'With the Inquisition involved, I'd like to know what you've gotten us into.'

'It is just a mission,' the Colonel says, his expression sharp with anger. 'News of our success with the Brightsword operation was recognised by individuals in the hierarchy of the Inquisition and the decision was made to give me the opportunity to effect an attempt.'

'Kage has got a point,' says Kin-Drugg, walking just ahead of the group. He stops and turns, arms crossed. 'A full assault on Acheron wouldn't work, I can see that, but there are all kinds of specialist forces on Armageddon. What about the Space Marines, for instance? Or Stormtroopers? I would think that they could probably do a pretty successful raid to take out this von Strab.'

'Any kind of regular forces are out of the question,' the Colonel says, staring flatly at Kin-Drugg. 'The Inquisition is doing all that it can to suppress knowledge of von Strab's personal army. If this information were to become more widely known, it would lead to uncertainty at best, and at worst, we would be facing the possibility of mass desertions, even fighting within our own ranks. Our efforts here cannot tolerate such a situation. Even the intervention by non-line forces would cause questions to be raised. Their absence from the fighting for any period of time would be noticed and have to be accounted for, as would any failure of them to return.'

'I get it now,' says Brownie. 'Nobody knows we're here, so nobody's going to miss us when we're dead, is that it?'

'That is one way of looking at it, yes,' says the Colonel, resuming his walking. 'The other is that there has been no chance of us developing any kind of pro-liberation sympathies. We have been free of exposure to the propaganda put out by von Strab.'

'And what if we fail?' says Lorii, casting a sideways glance at me. I'm not sure whether the look is one of accusation, or seeking support. I keep my expression blank.

'I have already spoken of the potential disaster to the war effort if von Strab is indeed a traitor and allowed to continue,' the Colonel says, looking away.

He seems uncomfortable with the questioning, but he's not got much choice. This is the part of the mission when everything hangs in the balance for him. Up until now, we've had no choice but to follow his orders. They have been backed up by the full force of the Imperium, from the Commissariat provosts on the ship to the Imperial Guard we've been amongst since reaching Cerberus Station. Now there's nothing except discipline and his own force of will to stop us simply walking away. We're covert, so nobody knows we're here, there's nobody to back him up. He can't threaten us any more, so now he has to get us to understand what it is we're doing, and why we have no choice but to comply.

'You know what I mean,' says Lorii. 'There is always a last resort, a fall back plan. What will happen if we can't take out von Strab?'

The Colonel doesn't answer straight away; instead he looks at each of us. He has our full attention.

'Considering what is at stake, the Inquisition will use extreme measures to ensure that von Strab cannot turn the course of the war against us,' he says, expression impassive. 'If we fail, they will have no choice but to ensure the complete destruction of Acheron Hive.'

'But surely that would be a blow just as deadly?' says Fenn. 'If only for morale, which is everything in this war at the moment.'

'Then we must not fail,' says the Colonel briskly, regaining his usual business-like self. He turns to me. 'You will work with Armourer-scribe Spooge to draw supplies suitable for the remainder of the mission. I want every eventuality covered.'

'Right, sir,' I say. I look at the others and then sweep open my arms in a gesture that encapsulates the whole warehouse. 'Let's find out what we've got to play with.'

ASH WASTES

CHAPTER ELEVEN
ACROSS THE WASTES

WE SPEND TWO days getting ready. The secret storehouse has pretty much anything we want: there are weapons and ammunition obviously, but also rations, canteens, blankets, packs, picks, shovels, knives, mugs, bowls, magnoculars, cold weather suits, mountaineering equipment, gas masks, rebreathers, eyeshades, portable cookers, lanterns, tents, poles, rope and a hundred other things besides.

The time not spent hunting down rogue boxes of ammunition or searching through piles of foil-wrapped bagging for ration bars we spend asleep or resting. We find blankets and bedrolls and make ourselves a cosy little camp in one corner of the warehouse amongst the shelves of crates. The Colonel seems pretty lax about keeping watch, but

I continue to keep the practice going so that we stay sharp. I get the impression that he's giving us the time to regain our strength and build up our energy reserves for the next push.

At first it looked as if there wouldn't be any problems, but then we worked out just how much this stuff weighed. There was no way we would be able to carry it on foot. The problem is, the heavier your pack, the slower your progress. And the slower your progress, the more water and rations you need, which in turn weigh more and take up more space. We can't rely on getting any kind of re-supply until we reach the hive, and given the uncertain terrain we'll be crossing, as well as the possibility of bad weather, we could be hiking for anything up to three weeks to cover the hundreds of kilometres to Acheron.

We lay out each pack and its contents in the small antechamber, and it becomes obvious that some things are just too big to carry. In the end, with the help of Spooge and advice from Fenn – who knows a thing or two about extended missions – we narrow our needs down to essentials, and then we all have a little space to bring some of our own preferences.

Brownie, for example, insists that as well as the heavy stubber he's dragged all the way from the jungles, and five hundred rounds for it, a light mortar would be extremely useful. Fenn, on the other hand, is all for carrying extra water to be on the safe side. Hidden in a dusty corner, amongst piles of tent poles and coils of rope, I found a few innocent-looking boxes not even listed on Erasmus's inventory. Prying one open, I discovered that it was full of gold coins. I guess the Inquisition isn't above greasing a few palms.

A few years ago, such a find would have seemed a golden opportunity to make something for myself, but not now. Where the hell am I going to be able to exchange coin? What am I going to spend it on? For a start, I'd have to desert from the Colonel, and that's a lot harder than you might think. I got away from him once, legitimately, but he was waiting for me as soon as I screwed it up. However, you never know what fate might deal you, so I make a secret compartment inside the lining of my pack and stash twenty of the coins.

The others take a selection of spare side-arms, ammo, or extra rations, according to their own needs and desires. While the others are packing the Colonel goes over our planned route to Acheron with Fenn, Oahebs and me. I have to say it doesn't look appealing.

To get down from the Diablo Mounts, we have to get past the lovely-titled Ork Mountain. It's a huge volcano not far north of where we are, and it is teeming with feral orks. Down on the plains, we'll be south of the ruins of Hades Hive. It's too risky to join the Hades-Acheron highway, because it's bound to be used by both Imperial forces and orks as the battle lines shift back and forth between the two hives. And the nature of our mission means we have to stay away from both sides.

We'll be cutting across the wastes south of the highway, until we reach Avernas, a forge complex that sits across the road outside Acheron. From there, the Colonel tells us, there's a disused pipeway that leads across the wastes to the Acheron under-hive, allowing us to infiltrate von Strab's domain from within. It'll neatly bypass the Imperial forces around the hive, as well as the long-ranging patrols from the heavily fortified Hemlock cordon. The whole area is also littered with ork drop sites, so the greenskins are constantly sallying forth from landed rok fortresses across the ash wastes and along the rivers.

Generally I'm confident, though far from happy. It's not the orks that are going to be the problem. Nobody's going to find a small group like us in those vast stretches of wilderness unless they happen to roll straight into us, and we're more than capable of dealing with the odd scouting force or roaming ork band.

No, the problem is the wilderness itself. The terrain is going to be hard going all the way, and there'll be no respite until we reach Avernas. If we can get that far in good time, we'll have broken the back of the trek and we can start preparing for Acheron itself. But I won't dwell on what we can do once we reach the hive itself. It's far better just to concentrate on getting us there.

Oahebs proves to be a brilliant navigator: he studies the sketchy maps constantly and questions the Colonel or Fenn about landmarks, route and the conditions we're likely to encounter. Throughout the discussion I feel that same uneasy feeling I get when I'm around him. I can't shake the notion that he seems to be keeping an eye on me for some reason. I still don't know anything about him, or why Oriel saw fit to send him to Schaeffer. I'll be watching him just as closely from now on. Anyone who's had dealings with the Inquisition deserves scrutiny, because you can be sure they've got some hidden plan or agenda. You just have to wait it out, and hope they aren't out to frag you too much.

Although we'll be almost impossible to spot, particularly since nobody should be looking for us, the Colonel decides to travel by night and hole up during the day. Fenn warns us that it can get freezing cold in the wastes and that we should not skimp on cold weather clothing. Later we sit down with the rest of the squad, and I pass the message on.

'It'll be tricky,' says Fenn, who is leaning against the wall, with an unopened ration pack in his hand. 'It'll be hot during the day and cold at night. We need to look for shaded campsites wherever possible. Storm season is just around the corner too.'

'This just gets better and better,' says Kin-Drugg, shaking his head. He nurses his wounded leg. 'Perhaps I should have stayed at Infernus Quay, I'm not going to be making good progress on this.'

'If you fall behind, you stay behind,' the Colonel says, standing in the doorway of the bare room. 'You carry your share, too.'

Crumpling his ration wrapper and angrily tossing it to the floor, Kin-Drugg hauls himself up and limps outside, muttering under his breath. We watch him go, exchanging glances. We know the Colonel's right: we can't afford to move at the speed of the slowest.

'I have intercepted a communication from high command on one of the comms sets,' says the Colonel, stepping forward. We look at him attentively. 'The orks have launched a serious offensive against Helsreach, so a lot of our forces will be drawn south. There will be a lot of activity, but it means that everyone's attention will be diverted from Hades and Acheron.'

'Have you heard anything about the weather?' asks Fenn, peeling open his rations and looking at it with a glimmer of distaste. 'What's the storm forecast like?'

'I haven't received any specific storm warnings,' says the Colonel. 'However, there is little comfort to be drawn from that. If we get caught in a storm, our priority must be to weather it. We have to make the best possible progress we can, because things will only get worse if we lag. We must reach Averneas before the season of storms begins in earnest.'

'And what news from Acheron?' I ask.

'No further intelligence,' replies the Colonel. 'However, there are rumours that Thraka himself visited the hive not long ago, with fresh instructions for von Strab. But these are unconfirmed.'

'Have we any idea what those instructions might be?' says Lorii.

'It is likely that the warlord is merely reinforcing his authority,' replies the Colonel. He pulls a chronometer from his pocket and snaps the case

open. 'There has been no change in activity to indi-
cate a new strategy. Sundown is in little over an
hour. Kage, have everyone ready to move out in
thirty minutes.'

'Yes sir,' I say, standing up, and dusting crumbs
from my trousers. 'Okay Last Chancers, eat up and
gear up. Last one ready carries the heavy stubber.'

THE SQUAD ASSEMBLES outside in a ragged line in the
descending darkness with their bulging packs at
their feet. The jagged silhouettes of ruined buildings jutting up above the warehouse merge into the
night sky. I head back into the storehouse and find
the Colonel in conversation with Spooge and
Kelth.

'But my orders were to take office here in Diabolus Forge,' Erasmus is saying. His skin is reddened
from exposure, but the flabbiness has disappeared
with his recent exertions. 'I cannot disobey the
directives of my masters.'

'Do you have a copy of your orders?' says the
Colonel, holding out a hand. Spooge delves into
the recesses of his clothing, pulls out a tattered
scroll and hands it to Schaeffer. The Colonel reads
it briefly, and then hands it back to Spooge.

'It says you are to report to your post here for
duties,' says Schaeffer. 'And I am giving you your
new duties.'

'As much as I agree with you, Colonel, I'm afraid
it's impossible,' says Spooge. 'An Imperial Guard
officer does not hold authority over an adept of the
Departmento Munitorum.'

I pull my laspistol from my belt and stride forward, pointing it at Spooge.

'I think you can safely say that you've done everything you can to fulfil your orders,' I say, stopping with the pistol an arm's length from his face.

'You're not offering me any choice, are you?' he asks with gratitude on his face.

I shake my head and then pivot on the spot to aim at Kelth. The tall Navigator looks down his nose at me, and sneers.

'This is ridiculous,' he snorts. 'There is no reason to subject me to this imposition. What possible use can I be? I'm not a soldier, I have made that quite obvious.'

'Everyone is useful,' says the Colonel, walking over and placing his hand on my arm, to make me lower my weapon. 'Until now you have had no choice but to accompany me. I could force you to continue, but you are right, that would serve little purpose.'

'So let me go,' says Kelth, crossing his arms. 'Let me walk away.'

'For security reasons, I cannot do that either,' says Schaeffer, walking over to Kelth, his hands clasped behind his back. He pauses for a moment, then looks deep into the Navigator's grey eyes.

'What we're doing here is not a game,' the Colonel says finally. 'I do not dress up the importance of my missions, and this operation ranks amongst the highest I have ever led. Armageddon hangs in the balance, and the slightest nudge in either direction could turn the war.'

He walks away, head bowed, before turning again, an arm outstretched towards Kelth. The Navigator watches him with a wary expression, occasionally glancing at me with distaste.

'Von Strab is hiding out in the Acheron under-hive,' the Colonel says. 'The forces drawn into Acheron by his presence are far beyond any military threat posed by this so-called army of liberation. However, the moral threat he poses is greater than any other on the planet. We cannot allow Ghazghkull to have such a man under his sway, whether it be as a pawn or an ally.'

'I am not trained for your war,' says Kelth with a heavy shrug. 'I am of the Navis Nobilite, and I have a higher calling than crawling around in the dirt dodging bullets. I was born to steer mighty ships through the ether, and to bring warships to battle. I am no use to you.'

'I'll say it again,' says Schaeffer. 'Everyone is useful. None of us can see how this will end. It may be that the Emperor has some part for you to play. You are here, now. All the starships in the fleet, and all the soldiers of the Imperial Guard, have battered them-selves against this ork horde, grinding this war into a stalemate. Now we have a chance, a lone, slim chance, to be victorious. Can you honestly walk away from this? Would you ever forgive yourself for passing up an opportunity to do something real, something genuine in your life? Will the Emperor forgive you?'

Kelth is amazed by the passion in the Colonel's voice. But his expression changes back to its usual one of superiority and suspicion. I don't know why the Colonel's so keen to have him with us, perhaps he really believes we have been brought together by the Emperor. It doesn't matter. If the Colonel wants him, I'll deliver him.

'We're called the Last Chancers,' I say, and Kelth turns on me, eyes narrowed. 'We're all given a last chance because we have wronged the Emperor with our crimes. Perhaps you deserve a last chance to do something truly exceptional with your life. Even if you don't do it for the Imperium and the Emperor, think of yourself and your family. Few people will know what we do here, but those in power, those whose words shape our futures, they will find out. Think what good it will do for the standing of your family to be associated with a great victory. Those Imperial commanders, those nobles, will owe you a debt of honour, so your future can be prosperous.'

I'm surprised by my own conviction, and a turn of phrase I didn't think I was capable of. As a devious, calculating look enters Kelth's eyes, I wonder what's brought this sudden surge of loyalty in me. The Navigator interrupts my thoughts.

'I would need some form of assurance,' he says, stroking his chin. 'A letter. Write me a letter detailing the events that have occurred here. Have it sealed and sent to High Command. I want it to be forwarded to our estates on Terra.'

The Colonel thinks for a moment and then nods.

'Spooge, come with me and we will draft this letter,' he says. The scribe heads off into the recesses of the storehouse. The Colonel gives Kelth a hard look before turning and following him.

The Navigator looks at me, a smug smile on his face.

'The Colonel will be true to his word,' he says.

'Yes he will,' I say, walking right up to him to stare him right in the eye. 'And that means you're one of us now. One of his. One of mine. You can start by grabbing your pack.'

I ignore his disconcerted look and I walk off chuckling to myself.

WITH NEW UNIFORMS, boots and weapons, and carrying full belts and packs, we're ready to set off at last light. In single file, we keep to the shadows. In the dark sky above us, the odd flicker of a jet soars overhead, while the evening air echoes with the distant thump of heavy artillery. The sky to the south is illuminated by the detonations.

Lorii leads the way, a little ahead of the rest of us, as we make our way over cratered ferrocrete roads, and march between broken piles of brocks and half-ruined walls. Banks of earth are piled up as crude, abandoned defences across some streets. A deep dip in the ground turns out to be the footprint of a passing Titan. Its weight pulverised the brick into dust and compacted the mud into a rock-hard surface.

Erasmus starts panting under the weight of his pack after just a few minutes. Kelth falls to the rear alongside Kin-Drugg. At least the drop trooper has the excuse of a busted leg, the other two are just out of shape. After a few days' hard slog we'll soon see if they can make it all the way or not. If they're still with us in five days' time, I reckon they'll be good for the whole trek. If not, the scavenging rats of the ash wastes will strip every morsel of flesh from their bones.

While we march between the shattered shells of Infernus Forge, I marvel at how much destruction has been heaped upon Armageddon. I've been to war zones before – from the tyranid-scourged fields of Ichar IV to the trench lines of Coritanorum – but I've never seen a world so wholly torn up.

Fenn sees me looking around and drops back to fall in beside me.

'This all happened in the first few days of the invasion,' he says, waving a hand to encompass the ruined complex. 'It was once teeming with Adeptus Mechanicus, but then the gargants came. Only the adepts' Titans could match the firepower of the ork war machines. The whole place was virtually destroyed in the crossfire.'

We pass a toppled monument, a larger-than-life-size statue of a Space Marine, his ornate armour emblazoned with a winged blood drop.

'That's the Dante Memorial,' says Fenn, stopping to gaze sadly at the fallen sculpture. He shakes his head. 'The Blood Angels were our saviours in the second war, when Ghazghkull first came here. There are monuments right across the planet. There's even a shrine of thanks at Cerberus.'

'You seem bitter,' I say, noticing the deep frown creasing the ork hunter's forehead.

'Monuments, memorials, arches and statues!' he spits, rounding on me with a snarl. 'Instead of rebuilding our defences or repairing the factories, von Strab has squandered our resources on these effigies. And more than half of them are dedicated to him. We won't see it, but there's a huge arch on the approaches to Acheron, that commemorates his part in the second war; it was erected by his cronies after he disappeared.'

We stop as the Colonel signals from ahead. He is standing at a junction between the remnants of two huge smelting plants, and conferring with Lorii and Oahebs.

'You'll have to fill me in,' I say. 'History was never my strong point, especially not when it concerns events on the other side of the galaxy.' I squat down on a piece of fallen masonry. Fenn sits next to me, and pulls free his knife and whetstone, as he always does when we take a break. The others sense an opportunity for a quick rest, even though we've barely been going an hour, and they set themselves down on the side of the rubble-strewn roadway.

'Even in the last war, it was rumoured that von Strab had sided with the orks,' says Fenn. His words are punctuated by the scrape of the whetstone. 'Armageddon is so important, strategically, that his family have been given free rein for tens of genera-tions. Even before the wars, life here was never easy – except for the overlord's family and his so-called advisors. But the tanks rolled off the production lines, minerals were shipped out according to the tithes, so no one cared. Not until the orks arrived, anyway. Then von Strab suddenly became the centre of attention.'

He stops sharpening the knife and tests the blade with his thumb. A small bead of blood drops from its tip. He nods up ahead and I look to see the Colonel waving us on. Sheathing his knife, Fenn stands up and stretches. The rest of us pull ourselves to our feet, and help each other with the weight of our packs.

'If it hadn't been for Commissar Yarrick holding out at Hades, Ghazghkull would have overrun us last time,' Fenn says as we start walking again. 'Von Strab said he had some master plan to win the war; it turned out his family had a stash of virus missiles they'd been keeping secret for centuries. I don't know what they thought they might be used for, but I'm pretty bloody sure it wasn't in the event that the orks invaded. Anyway, that's beside the point. The missiles were so ancient that half of them malfunctioned and fell on our own troops. After that, Yarrick made moves to have von Strab removed from power but he disappeared with Ghazghkull after the Blood Angels' attack on the main ork headquarters. Nobody heard anything from him until Ghazghkull came back, transmitting his messages from Acheron.'

'What messages?' asks Brownie, who is just a little way behind us.

Fenn waves a hand for Kin-Drugg to join us, and he fishes around in the drop trooper's pack. He pulls out the compact comm-link receiver and switches it on. Static and chopped messages squawk out from the speaker message as Fenn twists the frequency dial. He stops and we listen to a reedy voice just discernible between the crackling and hissing.

'Brave citizens of Armageddon, I beseech you to unite with me and cast off the shackles of Imperial oppression! Join us in our holy cause. Your prince has returned to lead you to freedom!' There's more hissing and an audible clicking before the voice starts again. 'The glorious...'

Fenn snaps the comm-link off as the Colonel comes striding back down the road towards us. He snatches the comm-link and rams it back into Kin-Drugg's pack, a growl in his throat.

'Nobody uses the link!' Schaeffer barks, angrily tightening the cords on the pack. The force jerks Kin-Drugg backwards, and almost pulls him off his feet.

'Are you afraid we might get swayed by such persuasive rhetoric?' asks Kelth, coming up from behind.

'You should know better,' the Colonel says in a low hiss. 'Sound carries far at night. No talking until we are clear of the forges.'

He waves us on, but puts his hand on my shoulder to stop me. He turns me round to face him.

'You in particular should know what is at stake,' he whispers. Even in the darkness I can see the angry glint of his icy eyes. 'We must succeed.'

'Why?' I say, stepping out of his grasp. 'Why the frag are we so Emperor-damned important? I don't believe your crap about us being the only ones who can do this.'

The Colonel checks ahead and, once satisfied that the others are out of earshot, motions me to start walking. He strides alongside me on those long pegs of his, looking straight ahead, and not even glancing at me as he talks.

'There are currently those in the Inquisition who are working on a more drastic solution to the von Strab problem,' he says, the words quiet and clipped. 'We are to be the last attempt at a covert conclusion.'

'Covert conclusion?' I ask, glancing down as my foot catches a piece of rubble and sends it skittering over the rockcrete. The noise bounces back off the dark, hollow shells of buildings around us. Suddenly I feel very exposed and understand the Colonel's anger at the use of the comm-link.

'The troops inside Acheron have achieved nothing in their search for von Strab,' the Colonel says. 'There are inquisitors who believe that the threat he poses to the stability of the sector is such that any sacrifice pales in comparison.'

'Like Coritanorum?' I can tell where the Colonel is going with this. 'They want to destroy Acheron?'

'Yes,' the Colonel says, finally glancing at me for the briefest moment.

'We destroyed Coritanorum,' I say. 'If what you say is true, then perhaps these inquisitors are right.'

'Coritanorum was irrevocably infected,' Schaeffer replies. 'Even those who had not been directly corrupted by the genestealer infestation were exposed to its spiritual heresy. There is a strong resistance movement inside Acheron, not to mention the thousands of our own troops who are conducting operations in there.'

'Yes, but they'll be pulled out before any strike, won't they?' The Colonel shakes his head. 'Why the hell not?'

'To do so would let von Strab guess our intentions,' he says. 'Giving him the opportunity to escape justice.'

'That comms signal is obviously a recording, so how does anyone know that von Strab is still in Acheron?' I ask. Somehow a stone has worked its way into my boot and is pressing into my big toe. I wriggle my toes to shift it, trying to concentrate on the Colonel at the same time.

'Nobody knows if he is still there,' the Colonel says heavily. 'These hard-line inquisitors are prepared to sacrifice Acheron just to be sure. You were telling Kelth about the last chance. Well, we are the last chance for Acheron. One of the inquisitors opposed to this course of action is an old colleague of Inquisitor Oriel. When he heard about the operation against Brightsword he specifically requested that Oriel intervene and ask me to deal with the situation.'

'But who would be willing to carry out such orders?' I say. 'Surely there will be resistance to the annihilation of a hive full of people?'

'The resistance has been our ally, until now,' he says. He looks up into the cloud-covered night sky, as if to look into space. 'However, a battle barge of the Marines Malevolent is currently disengaging itself from its current duties and will be preparing for the bombardment.'

'So that's the great hurry,' I say, realisation hitting me. 'Someone's been buying time for us?'

'Buying it with the lives of Imperial soldiers and Space Marines,' the Colonel murmurs, his face grim. 'Despite our best efforts, time is running short. Desperately short, in fact. We have twenty days, twenty-five at the most, before the destruction of Acheron begins. In twenty days, if we have not removed von Strab, millions of soldiers and citizens in Acheron will die under Imperial guns.'

CHAPTER TWELVE
THE LONG MARCH

WE MARCH ALL night, taking short breaks every couple of hours to catch our breath, and take air from our breather tanks. It would have been impossible for us to carry enough air for the whole journey, and so all we can do is periodically clear our lungs of the gas and filth that clings to the Diablo Mounts like the tar on the rocks.

Our faces are covered in grime and our fatigues hang heavy with accumulated dust and filth. And this is after only the first night. My clothes are greasy on my skin and dirt stirred up by the wind has worked its way into every opening in my uniform. Grit inside the neckline chafes my throat, my hands are raw from scraping against the grip of my lasgun, and my heavy pack bites deep into my shoulders. My back aches, my calf muscles are

tighter than coiled steel and my eyes are gummed
up with sweat and dust. The wind is bitterly cold,
and the layers of clothes I'm wearing do little to
blunt its bite.

I'd rather be someplace else.

Dawn finds us huddled in a depression in a large
boulder. I'm on first watch, and as light slowly seeps
across the sky, dull through the thick clouds, I
finally get to see the pass in the ash wastes below.
Munching on a ration bar, I look down at the valley
that stretches down between two low, rounded
peaks. The rocks glisten like an oil slick in the yellow light. A few pale, twisted trees rise out of cracks
and crevices in large rocks.

Behind me I can hear the squad slumbering fitfully; their snorts, coughs and snores blend with the
shrill noise of the wind that comes down the mountainsides. I can barely see them – they are hidden
under their bedrolls in nooks and crannies.

*Tendrils that drip with blood erupt from the ground,
spraying the still bodies with gore and dirt. Blissfully
unaware of the danger, they continue to sleep. The grey tentacles wrap around them squeezing them tight. They awake
with chokes and screams. Their necks snap, and their
organs burst out under the pressure. Their faces are crushed
by the tendrils. Lifted into the air, the ragged shapes erupt
with blood that sprays from ruptured arteries. Their limbs
are pulled from their sockets and waved around as trophies.
A victorious scream fills the silent air as the tentacles swirl
the blood and dust into obscene patterns. The air starts to
shimmer, and half-seen forms appear out of the bloody mist
that wells up from the dismembered corpses. I realise the*

scream is mine, that I am revelling in the slaughter before
me, and am infused with the power of the sacrifice. I feel
hot, in the throes of ecstatic revelation, and energy courses
through my body.

'Your watch is over.'

I almost yelp with surprise. Oahebs is standing in
front of me, leaning down over the lip of the hollow
I'm secreted in.

'Where the frag did you come from?' I snap.
'Emperor's tits, man, I could have sodding shot
you!'

He eyes me darkly, his gaze lingering on my face.

'You look tired, Kage,' he says eventually. 'Your
eyes are very bloodshot.'

'Of course I'm tired, you meathead,' I say, rising to
my feet. 'I've been awake for the last twenty hours
straight. Are there any other meaningful observations you'd like to make, any other pearls of
wisdom you want to drop in my direction?'

'It looked like you were in a trance,' he says, obviously picking his words with care. 'You were staring
at the camp. I thought you were asleep with your
eyes open.'

I look sharply at him, trying to read his thoughts,
but his face is as passive as ever. I feel a cramp in my
stomach and dizziness momentarily grips me.

'Just keep yourself awake, alright?' I snap, pushing
past him.

He doesn't reply. I stomp down into the sheltered
depression where the others are still sleeping. Kin-
Drugg gives me a wordless nod as he comes in from
the other side, where he's been watching the route

we came in by. I give him a hurried wave and then throw myself down next to my pack. Pulling at my blanket, I roll over, with my back to the others.

My thoughts are racing. One moment I was looking down the valley, and the next Oahebs was right in front of me. There's no way he could have come up on me without making some kind of sound, and I'm pretty keen-eyed and keen-eared.

The nausea has subsided, but I'm left with a little edge of panic. Breathing deeply, I close my eyes. I am bone tired. I wish sleep would sweep over me, but the more I long for it, the more awake I become. I can hear the blood rushing in my ears, and I can feel every stone and lump underneath me. My heart is hammering in my chest. I sense a distant whispering, a voice just on the edge of my hearing, and I roll over and open one eye to see who it is. Everyone else is still asleep.

As my fatigue finally pulls me into sleep, the voices start to get louder.

LORII WAKES ME just before dusk. After a quick bite to eat and some water from my canteen, I'm ready to go. The Colonel leads off, heading down the pass to the left of the main track. He weaves a path through the scattered boulders and stubby bushes. After about an hour, the pass makes a bit of a hump – a last rise before plunging down towards the wastes below. Schaeffer heads further to the left, up the side of a steep ridge.

'Aren't we silhouetting ourselves?' asks Brownie nervously. 'It's not even dark yet.'

'There is something I want you to see,' replies the Colonel, pointing out to the north-east. In the evening gloom, we can see right across the wastes. Just before the horizon is a dark blot, from which hundreds of columns of smoke and vapour rise into the air. A small mountain-like shape rising out of the wastes, surrounded by smaller blobs. The place is lit from within by innumerable fires; some are just flickers, but others rise high into the air.

'Hades Hive,' says Fenn, bowing his head and making the sign of the eagle across his chest.

'There's nothing left,' says Brownie.

'On the contrary, millions of refugees, soldiers, Space Marines and orks are out there,' says the Colonel. 'It is still a constant battle for control of the ruins. Commissar Yarrick declared that Hades would never fall. Blood is spilt to ensure that he does not have to break his word.'

'Is that what could become of Acheron?' I ask. The Colonel glares at me. I'd forgotten he hadn't told the others about the Inquisition's plan to flatten the place.

'It is a possible fate for all the hives on Armageddon,' the Colonel says, smoothing over the subject. 'The orks will ravage this world, and without Armageddon's factories, without the forges and the hives, worlds a hundred light years from here will weaken and wane, in a long chain that stretches back to Holy Terra itself. Acheron could be the turning point in preventing that. Alternatively our failure could see the beginning of the end for the Imperium.'

'That sounds overly dramatic,' says Kelth. He's taken his pack off and has leaned it against a rock. To do so is a mistake, because he'll only have to struggle to put it on again.

'I wish this were a simple melodrama,' says the Colonel. 'And I wish I was merely making speeches to rouse you. But I am not. We are beset on all sides by a galaxy full of enemies. Our foes are held back only by the Emperor's vast fleets, his armies, and the might of the Space Marines. If those foes sense weakness, they will descend on us like a pack of scavengers and pick apart the Imperium piece by piece. A squad is only as good as its weakest member, and the Imperium is only as strong as the weakest world.'

We contemplate this in silence as the Colonel leads us back down the ridge. The sight of a smouldering, ruined hive that once teemed with hundreds of millions of lives is certainly one that I'll never forget. I've seen horror: in the eyes of a strangled woman and on a battlefield literally heaving with the wounded crawling over the dead. Even the crater that was left from Coritanorum, the death place of over three million souls, was nothing compared to the ruination of Hades.

I can understand why Yarrick won't abandon the desolate hive. He made his stand there against Ghazghkull's first invasion. Like the Colonel says, if you falter for just a moment, you're dead. If you show the smallest hint of weakness, or mercy, then you will be taken out and fragged, good and proper. In a small way, it's a shame that we're going to Acheron. I'd like to fight in defence of Hades. It somehow seems appropriate for the Last Chancers to fight for something broken.

'Hey, move your arse,' says Kin-Drugg from behind me, breaking into my melancholy thoughts. I realise I've slowed down.

'Piss off,' I say to him, without turning around. I pick up the pace, eager to put the ruins of Hades behind me.

IF I THOUGHT that the jungle was hard-going, and the Diablo Mounts an ordeal, then the ash wastes have to be the worst terrain I have ever had to cross – and that includes the our forced march across the ice fields of Kragmeer.

Discoloured sand and ash stretch as far as the eye can see. Heat shimmers off the undulating dunes. The wind blows constantly, whipping a constant mist of ash into your face; its touch burns the skin with alchemical pollution. With our hoods pulled tight over our heads, rebreathers in our mouths and our noses clamped shut, each of us is enclosed in our own personal world. We are unable to communicate even with the person just a few metres in front.

The ground is constantly shifting underfoot. Each step sees you sinking to your ankles into the orange and red ash. Our pace slows to a crawl. The Colonel pushes us on for longer than before so that we make camp only when the pre-dawn glow touches the horizon.

During the night, the temperature drops rapidly. Our sweat freezes on our skin, and our breath billows from our filters like tank exhaust fumes. It's the only moisture there is – the ash underfoot stays just the same, because there's no water in it to freeze. Occasionally we see explosions far off that we steer away from, or hear the roar of a jet passing low overhead. On the second night, a huge wave of Imperial bombers passed over us, attacking a position no more than ten kilometres away. We stopped to watch the display: cluster bombs and incendiaries lit up the sky for nearly an hour.

Each step is painful. I drag my foot from the sucking ash and plant it in front of me, hauling myself forward. The pack on my back seems to hold the weight of the galaxy. Breathing shallowly to conserve the air tanks, we claw our way up dunes on our hands and knees and the wind drags dust to obscure our tracks behind us.

Sometimes the ground is rockier, as we breast some ridge of escarpment, so we pick up the pace. Kin-Drugg is in almost constant agony, he is literally dragging his bad leg behind him towards the end of each night's hike.

At other times the wastes are like an ocean. The ash has no substance; it is just thin dust that the winds slice through, creating constantly moving waves. Just like water, we wade through it, or swim across the top of it on our stomachs, craning our necks back so that the toxic dust doesn't get into our rebreathers.

We almost lost Erasmus at one point. Crossing an ash lake, he forged forwards, with loops of heavy stubber ammo around his chest and waist and his malfunctioning servo-skull crammed under one arm. He lost his footing and slipped forwards. The weight of the bullets began to drag him under. Brownie managed to get his hands under Erasmus's chin and hold his head free while the rest of us clawed at the dust, trying to scoop him out. As the ground shifted and settled, we ended up waist-deep in the ash, and floundered around for a few minutes until Oahebs found some sturdier ground a little way off. Now we use our lasguns to probe the ground ahead of us, checking to see how solid it is.

He was lucky we found him. Visibility is no more than a couple of metres in the darkness. It was thanks to his shouts and the clanking of his bullet belts that we could zero in on his position. Emperor alone knows how the Colonel and Oahebs lead us in the right direction. Except for first and last light, the sun's glow is pretty much constant in all directions. We can only judge by the prevailing winds that come from ahead and to our left that we're not travelling in circles. Well, I hope we're not.

Each day as the light of the sun begins to glow through the clouds, we pitch our crude shelters to protect against the wind, each little more than a two-sided sheet held up on a pole. There's nothing for the pegs to bite into, so we hold down the guy ropes with ammo cans and packs. After setting camp each day, we break out the rations and use one of the low-detection stoves that the ork hunters take into the jungle. A ration bar crumbled into a little boiled water makes a passable broth. We cluster around the heat from the plate with our gloves off, taking it in turns to bask in the relative warmth.

With the coming of the sun, the heat of the day steadily grows, until it's like a furnace. We daren't remove our protective gear, any pieces of exposed flesh are touched by the elements are raw and blistered. We wear tinted goggles for the most part, which shade our eyes from the glare reflecting off the rising mounds and ridges on every side. My cheeks are cracked and started bleeding yesterday. Only four days into the march, and my eyebrows have started falling out.

We slumber fitfully in our shelters, each of us exhausted from the day's toil, but too uncomfortable to find solace in sleep. We don't even pretend to be keeping watch. We can barely see twenty metres in the dust and heat haze. Nobody's looking for us, and in any case they'd have to walk straight over us to spot us. Better that time is spent resting, digging into those reserves of energy for the next night's march, our bodies slowly thawing as the morning turns to afternoon.

The constant temperature changes are playing havoc with the equipment. I'm pretty sure the barrel of my lasgun has warped and points slightly to the right now. I don't think it'd be much use in a fire fight anyway, now that grit has got into the lenses and trigger mechanism. I make a point of remembering to tell everyone to clean and check their weapons before bedding down each day, so that if trouble does come along we might at least fire back.

When it's time to break camp, we almost have to dig ourselves out. Ash and dust gathers on the shelters, and leaves a layer over our packs. Each of us spends several minutes excavating in the dying light to find hidden magazines or spare boots.

SEVEN DAYS IN and we're all fit to drop. I'm so dog-tired I'm staggering from one step to the next, every fibre in my body, every moment of my concentration is focussed on taking the next step. I hear voices on the wind, but I know they can't be real voices: I would only to be able to hear the others over the wind and through my thick hood if they stood right next to me and shouted. The wastes turn into an undulating morass of greens and oranges, deep reds and blackened ash. The laces in my boots have been eaten away by the corrosive dust, and my coat is frayed and torn in places.

My face burns, my eyes water constantly and my throat feels as if red-hot needles have been shoved into it. Even taking off my rebreather to take a gulp of water is an arduous task. We have to try not to breathe in the toxic fumes that swirl around us.

We pass a lake of oil that burns with a green flame. There are remnants of twisted machinery at its heart. The heat is welcome in the freezing night so we stay there for a short while, not caring that we can be seen silhouetted against the blaze. There's nothing out here to see us. There's nothing out here at all.

Or so I think.

We're just getting ready to camp on the eighth dawn when shimmering figures appear in the gloom, about fifty metres away. I think I'm seeing things again, but they soon solidify into the shape of a small group of men riding on the backs of strange mounts. Despite our fatigued state and numbed brains, we react quickly.

I sling off my pack and drop to the ground, lasgun ready. Ahead and to my right, Erasmus hurries forward with the ammo for Brownie's heavy stubber. The Colonel has his pistol in his hand and waves Kin-Drugg and Kelth to circle to the left. Lorii and Fenn have already broken to the right. Oahebs takes cover behind his pack a few metres behind me and to my left. He rests his lasgun across the pack, and squints through his goggles along its length.

The riders see us and halt. One of them comes forward, pulling a rifle from a sling that hangs behind his leg. The six-legged creature he's riding is covered in long, shaggy fur, and has a pointed snout and heavy shoulders. Its broad, webbed feet step across the surface of the ash without sinking, and it tosses its head from side to side, snorting constantly. I can't see any obvious eyes or ears.

The rider is swathed from head to foot in ragged cloth. Over this he wears heavy black robes, two bandolers cross over his chest. His legs are protected by a long quilted skirt split to the groin, under which are heavy trousers. Dark goggles glint from under the scarf across his face, but I can see nothing of his expression. He rides forward with his rifle pointing up, his other hand on the reins of his beast.

He stops about fifteen metres away, glancing left and right. I train my lasgun on his chest, my finger easing on to the trigger. I spare a second to use my sleeve to wipe grime from my eyeshades, before taking aim again.

To the right, there's a stutter of autogun fire and muzzle flare in the swirling dust. The Colonel brings up his pistol immediately, but I've squeezed the trigger first. So too does Oahebs. The two las-bolts strike the rider almost simultaneously: my shot detonates some of the ammunition on a bandoler, and the other punches through his right shoulder.

The beast rears as Brownie opens up. The roar of the heavy stubber sounds over the wind and two of the riders further out pitch from their saddles. There's more autogun fire from the right, replied to with the zip of lasguns. Suddenly every one of my senses works just fine. I fire off shots at the cluster of riders, as they're turning their mounts to run. I catch one of their steeds in the flank and it jinks wildly, almost toppling its rider, before they both disappear into the gloom.

We continue to fire after them, not knowing whether we're hitting anything or not. The lead rider is slumped across the neck of his mount, which just stands there dumbly until the Colonel puts a bolt into its skull. It falls sideways in a cloud of ash and dust. Brownie lets off another couple of bursts before everything falls silent again except for the hissing of the wind.

There are another few shots from the right and I think I hear a shout, but I can't be sure. We wait to see if they've regrouped for another attack. A minute passes, then another, and another, and still we don't move. After days of monotonous slog, the sudden action infuses my body, making me almost twitch with energy. I strain every nerve to stay calm.

We all turn as two figures emerge from our right, dragging something between them. We relax when we see Fenn and Lorii, bringing back a trophy of their own fight. With Oahebs, Fenn, Brownie and Spooge still standing watch, we gather around the dead rider. He looks like the others we downed: hidden beneath layer after layer of clothes. Kelth pulls the scarf from the rider's head, to reveal a face pitted and worn with exposure; the skin thick and leathery. Scabs and boils are clustered around his lips, and his teeth are little more than blackened stumps. Lorii briefly pulls out her rebreather to speak, trying not to breathe in too much.

'There were four more of them, trying to get behind us,' she says, pausing to inhale through her rebreather. 'One of them saw Fenn and opened fire.'

The Colonel nods before pulling out his own mouth-piece.

'Nomad raiders,' he says. 'There could be more. We will move in case they return. Set watch during the day.'

I nod as he turns at me for acknowledgement. Placing his pistol in its holster, he waves for us to move out. His head turns from left to right as he scans for any sign of the raiders. Already the ash is covering up the bodies, and by the time we sort ourselves out and moved away in single file, the only evidence of them is a few dark mounds. As we slip away into the swirling dust, a distant, haunting cry carries along on the wind. It's a signal, there's no doubt. Clutching our weapons tighter, we cast nervous glances around us, and hurry off.

WE PRESS ON as fast as we can for the next two nights. Finally, as dawn approaches on the tenth day, a darkness can be seen on the horizon to the north. The coming of daylight sees us taking shelter in the shade of an overhanging cliff, the red face soaring out of the dunes to a hundred metres above us. There's been no further contact with the nomads, although occasionally one of us thinks we have glimpsed shapes in the distance, either ahead or behind us.

We find a small cave, half filled with sand and dust, at the foot of the cliff, and dig our way in. We find ourselves in a spacious cavern, high enough to stand in, and twenty metres across at its broadest. While the others make camp, the Colonel asks Oahebs and me to join him. Leaving the cave, we make our way along the cliff until it descends to a ridge that we climb up. With thick boots and gloved hands, the climb isn't easy, but we eventually make it to the top. From here, we can see kilometres around, over the layer of dust-fog that sweeps across the wastes below.

And there, about twenty kilometres away, we can see the Hades-Acheron highway as it cuts across the wastes on high pillars; it is like a ribbon of grey against the orange and red. And slightly to the east, Averneas Forge sprawls out into the dunes and hills, a black oily cloud of soot hanging above it. It looks like Infernus Forge, only much more intact. Chimneystacks hundreds of metres high pierce the dark cloud and a tangle of dome-roofed Mechanicus factory-temples radiate out from a large, slab-sided structure at the centre. It's impossible to make out any more detail from this distance.

The smoking remnants of a gargant – seventy metres of ruptured metal plates and jutting many-barrelled cannons – stand a few kilometres from the complex. There are swarms of movement around its base. Although it's impossible to make out any details through the dust cloud kicked up, it's obvious the orks are there in force. Flickers of light from the forges are accompanied a few seconds later by the tinny, distant thumps of heavy gunfire.

Oahebs points to the west of the forge, and there we can see the shadowy shapes of two Battle Titans; Warlord-class I'd guess by their size. They are standing watch over the industrial complex. Like huge sentinels, sixty metres tall; they stand immobile, their giant plasma reactors dormant and their huge weapons silent. A column of vehicles, tanks and personnel carriers is making its way along the highway in front of the nearest titan. They look like toys compared to the armoured titans; each is smaller than its head. I can imagine the crew in the carrier manning their stations, waiting for the order to unleash the destructive potential of their war machine.

Pulling out his map, the Colonel fumbles in his pocket. He produces a short pencil and makes a few notes on the map before passing it to Oahebs. I look over his shoulder as he traces a route under the highway west of Averneas, around the end of the ork lines and then into the complex itself. The Colonel nods, takes the map back and folds it away. We head back down the ridge to rejoin the others.

I DON'T SLEEP AT all well that day, thinking about ash wastes nomads finding us and knowing that a battle rages so close. We can hear the occasional explosion. We're going to have to sneak in to Averneas, and the battle may actually turn out to work in our favour. Nobody's going to give a squad a second thought as it hurries through the half-ruined complex – there are troops all over the place. The only concern is that we don't get too caught up in the fighting itself.

As day turns to night, the dark sky is once again lit by detonations and muzzle flashes. We cut across the wastes towards Averneas. Our progress is slower than normal as we make sure we don't run into anything unexpectedly. Myself, Lorii and Fenn each make regular forays ahead to scout out any enemy positions, but there's nothing for the first hour.

The noise of the ork attack is loud now; it's only a few kilometres away. We start to skirt west, away from the brightness of the battlefield. As we get closer, we can see lights from vehicles that move along the highway. They are the tanks and supply convoys that reinforce Averneas from other fronts. We pass under the highway itself between the huge supporting struts, and climb over mounds of debris and wrecks of vehicles. The rockcrete pillars are pocked with shell craters and bullet holes, and the tangled ruins of the combatants stretch out of sight to the left and right, testimony to the battles fought for control of the road.

We hear odd noises over the rumbling of vehicles above: the sound of scratching on metal, the skitter of a dislodged stone down a rubble pile. There are odd glimpses of movement in the gloom. They are probably just desert rats or solitary scavengers picking an existence from the ruin of war. Whatever it is, it knows better than to face us. As we clear the tangled wreckage, we make a quick sweep behind us, which reveals nobody following. Two kilometres ahead and to the east lie the outlying buildings of the forge complex. Its smokestacks jut from roofs, billowing fumes, and the glow of forges and furnaces spills out from shattered windows and shuttered doors.

With jets roaring above us and tracer fire crossing the sky, we sneak into Averneas, cutting our way through a battered mesh fence that surrounds a windowless building on the outskirts. We climb a wall on the far side into a dumping compound of some kind. Piles of warm slag smoke fitfully on the frost-hardened ground, illuminated by the flare of fire from an anti-aircraft gun on the roof of the nearby forge house.

A guardhouse stands at the gate into the access-way beyond the forge, and we slip around it, keeping to the shadows, before making our way along the surrounding fence. We duck into pools of darkness as a squad of Steel Legion troop past, following their Chimera APC along the road.

To our right, a spotlight springs into life; it points up into the air, and reflects off the clouds. It's joined by others, and soon a dozen patches of light criss-cross the night sky, occasionally showing up the silhouettes of large ork bombers. Flak and tracer fire screams up into the sky as we cut through the fence and push through. But the bombers don't attack; they disappear from view as they head eastwards towards Acheron Hive.

The Colonel points left and we hurry on, leaping over abandoned sandbag barricades into empty gun pits, into the heart of Averneas, skirting along gantries over dormant firepits. A misplaced shell explodes ahead of us, bringing down the wall of a brick outbuilding. We turn away as a fire crew appears on a steam-driven tender, and pick our way along another route to our objective. The Colonel leads us steadily north and east, taking a circuitous route to avoid contact with the defending forces.

About half a kilometre inside Averneas, a ruined refinery soars above the landscape, its chimneys and towers toppled, the maze of pipes and tanks now a dark warren of twisted metals and ruptured ferro-crete.

'This is it,' the Colonel says, voice muffled by his rebreather. He waves me to lead the way in.

Something crunches under my foot, and I look down to see a half-rotted ork skull. Other remnants lie close by, alien and human, and it's obvious that the refinery has changed hands several times before. A twisted, spire-like pumping tower leans precariously onto a bent network of high-level gangways. The Colonel leads us towards it, signalling that we are to enter the shattered building at its foot.

Passing through, we see faces reflected in blank, cracked display screens. We step past overturned chairs and have to avoid cracked plates and mugs that have been dropped on the floor. We find ourselves at the top of a spiralling staircase that plunges deep into Avernas. The Colonel pulls a small lantern from his pack and lights it with a match. Then he leads us down, pistol in hand.

Five storeys down, we come to another landing. The Colonel turns off the stairs, ducking through the collapsed arch of a doorway. Beyond, we come into a room full of pipes and gauges, the pumping machinery long silent. The length of the chamber is dominated by a single massive pipe, twice the height of a man. Near to where it comes in the wall is a maintenance hatch. It creaks alarmingly as Oahebs winds it open.

Shining his lantern inside, the Colonel reveals the interior of the dark pipe. The sides are smeared with scum and residue, and the bottom of the pipe is slicked with a thin stream of shiny, thick fluid. The smell is acrid; it stings my eyes and lips even through my protective gear. The Colonel ducks and steps through the hatch into the pipe, his boots ringing dully on the thick, corroded metal. Shining the lantern to the left, east towards Acheron, he waves us on.

CHAPTER THIRTEEN
NO LIGHT AT THE END
OF THE TUNNEL

THE AIR IN THE pipe is old and stale; it hangs with the cloying tastes of oil, but is purer than anything we've breathed since we arrived on Armageddon. We take off the rebreathers and talk as we walk. It helps to break up the monotony of trudging kilometre after kilometre, day after day. We follow the bobbing glow of the Colonel's lantern. After a kilometre or so underground when it has cleared Averneas, the pipeline rises sharply and breaks out overground into the ash wastes.

Occasionally the pipe takes a turn to the left or the right, or rises and dips over some obstruction. Here and there, battle has taken its toll and the pipeline is ruptured. We have to don the rebreathers as we pass such sections, through which the light from outside blinks. Our feet scrape on the dust and ash blown in from the wastes.

At one point, the pipeline is so mangled and torn by some huge explosion that we have to climb over the twisted remnants. We step out into the wastes from the shattered pipe to see Acheron rearing up in the distance, about thirty kilometres away. Thousands of metres tall, it spears the sky like a dark spear, the upper spires obscured by the low toxic cloud. Flames burn from its ravaged shell, and there are still signs of heavy fighting as artillery batteries bombard its lower reaches.

Like a giant stalagmite, it rises up from the wastes, pocked with shuttle docks and entryways. Even at this distance, we can see the smoke issuing from a million flues, the haze rising and clinging to the hive's upper reaches, adding to the smog that obscures its lofty pinnacle. Buttresses that housed tens of thousands splay outwards, scarred and ravaged with shell holes and craters. The ferrocrete skin is worn by millennia of erosion into strangely flowing, organic shapes. It looks like a massive fire-ant mount, excreted up from the core of the planet.

It reminds me of Olympas, my home, and not since fighting around the hives of Ichar IV have I felt so far from there.

The pipeline starts again less than a hundred metres away, but I take every second to drink in the dark majesty of Acheron. I can imagine the thousands of factories within, the millions of souls labouring in forges and mills, workshops and garages. The thump of engines, the clanging of hammers will be resounding through the hive city; the sounds of my childhood. Generations live and die without ever breathing air that has not been reclaimed for millennia, and without drinking water that has not been the piss of five hundred generations before. Most have never seen light except from a glow-globe. Many of them don't even know such things exist.

This could be last sight of a hive I see in all of its glory, a great mound of humanity's industry with a life and personality of its own. In just two weeks, it might not be there. It might become like Hades, a ruined wasteland of craters, testament to the orbital fury of the Marines Malevolent. Those millions – no billions – of souls exist in ignorance of the doom that hangs over them. They are condemned simply because it would be pointless trying to save them. So it has always been, and so it must be, for the Imperium does not count in millions or billions of lives. Such numbers are insignificant. What does the Emperor care, all-seeing from the Golden Throne of Terra, if a billion souls die so that a world is held against the darkness? It is a mere drop in a sea, amongst a million oceans.

Armageddon must hold.

I linger for a few seconds as the others clamber back into the pipe way and continue on. I can't let Acheron die. If Acheron dies, then so could Geidi Hive on Olympas. No matter what has happened to me, or happens to me, I've always felt sure that Geidi would live on, as old as the Imperium itself, enduring war, poverty, insurrection and upheaval.

The people change, regimes come and go, but Geidi will always be Geidi. Now that might not be true. Perhaps even now it is a flaming pyre for three billion people, destroyed by orks, or eldar, the tau or the traitors of Abyssal Chaos. Perhaps the soldiers of the Emperor have obliterated it. If Acheron can survive, then so can Geidi and part of what I am will last for eternity.

A FEW KILOMETRES on, after five days of walking, the pipeway dips sharply, and heads down into the rock beneath the ash wastes towards the Acheron underhive. We decide to rest for a few hours before making a concerted effort towards our goal on the next march. Everything is still down here, not even the wind brushing against the pipe to break the silence. I close my eyes but sleep refuses to come.

Hearing a scraping noise, I open one eye to see Brownie dragging his knife across his bald scalp, shaving off non-existent stubble. I sit up and he turns and looks at me. His eyes are white in his dark face, and they peer at me out of the gloom. Standing up, he shuffles past the sleeping form of Fenn and sits next to me.

'Nearly there,' he says, his voice kept low to avoid disturbing the others. I nod, not sure whether I'm in the mood to talk or not. 'How long do you think it'll take to find him?'

'Hard to say,' I shrug. 'There've been Guard regiments looking for him for almost a year now, without so much as a glimpse, or so Fenn reckons.'

'And so how are we supposed to find him?' he says with a frown. 'We could be here weeks, months, even years.'

'It won't come to that,' I say, and he looks at me sharply.

'How do you know? What have you heard?'

'The Colonel always has a plan,' I tell him. 'I bet he probably already knows where von Strab is, and if he doesn't, then he'll have a way of tracking him down in no time.'

'You seem very confident,' he says.

'Experience,' I reply after a moment. 'The Colonel's never failed.'

'I'd never heard of him before he turned up at the prison tower,' says Brownie, glancing over to Schaeffer's sleeping form. The Colonel is lying on his back with his head on his pack. His greatcoat is pulled up to his chin like a blanket. He looks as still as a corpse except for the shallow rising and falling of his chest. 'If he was such a hero, surely someone would know who he is, or where he's from?'

'Ever heard of a place called Typhos Prime?' I ask, leaning closer. He shakes his head. 'How about False Hope? Kragmeer? Deliverance?'

'Nope, never heard of any of them,' says Brownie. 'Why?'

'That's my point,' I say. 'You don't hear about the Colonel because he doesn't want you to. Does anybody know exactly where he's been? What he's done? Perhaps Inquisitor Oriel and few of his shadowy friends do. Maybe the odd Warmaster or sector marshal. I don't know him from the next man. He could be the son of a Terran High Lord, or the bastard spawn of a pit slave for all I know. We once thought that perhaps he was a daemon in the body of a man.'

Brownie laughs, before casting a nervous glance at the others.

'That's a bit much, isn't it?' he says.

'I saw him get his arm blown off by a plasma bolt,' I tell him. Brownie looks over, seeing the Colonel's arms crossed over his chest like a body waiting to be interred in its coffin.

'They look normal enough to me,' he says. 'Are you saying he's not human?'

'Don't listen to him,' says Lorii, rolling over to her side on my left. 'The Colonel's as human as you or me.'

Brownie can't stop himself from giving her a second glance. He is obviously looking at her alabaster skin and pure white hair.

'Why?' he says. 'Kage might have a point.'

Lorii gives me a long, hard look, and I glance away, wondering what she knows. What did Oriel tell her about me? What about Oahebs, for that matter? Oriel knows, or suspects, that I'm a witch. Did he voice those suspicions to anyone else? Lorii taps a finger into her temple and my heart skips a beat.

'Kage isn't quite all there, are you, Kage?' she says. I scowl at her. 'He's got a bit missing, cut out of him on his last mission.'

'What's that got to do with the Colonel?' I ask, raising my voice. 'You thought there was something not right with him too.'

A shadow looms over us in the yellow glow of the lantern. We look up to see the Colonel standing over us, his face in shadow. His head turns to look at each of us, the whites of his eyes barely a slit. With the fingers of his left hand, he pulls off his right glove and holds his arm out. I expect to see the metal of an augmetic, but the skin is tough and wrinkled; small hairs stand out from his wrist. He leans forward and waves it in front of my face.

'They grew a new one for me,' he says, bending close.

'Who?' asks Brownie, before flinching as the Colonel turns his gaze to him.

'The tech-priests, of course,' he says, pulling his glove back on. 'It took three weeks of constant pain, feeling bone growing, new flesh knitting to old flesh, and skin hardening under the glare of special lamps.'

'You never mentioned it before,' I say, and the Colonel straightens up.

'Why would I?' he asks. 'You may fear and loathe the Inquisition, but they are powerful allies and have their uses. A new arm took a while, but not as long as it took them to rebuild my spine after I was crushed by a tank.'

He leans forward again, centimetres from me.

'Do you think I was born with these eyes, Kage?' he asks, his whisper sending a shiver down my spine. 'Even they cannot grow eyes, did you know that? These were donated.'

'Who was the donor?' Lorii asks in a hushed voice, peering at the Colonel closely. Her hand unconsciously moves to touch him.

'A heretic who sinned against the Machine God,' Schaeffer says. 'A mindless servitor now, with no need of eyes to monitor the power fluctuations in a plasma reactor aboard a battleship.'

'That's so fragged,' I say, shaking my head. 'What else have they done to you?'

He gives me a confused look.

'You make it sound like a punishment,' the Colonel says. Behind him, I see that the others have woken up and are listening intently. Erasmus looks as if his eyes are going to burst, they're bulging so much. 'It is not a sentence, it is a gift. I have been kept alive for six times the natural span of a human, that's nearly three hundred years. Three centuries of service to the Emperor – three centuries of dedication.'

'Three centuries cheating death, and knowing nothing but war?' suggests Lorii, earning herself a bitter laugh from Schaeffer.

'Life is war, Lorii, you of all people know that,' he says. 'I was not created for battle like you, but in his wisdom the Emperor has granted me a gift that is seldom seen. I have never failed, and as long as I live, I never will.'

'What does he mean, you were created for battle?' asks Brownie, looking at Lorii. 'What does that mean?'

Lorii says nothing, she just grimaces at the Colonel.

'What is the matter, Lorii?' Schaeffer says. 'It is not a guilty secret to be ashamed of and kept hidden. Not like some low-born lover to a governess. Tell them who you are, and be proud of it.'

Her expression turns to one of sadness. She looks pleadingly at the Colonel, who steps back and looks away, arms crossed. She looks at the others, and then at me.

'I was one of five hundred brothers and sisters,' she says, looking down, head bowed. 'We were bred from the seed of Macharius himself in an incubator. We were fed on artificial stimulants, and combat doctrine was pumped straight into our minds.'

She falls silent, hands tightly balled into fists in her lap, her shoulders shaking with anger.

'They thought they could make a perfect soldier,' the Colonel says, without turning around. 'They took the seed of the great Macharius without his knowledge just before he died. For centuries they laboured in secret, their goal shunned by other tech-priests. They did well, considering. Five hundred healthy babies were created out of fifty thousand attempts. Five companies of soldiers were raised from their unnatural births to fight.'

'I'm the last one,' says Lorii, still gazing at the oil-slicked floor. Then she looks up, her eyes brimming with tears. She looks at me, and her anger returns. 'When Loron died, I was the only one left. You think you suffered, believing you were the only one of us to survive Coritanorum? What if you were the only living proof of an obscene experiment performed by outcasts and heretics?'

'The tech-priests understand the working of the body, even the mind, and the ways it can be manipulated,' says the Colonel. 'But they know nothing of the soul. In all their teachings they forgot about one thing. Faith. Faith in the Emperor.'

'So what happened to the others?' I ask. 'I know your company was all but wiped out in an air attack, but what happened to the other four?'

'Killed in battle, all of them,' says Lorii. 'On Ichar IV, Methusala, Lazarus Saecunda. They were on their own, shunned by the other regiments – easy targets.'

We absorb this in silence. Then Dunmore stands up.

'Well, since we seem to be getting everything in the open, I have something to tell you,' he says. 'Why do you think I'm called Brownie?'

'I thought it was because of your dark skin,' says Kin-Drugg, but Brownie shakes his head.

'First time I was in battle,' he says, looking at his feet. 'First time the firing started, I shit myself. Literally, shit myself. That's why they called me Brownie.'

We greet this in stunned silence, and it's Lorii who starts laughing first. Her cackle degenerates into snorts as we all join in, except the Colonel who stands there in stony silence.

'Seriously?' Lorii manages to say between gulps of air. 'You're called Brownie because you shed your cargo in your first fight?'

Brownie's laughing too; his teeth gleaming white in the gloom.

'Damn straight I cacked myself,' he says with a grin. 'A shell went off about twenty metres in front of me; it covered me in blood and guts. I dumped my load as I lay there screaming. That's when I decided that I was going to learn how to use the biggest guns we've got. I even tried to join an artillery regiment, but they found out I was already enlisted and kicked me back.'

'Meathead,' I mutter, slumping back against the side of the pipe, and closing my eyes. I've no desire to confess anything at the moment.

Everyone drifts apart again, some still chuckling. I drift away too, and sleep finally claims me.

IT DOESN'T FEEL like any time has passed before the shuffling of feet and scraping wakens me. I didn't realise just how dog-tired I was. My brain still numb, I gather my gear together and fall into line behind Kin-Drugg. It doesn't take much to start walking, swinging one leg in front of the other. I focus on the buckle of Kin-Drugg's pack a couple of metres in front of me.

Why do I feel so lethargic? Looking past Kin-Drugg's shoulder, I see that the others are stumbling and shuffling along too. We're all so tired; mindless zombies from the fatigue. My legs are cramping and I can feel a pain in my chest every time I breathe in. The sores on my face throb and open. Blood dribbles down my cheeks and chin. I see the Colonel sway slightly, and reach out a hand to steady himself. The lantern drops from his fingers and clatters into the skin of oil gathered in the bottom of the pipe.

That's when I realise there's more to this than just exhaustion.

'Rebreathers!' I croak, but nobody seems to hear me. I'm sweating hard, my face is burning hot, and my hands greasy with perspiration.

I stumble past Kin-Drugg and grab the Colonel.

'Gas,' I manage to wheeze, pointing to the rebreather at Schaeffer's belt. 'Bad air!'

He nods dumbly but does nothing. I fumble for my own rebreather, my fingers feeling thick and clumsy, like fat sausages. I manage to pull on the rebreather. The filtered air fills my lungs. A few short breaths clear my head enough to pull the Colonel's rebreather free and slip it over his face. He waves me away and I help Kin-Drugg with his. Slowly, like they're underwater or in zero-grav, the rest of the team begin to pull on their masks, flailing with the straps and buckles.

I haul off my pack and retrieve my goggles from a pocket. The filtered lenses blot out almost all the light from the lantern, but the stinging stops almost immediately. Fenn stumbles up to me, pointing desperately at his rebreather. Bending forward, I peer at his face and see a short crack in the mask, just under the nose filter. Ignoring my pack, I grab hold of him and drag him forwards, past the Colonel. I'm hoping that the gas pocket will come to an end shortly.

Fenn begins to convulse in my grasp. His fingers claw at my sleeve, his feet kick spasmodically as he tries to walk. I heft a shoulder under his arm and half-drag, half-carry him along. The light of the lantern fades behind us and we plunge into darkness. Something cracks and crunches underfoot and the floor becomes slippery. A couple of times the weight of Fenn overbalances me and we fall down into a heap. As I struggle up with him, I put my hand into a soft, furry mass. Things writhe under my fingertips and I snatch my hand back, gagging from the sensation. I pull us to our feet and hurry on as quickly as possible, part of me glad I can't see anything in the darkness.

I'm not sure how much further we have to go, or how long he's got. Occasionally the pipeline bends without me noticing, and it's only as I slip on the sloping sides that I know we've changed direction. At one point, I feel a gust of air on the side of my face, and I turn and look but can't see anything. Perhaps there's a secondary pipe or some kind of vent. I consider stopping, hoping that it'll be bringing in fresher air. I stop myself though, equally conscious that the toxins could be coming from there instead.

I can't tell how far we've gone, perhaps two desperate kilometres, before Fenn starts to calm down. I can't see him, so I risk pulling out my rebreather. I swallow a lungful of stale air, but it's the usual stale air of the pipe. I take off the ork hunter's mask and he's gulping it in. He bends double, hacking and coughing. Then he slumps sideways, falling from my grasp, and I fumble around in the pitch black until my hands find him again.

I dump myself down next to him. Both of us are panting heavily, not able to spare a breath for words. We sit in silence, in the total darkness, hoping that the others will catch up with us soon. Hoping that they're not all dead.

* * *

IT CAN'T ACTUALLY be more than half an hour until we see a glow from further up the pipe, though it feels like half a day to us. There are definitely things in the darkness, creatures skittering past, brushing under my legs, scratching at my boots.

As the light draws closer I make out the Colonel, and the others close behind him. He doesn't even give us a second glance as he walks past. Brownie dumps my pack at my feet and offers a hand to haul me up. Lorii pulls up Fenn. Nodding his thanks, Fenn falls into line. I pull on my pack and take up the rear, following behind Kin-Drugg as he limps along.

ACHERON HIVE

CHAPTER FOURTEEN
THE UNDERHIVE

THE PIPELINE IS teeming with rats that scurry underfoot and dart through the glow of the lantern into the darkness. Here, lower down the pipe, they swarm in front of us, hissing, screeching. Some of them are as long as a man is tall, their tails fat ropes of pink flesh.

Many of the rats are misshapen, with hunched backs, bony protuberances, overlong fangs and are covered in scabs and boils. They nip at our ankles, bare their fangs and whip their tails in agitation as we kick them aside. Here and there, the pipeline is cracked, and the rats hide in the shadows; their glittering eyes regarding us menacingly. They seem to plague Kin-Drugg more than the rest of us. Perhaps they sense that he is wounded and is the easiest prey. I have no doubt that had he strayed from the circle of light they would have been on him as quick as possible.

I reckon any one of us would probably be easy meat, for that matter, the hunger of the rats only kept in check by their fear of our numbers. I figure it was the skeletons of those that had unwisely ventured into the gas pocket that we had been crunching through in the pitch black.

After several hours, the rat population slowly begins to dwindle and we start to hear noises. The pipe shudders almost imperceptibly with a distant thumping. The rats here are leaner and more active than their cousins further up the pipe. As we march, the thumping becomes more pronounced and blends in with sounds of other machinery whirring and grinding.

The Colonel stops and shuts off the lantern for a while. As my eyes adjust, I detect a tinge of light from far ahead. It gets brighter as we walk, and I become steadily more aware of the clumping of our boots on the hollow metal of the pipe. I realise that it's no longer burrowing through the ground.

Smaller pipes spring off from the main one, heading left and right, up and down, to different parts of the Acheron underhive. The route branches into two pipes roughly half the size of the one we stand in and the Colonel leads us to the left, stooping and shuffling through the much narrower space. It's not far, less than half a kilometre and the pipe suddenly ends, opening out into a wide, low tank. Dropping to its bottom, we find ourselves knee-deep in thick, oily sludge that sucks at our boots. Dull light streams in from an open hatch in the roof ahead of us, and iron rungs, corroded and broken, stick out of the tank's wall. The Colonel switches off the lantern, stowing it in Lorii's pack and signals for me to lead the way up the ladder.

Poking my head out of the hatch, I find that we're in a high chamber, filled with similar rectangular tanks arranged in a regular pattern over a ferrocrete store. Dust, centimetres thick, lies over everything, stirred gently by large fans rotating solely behind grilles in the ceiling.

There's no sign of life so I pull myself out, readying my lasgun. I crouch on top of the tank and gesture to the others to come up.

We fan out across the room, securing the two wide doorways at either end, both barred from the inside with steel slide-locks. I look to the Colonel for further instructions but he just shakes his head and then points to the door next to me.

'We are inside the underhive,' Schaeffer says, keeping his voice low. 'From here we will have to establish our exact location and commence our search for von Strab. Remember that there are the native underhivers, Imperial forces, von Strab's Army of Liberation and the orks. And none of them will necessarily be sympathetic to our cause. We must acquire suitable disguises at the earliest opportunity and preferably a guide of some kind. We must not be discovered.'

He nods for me to slide back the bar on the door. It squeals as rust flakes off and drops into the dust. Kin-Drugg puts a hand on the door and thrusts it open. It swings out noisily on corroded hinges, revealing another chamber, much like the one we're in, but filled with spherical tanks ruptured from within. The floor is sticky with ancient chemicals. Flickering glow-globes cast moving shadows over the gauges and control panels, and reflect off another doorway opposite.

I scoot forward, my boots sticking to the tacky floor, holding my lasgun in a tight grip. The others follow, spreading out to the left and right, picking their routes between the abandoned machinery. The glass in the gauges is cracked; the pipes between them are split and frayed and a moss-like growth is spread over most of the tanks.

'Water reclamation,' I say quietly, remembering the parasitical algae that I was tasked with cleaning off the tanks when I was four years old.

The next door swings open with little noise; its hinges have more recently been oiled. Instantly, we're all alert, realising that whoever oiled them could be close by, perhaps living in the area. Oahebs points at the ground and I glance down, seeing obvious boot tracks in the grime of the floor. Behind me, Brownie whispers to Erasmus to prepare the heavy stubber ammo, and he pulls out the bipod from its barrel, ready to drop down and give covering fire at a moment's notice.

The roof is low, buckled inwards in places, sprouting coils of pipes and cables, covered with grilles and hatches. We're on some kind of landing, a stairwell spirals up through the roof and drops down beneath us. Other doorways open up from the walls around us, some into darkness, others into brightly lit areas. From below comes the flickering orange glow of flames.

As we move to the stairwell, we see that the handrail is dotted with small spikes, made from short nails crudely welded to it. Fenn motions for us to stop where we are and stalks forward, crouching; examining the steps. He bends down to look through the railing and then sits back.

'Trip-wire,' he says, running his finger along a fine wire strung across the front of the first step.

'Attached to what?' the Colonel asks, stepping forwards.

'Bolts, metal plates, spoons,' says Fenn. 'It's an alarm, not a booby trap. Everyone watch where they tread.'

He leads the way, the Colonel following, as we step carefully down the stairway. I glance over the rail into the darkness below, and there's an unmistakable glow of flames from near to the base of the stairs some thirty metres below. I'm sure I see movement, and Lorii's glance over her shoulder at me confirms that I haven't imagined it. Without a word, and trying to make as little noise as possible, we spread out, allowing a gap of a few steps to open up between each of us. Looking up, it's easy to see the crude tripwire and rattling, clanging alarm system suspended from the steps above.

Suddenly, Fenn freezes and we all stop immediately, weapons brought up to the firing position, ready for anything. He hands his lasgun back to the Colonel and draws his knife, keeping it behind his back to prevent any reflection from the firelight below. The Colonel lets him to disappear further down the steps. Shortly afterwards there's a muffled groan, and the sound of boots scraping on metal. Then a heavy sigh.

Receiving some signal from Fenn that we can't see, the Colonel carries on downwards, and we follow, catching up with Fenn a dozen steps on, stooped over a body, his lasgun reclaimed from the Colonel. The man is thin to the point of being wasted. He is dressed in ragged breeches and jerkin and his arms are tattooed with a pattern of interlocking black squares. On his head he wears a black and red scarf, tied in an intricate knot at the base of his skull. The tattered ends drip with blood from the ragged wound across his throat.

I glance at Fenn and he gives me a 'him-or-us' sort of look. I nod in understanding. We're close enough to the fire now to hear the crackling of flames and the murmur of voices. It's only about ten more steps down, and by crouching we can see into the low room below through the spiralling banister. The substantial fire is a little off to our right, and there are seven or eight figures sitting around it on blankets.

The room itself, ruddy from the firelight, is some kind of old slaughterhouse. Hooks on belts hang from the ceiling, rusted gears seized together from the ancient mechanism that used to move them. Blood channels are cut into the floor, angling down towards one wall into a gutter and down into a sinkhole, even redder than the rest of the room.

Along one wall is a long, rusted metal bench, covered with junk of all kinds: broken knives, hammer heads, corroded spanners, planks of wood, nests of wire and stretched springs, leaking power packs and pieces of broken glass.

At that moment, one of the figures by the fire half turns to look over its shoulder straight at me. It's a woman, she has long straggles of hair sticking out of her headscarf. Her mouth is open as if she's about to speak and her right hand is raised holding a bottle. Her eyes lock on mine for an eternity, and I can do nothing but stare back at her.

Her invitation for a drink turns to a shout of warning.

The others around the fire boil up from their places, grabbing weapons and shouting. Fenn leaps down the steps, followed by the Colonel and the rest of us. The crack of gunfire echoes around the room and bullets whiz past me as I jump down the last few steps, almost losing my footing.

Lasbolts and muzzle flares blot out the firelight as we return fire. A bullet plucks at the material of my trousers just below the knee. Hurling myself to the left, I fire from the hip, aiming at the woman who is crouched down with a pistol held in both hands.

The first shot is high, but the second takes her in the shoulder and the third low in the stomach. She sprawls backwards, pistols flying from her grip, and clutches her stomach.

Brownie curses to my right, sheltering behind the iron of the staircase, fumbling with the heavy stubber as Spooge slaps an ammo belt into the breech.

The Colonel's bolt pistol roars in my ear. One of the enemy is flung backwards by a hit in the chest, onto the fire. His ragged clothes erupt into flames and his piercing shrieks can be heard over the noise of the fire fight.

In a few seconds, all but one of them is down, dead or wounded and the last one bolts for an archway to the left of the fire.

'We need him alive,' snaps the Colonel, knocking aside Fenn's lasgun with his pistol as he takes aim.

'Got him!' I shout, and I sprint forwards after the getaway.

I don't spare a glance at the groaning wounded as I duck through the arch, which opens out into a high chamber, vaulted with buttresses and pillars. Ancient, defunct machinery fills the room, soaring above my head with banks of dials and gauges, creating a maze of pathways. Water drips down from rusted pipes that criss-cross the ceiling. A splash to my right sends me heading in that direction. I jog along, half-crouched and alert, wary of an ambush. To my left I see a deep puddle rippling against the base of the machines and turn to follow my prey.

I catch a glimpse of him in the gloom, about twenty metres ahead. He ducks to the right and out of sight. Speeding up, I leap over the puddle, lasgun grasped in both hands as I pound up the rockcrete aisle.

Skidding around the corner, I have to spin and twist to avoid the knife thrust at my face as the man jumps out of the shadows at me. Instinctively, I drop and roll to the left using the momentum of my run to come back up to my feet, grabbing my lasgun by the barrel and swinging it. The butt connects with the man's arm above the elbow; it knocks him off balance and jars the knife from his fingers.

I step in to drive the toe of my left boot into his family jewels. I almost lift him off the ground. With an agonised squeal he drops like a sack of synthi-spuds, grasping his crotch, coughing and choking. I loom over him, and he looks up at me, pleading in his eyes.

He's older than me, I would guess thirty-five years at least, his face thin, his premature wrinkles lined with grease and grime. His eyes are watery and weak. They are filled with tears from the pain in his nuts, his lips cracked and raw as he wordlessly mouths his agony. Like the others, he's dressed in breeches and jerkin, which is open to reveal a tight, wiry body tattooed with the same overlapping boxes design on the sentry. His scarf is pinned in place with gaudy brooches shaped as cogs and skulls.

I hear the others making their way through the room and I call out to them. Slinging my rifle over my shoulder, I offer him a hand and pull him to his feet. He stamps several times on the ground, trying to get his balls to settle properly. He is still bent over.

'What's your name?' I ask him, and he looks at me with hate-filled eyes.

'Derflan Kierck,' he wheezes. 'By the Great Cog, who are you?'

'We're your new best friends,' I tell him as the others gather behind me. 'Say hello to the Last Chancers.'

CHAPTER FIFTEEN
TRAITOR CITY

THE UNDERHIVE IS lit with thousands of burning braziers. They stand on poles and are slung from chains from the high plasteel rafters that soar above the small conglomeration of huts and hovels. They are wedged into spaces between the banks of gigantic pistons that seized up thousands of years ago.

We're standing at the top of a wide sweep of stairs that leads down into the vast hall. We are now dressed in rags and headscarves taken from the dead underhivers. Our packs have been swapped for ragged, rope-strapped sacks, our lasguns swathed in strips of dirty cloth to conceal their well-maintained appearance. It turns out that the group we killed were tool merchants, who scavenge and repair whatever they can find to sell. It was a workshop we'd found them in. They used to spend half their time travelling from settlement to settlement.

KIERCK STANDS AT the front of our group, the Colonel right behind him, ready to grab him if he tries to do a runner.

'Is Firehole,' the underhiver says, grinning and revealing his stubby, brown-stained teeth. 'Good tradin' at Firehole. Allas plenty of tradin' at Firehole.'

He looks at me and flinches. His expression changing into an oily, sycophantic smile before he looks away.

'We will circle around,' says the Colonel. 'We should avoid contact as much as possible.'

'No!' says Kierck, his voice a nasal whine wholly in keeping with his scrawny, withered appearance. 'They seen us already. Wonder why we not come in if we leave now. Is good, no worries. We trade, we go on, they not know where we go next.'

The Colonel considers this for moment and nods.

'We will do this your way,' he says. 'But if we run foul, you will be the first to die, understand?'

'No worries, Derflan not run you foul, you see, yes,' Kierck says, almost bowing because he's so hunched over, the same ingratiating smile on his face. 'Derflan talk, we sell, they buy. Is allas good, yes?'

The Colonel nods again and Kierck leads us down the steps. He pulls a small hammer from his belt and then produces a triangular sheet of metal hung on a chain. Holding the chain, he begins to rap the hammer against the sheet, ringing out a sharp clang every few steps. He begins to holler, his accent so broad I can't understand what he's saying.

'No talk,' he says, looking over his shoulder at us. He eyes us critically, obviously not pleased with our disguise. A leering look enters his eye as he examines Lorii. 'Mouths give you away as outsiders. I say you cousins, brother-keepers of the Great Cog. You learnin' tool tradin' from ole Derflan. You promise keep ears open and mouths shut, that why you not talk, yes?'

As we approach, people emerge from the hovels of Firehole. Most are semi-naked, dressed in leather aprons, heavy kilts and thick breeches, their chests bare. This goes for the women too, and like the men who emerge, they're also painted with orange and red flame designs from navel to shoulder. Some show branding scars on their faces, breasts and arms, and the men have a strange F-shaped runes burnt into their foreheads. A few have small children with them, unmarked as yet. In all, about thirty or forty gather around us as we walk into the middle of the settlement.

I can feel heat rising up from the ground and I guess that there are some kind of forges or furnaces below us, that once worked the huge pistons, but are now turned to some other use. The fact that they're fire-worshippers is as plain as the nose on my face, and their whole lives are based on this valuable resource so they've built their settlement on top of it.

One of them comes forwards from the group, his bald head glistening in the light of the braziers. His skin is swarthy. He looks at us with dark eyes. He's broad and muscled; the flame designs dancing as his chest and biceps twitch. He looks about thirty years old, no more.

'Praise the Imperial flame,' he says, holding his hands above his head. There's a murmured echo from the other gathered folk. 'Long has it been since the people of the Great Cog visited us. I am Firefather Supurnis, and you are welcome in my town.'

He extends a hand, his arm rippling with taut muscles and Kierck shakes it, bowing ever so slightly in his cringing fashion.

'The Great Cog has sent us,' says Kierck, nodding ferociously. 'Yes, with bounty he has sent us. Bounty for the tradin'. Our halls grow dim and cold, and we bring the gifts of the Great Cog to trade for the warmth of the Imperial fire. My cousins here, they come from the distant halls, strangers who allas wanted to see the magnificent Imperial flame.'

The leader of Firehole looks at us, head cocked to one side.

'You are welcome to Firehole, distant travellers,' he says. 'Perhaps I might show you the Imperial flame once we have completed out business?'

'Allas good to see,' says Kierck. 'Sorries for my cousins, for they have vowed not to speak except in the hall of the Great Cog, for none worthy of words except the Great Cog. Their thanks you have, I sure of. Tradin! Down to tradin', we here for that.'

As we pull forth our sacks of salvaged hammers and spanners, gears, shovels and other assorted junk, Kierck squats down and spreads out a large oil-stained sheet pulled from his pack. Taking our wares, he lays them out, carefully grouping them by function and, from left to right, in ascending order of repair. We lay out everything from broken bits of wood to fully functioning hand drills.

The people of Firehole crowd close, pointing at various items, and muttering to each other. Some items they pick up and pass around to examine, until all are happy with what's on display.

'Wares seen,' says Firefather Supurnis, looking over the crowd and receiving nods of agreement. 'Let the trading begin.'

Chaos breaks loose as a disorganised auction begins, with everyone bidding for different items, waving their fists in the air, bellowing their offers, pushing and shoving to point at the objects of their bids. The Firefather is in there with the rest of them, shouting his own bid.

Kierck squats, looking up at the press of bodies, mentally taking note, nodding, shaking his head, and bargaining with twenty people at once. Now and then, an agreement is reached and he picks up something from his sheet and hands it over. He receives a handful of tatty pieces of paper in return. Slowly, piece by piece, the sheet is emptied until only a few items remains and the crowd has drifted away, content with their purchases.

Firefather Supurnis and a few of his devotees linger as Kierck packs his sheet away, handing back the items to those who gave them to him. He presses a greasy length of chain into my hand.

'Tradin' over,' Kierck says happily, waving a fistful of notes above his head. He grins at us. 'Allas good tradin' in Firehole, dint I say, yes? Allas good tradin'.'

'Come,' says Supurnis, waving an arm in a broad sweep to usher us forward. 'You shall see a sight that has become one of the marvels of Acheron.'

He leads us through the twisting maze of pistons and hovels, his henchmen behind us, until we come to a great block in the centre of the settlement. Archways have been carved into it, the ferrocrete structure daubed with bad paintings of flames, scrawled script written across it like graffiti.

Entering into the hollowed-out block, we find a conveyor cage, its open ironwork box is suspended on chains that are looped around gears hanging from the ceiling above us. From the shaft billows smoke and heat, causing sweat to spring up on my face. Distant sounds of industry, the clanking of metal and the crackle of flames, echoe up from below. Swinging open the conveyor door, he waves us inside. We cram into the small space, and Supurnis pulls a brake lever. The gears begin to slowly shift into motion, lowering us down into the shaft.

The elevator is obviously not part of the original piston room above. The walls are chipped and hand-carved from the ferrocrete. Small alcoves here and there contain burning lamps that scarcely illuminate the dark passage. We pass down about twenty or thirty metres until the shaft opens out, replaced with metal girders that guide the elevator.

Beneath us stretches a massive furnace room that eventually disappears into the smoky gloom. The heat is intense from the high open furnace doors; everything is bathed in a red glow. Hundreds, perhaps thousands, toil at great coal heaps, with pails and shovels, to feed the furnaces. From young children to old women, their painted flames are smeared with sweat and toil. Their labour keeps the fires burning. Braziers gutter everywhere, lending their smoke to the fumes of the furnaces.

As the elevator touches down with a loud crunching clang, Supurnis opens the door and we step out. He swings the door shut and slaps loudly on the framework of the cage, which lifts off a moment later, clanking back up into the gloom.

It's then that the noise hits me properly. There's the crackle of flames, the creaking of great steam wheels and the hiss of boiling water. But there are also groans, moans and the crack of whips. Through the gloom I see large, stooped shapes shuffling amongst the lines of workers, barbed whips in their hands, cudgels and clubs occasionally raised to beat a flagging worker about the back and shoulders.

They're unmistakeably orks.

I look to the Colonel, who's also spotted them. Before he can do anything, shapes loom out of the shadows behind us. More orks, five of them, are carrying heavy cleavers and maces. Their thick green skin catches the red hue of the furnace fires and the flames glint off their dagger-like tusks and pug-like noses. Their red eyes regard us malignly.

We freeze, none of us willing to make a move for our weapons. They have the advantage of surprise. A look from the Colonel warns us to play it cool. Kierck begins to whimper, and there's a wet, dripping noise as he soils himself. He cowers on the ground, covering his head with his arms. I catch Brownie's eye as he shifts nervously. A heavy poncho over his shoulders conceals the loaded heavy stubber and loop of ammo trails from his pack.

'Behold the Fires of Supurnis!' the Firefather declares, spreading his arms wide, his face a picture of exultation. 'The Imperial flame was great, but the flames of Supurnis are mightier still. See the fires that never dim, hotter and brighter than ever before under a hundred Firefathers.'

We say nothing, and he reads the fear and anger in our eyes. The zealous look is replaced by a business-like expression.

'I know you, assassins,' he says with a cruel smile. '*Emperor* von Strab warned me that you would come for me.'

'Emperor von Strab?' blurts Kin-Drugg before he can stop himself. A triumphant gleam enters the Firefather's eyes, or perhaps it's just a trick of the light.

'I knew you were no cousins of this wretch!' he says. He bends down and snatches the notes still gripped in Kierck's hand and waves them at us. 'Jealous out-hivers, that's who you are, isn't it? You heard that Firehole was strong again, bringing warmth and life to everyone. The great Emperor von Strab is generous in his gifts and you wish to claim them for yourselves.'

He looks at the orks and smiles.

'His needs are great, and he must protect his interests,' he says. 'Without them, the fires would dim, the furnaces would grow cold and the palaces of the Emperor would be lifeless. Bountiful was the great day when the messengers of the Emperor came to me. See what I have here? These labourers, they labour for me and me alone.'

'Slaves,' the Colonel snaps. 'You have made slaves of your own people.'

'Oh no,' says Supurnis with a horrified look. 'They are new converts, brought together under the fires of Supurnis. My people share in the generosity of Emperor von Strab, for I am not a tyrant.'

The Colonel snorts.

'And what of us?' he says. 'What do you think you will do with us?'

'You shall pass through the cleansing flames and join the great works of Supurnis,' the Firefather says. 'Is it not fitting that those sent to slay me should end their lives in the great furnaces they tried to quench?'

The Colonel says nothing, and I look around, desperately seeking some way out. The conveyor has gone, the orks are behind us and there is nothing in front of us except an endless stretch of furnaces and slaves, with more orks among them.

I can't see any obvious route of escape.

'Bind them,' Supurnis says, receiving a questioning grunt from one of the orks. He shakes his head in disbelief. He grabs Kierck's arms, drags them behind his back and imitates wrapping something around his wrists. 'Tie their hands up, you idiots.'

The orks step forwards, and one reaches out and grabs my left arm. I act without thinking, wrenching my knife from my belt, driving it up into the soft underjaw of the alien. It becomes buried to the handle. Lorii's clubbed down by a brutal backhand slap, she spins to the floor with blood flying from her split lips.

The Colonel whips out his power sword, turning the motion into a sweep that cleanly severs the arm of the closest ork. It bellows and punches him in the face, knocking him backwards. Brownie grabs Spooge and they dive clear of the scrum, trying to drag the heavy stubber free. Kin-Drugg is knocked from his feet by a club to the back of his head, smashing his nose on the bare ferrocrete.

I just have time to pull my knife free and duck as another ork swipes at me with its cleaver. The blade whooshes past my right cheek and tears through the fleshy part of my shoulder. The Colonel spins and chops the ork's head off in a single stroke, the blood fizzing and spitting along the length of the power sword's glowing blade.

I see Kelth huddled on the ground, trying to crawl away, but he catches a boot in the ribs that rolls him over with a shocked shout. Another ork lunges for me and I spin away, coming face to face with Supurnis. The Firefather batters a huge fist into my jaw. My legs threaten to buckle under me.

With a roar I drive my left fist into his nose, splintering the bridge and driving the cartilage into his skull. He flies backwards, blood spraying from his broken nose and I dive on top of him, my knife at his throat. I wrestle him between myself and the ork.

'Stop or your master dies,' I shout, and the ork pauses for just a second before bringing its blade down onto the Firefather's head, splitting it to the cheek. It gives a guttural chuckle as it wrenches the blade free, blood and brain fluid dripping from its hand.

'Not master,' it says, its large jaw twisting obscenely to form the words. 'Slave.'

I throw the Firefather's body into the ork and scramble away. I manage to get to my feet as the ork flings the corpse of the Firefather aside. Lorii rears up behind it, swinging her lasgun like a club with all her strength. The stock connects with the back of the ork's head. The creature merely grunts before turning around and swinging wildly with its broad cleaver. The blade chews a notch in the lasgun and sticks. The ork pulls towards it, tearing the lasgun from Lorii's grasp. I dive towards its exposed back, my knife held fast in two hands, and plunge it downwards into its skull. The force of my charge bowls it forwards into the ground.

By now, other orks are running towards us from the slave lines, yelling and growling. They wade through the press of bodies with their clubs and whips, clearing a path. That's until a woman, younger than me, her long black hair matted with blood and filth, drives the edge of her shovel into the face of one of her enslavers. Another ork batters

her across the side of her head with its cudgel,
smashing her face in and toppling her. But her act
has ignited the whole mob. Like a ripple in a pool,
her resistance spreads through the slave mob.

Flailing with buckets and shovels, clawing and
biting, the slaves rise up against the orks. Emperor
knows how much degradation and impoverish-
ment has turned to hatred and anger in an instant.
The two dozen or so orks react viciously, breaking
bones, crushing skulls and tearing off limbs. But the
mass of humanity is too much for them as the
seething crowd overwhelms them; their raw
loathing demands the destruction of its creators.
The orks disappear under a pile of bodies, some
dead, some alive, but all crushed by the sheer
weight of their foes.

We watch in stunned silence as the crowd begins to
part. Some of the slaves wield gory trophies such as a
severed head or hand, and wave them in the air. It is
all over in less than a minute. The cheering begins,
and the bodies of the orks are hoisted into the air and
over the heads of the freed slaves before being tossed
into the furnaces. Some start singing and dancing, but
most of them flood towards us, and we retreat quickly
until our backs hit a metal wall behind us.

The celebrating mass presses in towards us, shouting thanks, clamouring for a touch. I fear for my life
more than ever. It looks like they'll mash us to
death with their praise. I step on something soft,
and glance down to see Kierck cowering behind me,
my foot on his hand. I drag him to his feet, and
push him away from me.

'Get back!' the Colonel bellows, brandishing his power sword.

The crowd falters for a moment and then sweeps on. The people at the front are pushed into us by the weight of those behind. We thrust them away as best we can, shouting for them to stay back. After a few minutes of breathless wrestling with the mob, we manage to push them back far enough to get some breathing space There's still shouting and cheering, and a sea of grinning yelling faces and waving hands in front of us. The Colonel grabs one of the freed slaves, an elderly man with whip marks across his shoulders; his face caked in coal dust and soot.

'How do we get out of here?' Schaeffer demands, sheathing his sword and grabbing hold of the man's arms.

'Out?' the man says, his eyes crazed, half-vacant. 'No way out. No, stay here, no way out.'

'The coal ramp,' says a bearded man from behind the old-timer. 'We can climb out of there.'

He turns and speaks to the people behind him, pointing over their heads. The message is passed through the crowd. Eventually the consensus is reached and the mob begins to move away, flowing down the wide aisle between coal piles and furnaces like a filthy tide. They begin to scramble up over the fuel, some forging ahead, others stopping to help the children and the elderly.

We look at each other, dumbfounded by the rapid turn of events.

'Ever started a revolution?' Kin-Drugg asks of no one in particular.

'Twice,' says the Colonel, walking forward to peer up the conveyor shaft. 'The Firefather must have had some way to call down the elevator.'

'Perhaps he just shouted,' suggests Brownie, craning his neck to look up into the darkness.

'Unlikely,' says the Colonel.

'Why don't we just follow them?' I ask, pointing to the men and women clambering up the ramps where the coal is dumped.

'We are here to hunt von Strab, not liberate the hive,' says Schaeffer. 'We must avoid complications.'

'Won't they wonder who we are?' says Kin-drugg. 'Word's bound to spread.'

'All the more reason to get as much distance as possible between ourselves and this place, then,' says the Colonel. 'Now, look for something to call the elevator.'

We examine the area, looking for some kind of comms or lever, but there's nothing but battered old pails, broken shovels and dirt.

'He must have been worried that the slaves might try to storm the lifter,' says Lorii. 'Perhaps it's hidden.'

We recommence our search, examining the walls and floor. Oahebs gives a cry of triumph as he peels back a piece of sacking hanging from a large nail. Suddenly it seems so very out of place. Behind it is a small rope hanging from a hole in the wall. Oahebs tugs the rope, and far above rings a tinny bell that echoes down the conveyor shaft. A few seconds later machinery grumbles into life and we see the elevator rumbling down towards us.

We step back and ready our guns in case it's carrying more orks or some other hired thugs in the
dead Firefather's employ. As it rattles into view, we
see a single man in the elevator; his wide-eyed
astonishment makes me chuckle. He desperately
looks around, as if to magically find some way of
stopping the conveyor.

'Don't think about shouting,' I warn him, my lasgun pointed at his head as the conveyor shakily
drops down the last few metres. He holds up his
hands as Kelth steps forward and pulls open the
door; waving him out with the barrel of his laspistol.

'We heard fighting, I thought the Firemaster was
in trouble,' he says, looking around. His gaze rests
on the corpse of Supurnis and his shattered skull.
He looks at us with horror. 'You killed the Firefather!'

'Actually, that did,' says Brownie, pointing to the
dead ork I knifed in the neck.

'You profited from this slavery,' the Colonel says,
his voice deathly quiet. The angrier he gets, the quieter he gets, and his voice is barely a whisper. He
raises his pistol.

'I... I...' the man stammers, stepping backwards.
The Colonel's bolt pistol booms and the fire worshipper's head disintegrates in a cloud of blood and
splintered bone, his headless corpse collapsing to
the floor in front of the conveyor.

'Bring him,' the Colonel says, pointing to Kierck,
who's curled up by the wall, one hand over his eyes,
the other clutching and wringing his tunic nervously.

Lorii grabs the underhiver by the collar and drags him up, guiding him into the lifter. We follow and the Colonel shifts the lever. The cogs above hoist us into the air. We ready our guns, crouched and standing around the outside of the conveyor. We're sitting targets in here if anyone has a mind to attack.

It's a tense half-minute as we clatter up the shaft, waiting for some shout that we've been spotted, anticipating the gears to clank to a halt and the conveyor cage to be sent plummeting to the ground below. Nothing happens though, and as we top the shaft, we can see that the block room is deserted, save for the two twisted corpses in the corner. Blood is pooled over the floor and leads out the door in the prints of several pairs of bare feet. The slaves got here first then. The fire worshipper was the lucky one, judging by the battered and bloodied bodies. At least he died quickly.

We cautiously exit the conveyor room and find Firehole living up to its name. The hovels are ablaze, some with burning corpses visible inside, others empty. The screaming and shouting of the slaves as they tip over braziers and put the settlement to the torch can be heard a short distance away. It's a form of justice, that Firehole should die by the flames that were kept burning by the labour of its slaves.

'This way, this way,' says Kierck, suddenly animated and pointing out of the settlement. 'We go quick, tetraptors wake up soon, must cross valley first.'

'The what?' asks Oahebs. 'Tetraptors? What are they?'

'Not matter, we not see them, we go quickly, now!' says the underhiver, heading off at a trot, waving us to follow. 'Come, we cross valley then sleep.'

CHAPTER SIXTEEN
EVIL AWAKENING

'THE VALLEY', IT turns out, is a great gash across the underhive. At some distant time in the past, the crust of Armageddon gave way under the weight of the hive city, and opened up a fissure that plunges down several kilometres. Heat and steam issue forth and the glow from deep lava illuminates the whole chasm. For level after level below us, and soaring half a kilometre above us, the rip extends. Like a ragged cross-section of the whole underhive, you can see the twisted, crushed depths and the more spacious, populated upper levels, before the fissure heals itself far above us meeting the hive city proper.

The levels just stop, chambers broken in half, walls crumbling from centuries of subsidence. The gap, some two hundred metres wide, is criss-crossed with bridges of all types, from ferrocrete spans to chain-link, rope bridges to metal structures, all bowing under their own weight.

The lip of the fissure is teeming with crowds and other life. Spiders the size of dogs scuttle out of holes and drop from above to feast on discarded rubbish, and bats swirl overhead; darting from shadow to shadow and feasting on the clouds of insects hovering in the thermal updrafts. Small birds, no larger than my thumb, flit to and fro, their chirps resounding along with the chirruping of fire crickets.

Gantries extend across the gap, from rickety wharfs made of charred wood to elegant half-arches jutting out from several levels above us. There's a great throng of people gathered over the fiery chasm, some with nets trying to catch the flitting birds, others on their knees praying.

As we walk onto the rubble-strewn lip, a priest dressed in a red robe is performing a wedding a few metres to our right, mumbling the rites in High Gothic. The couple, dressed in their best rags by the look of it, offer him two dead rats, which he casts into the molten rock below, blessing their unions. Others are casting their possessions into the flames, chanting, slapping themselves, baring their loins and indulging in all manner of other bizarre behaviour.

Kierck stops and we admire the view for a moment, shaking our heads. Sweat prickles on my face from under the headscarf; it runs down my cheeks and the back of my neck. There are lots of people here, I guess thousands, if not tens of thousands stretching up, down, left and right as far as I can see; those more than about half a kilometre away disappearing in the heat haze.

In front of us is a swaying rope bridge with metal bars for a floor. On it people squeeze past each other as they meet coming in opposite directions. It attaches to a metal A-frame dug into the ferrocrete of the opposite floor, and leads into a low, dark tunnel. We have to wait for a short while as a large group of men swathed in robes and hung with chains made from finger bones, hurry across the bridge, casting nervous glances downwards.

Walking out over the inferno, I feel a tremor of fear, but it's more than just the natural disquiet of walking across a ramshackle bridge over a raging inferno two kilometres down. No, I'm reminded of the warp-dream, in which I fall into a purifying inferno.

I glance over the edge of the bridge, one hand grasping the rope guideline tightly. My eyes sting from the heat. I can't see anything except the red glow and the roiling steam.

Then I notice the silence. Suddenly the chasm is deserted. Even the birds and insects have disappeared. Lorii has her head craned up to see above us, and the Colonel turns, shoulders his way past me and grabs Kierck by the arm.

'What happened?' he demands. 'Where have they gone?'

'Too late!' wails Kierck, flapping his hands against the top of his head with terror. 'Run! Run now!'

He tears himself free from Schaeffer's grasp and, head down, ploughs past me, his spindly little legs moving at speed. Below us is an ominous rumble and the walls of the chasm begin to shiver. Stones topple off the edge into depths. The rumbling grows louder, and steam belches up around us. I glance over the edge and see a dark cloud racing up towards us. After a moment I realise that it's thousands of winged creatures, rushing straight up out of the chasm. These must be the tetraptors.

'Run!' I bellow, sprinting after Kierck.

The others need no encouragement, and as fast as we can, we haul ourselves across the bridge, which sways violently from side to side, causing us to lose our footing, slipping forward on the metal rungs polished smooth by generations of feet.

We're not fast enough.

With a deafening flap of wings, the tetraptor swarm engulfs us. Each is only the size of my hand, with four broad bat-like wings. On thin necks, their beaked heads swivel and peck, tearing at our clothes and skin, their small claws shredding and gripping. Several are biting at my headscarf, their wings battering my face; others hang from my arms as I flail around. My face is bleeding from a dozen tiny cuts in an instant, bitten, or caught with the tip of their talons as the things fly past.

I can't see any of the others in the black morass of flying beasts. I bow my head and charge, stomping tetraptors underfoot, stumbling forwards with no idea how far it is to the other side. I can feel their greasy, furred bodies pushing at me through tears in my flesh. I have to pause to rip one free; it is trying to claw its way through the groin of my trousers. I fling it aside in disgust. I'm snorting heavily as I run, breathing through my nose. I am scared of opening my mouth in case one of them gets in there.

My foot lands on solid ground and, not expecting it, I trip, falling forwards, crushing more tetraptors underneath me. Scrabbling forwards on all fours, I feel someone grab me under the arms and haul me to my feet. I half-run, half-dive, suddenly finding myself clear of the living cloud in a small passageway, lying on top of Kierck. A couple of the creatures are still attached to me and I stand up to pull them free, throwing them down to the ground. I grind them to pulp with the heel of my boot.

The Colonel bursts out next, swiping with his hands at lingering tetraptors. He is swiftly followed by Lorii and then Spooge, who's whimpering from the dozens of lacerations torn into his flesh. Brownie comes out next, panting heavily, dragging the weight of the heavy stubber behind him. He collapses to the ground next to me, dabbing a ragged sleeve at the cuts on his forehead. His headscarf has gone completely.

The others appear in a large clump, falling over each other in their desperation to get clear. Kelth yells as the rest land on top of him in a heap at my feet. We watch in horrid fascination as the swarm continues: thousands upon thousands of the creatures all heading up the chasm, until it begins to slow after another minute or so. Two minutes later they're gone, having disappeared up beyond our view.

'What in all holy crap was that?' moans Kin-Drugg, cradling his leg, blood streaming down from his reopened wound.

'Tetraptors,' says Kierck. 'I warn you, we be quick, but not quick enough, yes?'

'What are they?' says Lorii, still looking up the chasm, as if expecting them to return. 'Where did they come from?'

'Live down in the depths of the valley,' says Kierck. 'In holes and gutters, nooks and crannies. Each night the valley rocks, the river of fire surges, and they come free, flying higher for food. Each morning they return. Not good to be in the valley when that happens, yes?'

He gives a guttural chuckle, and slaps his thigh.

'You think Derflan look ragged, eh?' he says, pointing at us. 'You proper underhivers now, yes? Ha!'

As the others pick themselves up, tugging at torn clothes and nursing their wounds, the colonel grabs Kierck by the shoulder. He pulls him close, his voice harsh.

'If I were a suspicious man I would say you were trying to betray us,' he says.

Kierck recoils from the Colonel's anger. 'First there is the debacle at Firehole, and now this. I said that if we run foul, you would be the first to die.'

The Colonel pulls his pistol out and thrusts Kierck against the wall. The tool trader flings himself prostrate at the Colonel's feet, sobbing and muttering, stroking the Colonel's bloodstained boots.

'No, no!' he gibbers. 'Not betray the Colonel. Derflan like Last Chancers, he does. Free those people, go to kill the overlord, yes? Derflan not lie, he almost slave in the firepits, yes? Not know evil in Firefather's heart, not know anythin', not been to Firehole for many years. Overlord to blame, not poor Derflan. Must cross the valley to get to the overlord, oh yes we must!'

The Colonel looks down at him with a disgusted expression and then kicks him away, holstering his pistol.

'How far to von Strab?' he asks, crossing his arms.

'One more day, Colonel, one more day,' Kierck says, his forehead still pressed against the metal mesh of the floor. 'Rest tonight, Derflan know good place for sleepin'. Tomorrow we go through the tunnels, then we by the overlord palace, tomorrow night at latest.'

'And where are these tunnels?' says Schaeffer. 'What will we find in them?'

'Nothing in tunnels, nothing 'cept rats,' says Kierck, trying to cringe even lower. 'Only way to overlord, less you wantin' more orks. Orks everywhere, Overlord army everywhere this side of the valley.'

'How dangerous is it?' the Colonel says.

'Derflan not lie, is dangerous, yes, dangerous,' he says. 'But Derflan travel the valley side many times, I know secret ways, rat ways. Orks not find us, overlord army not find us.'

'Lorii, Kage, scout out tonight's camp,' says Schaeffer. 'Come back here if it is clear.'

'Is close,' says Kierck. 'Down this tunnel, take first tunnel on right. Crawl tunnel, big enough for us and rats. Too small for orks. Derflan hide there before. Is sixth gratin' on floor, drops down into fan well. Yes, sixth gratin'. Fan well has other tunnels, check them too. Find rats, no orks I reckon.'

'Did you get that?' I ask Lorii and she nods.

'Come on, let's not hang around,' she says with a strangely expectant expression.

KIERCK WASN'T LYING, the tunnels he sends us to are a complete rat's nest of interlocking passages, ducts, sewers and alcoves, teeming with giant rodents. They flee when we approach, their chittering echoing off the metal and stone walls. Using hand-held glowstrips, we find the fan cover he talked about, and, prising it open, drop down into the room below. The fan is motionless, its hub a solid mass of rust; the blades broken and lying on the ground. The chamber itself is low, forcing us to crouch, but broad enough to accommodate all of us. Vents, some large enough to crawl through, radiate out from the chamber, some head up, others down. A large access hatch lies off its hinges on one wall, revealing a dark room beyond.

'Looks quiet enough,' I say, and Lorii grunts in agreement. She shines her torch at the hatchway.

'We should look through there, to make sure nothing's in there,' she says. 'You first.'

Ducking through the door, lasgun in one hand, torch in the other, I find myself in a room high enough to stand up in. Walkways lead up to doors on each side, and old factory machinery lies dormant; it is a labyrinth of conveyor belts, gears and metal boxes.

Something cannons into my back, sending me flying forward. Spinning to my back, I drop my torch and reach for my lasgun.

Lorii steps forward, lashing out with her foot to send my weapon tumbling out of my grasp. She pulls up her lasgun, the barrel pointed straight at my face.

'Go for your knife,' she says. 'Please.'

I slowly pull the dagger free, and as her finger closes around the trigger of her lasgun, I toss it away, clattering under a machine that looks like a splayed ribcage.

'What are you doing?' I ask, keeping my voice steady.

'I've been waiting for this for over a year, you bastard,' she says, spittle flying from her lips. 'In fact, ever since you left Typhos Prime.'

'This is about Coritanorum, isn't it?' I say. I start to sit up, but she signals me to lie back down with a thrust of her rifle.

'You guessed that all on your own, did you?' she says, sneering. 'Whatever gave you that idea?'

'Loron's death wasn't my fault.'

'No, it was the bullet through his head that killed him,' she says, her voice dripping with bitterness.

'He got slack, didn't pay attention,' I utter, slowly edging away. 'I'm not responsible.'

'It was a war, idiot,' she snaps. 'You heard how we were brought up. We were bred for fighting. We expected to die in battle.'

'And that's what happened to Loron,' I retort.

'Yes,' she says. 'But this isn't about Loron, it's about me.'

'Look, I'm sorry that you're the last one left, but it's better than being dead, isn't it?' I cast around for some kind of weapon. There's nothing.

'Are you really sorry?' she asks.

'Actually, no,' I admit with a shrug. 'It's not my fault, is it? It's your problem, you deal with it.'

'I'm about to,' she says. 'But the only reason I'm here is because of Inquisitor Oriel. He was the one who got me out of there. You left me behind.'

'We thought you were dead!' I snap, my anger rising. 'You charged off and we thought you were shot!'

'You didn't check, did you?' she snarls, her pale skin yellow in the light of the glow-strip. 'I might have been wounded, but you didn't care. Just one more dead freak, I bet.'

'I never thought that,' I say, shaking my head. 'You were a Last Chancer. We're all freaks one way or another.'

'You didn't think anything, did you?' she says, taking her hand away from her lasgun for a moment to swipe away a frond of hair. A moment later, she's focussed on me again, her eyes daring me to make a move. 'There wouldn't have been one of us left, would there? None of us, none of us to remember what we were, where we came from. Just a bunch of dead soldiers.'

'Don't blame me,' I say with a curl of my lip. 'I didn't make you. Frag you!'

I stand up slowly, my stare fixed on her.

'So what?' I snap. 'You're going to kill me because I was more concerned with my own survival than some stupid woman who ran off? Because you're a freak of nature that should never have existed?'

'Because you're so proud you're still alive,' she says. 'You're a survivor, aren't you? Inviolable, painless, survivor Kage. That's you isn't it? You'll outlast the Colonel, you think. But you don't deserve it, do you? You've done nothing, you even threw away your Last Chance.'

'I've never pretended otherwise,' I say, exasperated. 'Just fraggin' shoot me and have done with it, for Emperor's sake.'

'Oriel told me about you,' she says with an arch expression. 'You're tainted, evil. I'll be doing you a favour.'

'Oriel can fraggin' talk!' I sneer. 'He reads minds, you know.'

'Actually, he just lets people read his,' she says. 'Otherwise he would have never let me rejoin the Last Chancers, he'd know I wanted to kill you.'

'Perhaps he did know, I wouldn't be surprised,' I say, crossing my arms. 'He's not the type to do his own dirty work, is he?'

'No, he didn't know,' she says confidently. 'It's why he sent Oahebs. He's to keep an eye on you, and make sure your evil doesn't take you over.'

'You're either going to shoot me or not, so get it over with,' I say, staring straight at her.

'I'm not going to shoot you,' she says, grabbing her lasgun by the barrel and letting it drop beside her.

'So what the soddin' hell was that all about?' I gasp.

'I'm going to use my hands,' she says.

LORII CRACKS HER knuckles and smiles at me.

'You're good, but you'd best shoot me instead,' I say with a laugh.

Her first punch is lightning fast, and as I pick myself up rubbing my jaw, I remember just what she was like in Coritanorum. Deadly with her hands and feet.

I duck the next punch, only to find out it's a feint as the toe of her right boot cracks into my chin, snapping my head backwards and sending me back on to my arse again. This isn't funny any more.

She lets me stand up, and I launch myself at her, throwing a quick left-right-left combo that she bats aside with her forearms, twisting quickly and sending a back heel kick to my knee. I topple to the ground. She says nothing, just stands there bouncing on her toes as she waits for me to get back to my feet.

The bitch is just taunting me. She thinks she can kill me; she wants me to feel pain. No holding back any more. I'll teach her pain. I claw my fingers and rake at her face, grabbing the wrist of the arm she shoots out to stop the blow. Bending sideways, I twist, wrenching her arm out of the socket. Her shrill cry sounds like sweet music in my ears.

She tries to punch me and I block the blow, slapping her arm away, driving the fingers of my free hand into her stomach, just below the ribs. She falls, gasping for breath. I kick her in the face, splitting her nose open. Her head slams against the floor, the red blood vivid against her pale skin. The sight of it sends a thrill down my spine. Leaning forward I grasp her hair, longer after a month without being cut, and drag her head forwards. My fingers find her eyes, and I dig deep into the sockets.

I wonder whether to stop, but the sight of the crimson patterns across her white flesh brings out an urge from deep within me. This is what I exist for.

Leaving her mewling on the ground, I get up and stalk across the room, stooping to fish out my discarded knife from where it lies. The blade feels cold as I hold it against my cheek. I walk back over to her, as she tries to crawl away. I grab a leg and haul her back, and she twists, trying to kick me; her good arm flailing in thin air. I can hear the breath whistling out of her lungs. I want to see them.

I LICK THE *knife clean when I'm finished. Blood tastes saltier than I remember.*

I CAN TASTE blood as I wake up, and in a moment of recollection, I remember the fight with Lorii. I snap my eyes open, disorientated. There's blood on my hands, and my knife lies next to me. I'm sitting with my back propped up against a machine, and I can see the toe of a boot poking out around the corner. Not sure what I'll find, I pull myself up, feeling dizzy. Leaning on the machine, I stagger to the corner, trying to ignore the pounding in my head.

What I find is a ragged, bloody mess, almost unidentifiable. All except the shock of white hair on the scalp.

I throw up.

FUGITIVE

CHAPTER SEVENTEEN
THE REALM
OF THE OVERLORD

I RUN. IT's the only thing I can do. I don't care where I'm going. I twist, turn and crawl through air vents, and splash along sewer pipes, just trying to get as far away as possible. I tell myself it's for the safety of the others, that there's something I can't control happening. I know that it's really just to save my skin. When the others find out what's happened they'll kill me for sure. Perhaps I deserve it, but I'm not going to wait around for it to happen.

I enjoyed every minute of it. Every touch, every scream, every whimper, every drop of blood and bile. It was like a symphony of the senses.

I shudder, images appearing in my mind as I duck under coils of cables and squeeze between filtration tanks. I want to bury myself in the industrial morass of the underhive. For hours I keep moving, in the same general direction, ignoring the squealing of the rats, and the flutter of things against my face in the darkness. Here and there I pass through a lighted section, flickering glow-globes casting a sickly yellow light over a tunnel junction or sewer entrance. I abandoned my pack a while ago, unable to squeeze it through an observation hatch. I took only the rations I could fit in my belt, and the gold coins taken from the Inquisition stockpile in Infernus Forge. My flight takes me up and down, through wells and sinkholes lined with algae, across swaying bridges of rope and wood, skirting the glow of fires, and the indistinct babble of voices.

I stop as I'm crawling through a ventilation duct. It ends in a grille, and through the mesh of wire I can see an open area beyond, brightly lit from above. It looks like some kind of forecourt. As I look to the right, I can see two large gates made from plates of steel, heavily riveted. There's a handful of orks outside, carrying large calibre guns, and a few men with red forage caps on, autoguns and lasguns in their hands.

Without trying, I've found von Strab. This is obviously a major entrance to his domain. It's hard to see how the Imperial forces could have failed to find it after months of looking. Perhaps it's better hidden than it seems. This is the last place I want to be, on the edge of the fortress of the man I was sent to kill.

This is perfect. Von Strab will give me sanctuary. He will protect me from the Colonel and the others. All I have to do is go and warn him, show him my good intentions. I don't want to kill him, not now. Now he is my saviour.

I kick out the grille, which clatters noisily to the ground. The guards come running over, the orks lumber up behind, grunting and growling. I throw down my lasgun and hold up my hands in surrender.

'Who are you?' demands one of the sentries, a young man with a pointed black beard and a tattoo of a dagger on his cheek. 'What are you doing here?'

'I need to see the overlord,' I say, lowering my hands. 'I have important news for him.'

'You can tell me,' the guard says.

'No, it's too important,' I reply. 'I have to speak with von Strab himself. I'm from outside the hive.'

'I can see you're an outhiver,' the man says, glancing over his shoulder towards the gate. 'Curfew's on, I can't let anybody inside, especially not some outhiver stranger.'

I step closer, fixing the man with an intent stare.

'This is important,' I say to him, speaking slowly, earnestly. 'The overlord could die if you don't let me see him right now. You can't ignore this, not with witnesses to say that you met me.'

The man shuffles nervously. He looks at his companions, who offer him only shrugs and shakes of the head for support. The orks look on, bemused, perhaps not understanding the conversation. They look to the man I'm talking to, waiting for the order to smash me to a pulp.

I toss my knife to the ground in front of him. I spend a moment wistfully remembering the feeling of the sharp blade slicing through Lorii's white skin. I recall carving an elegant tracery of red on the canvas of her naked body.

'I'm unarmed,' I say, focussing on the matter in hand. 'You can search me.'

'I will,' the guard says.

'So you'll let me in then?' I say.

'If the overlord is displeased, you'll die before me,' he says with a scowl. 'Follow me.'

He turns and the whole group of us troop to the gate. One of them has picked up my knife and lasgun. I can see now that there's a watchtower behind the gates, mounted on the side of a white marble pillar that stretches up to the roof. The snouts of three heavy weapons poke through vision slits cut into the sheets of metal. The sentry leader signals to the tower and I hear a muffled voice calling out. A short while later, metal grinds on metal and the gate is pushed open. The man grabs me by the arm and leads me inside. With a clang the gates shut behind me again, and I see two men lowering a thick iron bar into place.

The four of us are in a wide plaza, lined with marble pillars, littered with broken and toppled columns and statues. Cracked flagstones line the floor, thick red moss growing between them. At the far end, a wide set of steps leads up, also made of marble. At the top is a set of high double doors, carved from wood. They are decorated with Imperial eagles that have been burnt and hacked at; the symbols of the Emperor defaced by the ancient cathedral's new occupants. Headless busts of saints line the stone wall; obscene graffiti scrawled over the frescos of great triumphs of the distant past. Guttering torches are mounted on the pillars, and in the shadows I see movement. I can hear grunts and crude, barking words. More orks.

The guard leads me up the steps and opens a small porter door in the cathedral entrance, pushing me through before stepping in behind me. The inside of the cathedral is crumbling and ruined. Tapestries have been torn down from the walls and scorched, the stained glass windows have been shattered. More torches in sconces bathe the interior with fluttering red light. Four more men emerge from the left to join us. They wear red forage caps too, and makeshift uniforms scavenged from various Imperial regiments. 'Strip,' says the bearded man.

I pull off my headscarf and drop it to the ground, and follow with the ragged clothes taken from the tool merchants. I stand naked while they search through the garments. They find the rations in my belt, and then one of them empties out the pouch containing the gold coins.

'What do we have here?' says the man in the white tunic.

'Gifts for the loyal soldiers of the Army of Liberation,' I say.

They look at me with suspicion for a moment, and then their greed takes over. They count the coins and divide them between them, hiding them away in pockets and pouches.

'Okay, get dressed,' says the bearded man.

This done, he leads me down through the pews, on which more men sleep, grey blankets over their still forms. A few wake with coughs and snorts, and watch us as we walk down the aisle towards the overturned altar at the far end.

'This way,' he says, pointing to a winding staircase that leads up to the right.

Halfway up, the staircase is replaced by a metal ladder, which enters a hole in the roof. The ceiling is shored up with metal beams and timbers. There are cracks in the plaster and stone – evidence of the great weight that crushes down upon the ancient cathedral. That's how it is in the underhive. One generation's homes become the sewers and basements of the next. And then another layer is built right on top of that, and another and another. For thousands of years the hive grows, its foundations the rubble of the buildings below, until it becomes the mighty tower that today stretches up into the clouds.

The ladder leads us into a small, bare room with a single door leading from it. Following the guard, I walk through the door into a narrow corridor lined with portraits that have been scrawled over and ripped. At the far end of the gallery we pass through another door and down a short flight of steps.

For several minutes we walk, sometimes passing the silent machines of a factory workshop, other times we return to the spires of the cathedral. Up ladders and down stairs, through the maze. I wonder if he's deliberately taking the long route, trying to disorientate me. If he is it's working admirably, because I haven't got a clue where I am now.

He brings us to halt in a small chamber with thick red carpet on the floor, muddied and trampled by many booted feet. A low couch lies along one wall, with a small table next to it. On the table sits a crystal decanter and a glass.

'Sit down,' he says, directing me towards the couch. I do as he says. He pours a clear liquid from the decanter into a glass and hands it to me.

'That's very civil of you,' I say, sniffing the liquid. It's odourless.

'It's water,' he explains. 'The overlord insists that his visitors be refreshed when he greets them.'

'Very sensible,' I say, not sipping the water. It could be poisoned or drugged. The guard sees my distrusting look and, with an annoyed sigh, grabs the goblet from my hand and takes a swig.

'It's perfectly safe, what do you take us for? Barbarians?' he says.

Still unsure, I take a small sip. It's clear, tasteless, unlike the scummy liquid I've been surviving on since boarding the starship over a year ago.

'Yes, it really is fresh,' the man says with a smile, reading my expression. 'The overlord had a few tankers full before... before his unplanned migration. We managed to bring one with us. It's almost used up now, so make the most of it.'

I nod in thanks and take another sip while the guard knocks gently on the door and then lets himself in. The door closes with a click behind him and I can hear a muffled conversation. Suddenly there's the sharp retort of a pistol, and something bangs against the door. A moment later, the door opens and another man steps out, an old style revolver smoking in his hand. This one looks mean, with a hard edge about his grey eyes. He has a scar across his chin and his greying black hair is slicked back over his head. He's dressed in a long gown of patchy purple velvet, the leather belt with a holster looking out of place around his waist. I stand up to meet him.

'I am Sorious von Spenk,' he says with a cursory bow of the head. 'I am Emperor von Strab's chancellor.'

'Ex-Lieutenant Kage, formerly of the Imperial 13th Penal Legion,' I say, bowing stiffly with my hands by my side, in the manner I've seen a certain type of officer use in the past.

'A penal legionary?' says von Spenk, cocking his head to one side and examining me. 'How interesting.'

'Can I see von Strab now?' I say. 'It is urgent.'

'The Emperor will see you in a moment,' he says, emphasising von Strab's new self-proclaimed title. 'Please, finish your water.'

We stand in silence, with me pretending to examine the interior of the antechamber and von Spenk blatantly looking me up and down, his brow furrowed. After what seems like a long while, he holsters the revolver. After a tortuous wait, which must have only been a few minutes but felt like an eternity, there's a bellow from inside the door. Von Spenk opens it and I step through, almost stumbling over the body of the bearded guard who is lying next to it, blood dribbling out of a hole in his forehead.

'I apologise for the mess,' murmurs von Spenk, steering me forward with a hand on my shoulder, closing the door with the other. 'The Emperor does so dislike being disturbed at this hour.'

The walls of the short, wide chamber are hung with deep red drapes, looped over rails. It's only at a second glance that I notice that the rails are made from wired-together bones. The carpet underfoot was once white, but now is stained with mud, blood and who knows what else. Two sets of double doors lead off from either side, and I note with fascination that the handles have been replaced with small jaw bones. I look up and see a *chandelier made from fused ribs, and I can guess what fat was used to make the candles by the distinctive smell. At the far end, sitting on a throne-like chair carved from dark wood, sits von Strab. Other than him and us, the room is empty.*

He is heavily built, his jowls wobbling as he sits forward to peer at me out of one piggy eye. The other has been replaced with an artificial lens, the glass and metal protruding from his pallid, veiny skin. He sits with his hands on his knees in what I supposed is meant to be a regal pose. The whole effect is somewhat spoiled by the fact that the so-called Emperor is dressed in a grubby off-white bed robe and a pointed nightcap, complete with tassel.

'Humble greetings, your excellency,' says von Spenk, with a low bow. 'My profuse apologies for this disturbance. May I present Lieutenant Kage, a messenger from the outside.'

Von Strab lifts a hand and waves me forward. He speaks quietly, his voice strong and proud.

'Let me see you,' he says, leaning forwards.

I stand in front of him, hands clasped behind my back, waiting patiently. He looks at me from toe to scalp, lips moving wordlessly. He gives a grunt and sits back.

'Ugly sort, aren't you, lieutenant?' he says.

'Kage,' I say automatically.

'Hmm? What's that?' says von Strab.

'Just call me Kage, your excellency,' I say. 'And yes, my features are as harsh as my life has been.'

'Well, Kage, don't keep me waiting,' the overlord says. 'What do you want?'

'I have been sent here to kill you,' I say.

Von Strab recoils in horror, and instantly von Spenk is by my side, his revolver pointing at my right temple.

'Do not move, assassin,' says von Spenk. I sigh.

'Obviously I'm not going to do it,' I say, keeping my eyes on von Strab. 'I'm here to warn you.'

Von Strab recovers slightly, and peers at me suspiciously. He waves a hand at von Spenk, who lowers his pistol, though I note he doesn't holster it.

'Warn me that you are sent to kill me?' says the overlord.

'The rest of my team are still in the underhive, and they intend to either kill you or abduct you,' I say. And then, as if that would explain everything, 'We were sent by the Inquisition.'

'The Inquisition, you say?' says von Strab. He laughs, a soft, gurgling sound. 'Well, that's no surprise at all, is it von Spenk?'

'No your excellency,' says the chancellor-bodyguard. 'I imagine it is they who are responsible for the previous attempts on your life.'

'Of course they are,' I say. 'They think that the fate of Armageddon could rest in your hands. You are quite a threat to them.'

'This team of yours, tell me about them.' says von Strab.

I tell him everything. Everything about the Last Chancers, the Colonel, our journey here and our arrival. I explain about Derflan Kierck and his tunnel system. I save the best until last.

'And if we fail, then you're still doomed,' I say. 'A Space Marine battle barge is readying to flatten the whole of Acheron from orbit.'

Von Strab accepts this with a nod. He rests his elbows on the arms of the chair and steeples his fingers under his chin.

'You're not surprised?' I say.

'Of course not,' says the overlord. 'Everything they say is true. My grand Army of Liberation is fast becoming a force to be reckoned with. Do you know why they haven't found me yet? Deserters, like you. I'm always a step ahead of them. The rewards for loyalty to me are worthwhile, as I'm sure you'll find out. I have ten thousand trained soldiers, natives and others, and ten times that number as auxiliaries. The hive will be ours again.'

'You can stop the Colonel, with my help,' I say, stepping forward. Von Spenk tenses but I ignore him. 'But there's nothing you can do about that battle barge. In less than two weeks there'll be no hive to retake.'

'Let me worry about that, Kage,' says von Strab. He smiles and nods. 'I think I like you, Kage. I think I'll let you live, for now.'

'For now?' I say, raising an eyebrow.

'For now,' he says. 'Be thankful for that. Now, I must retire, I am bone-weary. Von Spenk will find you suitable quarters for tonight, and I'll see you bright and early in the morning. Oh, and make sure you get him cleaned up, von Spenk, he smells as bad as he looks.'

'Yes, your excellency,' von Spenk says with another bow. 'I'm sure we can accommodate your guest.'

He leads me through the door to the left and we pass through a series of rooms, each decorated in the same macabre opulence as the audience chamber. One is a trophy room, and amongst the strange and mutated rat skulls, stuffed lizard heads and other creatures are a number of human skulls and half-decayed heads.

'Hunting has always been the sport of the Emperor's forefathers,' explains von Spenk, noticing my gaze lingering on the contorted face of a woman. I can see maggots crawling in her empty eye sockets, making her cheeks twitch with a semblance of life. 'He refuses to let circumstances stand in the way of family traditions and makes do with what he can.'

After passing through several rooms, von Spenk brings me into a bare stone corridor, the walls slimed with mould. Rickety wooden steps lead down into a small basement with barred doors leading off. Von Spenk opens one and shoves me through. I bang my head on the low ceiling, and see a bare room, no larger than two metres square.

'Surely von Strab…' I begin, turning to von Spenk. He smashes me round the head with the butt of his pistol.

CHAPTER EIGHTEEN
THE MAD COURT

I WAKE UP, my head thumping with pain. I raise a hand to my forehead to feel a lump the size of an egg and scabbed blood. It's dark, a thin trickle of light seeps out of a door in front of me. I stand up and crack the top of my skull against a ceiling. Crouching down, I crawl across the cold, hard floor, feeling with my hand in front of me. I feel the grain of wood on the door, and by moving to the left and right find that I'm in a cell just a little wider than my outstretched arms.

Where am I?

More to the point, how did I get here? I try to concentrate through the pain of my throbbing head, trying desperately to remember. I mentally recoil from the image of Lorii, and try to recall what happened after that. My memory ends in an air vent, looking at the gates to von Strab's realm. After that, I haven't got a clue. I consider banging on the door, but disregard the idea. In my experience, if someone puts you in a cell, they intend you to stay there until they're ready for you to come out. If you make a fuss, you're just as likely to increase the length of your stay. With this in mind, I sit with my back to a wall, hugging my knees to my chest as I try to think.

It's pointless. I can't remember a damned thing. I don't know where I am, whether I actually want to get out of here, or what's waiting for me beyond that door. As has happened so many times in my life, I'm left with just one option. I have to sit and wait to see what happens.

I don't have to wait long. Soon there's the rattle of a key in the lock and it swings inwards, dim light streaming in. A man stands there in a faded purple robe, a gun belt at his waist.

'Come and get washed up for the emperor,' he says, stepping back. 'We'll see if he's still approving of you this morning.'

I think it best to say nothing yet. Anything I do say is bound to get me in more trouble. If I just play it steady, go along with whatever happens unless it gets life threatening, I could come out of this without too much pain. I just hope there isn't a test later.

I'M LED OUT of the cell and up a set of steps, and we turn into a shower block. The water is freezing cold but I don't mind. It's the first opportunity I've had to wash the grime of the ash wastes and the pipeline and the underhive out of my hair and from under my fingernails. I realise just how filthy I am as the blackened water spills down the plughole. I'm not one to worry about getting dirty, but it is nice not to be caked in crap like this every once in a while.

My rags have been replaced with robes of black silk, patched in a few places, with a white belt. It feels airy and light, and quite strange after a lifetime of combat fatigues and constricting uniforms. Lastly, there's a red forage cap, which I ram onto my head.

'The emperor will approve, I'm sure,' says the scarred man, looking me up and down, then leaning forward to straighten my collar. 'Follow me.'

He leads me through a succession of rooms decorated with ghastly human remains. Bones, foetid organs and rotting skulls are used to adorn portrait rails, chandeliers, doors and furniture.

The stench is unbelievable, and it sticks in my throat. I try to hold my breath, but soon that doesn't work and I resort to merely breathing through my mouth. Now I can taste the sickness in the air.

We finally enter a crowded room, filled with men and women of all ages; some dressed in simple robes like I am, others with gaudy officers' uniforms. Young boys wind through the crowd with tarnished silver trays, offering up a selection of local delicacies. My escort has disappeared into the throng, and one of the serving boys comes over and proffers the tray beneath my nose. It is dominated by a pyramid of small brown balls, edged with slices of meat.

'What's that?' I ask, pointing at a small, grey sliver of flesh.

'Sandrat bladder,' he chirps. 'Broiled over sump-oak branches. Very bitter, they say.'

'And these?' I say, using my fingertips to pick up one of the balls, which looks like excrement rolled in wood shavings.

'Oven-roasted kernuckle, with a savoury coating of fresh mudstool,' the young waiter replies.

'Kernuckle?' I say.

The boy sighs and despite being less than half my age, gives me a superior look.

'It's taken from the loins of a phundra,' he says with a condescending tone.

'The loins?' I say, plopping it back onto the plate and wiping the grease from my fingers on the boy's white smock. 'It's a bollock, you mean? Must be rare.'

'They have six each. It is an acquired taste,' answers the boy. With a mock sorrowful shake of his head he turns away and melts into the crowd, in search of someone who's obviously acquired more taste than I have.

The crowd is gossiping and mingling, but soon a hush spreads out from the far corner of the room. I shoulder my way through the people, earning myself the odd elbow in the ribs in the process, until I can see to the front.

I see a balding fat man dressed in a grey greatcoat lined with red thread. He wears a long parade sword at his belt, and a pistol grip inlaid with glittering gems protrudes from a leather holster. If he ever tried to fire that it'd rip his palm to shreds. His right eye has been replaced with a mechanical implant, the lens glowing with inner energy. He has a napkin tucked into the front of his coat, stained dark red. The man who took me from the cell appears at his shoulder and plucks the napkin free, using a corner to dab at a couple of specks at the corner of his master's mouth.

'Thank you, von Spenk,' the man says, the crowd parting in front of him as he waddles forward. He sees me and I flinch trying not to catch his attention. But he marches straight towards me, and suddenly I'm right in front of him.

'Glad you could make it, Kage,' he says, and my heart begins to pound in my chest. How the frag does he know my name? What the hell has been happening to me? 'I trust that your new vestments are to your liking.'

I look down at the flimsy robe, suddenly uncomfortable as I realise that it barely hides my nakedness.

'I'm more used to a uniform,' I say, looking at the fat man and shrugging. There's an almost inaudible murmur of disapproval from the crowd.

'This robe belonged to the youngest half-son of his excellency, Gabro von Strab,' says the man in the velvet robes. 'It is an honour to wear it.'

Von Strab? This is overlord von Strab? I'm about to open my mouth to apologise but the overlord speaks first.

'Nonsense, von Spenk!' says von Strab, pushing him away and stepping closer to me. He lays a beringed hand across my shoulders and turns me to face the crowd. 'Gabro was a noisome little prick who didn't even have the decency to scream when I throttled him. Kage is a military man, through and through, aren't you?'

'I… I've never been anything more than a soldier,' I say, hoping it doesn't look like I'm squirming too much.

'Such humility!' booms von Strab. 'See, Kage is a fighting man, a veteran of the hack and slash of war. He doesn't want the throw-offs of some poxy boy-lover. Take it off, I'll find you something better.'

'Now?' I whisper. 'Take it off now?'

I'm not usually self-conscious. I've spent untold hours in the shower blocks in a garrison or aboard a ship in front of my fellow soldiers, men and women. But there's something about the expectation, the leer in the eyes of these lackeys that makes me want to keep myself covered up. Von Strab unbuckles the belt and whips up the robe.

'You've certainly got nothing to hide, Kage,' he says, casting the silk robe aside. I stand there covering my troopers with my hands as a gasp ripples through the audience. 'Why, look at all these scars. I thought it might have just been your face.'

A short, thin woman steps forward. She is wearing a wig that makes her twice as tall as she should be.

'Are you… intact?' she asks, glancing suggestively at my crotch. I pull my hands away and she titters and grins. 'Oh no, most intact!'

'You there, von Guerstal,' says von Strab, pointing to a man in a bright blue uniform with a thick moustache, his thinning grey hair plastered over a scalp shining with perfumed lotion. 'You've let a bunch of assassins into the underhive. I'm stripping you of your title and giving it to Kage.'

The man stands mouthing wordlessly, his hands flapping ineffectually at his sides. Von Strab clicks his fingers and his henchman, von Spenk, steps forwards with a revolver in his hand. A single shot through the left eye blows the man's brain out and he flops to the floor.

'As well as your title, I'm stripping you of your clothes,' von Strab continues, as if the man could still hear him. He turns to me. 'Congratulations, Marshal Kage.'

Standing there naked, with everyone's gaze upon me, I'm not sure what to do. I bow formally and murmur my thanks. Von Strab rounds on the crowd,

'Well, don't leave the man standing there with his pride hanging out,' he bellows.

The crowd surge around the dead man like scavengers, fighting each other to pull off his clothes. They pounce on me next, lifting me up and turning me as they dress me. Having been pinched, pulled and spun around a few times, I'm deposited back on my feet a little unsteadily. I stand swaying in front of von Strab. The uniform, with its bright blue jacket and red sash, is a little too big for me: the cuffs hang past my wrists, the hose wrinkles around my ankles.

'Splendid, now you look like a Marshal of Acheron,' von Strab says, grabbing me by a shoulder and slowly turning me around. 'Once we're done here, you can assume your duties.'

'Duties?' I say.

'Well, von Spenk will fill you in on the details, I'm sure,' says von Strab. 'But a damned good start would be hunting down these assassins of yours.'

THE 'EMPEROR' IS listening to petitions from his court, and judging a few cases brought to his attention by underhivers brave enough to dare enter his lair. While von Strab settles a dispute between a small man dressed in a red smock with a golden laurel nailed into the flesh of his head and a tall, pinched-faced man with a ridiculous blue wig, von Spenk takes me to one side.

'You do nothing,' he says, the fingers of his hand digging painfully into my arm. 'If the emperor asks anything, just say that it is all in order and being looked after. I arrange the security around here, you just have to take the credit.'

'Or the blame?' I say.

'Look at him,' von Spenk says, nodding towards von Strab, who now has the two plaintiffs balancing on one leg, to see who falls over first. 'Centuries of intra-family breeding never gave him the best start in life, but this whole business with the beast has made him worse than he ever was.'

'The beast?' I stammer.

'Ghazghkull, you halfwit,' snaps von Spenk, his voice a whisper. 'Didn't Oriel tell you anything?'

I stay silent, stunned by the question. How does he know Inquisitor Oriel? What have I got myself into?

'Look,' he says, calming down. 'I'll make it simple for you. Oriel recommended the Last Chancers to me for this job. I'm the one trying to make sure this place doesn't get blown to hell and back, so for Emperor's sake, listen carefully.'

'You could've killed him last night,' I say, stepping back. 'One shot, and this'll be over.'

'That's my back-up plan, yes,' says von Spenk. 'Ideally, I want to take him alive. We need him on board, and to find out what he knows.'

'And risk millions of lives?' I snap, glancing over my shoulder as I realise how loud I spoke.

'Yes,' says von Spenk, his face set. 'Like you say, I can finish this any time I like. I'm his bodyguard, I have been for twenty years, you idiot. Do you think I just happened to be in the right place at the right time? If we can't get him out alive, his corpse will do fine, and we still have sixteen days.'

'I didn't realise,' I say.

'You're not meant to – you're a trooper, Kage, just stick to following orders,' says von Spenk. 'I'll make sure Schaeffer and the others can get to von Strab, you just keep your head down and cover for me. It's your neck on the line, not mine, so you best play the…'

He stops suddenly and looks up. I follow his gaze. Von Strab is looking at both of us, arms crossed, tapping his foot.

'What are you two colluding about, eh?' he barks.

'Marshal von Kage was just outlining his plans for tracking down and detaining the interlopers, your excellency,' von Spenk says, giving me a gentle push in the back.

'Von Kage?' I whisper, holding my ground.

'It's the name of a noble, get used to it,' von Spenk whispers back. 'Everyone's bloody von something or other around here, so pay attention or you'll get confused.'

I totter forward after a more hearty push from von Spenk. Glancing past the overlord, I can see two men wrestling on the ground, clawing and biting at each other, tearing out lumps of hairs and scratching at each other's faces. Von Strab notices my gaze.

'A stroke of genius, though I say it myself,' the overlord says with a smug grin. 'If they can't decide which of them gets the woman, they should fight like women for the right.'

The woman in question is watching the fight with distaste, her loose white gown open at the front to leave little to the imagination.

'Of course,' says von Strab, leaning close to whisper in my ear. 'I might just take the girl myself. What do you think?'

'She's certainly a fine woman,' I say.

The two men are panting heavily, bleeding from dozens of cuts and scratches, their tussling grows slower and weaker. Von Strab watches them, a finger held to his pursed lips in a studied pose of thought. He glances at me and winks. He claps his hands together and the two wrestlers stop and look up at him.

'Abysmal, absolutely abysmal,' the overlord says in a matter-of-fact tone. 'Von Spenk, since neither of these two is man enough to claim her, I claim her for myself. And since they're not man enough for that, I claim their manhood too. Have them castrated.'

The two men haul themselves to their feet. They grasp at their ragged robes, protesting and pleading. Red-capped guards appear as if from nowhere and haul them off, their screams resounding from the white-plastered walls and ceiling.

Von Strab beckons the woman forward with his finger. She has long dark hair that hangs around her shoulder in curls, and her stomach is tattooed with an interweaving snake and rose.

'You can have her, Kage, as a reward for dealing with this whole matter so well,' says von Strab. The woman looks at me, and her expression is none too pleased as she takes in my scarred face and blunted nose.

'You are very generous,' I manage to say. It's been many years since I've been with a woman, I'm not sure I remember what to do.

'Well, don't mess about, Kage, get on with it,' says von Strab, and my mouth gapes in disbelief. He wants me to do the deed right here? Then to my relief he says, 'That door behind us, you'll find your new bedchamber through the hall and the second door on the left. Take your time, I'm sure you've earned it.'

Seeing a hint of annoyance in the overlord's eye, the woman steps forward, eyes cast demurely to the ground, and takes my hand. The gathered mock officers and gentry begin to clap and cheer as she leads me out through the door. My heart begins to race, the feeling of her hand in mine causing a sweat to prickle on my skin. Desires I've not felt for a long time begin to rise.

The female's hand is hot and clammy, and I can feel her blood rushing through her veins. Her heart pounds as fast as mine, and I can hear her breath begin to shorten from fear or excitement. I don't care which. She opens the door to my chamber, revealing a wide, high-ceilinged room with a ragged-looking pair of armchairs, an ornate night stand and a bed the size of a small spaceport. It's covered in stained white covers decorated with fraying embroidered flowers.

The woman lets go of my hand and crosses to the bed, slipping the robe from her shoulders. She turns and reveals herself to me, before lying back onto the sheets. She looks at me past her generous breasts. I can sense her fear, her unwillingness.

'You can do what you like with me, marshal,' she lies. Her voice betrays her coldness. I notice cloudy glass goblets and tarnished silver cutlery on a tray on the night stand. I smile at her.

'I will,' I say.

I LEAVE THE *bloodied cutlery and shards of glass in a crimson pool on the tray. Someone will clean it up for me, I'm sure. I feel spent, exhausted, but I know there's something I've got to do before I can rest.*

I leave the bedchamber with its blood-soaked sheets and the ragged corpse of the harlot, and walk back to the room where I met von Strab. Opening the door, I find it empty, except for the serving boy who is now crawling across the floor on his hands and knees, picking up crumbs, bones and pieces of discarded food.

'Where is von Strab?' I ask him and he shrugs.

'Dunno,' he says, his pompous tone now gone.

I walk over to him and grab his curling golden hair in a fist, dragging him to his feet. He squirms in my grasp and I give him a little shake to quieten him down. When he goes limp, I twist my wrist so that he's looking at me.

'Don't make me ask again,' I say. Something wet dribbles down his leg onto my foot. He begins to cry.

'He'll be in the throne room,' he stammers between sobs, pointing to an archway on my right. I let him go. As he turns to crawl away, I kick him in the stomach, turning him over. Pinning him to the ground with my soiled boot, I give him a look. Pulling a cloth from the belt of his tunic, he wipes the piss from my shoe. With another kick, I send him on his way.

Walking through the arch, I find myself in a columned gallery overlooking a deep pit on one side. Naked bodies writhe and moan on the ground. At first I think it's sounds of pleasure, but then I notice the fattened, blood-slicked forms of rats weaving their way through the morass of exposed humanity. They're being eaten alive. None of them seem to be putting up any kind of fight as the rats, some with multiple tails, two heads, elongated fangs and other mutations, gnaw at their skin, nibble on fingers and toes, or burrow their way into their warm guts. I stand watching the tableau, caught up in the decaying artistry and beauty of the scene. I have to tear my gaze away, remembering that I have an important errand before I can take all this pleasure for granted.

I find the throne room at the far end of the gallery. It looks to have been a warehouse some time in the past. A mezzanine runs around for a higher level, partly blocked off by the collapsed roof. Metal girders criss-cross the wide span of the ceiling, held up by more steel beams. Light green paint peels off the walls, revealing crumbling dark red brick. The floor is tiled with white squares, greening at the edges. The wide space is littered with detritus. A few decaying bodies are slumped here and there, and there are clothes scattered all over, some of them neatly folded and stacked, others ripped and torn, thrown haphazardly everywhere or in half-burned piles.

At the far end of the hall von Strab is sitting in a large plain chair, vacantly looking around the room. He hears my boots clicking on the tiles as I cross to him, and looks up quickly, a haunted expression on his face. He seems to recognise me only after a moment, and then relaxes. His left cheek is bruised and his eye red-rimmed as if he'd been crying.

'Where's von Spenk?' I ask, looking around.

'Oh, he had something to attend to, over in the oil sump district,' says von Strab.

'How much do you trust him?' I say, bending forward and whispering in a conspiratorial fashion.

'With my life, every day,' he replies, looking at me with a quizzical expression. 'Why?'

'I think he's a traitor,' I say, looking to the left and right as if someone might overhear us. 'I think he wants to kill you.'

'I don't believe you,' von Strab says, shaking his head.

'But he confided in me earlier, about a plot of his,' I say, taking the gamble. 'He's in league with Colonel Schaeffer.'

'I know he is,' hisses von Strab. 'Keep your voice down! He's trying to get me out of here, isn't he.'

I can't think of anything to say for the moment, taken aback by this admission.

'You mean you want to go back?' I say, amazed. 'They'll kill you for sure.'

'I have nothing to fear,' von Strab says, pulling himself up haughtily. 'Yarrick may be their golden boy at the moment, but he has no breeding. No breeding at all, and that will shine through. Besides, what makes you think Schaeffer will keep me? Once I'm out of Acheron, that's another business entirely.'

'But why risk it?' I say, trying to keep the pleading out of my voice.

'If I stay here, they'll kill me for sure, you know that,' says von Strab.

'It doesn't have to be that way,' I say, crouching in front of the overlord, leaning forward with a hand on the arm of his chair. 'I can get you out of here. I'll deal with von Spenk and Schaeffer, no problem. You'll be a lord again, and I'll be your right hand man. Think of the pleasures we could indulge in!'

'And the orks, what will you do about them?' he says, spittle flying from his lips.

'What about them?' I say, rocking back on my heels. 'Ditch them or bring them with us, it's up to you.'

'You don't understand,' says von Strab, nervously looking past me. 'Who do you think von Spenk is trying to rescue me from?'

I SQUAT THERE in silence, absorbing this information, trying to work out what it means. I give up.

'What does that mean?' I ask von Strab, who has a manic look in his eye now, and is gripping the arms of the chair so tightly his pudgy knuckles have gone white.

'I didn't have any choice, did I?' he says. His eyes rove around the large hall. 'Yarrick was going to have me tried as a traitor. I tried my best, I really did. This is my planet, not his, damn it! But he wanted me dead, so I had to get away. It seemed the only choice was with Thraka. When he said he was going to return, I was overjoyed. But he was going to kill me. I had to tell him about the orbital defences, about the battle fleet. What was I supposed to do?'

'You did the right thing,' I say to him, soothing him with my soft tone. 'Like you said, you would have died. You have to look after yourself.'

'Precisely, Kage, precisely,' he says, finally meeting my gaze. 'He gave me Acheron back, and the nobles flocked here, but he didn't leave me alone. You think those green-skinned thugs are my guards? They're my jailers. They have a leader, Urkug they call him. He's as brutal as Thraka himself. He's not stupid, not like you would think an ork to be. He thinks, he listens and he tells Thraka what I'm up to. I had to concoct the whole Army of Liberation scheme so I could at least get some of my own men. But Urkug keeps me away from them; his brute squads are barracked with them and they intimidate them.'

'We'll take care of it, you and me,' I assure him, radiating confidence. 'I've been in deeper shit than this in the past. I'll have your army licked into shape in no time, and I'll personally take care of von Spenk and this Urkug if you want me to.'

There's a clatter of heavy boots from behind me and von Strab falls silent, sitting back in his chair and assuming an air of indifference. I swivel round on my *haunches and see a group of six orks entering through the archway. The one in front is a head taller than the rest, an immense green bastard with arms as thick as my legs. Scalps hang from his heavy belt and his hands are covered with thick spiked knuckledusters.*

'Ah, Urkug, there you are!' beams von Strab, stepping off the chair and bringing me to my feet with a hand on my arm. 'I was just telling Kage here who you are. He's my new marshal, by the way.'

'Shut up!' grunts the ork leader, shoving me aside and barging into von Strab. He forces him back into his chair. 'My boys 'ave been tellin' me fings. Who are dese killers dat have come fer you? Who's 'im?'

He jabs a clawed thumb over his shoulder at me. I'm suddenly acutely aware of the green hunks of muscle looming up behind me. I feel nothing from them, except their stench. You'd think I could sense their rage, their bestial hungers, but they're as blank as the chair von Strab sits on. It's not like they love violence, or loathe their enemies. It's just what they do, without thought and without feeling.

'That's Kage, I just told you, Urkug,' says von Strab, squirming as a rope of saliva drips from the ork's jutting jaw onto his face. 'He's the one who told me about the assassins. That's why I made him a marshal.'

'He killed some of my boys,' says Urkug, turning on me. Behind him, von Strab gets to his feet and tries to walk away, but he stops as Urkug reaches back with a clawed hand and plants it on his chest, thrusting him back into the chair.

'I killed them,' I say. Stepping forward, and staring the ork straight in his red eyes. 'With my knife, not a gun.'

'Yer look too small,' the ork says. 'My boyz could eat you alive.'

There's only one thing orks really understand. I drive my forehead into Urkug's jaw, snapping a tooth. The ork squints down at me, his jaw working as he thinks, his fangs carving grooves in the thick flesh of his lips. He starts to laugh, a rolling, gurgling noise, and slaps me hard on the shoulder.

'You got a good wun dis time,' Urkug says, his congratulatory slap sending me staggering away. 'I like 'im.'

With the ork won over, my next job becomes a little easier.

'Would you like to join us?' I say, looking at Urkug. 'We were just about to conduct an inspection of the oil sump district, check on security, that sort of thing.'

Von Strab's eyes widen as he remembers that's where von Spenk is waiting for the Colonel.

'I'm sure Urkug and his boys have something else they should be doing, isn't that right, Urkug?' he says quickly, frowning in concentration. He's probably trying to work out whether I've intentionally betrayed him or not, or whether this is some elaborate plan to help him escape.

'Inspekshun sounds gud,' says Urkug. 'Me an' the boys will come wiv you.'

'Lead the way, your Excellency,' I say to von Strab, and I see the horror in his eyes as it dawns on him that we're not playing for the same team any more. There's only one player on my team, and that's me. Just like old times, looking out for number one. Frag the Colonel and his mission, it's time I put myself first again.

CHAPTER NINETEEN
BETRAYAL

VON STRAB TRIES to come up with something else for Urkug to busy himself with, but the ork leader is single-minded and determined to make a sweep of the sumps located a few levels below us. Ultimately, von Strab is just selfish and power-hungry. Once von Spenk and the Colonel are dead, he'll probably forget all about this stupid idea of giving himself up. With my help and encouragement, we'll get out of Acheron before the bombardment hits, and start anew someplace else. Perhaps we'll be able to make something in Hades, perhaps we could return to Acheron after the devastation has been unleashed and lead the scattered survivors to a great new life in gratitude and servitude. People in that position need strong leadership, and will accept it from just about anyone who shows them the way. Yes, with the fires still burning in the hive, Acheron will be ripe for the plucking.

I try to urge the orks on, without making it look as if that's what I'm trying to do. I've got no doubt that von Spenk is down here waiting to meet up with the Colonel. With any luck we'll catch him before the rendezvous and we'll be able to set a trap for the Last Chancers. I'm also interested to see whether von Spenk blows his cover. I reckon he won't.

The orks seem to know their way around pretty well, which isn't all that surprising since they've been in Acheron since the invasion began and von Strab returned. We haven't passed any substantial doors or gates and I haven't seen any boundary walls so I guess we're still inside the overlord's 'palace'.

We pass by areas plunged into blackness and I can feel chill draughts flowing from darkened doorways, the air damp and clinging. I guess the episode at the Firefather's little slave empire has begun to have its effects. The power from his furnaces is gone now, leaving areas of the underhive devoid of light and warmth.

The air gets even more stale as we descend, mildew and the tang of oil hanging in my nostrils. We pass between huge riveted steel tanks, the steady thump-thump-thump of unseen engines vibrating the floor and walls. This must be the oil sump district.

There are a few of von Strab's red-capped Army of Liberation soldiers stationed at intersections and doorways. They give us surprised, nervous looks as we approach. They look especially worried when Urkug and his boys give them menacing stares and growls. I wonder if they're in on the whole plan, or if they've simply been duped by von Spenk. I bet their loyalties would be different if they learned that Acheron was soon going to be turned into a smouldering lump of molten metal and rock, reduced to rubble by plasma and cyclotronic bombardment.

In fact, as soon as I sort out this current situation, I think I'll make it a priority to spread the news as far as possible. Not only will there be a stampede and chaos of godly proportions, resulting in thousands of wonderful deaths, but the uproar should give us the opportunity to take our leave of this god-forsaken place.

As we take a right down a flight of steps to another sub-level, the walls oozing with sticky green fluid, the corpses of rats and other vermin stuck in the adhesive flow, I wonder whether we should take Urkug and his boys with us. It might be worth getting them to help in the escape. They might not be that bright, but they are good hired brawn, which could come in handy. Once they've outlived their usefulness they can be disposed of easily enough. I don't want to feel Ghazghkul leering over my shoulder watching my every move through the eyes of his green-skinned enforcer.

The sump area is a maze of intersecting corridors, and we ask after von Spenk. The men of the Army of Liberation wander around guarding doorways and access shafts. Following their grunted directions, some of them contradictory, we eventually make our way down a winding set of steps. I note that it's been several minutes since we've seen any of the red-capped soldiers.

Through an archway ahead I can see von Spenk. He's pacing back forth in an open chamber that has a sump overflow pipe jutting down towards the centre from one of the walls. He seems agitated, stepping from foot to foot, glancing around. I know he's waiting for Schaeffer

to make contact somehow, and it looks like the Last
Chancers are running a little late. When he sees us, he
freezes.

'Just seeing how your sweep is getting along, von
Spenk,' says the overlord with a weak attempt at a cheery
wave. 'It looks like everything is in hand, so we'll be getting along now.'

I have to stall them. I know Urkug won't want to
hang around too long, so I need to keep him busy. I turn
to the ork, keeping one eye on von Spenk at the same
time.

'So, you're one of Ghazghkul's top boys then?' I say.
He squints down at me with his blood red eyes.

'Da boss knows I can take care of meself,' he grunts.
He stomps forward and slaps a meaty paw onto von
Strab's shoulder, making him wince. 'Emperor and me
'ave got everyfing stitched up, ain't we?'

Von Strab has begun to regain some of his senses, and
a cunning look enters his eye. The broken, slumped man
I found in the throne room is disappearing as he straightens his shoulders, then glances at von Spenk before
addressing the ork leader.

'Certainly, Urkug, certainly,' the overlord says. 'We
need each other, don't we? And to make sure that nothing happens to me, we need to search this area
thoroughly.'

'You 'eard summink?' Urkug says, cocking his head to
one side, his lips rippling as he thinks.

'Assassins might be coming here to kill me,' says von
Strab. 'I'm sure von Spenk has everything under control,
and his soldiers are doing a fine job, but I would feel
safer if you were to have your boys join the search.'

Von Spenk and the overlord are trying to get rid of the orks, but I definitely want to be around for the meeting with the Last Chancers. I haven't got a weapon, and if Urkug leaves I'll be alone with von Spenk. The Colonel will be here soon and the overlord will be whisked away. Then I'll be stuck here. Or worse.

'On the other hand,' I say quickly, stepping forward,' It might also be good to make sure the emperor has his bodyguards close, in case the killers slip through the net.'

Urkug pauses, trying to decide what to do.

'I'll have von Spenk to watch out for me,' says von Strab, walking over to pat the gunman on the shoulder. 'I'm sure he won't let anything untoward happen to me.'

Urkug is still undecided. A glance at von Spenk confirms that he's getting increasingly nervous. His lack of calm is betrayed by his furtive glances towards the outflow pipe, and his fingers hovering over his holster. Von Strab, on the other hand, is a picture of calm composure, the statesman in him coming to the fore.

'The emperor must be our primary concern,' I say, crossing the chamber to stand on the other side of von Spenk. 'I've been with this team. They have a native guide, and will slip into our midst without warning. They're like shadows, like ghosts.'

Just as I finish, Urkug's nostrils flare and his pointed ears twitch as he frowns. He looks at the other orks, who are also sniffing the air. There's a resounding thump from beyond the wall that echoes along the pipe to us; it is accompanied by a small cloud of dust and shower of gravel spilling from the end. A moment later, Erasmus comes tumbling into view, his servo-skull flying from his hands and clattering across the floor.

I pounce first, clamping a hand over his mouth and dragging him to one side. There's a pregnant pause as Urkug and his greenskins pull pistols and cleavers from their belts.

'We should take them alive,' hisses von Spenk, and surprisingly the ork nods in agreement.

Spluttering on the cloud of dust, Brownie follows next, his look of astonishment when he sees us is priceless. Urkug steps forward and smashes his pistol across Dunmore's jaw, hurling him to the ground, out cold. There's scuffling and rattling inside the pipe, and I guess the others are trying to decide whether to come down or not. Urkug waves his orks to close in around the opening, waving them to step back out of sight.

'It's Kage,' I say in a loud whisper that echoes up the pipe. 'I've got something waiting for you down here.'

I hear a muffled exchange of words that I can't quite make out, followed by a series of bumps. My ruse has worked, as first Fenn, then the Colonel drop out of the inflow. The Colonel takes everything in with a single glance, his gaze resting on me. There's no accusation in his eyes, no resignation. He simply looks at me with his blank expression and raises his hands away from his bolt pistol and power sword.

Kin-Drugg is next, still nursing his wounded leg, along with the underhiver, Derflan Kierck. The tool trader gives a panicked squeak and turns to haul himself back into the pipe, but one of Urkug's boys grabs his ragged robe and hauls him back, dumping to the ground and placing a heavy boot on him to stop him crawling away.

Next is Kelth, who delicately slithers out of the pipe with his back to us. As he turns around, his jaw drops.

Without hesitation, he sweeps his hand up, pulling back his headscarf to reveal his warp eye.

To my left, von Strab and von Spenk both start screaming, flinging themselves to the ground with their hands clawing at their faces. Urkug stands mesmerised for a moment, his eyes glazing over, and a rope of drool dripping from his jaw. Then he topples to the ground, stiff as a board. The other orks react with a mixture of terrified wails and angry roars, firing their pistols at unreal phantoms. One of them stares for a long moment before its eyeballs explode and it crumples into a heap on the ground. The other Last Chancers are in similar comatose or panicked sates. Brownie is squatting on the ground gibbering softly. Kin-Drugg starts tearing wildly at the bandages on his leg, driven by some personal mania.

I just look at the Navigator, the swirling, ever-changing deep vortex in his skull nothing new for me. I can feel the warmth of his immaterial stare wash over me as he turns in my direction. This time it is Kelth whose eyes widen in horror as he looks at me with his warp eye for the first time, seeing my true form.

'Daemon!' he hisses, recoiling, his natural eyes scanning left and right for some avenue of escape. 'Get away from me, foulest of the foul!'

'That's enough of this bollocks,' I say, stepping forward and delivering a sharp punch to the navigator's face, breaking his nose and sending him to the ground.

I kick him in the side of the head and he rolls over. Snatching the scarf from his limp hand, I quickly bind his third eye again, pulling the rope belt from his rags to tie his hands behind his back. Looking up, I see that everyone else in the room is starting to recover.

His boots thumping on the ferrocrete, Oahebs leaps out of the pipe, wrapping his arms around my shoulders and bundling me to the ground.

THE NEEDLES BEING driven through my head are total agony and I scream at the top of my lungs, wrestling against the weight bearing down on me. My eyes are dark, full of stinging pain, and my own yelling voice feels muted and distant in my ears. I thrash around, feeling something constricting me as my sight slowly returns. Suddenly the weight lifts and I see the face of Oahebs close to mine. He is crouched over me. A trail of blood dribbles from his nostrils and one of his eyes is cloudy, the pupil almost obscured.

'What?' I manage to say, my voice suddenly unnaturally loud, ringing in my ears. More pain stabs through my head but I ignore, it, concentrating on Oahebs. He covers my mouth with his hand to stop me speaking.

'Shut up, listen hard,' he says, the words coming so quickly and quietly I almost can't understand them. 'You're a psyker, you've been possessed by a daemon. I'm a soulguard, an earthing rod for psychic energy. When you're away from me, the daemon will try to come back. You must fight it. Believe me, try with all your will and soul!'

I'm in a bare chamber, looking at a wide pipe jutting in from one wall. Just ahead of me, the other Last Chancers are lying on the ground, moaning and clutching their heads and faces. There is a handful of orks nearby, recovering from something.

I see von Strab beyond them, kneeling on the ground and vomiting. His bodyguard, von Spenk, is crouched behind him with his revolver pointing at me.

One of the orks has regained enough presence of mind to drag Oahebs from me. Retching, the Last Chancer doubles up, and I see blood clotting in his ears and strange burn-like marks on the back of his neck. He glances back at me, his left eye now completely white, pain etched across his face. I feel weak, sickened and dizzy and push myself to my feet to stagger away from him. The orks have their pistols in their hands again, surrounding the Last Chancers. I fall to all fours, resting my head against the cold, slightly damp floor, feeling trembling exhaustion course through my body.

Then I notice my hands.

They're almost claw-like, the nails extended and pointed, the skin thin and brittle; the bones threatening to break through the wasted flesh. Shaking uncontrollably, I push myself to my feet and stagger to the wall, leaning against it, breathing hard. I look over my shoulder, vaguely remembering Oahebs's words. Something about a daemon.

The largest ork is disarming the Last Chancers, casually tossing their weapons aside. Three red-capped soldiers run into the chamber, lasguns ready. They stop short at the sight that meets them. They look at the orks, and then von Spenk and the overlord, trying to work out what's going on. It's von Strab who takes the lead.

'These are the assassins,' he says. 'Lock them up! We shall deal with them later. Von Spenk, Kage, Urkug, we have plans to make. Acheron is proving far too troublesome. It is time the Army of Liberation made its mark!'

CHAPTER TWENTY
FREEDOM

THE LAST CHANCERS have been bundled away, presumably to the cells where I woke up. Von Strab leads myself, von Spenk and Urkug back up through the sumps and then through the halls and galleries of his palaces, with their grisly, bloody decorations. A throne carved from dark reddish wood sits at one end. The walls are covered with heavy drapes. There are only the four of us here.

Von Spenk carefully closes the door behind us after we enter. I have only flashes of recollection from after the last time we were together. I remember there was a girl, and I have an image of von Strab on a throne weeping, but nothing else. Outwardly, I try to keep my expression as calm as possible, but on the inside my thoughts are in turmoil. Oahebs's warning comes back in full. A daemon is inside me! I don't know when or how, but it doesn't really matter. I thought the blackouts, the nausea, were tied to my witching abilities. Now it makes more sense. Something inside me is wrestling for control of my body. Even now its corruption is lurking inside me. He said to fight it, but how? How can I fight something I don't even begin to understand?

Already I'm changing. Its presence inside me is warping my flesh. I can feel it now that I know it is there. My hands are becoming obscene claws, and I can feel bones breaking and knitting inside them and elsewhere. The thump of my heart sounds different, faster, more erratic. There's a pain in my chest I've never had before; it feels like my ribs are fusing together. Never before have I been so aware of myself and my body. Like a cancerous growth, the essence of the daemon is sitting inside me, gripping my body and soul.

'The assassination attempt has failed,' declares von Strab, sitting down in his chair with a flourish, his good eye staring at me manically. 'Thanks to the prompt, nay miraculous, action of Marshal Kage, we are still alive. This is a state of affairs we wish to continue long into the future. Acheron itself is under threat, and we must therefore concede to quit our palaces and locate to fresher ground.'

Von Spenk is agitated in the extreme. Not once does he tear his gaze from me except to glance cautiously at Urkug. His fingers are hovering above his holster pistol in anticipation of drawing the weapon. He looked dangerous enough when I saw him before, but in this mood he looks downright murderous, and totally unpredictable.

As they discuss their withdrawal from the hive, I let my mind dwell on other plans. The overlord, the inquisitor-cum-bodyguard and the ork leader are all ignoring me, so I try to straighten things out in my head, although my thoughts keep returning to the creature festering inside me.

I've never been one for politics, but I think I can figure what is going on by piecing together snippets of remembered observations and conversations. Through von Spenk, or whatever his real name is, von Strab has heard about the planned bombardment of Acheron. He wants to get out, understandably, and having gained von Spenk's confidence will double-cross him before he is handed over to the Imperial authorities. That much makes sense so far, and explains his remarkable recovery when things turned awry.

Though he's as mad as a bag of spanners, the overlord is certainly not inexperienced when it comes to scheming. He probably has at least one back-up plan at any given time. His allegiance however temporary, with von Spenk and the Colonel allow him to shake off the orks and the grip of Ghazghkull.

For his part, as far as I know, von Spenk is trying to get von Strab out of Acheron as well, to prevent its destruction and win a little coup of his own over his rivals who want to flatten the hive. He said that he'd kill the overlord if necessary, but I'm doubtful. He seems more likely to throw caution to the wind and just cut and run. I'm pretty sure there's more than a little self-interest here and he obviously wants to save his own skin. With Urkug hanging around like a fart in an APC, I don't think he's willing to pull the trigger and risk his own neck.

And as far as I can tell, Urkug is the only straightforward one here, which isn't surprising. His orders from Ghazghkull are to keep von Strab alive and well, and to keep an eye on him so he can't betray the warlord. Von Strab thinks he's playing a subtle game, with his Army of Liberation and his plotting, but he's admitted that Urkug is smarter than he appears. Even he hasn't figured out what's going on, it's clear that Ghazghkul is intelligent enough to be aware of von Strab's potential double-crosses.

And stuck in the middle of all this are the Last Chancers, locked up somewhere below us, probably condemned to death. I don't know how it all went wrong, or why Urkug turned up at the meeting point, but it's obvious that the plan's gone to hell and isn't coming back. All of which leaves me thoroughly fragged as far as I can tell.

I have no weapon, and little chance of getting one at the moment. I haven't a doubt that if I make the wrong move, von Spenk will take me down in an instant.

Trouble is, I haven't got a fragging clue what the wrong move might be. Urkug's the same, so that's double the fun, and I can't even begin to work out how I'm going to figure in von Strab's schemes. At best the three of them consider me a disposable asset, at worst a potential threat.

The obvious course of action is to get the frag out of here and leave them to it. That's easier said than done though, with von Spenk and Urkug both keeping an eye on me. The only friends, for want of a better term, that I have are the Last Chancers, and I'm not even sure where they are. As far as I can tell, the only way out of this for me is to get the plan rolling again. If I can kill or seize von Strab, the Colonel and the others will be the best way of getting out of here. So I'd best start listening to what's happening, otherwise things could get even further out of my control.

'...narrow thinking,' von Strab is saying. 'What should we care if they all die? They are my army, and their duty is to protect me. If that is to be a diversion, then so be it. You never know, it might actually come good and do some damage to the lap dogs of Yarrick.'

'If dere's a fight, my boys will show you what dey're made of,' says Urkug, thumping a clawed fist into the palm of his other hand. 'We's not had a proper fight for ages, and the lads is getting bored.'

'But throwing away your forces just to cover your escape could prove unwise, your excellency,' says von Spenk, his smooth tone having returned as he tries to manipulate the overlord. 'We cannot guarantee what sort of reception you will receive wherever we end up relocating to.'

'I think I know how to do this,' I say, trying not to flinch as they all suddenly turn their attention on me. Von Spenk has his eyebrows raised in doubt, von Strab is looking at me with one narrowed eye and Urkug is frowning, although he seems to do that most of the time.

I feel something squirm inside me, not physically but in my mind, in my soul. I ignore it, fighting it back into the dark recesses.

'Colonel Schaeffer must have had some plan for getting out again, he always does,' I say, the idea only forming properly as I talk. 'I might be able to get it out of him. At the moment, his mission has failed. If I can offer him a chance to succeed, he might just take it.'

'What makes you think he'll trust you, a traitor?' says von Strab, leaning back in his chair. 'After all, you have betrayed him twice now.'

I have? I don't remember anything like that. That makes things more complicated, but as I'm trying to concoct an argument, it's von Spenk who steps in. He is pointedly not looking at me now, but something tells me he's guessed what I have in mind.

'He may have something, your excellency,' says von Spenk. 'There is nothing to lose by trying, as I see it. I will personally escort him to the prisoners, to assist if necessary.'

'I dun like it,' grunts Urkug. 'We should kill 'em before dey make more trouble.'

'We'll get rid of them, one way or the other, when they are no longer useful,' says von Strab.

Urkug stands his ground, his muscles flexing as he tenses, glaring at the overlord.

'I dun trust anywun any more,' he says. 'Dere's been too much secret talking, and I dun want no more of it.'

'You can come with me as well,' I say, and the ork's bucket-jawed head swings in my direction, fixing me with an evil stare. Behind him, von Spenk gives an almost imperceptible nod, confirming that he thinks we can take the ork out between us if necessary. In fact, as I think about it, it could be to our advantage to remove the ork leader as early as possible. 'If you don't trust us, that is.'

'I dun,' Urkug says. 'Let's do it now, no more talking!'

I WAS RIGHT: they are being kept down in the same cells where I had been for Emperor-knows how long. Von Spenk leads the way, down through the ornate audience chambers and portrait galleries, and then into the slime-covered stone depths in the levels below. The three of us stop at the bottom of the steps leading into a cell-lined hallway. Urkug pulls his pistol from his belt as von Spenk hands me the keys.

'I fink you doin' summink wrong, I plug you, right?' the ork says and I nod.

I walk down the line of cells, to the third on the left, which von Spenk tells me is the one where I'll find the Colonel. I pause outside the door, the heavy brass key between my fingers, figuring out how to make this work. I can't guarantee that von Spenk can take out Urkug with his revolver. Even a point blank shot to the head isn't always fatal to an ork.

On the other hand, if Urkug nails one of us with his heavy pistol, it's going to be all over pretty damn quickly.

I think perhaps the best way will be to lure Urkug towards the cell so that von Spenk can perhaps shoot him in the neck while the Colonel and I tackle him from the rear. A quick shout should bring the huge ork running in our direction, and then it'll be up to von Spenk. After that, we'll release the others and set about getting von Strab out of here.

If we can get von Strab out on his own, I doubt we'll have a problem keeping him safe and sound. He may be planning to double-cross von Spenk and avoid being taken in, but with the Last Chancers around that'll be near impossible. Of course, we'll still have to get him back to friendly lines intact, but since we managed to actually get here against the odds, a few kilometres to the Imperial cordon outside Acheron shouldn't be too difficult.

I slip the key into the lock, trying to keep my hand steady. The lock clunks loudly as I turn the key, and I tense as I pull the door outwards. As the sickly light from the glow-globes seeps into the room, I see the Colonel. He's sitting with his back to the wall facing the door. His eyes bore straight into me from the dim light. I stand there for a moment as we just look at each other, the Colonel's blank face betraying no clue as to his mood.

He stands up slowly to straighten his rags as if he were still in uniform, and takes a step forward. I hold up a hand to stop him, swinging the door almost closed behind me, cutting off all but a sliver of light.

As I turn round, the Colonel leaps forward, his right fist slamming into my jaw, knocking me backwards. I throw up my right hand to block the next punch, a fraction too late. Blood wells from a cut on my lip as his knuckles smash into my face, knocking back another step.

I open my mouth to tell him to stop, but he wades in with a boot, forcing me to sway to one side. I catch his ankle in my left hand. Instinctively, I bring my leg round to sweep away his standing leg, but he leans forward and catches my knee with a blocking forearm, spinning on his heel and wrenching himself free from my grasp.

Without pause, he attacks again, raining punch after punch towards my throat and face, forcing me to duck and weave, blocking with my hands and shoulders, slowly forcing me away from the door. A feint and a right uppercut catch me off guard, slamming my head back against the wall and stunning me. As I blink sweat out of my eyes, I see him stepping towards me, his face filled with murderous intent, his lips twisted into a snarl. It's the first time I've ever feared for my life at the hands of another man.

With a smile, I lunge forwards, the fingers of my hand driving towards Schaeffer's eyes. I can get this body to work faster than he ever imagined. I go on the offensive, striking with left and right blows, taking him on the chin and above the eyes. Turning my attention lower, I drive a fist into his gut, lifting him to his toes, and then slam a punch into the side of his head, making him stagger sideways.

'Idiot,' I hiss at him, driving a booted foot into his chest, leaving him leaning up against the wall gasping

for breath. 'I was going to get you out of here. Now that's never going to happen. I'm going to enjoy watching you die.'

He looks up at me, chest heaving; his face a picture of hatred.

'He is one of mine,' he spits. 'I want him back!'

He takes me by surprise, hurling himself off the wall, driving a shoulder into my midriff and bundling me into the far wall. My spine cracks against the stonework. The pain is easy to ignore, as he batters my face with combinations left and right punches. My right eye swells and closes up, my nose spills blood down onto my lips. He's panting badly now and I slap him with the back of my hand, my bony knuckles tearing the skin from his cheeks.

Clawing my fingers, I rake my hand across his face. My new talons tear off the lobe of his left ear and he sways to avoid the blow. He throws out a hasty punch, which is easily stopped. Grabbing his wrist, I trap it under my arm and wrench upwards. His elbow bends the wrong way with an audible snap. He hasn't once groaned or cried out in pain yet. That's a shame.

'You can't blame me,' I say, grabbing the front of his ragged clothes and slamming him into the wall. 'I'm not the Kage I used to be.'

He breaks my grip and forces his arms between us, throwing me backwards.

'I know,' he says. 'You are a creature of the abyss, a weak, despicable cacodaemon. I want him back, fiend of Horus, leech of the void!'

'But I'm right here,' I say with a laugh. 'I am Kage, you know it. This is what I'm really like. This is what I want to be like. This is what is inside me, in my soul. It

was easy to release myself, my psychic gifts saw to that. Now I can be free, from you, from the accursed Emperor, from duty and guilt.'

'You are never free from me,' snarls Schaeffer, smashing a fist into my chest, and cracking a rib. I laugh. It won't take long to heal, not now that I've unleashed my true potential. A few more modifications and this body will be perfect for me.

I stop his next punch in the palm of my hand and my long fingers close around his fist, crushing knuckles and pulverising the flesh. I force him down on to one knee and then let go, bringing my hand across his face with the same movement, splitting his bottom lip.

'Ever since I first met you, I wanted to do this,' I say, cracking my bloodied knuckles. 'Sure, you remember? I stuck a knife in you. This time I won't bother with the knife.'

I take a step forward, but at that moment light spills into the room, and I freeze. Urkug and von Spenk crowd into the door, their pistols drawn. I step back and lower my hands to my sides.

'He wouldn't co-operate, so I'm trying to force it out of him,' I say quickly, possibly too quickly as von Spenk's eyes narrow in suspicion. 'I just need a couple more minutes.'

'I think you've done enough,' von Spenk says, pushing past Urkug into the room. The ork grunts in annoyance and shoves him to one side to cram his bulk through the narrow space.

'I dun like dis, you stop it now,' Urkug says, waving me towards the door with his blunt-barrelled pistol. 'I say we just shoot dem now and forget about dem.'

'No!' says von Spenk, stepping in front of the ork's raised pistol. 'The emperor wants to dispose of them himself, you heard him say so. We'll get rid of them his way, and then we will get out of here and start again.'

Something gurgles in the ork's throat as he considers this and then he backs off, lowering his pistol.

'We go soon,' he says. 'Tonight. I might just get bored of your emperor if I have to hang around ere any longer. I get rid of fings when I'm bored wiv dem.'

Schaeffer is lying on the ground, clasping his broken arm. He is looking up at us with simmering abhorrence. Von Spenk motions with his pistol for me to leave the cell, but before I do, I crouch down next to Schaeffer and whisper in his bleeding ear.

'You always knew it would be one of your own that did for you,' I say. 'You made me, and now I've destroyed you. I hope you think about that when you're dying.'

VON STRAB DOESN'T seem too put out by the news of what happened when we return to the audience chamber. The manic look has returned to his eyes, and he looks at me closely as von Spenk informs him of what they found in the cell.

'Couldn't pass up the opportunity to settle the score, eh, Kage?' he says with a chuckle. 'It's quite naughty lying to me like that, but I can understand your reasons. I bet he made your life a living hell.'

'Yes he did,' I say. 'And he's overseen the deaths of hundreds, thousands of good soldiers and innocent civilians. If ever there was a man who embodied the evil that the Imperium represents, Schaeffer was that man. The sooner we're rid of him, the better.'

'Well, yes, but let's not be too hasty,' he says and I try not to show my disappointment. 'I have something special planned for these Last Chancers and their commander. Tonight, they'll be seeing the valley again, although I doubt they'll enjoy the view much.'

TRUE TO HIS word, a few hours later, a great entourage is making its way through the underhive to the massive fire chasm called the valley. Soldiers and courtiers numbering over a hundred file through the twisting corridors, across silent machine rooms, down spiralling stairs and along crumbling boulevards.

Von Strab walks at the head of the procession, and some of the Army of Liberation are obviously clearing the route ahead. With him are four bearers, carrying a patched canvas shelter over his head. The purpose of this becomes clear when we pass through a high chamber, its vaulted ceiling about two hundred metres above us. It writhes with bats, millions of them, and their shit rains down on us in steady drips, spattering our uniforms and robes. I try not to look up.

Flanked by orks and redcaps, we wind our way up a twisting causeway that arches out over a desolate, cratered hall. I can see a few ragged figures slipping between the shadows, digging in the pocked earth with small shovels.

'Who are they?' I ask, looking over the balustrade into the dim depths. The man behind me stops and leans over. He's dressed in a bright orange uniform coat, with jewelled roses set into the lapels. A cluster of medallions, many of them tarnished, hang on his chest, and he holds a cockaded hat under his arm. I can't help but notice *that he has no trousers or boots on, and his left big toe is pointing out of a hole in his damp, stained hose.*

'Bone prospectors,' he says, and then seeing my ignorance, continues. 'The fighting in the underhive has moved around a lot in the last three years. This was one of the earlier battles. About a hundred and fifty dead orks, maybe a thousand human remains. They were all buried in the mud when the level above collapsed, dropping the contents of the sewer tanks onto them. They dig around in the stuff looking for valuables. Apparently there are some people who cook the bones down, to eat, for glue, that kind of thing.'

'Just my sort of place, shame it has to go,' I say.

'Hmm? Go?' my new companion asks. 'What's going?'

'Nothing, nothing really,' I say with a smile, turning away and rejoining the column.

At the front of the line, chained hand and foot, come the Last Chancers. Kelth is easily picked out, a head taller than the rest with a crude iron mask, a lot like a pail, chained over his head. I guess von Strab doesn't want another attack of the warp-jeebies. The Colonel walks proudly at their head, the others either skulking along avoiding any attention, or looking around at their surroundings with startled gapes. Brownie looks like he hasn't got a clue what's going on. He keeps stopping and looking over his shoulder to talk to Erasmus behind him until the orks turn up and club him into moving again.

Somehow, Spooge is still carrying that bloody broken servo-skull, tucked under his arm. Before the little fragger dies, I want to smash it into pieces in front of him. I want to tear out all the mechanics and gears and cognitive analysers and scatter them to the winds.

Maybe then he'll understand that it's not fun and games to be a soldier.

The others are obscured by the press of people; mock military officers and the local dignitaries, some of them prodding the prisoners with walking canes, or spitting on them. We eventually reach a large semi-circular area with an ornate iron fence around the outside. Beyond that, I can see the jagged, bridged chasm of the valley, bathed in a red glow from below. A walkway juts out about fifty metres over the artificial canyon, lined with ropes on each side.

The overlord's lackeys and retainers spread out across the large balcony, pushing and elbowing each other to get the best view of the coming proceedings. Von Strab beckons for me, von Spenk and Urkug to follow him out onto the gangway. Ahead of us, the Last Chancers are herded along the pathway to its end. It's immediately clear what von Strab is intending to do.

It's a wonderful feeling, standing above that massive precipice, looking down over the edge into its ruddy depths. The heat drifts up and around me, the air dry on my skin. It's the closest I've come to remembering the soaring, gliding freedom of the warp. It's an odd memory, tinged with senses that my body no longer possesses.

I look up, seeing the roof has collapsed just a few levels above our heads, jutting stalactites of metal and ferrocrete point down at me. There's a wonderful stillness, a momentary hush of the underhive.

I turn to von Strab, who stands in front of the Last Chancers, von Spenk on one side, Urkug on the other. He opens out his arms; palms held up to the low artificial sky, his head arched back.

'Behold the great valley of Acheron!' the overlord declares. 'For a hundred generations, it has brought life and light and warmth to the underhive. Gods have been born in its depths, and blessings bestowed by robed priests basking in its holy heat. It has spawned its own creatures, its own tribes, its own prophecies. It is an extension of the will of Armageddon itself. These fiery depths have witnessed births and deaths, marriages and dissolutions, miracles and martyrdoms! And now it is time to commit the bodies of Armageddon's enemies to its burning embrace.'

A great cheer resounds from the gathered dignitaries, echoing off the roof, resounding back from the far wall of the valley. But I can sense the hollowness in their voices. The cheer is as much for the orks behind them as for their ruler and his rites of execution. Acheron is under the heel of von Strab, and if only it wasn't going to get annihilated in fourteen days, I would have had it made here. Still, there are other things to look forward to.

Brownie is the first in the line of Last Chancers, and he's starting to realise his predicament. He tries to wipe a hand over his bald scalp, but the chains between his wrists and ankle stop him. Sweat drips down his face as he looks over the edge. He shuffles backwards, and tries to run as Urkug steps forward and grabs him.

He shouts; his voice cracking into a scream as the burly ork hauls him towards the lip of the half-bridge, holding him out over the valley. Von Strab makes a theatrical flourish with his hand and Urkug shoves Brownie over the edge, flinging him into the empty space. In my mind's eye he hangs there for a second, mouth stretched open. He tries to flail his arms and legs, and drops from view, his shriek growing quieter and more hoarse as he falls to his doom.

There's baying and clapping from the crowd, and cries of 'Shame!' and 'Kill the traitors!'

Their fear-fuelled anger washes over me. It is mixed with genuine hatred. I shudder and my eyelids flutter. I glance around to make sure no one noticed.

Urkug turns and gives a gurgling laugh, and von Strab claps his hands quickly like an excited child about to receive a present. Beside the overlord, von Spenk looks decidedly irritated, his arms folded across his chest. The Colonel looks typically stoical, jutting his chin forward and regarding von Strab coolly.

Erasmus, behind the Colonel in line, gives an agonised shout and tries to rush forward, but one of von Strab's guards steps in and batters him around the side of the head with the butt of his shotgun.

Next up is Kelth, standing there with his head covered, unaware of what's going on. I wonder whether it's a cruelty or a kindness that he can't see what's happening. It's probably better for him, which is a shame because the arrogant bastard deserves more suffering in his life.

There's polite clapping from the crowd this time, following the overlord's lead. The ripple of applause seems civilised and tame compare to the emotions I can feel emanating from the frightened, heated mob.

Urkug hoists the lanky Navigator above his head with a roar and strides to the precipice. Kelth struggles vainly in the grip of the green monster, his chains rattling *against the ork's skull. With a triumphant shout, Urkug flexes his powerful arms and flings the Navigator into the void. I laugh, feeling the waves of fear washing from the remaining Last Chancers. It's like a drug, swilling around inside me, buoying up my released soul.*

Casually, the ork strolls back towards the line and grabs the rags of the underhiver, Derflan Kierck. The scrawny little man writhes in Urkug's clawed grasp, but to no effect. With almost contemptuous ease, the ork hurls Kierck over the edge into the chasm, holding up his other fist over his head in celebration. There's another great cheer and brash hooting from the audience, and hats are tossed into the air in celebration.

I stop when I see that it's to be the Colonel next. Urkug is stomping back from the end of the walkway, clenching his fists in anticipation.

'Wait!' I shout out, and the ork pauses. Everyone looks at me as I stride forwards. 'I think the honour of this should be mine!'

Von Spenk gives me a curious look, perhaps thinking this is some last minute gamble to save the Last Chancers. I'm happy to disappoint him.

'Of course, Marshall Kage,' says von Strab with an extravagant wave of his hand towards Schaeffer. 'You not only deserve it, but you have earned it.'

I walk forwards, my eyes focussed on the Colonel, and he returns my stare. Cold hatred burns there, willing me to explode from his sheer force of will. I smile at him, and then the smile turns into a grin, exposing my newly reshaped fangs. I hear a hiss from von Spenk behind me and a shout from one of the other Last Chancers. I ignore them.

I'm a few metres from the Colonel, when I remember Oahebs is still alive.

Frag.

LIKE A DROWNING man bursting to the surface of a tossing sea, I awake with a gasp for breath. With a force of will I cling on to the memories of the departing daemon, and through the pain surging through my heart and head, remember everything. In a single moment of clarity, I feel myself, more aware of who and what I am than I have ever been in my life.

In a single glance, I see the Colonel looking at me, a snarl on his lips. Next to him, Erasmus cowers, tears streaming down his now-sunken cheeks. To my right is von Strab, with von Spenk just behind him. And ahead of me is the massive ork, Urkug. I can feel the heat of the distant fire chasm washing up over the edges of the walkway. Sweat prickles on my skin. I can taste the blood from my bleeding gums where my sharpened fangs bite into them. My body feels tense and strong, twisted and warped by the daemon.

In that single moment, my entire soul becomes focussed in on itself, like a collapsing warp hole. I suddenly understand everything. I look at Oahebs, and see the blank white orb of his eye and the scars left across his face from the psychic energy that is coursing through him from me.

I see Fenn, standing tall beside the anti-psyker, a haunted look in his eye as he gazes out into the wideness of the valley, his nightmare of open spaces about to become a reality. Then there's Spooge, the last weeks of hardship etched onto his face. Gone are the rounded edges the blubbery cheeks. Still mortally afraid, and caught up in something far beyond what he could have comprehended a year ago, he nevertheless manages to spit at me. He cradles the servo-skull of his father like a totem, protecting it to the last.

And then there's the Colonel. Cold, hard as rock, unflinching and remorseless. A man who has endured pain, hardship and injury for over three centuries. A man who has dedicated his life to the Emperor and never once asked why; his faith is more solid than the foundations of a hive city. His body has been broken innumerable times and yet he's stayed alive; they have healed him and thrown him back into the eternal war.

He has never failed.

It all becomes as clear as crystal in that moment of awakening. Sacrifice, the Imperium is built on it. The sayings are all true. The Blood of Martyrs is the Seed of the Imperium. The Loyal Slave Learns to Love the Lash. Only in Death does Duty End.

For ten thousand years we have endured, sometimes we have thrived, other times merely survived. For a hundred centuries we have fought and died, spilt the blood of our enemies and our own over an uncountable number of battlefields. Mankind has sacrificed itself, for itself, so that it might last for another generation, and another, and another. Those sacrifices are for no greater cause than for the acts themselves. It is done in the unspoken hope that some day, perhaps in another ten thousand years, a generation will live without sacrifice and mankind's destiny is fulfilled for eternity.

The Emperor will not remember you by your medals and diplomas, but by your scars.

It is not only in death that we offer up our lives to Him, but also in life. We are not judged merely by the manner of our deaths, we do not earn His eternal grace merely by dying in His name. It is by the way we live out our lives before we die that defines who we were. It is easy to sacrifice a body, for it's nothing more than a mortal shell for our soul. To sacrifice your life, not your death, is the ultimate test of faith.

It is a test I have always failed. I have lied and cheated and killed my fellow men for my own reasons. I have squandered the opportunities for glory that I was given. Time and again I have stood upon the precipice of true sacrifice and turned away.

Von Strab's look of triumph turns to horror as I fling my arms around him, lifting him off the ground. I see von Spenk's astonished face flash past as I drive forwards with the overlord in my arms, the panicked bellows of Urkug sounding in my ears.

His legs hit the rope barrier and buckle, and my momentum carries us forward, toppling us head over heels into the precipice.

Now I truly understand what it means to have a Last Chance. I'm glad I finally took it.

Also from the Black Library

13ᵀᴴ LEGION

The first Last Chancers Novel
by Gav Thorpe

THE GUARDSMAN'S NOSE explodes with blood as my fist crashes between his eyes. Next, I hit him with a left to the chin, knocking him backwards a step. He ducks out of the next punch, spitting blood from cracked lips. My nose is filled with the smell of old sweat and fresh blood, and perspiration from the blazing sun trickles down my face and throat. All around I can hear chanting and cheering.

'Fraggin' kink his fraggin' neck!' I recognise Jorett's voice.

'Break the son of an ork apart!' Franx yells.

The guardsmen from Chorek are cheering their man on too, their flushed faces looking dark in contrast to their white and grey camouflage jackets and leggings.

He makes a lunge at me, his face swathed in blood, his dusty uniform covered in red stains. I easily side-step his bullish charge, bringing my knee up hard into his abdomen and feeling some ribs crack under the blow. He's doubled up now, his face a mask of pain, but I'm not going to stop there. I grab the back of his head with both hands and ram my knee up into his face, hearing the snap of his cheek or jaw fracturing. He collapses sideways, and as he falls, the toecap of my standard-issue boot connects with his chin, hurling his head backward into the hard soil. I'm about to lay into him again when I realise every-thing's gone dead quiet. I look up to see what the hell's happening, panting hard.

Pushing through the Chorek ranks is a massively muscled man, and I spot the insignia of a master sergeant on the blue sleeve of his tunic. He's got the black pelt of some shaggy creature tied as a cloak over his left shoulder and his eyes are fixed on me with murderous intent. In his hand is a sixty-centimetre metal parade baton, red jewels clustered around one end, and as he steps up to me he smashes the point of it into my guts, knocking the wind out of me and forc-ing me to my knees.

'Penal legion scum!' the Chorek master sergeant barks. 'I'll show you what they should have done to you!'

He pulls his arm back for a good swing at me but then stops in mid-strike. Just try it, I think to myself, I've killed harder men and creatures than you. I'm still fired up from the fight and ready to pounce on this jumped-up bully of an officer. I'll give him the same treatment I've just dealt out to his man. He glances over my head and a shadow falls over me. A prickly sensation starts at the back of my neck and turns into a slight shiver down my spine. I turn to look over my shoulder, still clutching my aching guts, and see that he's there. The Colonel. Colonel Schaeffer, commanding officer of the 13th Penal Legion, known by those unlucky enough to be counted amongst its number as the Last Chancers. The swollen dusk sun's behind him – the sun always seems to be behind him, he's always in shadow or silhouette when you first see him, like it's a talent he's got. All I can see is the icy glitter of his sharp blue eyes, looking at the master sergeant, not me. I'm glad of that because his face is set like stone, a sure sign that he is in a bad mood.

'That will be all, master sergeant,' the Colonel says calmly, just standing there with his left hand resting lightly on the hilt of his power sword.

'This man needs disciplining,' replies the Chorek, arm still raised for the blow. I think this guy is stupid enough to try it as well, and secretly hope he will, just to see what Schaeffer does to him.

'Disperse your troopers from the landing field,' the Colonel tells the master sergeant, 'and mine will then be soon out of your way.'

The Chorek officer looks like he's going to argue some more, but then I see he makes the mistake of meeting the Colonel's gaze and I smirk as I see him flinch under that cold stare. Everyone sees something different in those blue eyes, but it's always something painful and unpleasant that they're reminded of. The Colonel doesn't move or say anything while the master sergeant herds his men away, pushing them with the baton when they turn to look back. He details two of them to drag away the trooper I knocked out and he casts one murderous glance back at me. I know his kind, an unmistakable bully, and the Choreks are going to suffer for his humiliation when they reach their camp.

'On your feet, Kage!' snaps the Colonel, still not moving a muscle. I struggle up, wincing as soreness flashes across my stomach from the master sergeant's blow. I don't meet the Colonel's gaze, but already I'm tensing, expecting the sharp edge of his tongue.

'Explain yourself, lieutenant,' he says quietly, folding his arms like a cross tutor.

'That Chorek scum said we should've all died in Deliverance, sir,' I tell him. 'Said we didn't deserve to live. Well, sir, I've just been on burial detail for nearly a hundred and fifty Last Chancers, and I lost my temper.'

'You think that gutter scum like you deserve to live?' the Colonel asks quietly.

'I know that we fought as hard as any bloody Chorek guardsman, harder even,' I tell him, looking straight at him for the first time. The Colonel seems to think for a moment, before nodding sharply.

'Good,' he says, and I can't stop my jaw from dropping in surprise. 'Get these men onto the shuttle – without any more fighting, Lieutenant Kage,' the Colonel orders, turning on his heel and marching off back towards the settlement of Deliverance.

I cast an astonished look at the other Last Chancers around me, the glance met with knotted brows and shrugs. I compose myself for a moment, trying not to work out what the hell that was all about. I've learnt it's best not to try to fathom out the Colonel sometimes, it'll just tie your head in knots.

'Well, you useless bunch of fraggin' lowlifes,' I snap at the remnants of my platoon, 'you heard the Colonel. Get your sorry hides onto that shuttle at the double!'

As I JOG TOWARDS the blocky shape of our shuttle, Franx falls in on my left. I try to ignore the big sergeant, still annoyed with him from a couple of days ago, when he could have got me into deep trouble with the Colonel.

'Kage,' he begins, glancing down across his broad shoulder at me. 'Haven't had a chance to talk to you since… Well, since before the tyranids attacked.'

'You mean since before you tried to lead the platoon into the jungles on some stupid escape attempt?' I snap back, my voice purposefully harsh. He wasn't going to get off easily, even if I did consider him something of a friend. A friendship he'd pushed to the limits by trying to incite a rebellion around me.

'Can't blame me, Kage,' he says, with a slight whine to his deep voice that irritates me. 'Should've all died back then, you know it.'

'I'm still alive, and I know that if I'd let you take off I wouldn't be,' I reply, not even bothering to look at him. 'The Colonel would've killed me for letting you go, even before the 'nids had a chance.'

'Yeah, I know, I know,' Franx tells me apologetically.

'Look,' I say, finally meeting his eye, 'I can't blame you for wanting out. Emperor knows, it's what we all want. But you've got to be smarter about it. Pick your time better, and not one that's gonna leave me implicated.'

'I understand, Kage,' Franx nods before falling silent. One of the shuttle crewmen, looking hot and bothered in his crisp blue and white Navy uniform, is counting us off as we head up the loading ramp, giving us sullen looks as if he wishes they could just leave us here. It's hot inside the shuttle, which has slowly baked in the harsh sun until the air inside feels like a kiln. I see the others settling into places along the three benches, securing themselves with thick restraint belts that hang from beams that stretch at head height along the shuttle chamber's ten-metre length. As I find a place and strap myself into the restraining harnesses, Franx takes the place next to me.

'How's Kronin?' he asks, fumbling with a metal buckle as he pulls the leather straps tighter across his barrel chest.

'Haven't seen him. He went up on the first shuttle run,' I tell him, checking around to see that everybody else is secured. Seeing that the survivors of my platoon are sitting as tight as a Battle Sister's affections, I give the signal to the naval rating waiting at the end of the seating bay. He disappears through the bulkhead and the red take-off lights flash three times in warning.

'I haven't got the full story about Kronin yet,' I say to Franx, pushing my back against the hard metal of the bench to settle myself. Franx is about to reply when the rumble of thrusters reverberates through the fuselage of the shuttle. The rumbling increases in volume to a roar and I feel myself being pushed further into the bench by the shuttle's take-off. The whole craft starts to shake violently as it gathers momentum, soaring upwards into the sky above Deliverance. My booted feet judder against the mesh decking of the shuttle and my backside slides slightly across the metal bench. My stomach is still painful, and I feel slightly sick as the shuttle banks over sharply to take its new course. The twelve centimetre slash in my thigh begins to throb painfully as more blood is forced into my legs by the acceleration. I grit my teeth and ignore the pain. Through a viewport opposite I can see the ground dropping away, the seemingly haphazard scattering of shuttles and dropships sitting a kilometre beyond the walls of Deliverance. The settlement itself is receding quickly, until I can only dimly make out the line of the curtain wall and the block of the central keep. Then we're into the clouds and everything turns white.

As we break out of the atmosphere the engines turn to a dull whine and a scattering of stars replaces the blue of the sky outside the viewport. Franx leans over.

'They say Kronin is touched,' he says, tapping the side of his head to emphasise his point.

'It's bloody strange, I'll give you that,' I reply. 'Something happened to him when he was in the chapel.'

'Chapel?' Franx asks, scratching his head vigorously through a thick bush of brown curls.

'What did you hear?' I say, curious to find out what rumours had started flying around, only a day after the battle against the tyranids. Gossip is a good way of gauging morale, as well as the reactions to a recent battle. Of course, we're never happy, being stuck in a penal legion until we die, but sometimes some of the men are more depressed than usual. The fight against the alien tyranids at the missionary station was horrific, combating monsters like them always is. I wanted to know what the men were focusing their thoughts on.

'Nothing really,' Franx says, trying unsuccessfully to shrug in the tight confines of the safety harness. 'People are saying that he went over the edge.'

'The way I heard it, he and the rest of 2nd platoon had fallen back to the chapel,' I tell him. 'There were 'nids rushing about everywhere, coming over the east wall. Most of them were the big warriors, smashing at the doors of the shrine with their claws, battering their way in. They crashed through the windows and got inside. There was nowhere to run; those alien bastards just started hacking and chopping at everything inside. They lost the whole platoon except for Kronin. They must have left him for dead, since the Colonel found him under a pile of bodies.'

'That's a sure way to crack,' Franx says sagely, a half-smile on his bulbous lips.

'Anyway,' I continue, 'Kronin is cracked, like you say. Keeps talking all this gibber, constantly jabbering away about something that no one could work out.'

'I've seen that sort of thing before,' says Poal, who's been listening from the other side of Franx. His narrow, chiselled face has a knowing air about it, like he was a sage dispensing the wisdom of the ancients or some-thing. 'I had a sergeant once whose leg was blown off by a mine on Gaulis II. He just kept repeating his brother's name, minute after minute, day after day. He slit his own throat with a med's scalpel in the end.'

There's a moment of silence as everybody considers this, and I carry on with the story to distract them from thoughts of self-murder.

'Yeah, that's pretty grim,' I tell them, 'but Kronin's case just gets weirder. Turns out, he's not mumbling just any old thing, oh no. He's quoting scripture, right? Nathaniel, the preacher back in Deliverance, overhears him saying out lines from the Litanies of Faith. Stuff like: "And the Beast from the Abyss rose up with its multitudes and laid low the servants of the Emperor with its clawed hands". Things like that.'

'Fragged if I've ever seen Kronin with a damned prayer book, not in two fragging years of fighting under the son of an ork,' Jorett announces from the bench down the middle of the shuttle, looking around. Everybody's lis-tening in now that we can be heard over the dimmed noise of the engines. Forty pairs of eyes look towards me in anticipation of the next twist of the tale.

'Exactly!' I declare with an emphatic nod, beginning to play to the audience a little bit. I'm enjoying having a new tale to tell for a change, and it keeps them from falling out with each other, which usually happens when we wind down from a mission.

'Nathaniel sits down with him for a couple of hours while we bury the dead,' I continue, passing my gaze over those that can see me. 'I heard him explaining his view on things to the Colonel. Seems Kronin had a vis-itation from the Emperor himself while he lay half-dead in the chapel. Says he has been given divine knowledge. Of course, he doesn't actually say this, he's just quoting appropriate lines from the Litanies, like: "And the Emperor appeared with a shimmering halo and spake unto His people on Gathalamor." And like you say, how in the seven hells does he know any of this stuff?'

'There is nothing mystical about that,' answers Gappo, sitting on his own towards the rear of the shuttle. Nearly everybody seems to give an inward groan, except a couple of the guys who are looking forward to this new development in the entertainment. Myself, I've kind of come to like Gappo – he's not such a meathead as most of the others.

'Oh wise preacher,' Poal says with a sarcastic sneer, 'please enlighten us with your bountiful wisdom.'

'Don't call me "preacher"!' Gappo snarls, a scowl creasing his flat, middle-aged features. 'You know I have left that falsehood behind.'

'Whatever you say, Gappo,' Poal tells him with a disdainful look.

'It's quite simple really,' Gappo begins to explain, patently ignoring Poal now. 'You've all been to Ecclesiarchal services, hundreds even thousands of them. Whether you remember them or not, you've probably heard all of the Litanies of Faith and every line from the Book of Saints twice over. Kronin's trauma has affected his mind, so that he can remember those writings and nothing else. It's the only way he's got left to communicate.'

There are a few nods, and I can see the sense of it. People's heads are half-fragged up anyway, in my experience. It doesn't take much to jog it loose, from what I've seen. Emperor alone knows how many times I've felt myself teetering on the edge of the insanity chasm. Luckily I'm as tough as grox hide and it hasn't affected me yet. Not so as anyone's told me, in any case.

'Well I guess that makes more sense than the Emperor filling him with His divine spirit,' says Mallory, a balding, scrawny malingerer sitting next to Poal. 'After all, I don't think the Emperor's best pleased with our Lieutenant Kronin, 'specially considering the fact that Kronin's in the Last Chancers for looting and burning down a shrine.'

'Of course it makes sense,' Gappo says, his voice dropping to a conspiratorial whisper. 'There might not be an Emperor at all!'

'You shut your fragging mouth, Gappo Elfinzo!' Poal spits, making the sign of the protective eagle over his chest with his right hand. 'I may have murdered women and children and I know I'm a lowlife piece of ork crap, but I still think I shouldn't have to share the same room with a fragging heretic!'

Poal starts to fumble at his straps, having trouble because his left arm ends in a hook instead of a hand. I can see things might be getting out of control.

'That's enough!' I bark. 'You all know the score. Doesn't matter what you did to wind up as one of the Colonel's doomed men, we're all Last Chancers now. Now shut the frag up until we're back on the transport.'

There are a few grumbles, but nobody says anything out loud. More than one of them here has had a cracked skull or a broken nose for answering me back. I'm not a bully, you understand, I just have a short temper and don't like it when my men start getting too disrespectful. Seeing that everybody is calming down, I close my eyes and try to get some sleep; it'll be another two hours before we dock.

THE TRAMP OF booted feet echoes around us as the Navy armsmen march us back to our cells. Left and right, along the seemingly endless corridor are the vaulted archways leading to the cargo bays, modified to carry human cargo in supposedly total security. There are twenty of the massive cells in all. Originally each held two hundred men, but after the past thirty months of near-constant war, nearly all of them stand empty now. It'll be even emptier for the rest of the trip; there's only about two hundred and fifty of us left after the defence of Deliverance. The armsmen swagger around, shotcannons grasped easily in heavily gloved hands or slung over their shoulders. Their faces are covered by the helms of their heavy-duty work suits, and their flash-protective visors conceal their features. Only the name badges stitched onto their left shoulder straps show that the same ten men have been escorting my platoon for the past two and a half years.

I see the Colonel waiting up ahead, with someone standing next to him. As we get closer, I see that it's Kronin, his small, thin body half-hunched as if weighed down by some great invisible burden. The lieutenant's narrow eyes flit and dart from side to side, constantly scanning the shadows, and he flinches as I step up to Schaeffer and salute.

'Lieutenant Kronin is the only survivor of 3rd platoon,' the Colonel tells me as he waves the armsmen to move the others inside, 'so I am putting him in with you. In fact, with so few of you left, you are going to be gathered into a single formation now. You will be in charge; Green was killed in Deliverance.'

'How, sir?' I ask, curious as to what happened to the other lieutenant, one of the hundred and fifty Last Chancers who was alive two days ago and now is food for the flesh-ants of the nameless planet below us.

'He was diced by a strangleweb,' the Colonel says coldly, no sign of any emotion on his face at all. I wince inside – being slowly cut up as you try to struggle out of a constricting mesh of barbed muscle is a nasty way to go. Come to think of it, I've never thought of a nice way to go.

'I am leaving it to you to organise the rest of the men into squads and to detail special duties,' the Colonel says before stepping past me and striding down the corridor. A Departmento flunky swathed in an oversized brown robe hurries down to the Colonel carrying a massive bundle of parchments, and then they are both lost in the distant gloom.

'Inside,' orders an armsman from behind me, his nametag showing him to be Warrant Officer Hopkinsson.

The massive cell doors clang shut behind me, leaving me locked in this room with ten score murderers, thieves, rapists, heretics, looters, shirkers, desecrators, grave-robbers, necrophiles, maniacs, insubordinates, blasphemers and other assorted vermin for company. Still, it makes for interesting conversation sometimes.

'Right!' I call out, my voice rebounding off the high metal ceiling and distant bulkheads. 'All sergeants get your sorry hides over here!'

As the order is passed around the massive holding pen, I gaze over my small force. There's a couple of hundred of us left now, sitting or lying around in scattered groups on the metal decking, stretching away into the gloom of the chamber. Their voices babble quietly, making the metal walls ring slightly and I can smell their combined sweat from several days on the furnace-hot planet below. In a couple of minutes eight men are stood around me. I catch sight of an unwelcome face.

'Who made you a sergeant, Rollis?' I demand, stepping up to stand right in front of his blubbery face, staring straight into his beady black eyes.

'Lieutenant Green did,' he says defiantly, matching my stare.

'Yeah? Well you're just a trooper again now, you piece of dirt!' I snap at him, pushing him away. 'Get out of my sight, you fraggin' traitor.'

'You can't do this!' he shouts, taking a step towards me and half-raising a fist. My elbow snaps out sharply and connects with his throat, sending him gasping to the floor.

'Can't I?' I snarl at him. 'I guess I can't do this either,' I say, kicking him in the ribs. Forget about the murderers, it's the out-and-out traitors like him that make me want to heave. With a venomous glance he gets to his hands and knees and crawls away.

'Right,' I say, turning to the others, putting the fat piece of filth from my mind. 'Where were we?'

ALARM SIRENS ARE sounding everywhere, a piercing shrill that sets your teeth on edge. I'm standing with a pneu-mattock grasped in both hands, its engine chugging comfortably, wisps of oily smoke leaking from its exhaust vents.

'Hurry up, wreck the place!' someone shouts from behind me. I can hear the sound of machinery being smashed, pipelines being cut and energy coils being shattered. There's a panel of dials in front of me and I place the head of the hammer against it, thumbing up the revs on the engine to full, the air filling with flying splinters of glass and shards of torn metal. Sparks of energy splash across my heavy coveralls, leaving tiny burn marks on the thick gloves covering my hands. I turn the pneu-mattock on a huge gear-and-chain mechanism behind the trashed panel, sending toothed wheels clanging to the ground and the heavy chain whipping past my head.

'They're coming!' the earlier voice calls out over the din of twisting metal and fracturing glass. I look over my shoulder to see a bunch of security men hurrying through an archway to my left, wearing heavy carapace breastplates coloured dark red with the twisted chain and eye mark of the Harpikon Union picked out in bold yellow. They've all got vicious-looking slug guns, black enamelled pieces of metal that catch the light menacingly. People hurrying past jostle me, but it's hard to see their faces, like they're in a mist or something. I get a glimpse of a half-rotten skull resembling a man called Snowton, but I know that Snowton died a year ago fighting pirates in the Zandis Belt. Other faces, faces of men who are dead, flit past. There's a thunderous roar and everybody starts rushing around. I realise that the Harpikon guards are firing. Bullets ricochet all over the place, zinging off pieces of machinery and thudding into the flesh of those around me. I try to run, but my feet feel welded to the floor. I look around desperately for somewhere to hide, but there isn't anywhere. Then I'm alone with the security men, the smoking muzzles of their guns pointing in my direction. There's a blinding flash and the thunder of shooting.

I WAKE UP from the dream gasping for breath, sweat coating my skin despite the chill of the large cell. I fling aside the thin blanket that serves as my bed and sit up, placing my hands on the cold floor to steady myself as dizziness from the sudden movement swamps me. Gulping down what feels like a dead rat in my mouth, I look around. There's the usual night-cycle activity – mumbles and groans from the sleepless, the odd murmured prayer as some other poor soul is afflicted by the sleep-daemons. It's always the same once you've dropped into the Immaterium.

I've had the same nightmare every night in warp-space for the past three years, ever since I joined the Imperial Guard. I'm always back in the hive on Olympas, carrying out a wreck-raid on a rival factory. Sometimes it's the Harpikon Union, like tonight; other times it's against the Jorean Consuls; and sometimes even the nobles of the Enlightened, though we never dared do that for real. There's always the walking dead as well. Folks from my past come back to haunt me: people I've killed, comrades who have died, my family, all of them appear in the nightmares. Lately I've realised that there's more and more of them after every battle, like the fallen are being added to my dreams. I always end up dying as well, which is perhaps the most disturbing thing. Sometimes I'm blown apart by gunfire, other times I'm sawn in half by a poweraxe or a chainsword, sometimes I'm burnt alive by firethrowers. Several people have told me that the warp is not bound in time like the real universe. Instead, you might see images from your past or your future, all mixed together in strange ways. Interpreting warp dreams is a speciality of Lammax, one of the ex-Departmento men. I think they threw him into the penal legions for blasphemy after he offered to read the dreams of a quartermaster-major. He says it's my fear of death being manifested.

Suddenly there's a demented screaming from the far end of the cargo hold where we're held, down where the lighting has gone fritzy and its arrhythmic pulsing gives you a headache. Nobody's slept down there for months, not since there was enough room for everyone to fit in at this end. With everyone gathered in one cell now, someone must have had to try to get to sleep down there. I push myself to my feet and pull on my boots over my bare feet. As I walk towards the commotion, I rub a hand across my bared chest to wipe off the sweat. My body tingles all over with a bizarre feeling of energy, the map of scars traced out across my torso feels strangely hot under my fingertips. I look down, half-expecting the old wounds to be glowing. They're not.

I tramp into the gloom, watched by most of the others. The screaming's loud enough to wake up the Navy ratings on the next deck up. I understand their suspicion and morbid curiosity, because sometimes when a man starts screaming in warpspace, it's not with his own voice. Luckily it's never happened to anyone I know, but there are guys here who tell tales of men being possessed by creatures from the warp. They either go completely mad and kill a load of people before collapsing and dying, or they get taken over totally becoming a body for some strange creature's mind, in which case they'll stalk along the corridors calmly murdering anyone they come across. And that's even when the Immaterium shielding is still working. You don't want to know what happens on a ship whose warp-wards collapse under the continual assault from formless beings intent on the death of the ship's crew.

'Emperor of Terra, watch over me,' I whisper to myself as I'm halfway towards the source of the screeching. If it is a Touched One, this could be some really serious trouble. They don't allow us anything that can be used as a weapon, so we're virtually defenceless. Still, that's just as well really, because there'd be a hell of a lot less of us left if we were armed. Fights break out a lot, but despite what some people think it takes a while to beat someone to death and somebody usually breaks it up before there's a casualty. That said, if I wanted to kill someone I could, particularly if they're sleeping.

My whole body's shaking, and I'm not quite sure why. I try to tell myself it's the cold, but I'm man enough to admit when I'm scared. Men don't scare me, except perhaps the Colonel. Aliens give me shudders now and then, especially the tyranids, but there's something about the idea of warp creatures that just shivers me the core, even though I've never had to face one. There's nothing that I can think of in the galaxy that's more unholy.

I can see someone thrashing around in a blanket ahead, just where the lights go gloomy. It's hard to see in the intermittent haze of the broken glowglobe, but I think I see Kronin's face twisting and turning. I hear footsteps behind me and turn suddenly, almost lashing out at Franx who's got up and followed me.

'Just warp-dreams,' he tries to reassure me with a crooked smile, his big hands held up in reflex.

'Like that makes me feel better,' I reply shortly, turning back to the writhing figure of Kronin. I can just about make out words in the shrieks bursting from his contorted mouth.

'And from the deeps… there arose a mighty beast, of many eyes… and many limbs. And the beast from the… darkness did set upon the light of mankind… with hateful thirst and unnatural hunger!'

'Don't wake him!' Franx hisses as I reach out a hand towards the struggling figure.

'Why not?' I demand, kneeling down beside Kronin and glaring back at the sergeant.

'Preacher Durant once said that waking a man with warp-dreams empties his mind, allows Chaos to seep in,' he says with an earnest look in his face.

'Well, I'll just have to risk a bit of corruption, won't I?' I tell him, annoyed at what seems like a childish superstition to me. 'If he carries on like that for the rest of the cycle, I'm not going to get any sleep at all.'

I rest a hand on Kronin's shoulder, gently at first but squeezing more firmly when he continues to toss and turn. It still doesn't do any good and I lean over him and slap him hard on the cheek with the back of my hand. His eyes snap open and there's a dangerous light in them for a second, but that's quickly replaced by a vague recognition. He sits up and looks straight at me, eyes squinting in the faltering light.

'Saint Lucius spake unto the masses of Belushidar, and great was their uproar of delight,' he says with a warm smile on his thin lips, but his eyes quickly fill with a haunted look.

'Guess that means thanks,' I say to Franx, standing up as Kronin lowers himself back down onto the blanket, glancing around once more before closing his eyes. I stay there for a couple more minutes until Kronin's breathing is shallow and regular again, meaning he's either really asleep or faking it well enough for me not to care any more.

Why the hell did Green have to get himself killed, I ask myself miserably as I trudge back to my sleeping area? I could do without the responsibility of wet-nursing this bunch of frag-for-brains criminals. It's hard enough just to survive in the Last Chancers without having to worry about everyone else. I guess I'll just have to not worry, let them take care of themselves. Hell, if they can't do that, they deserve to die.

ABOUT THE AUTHOR

Gav Thorpe works as Warhammer Loremaster at Games Workshop, as a member of the Key Design team. He has recently admitted that his books are ghost-written by Dennis the mechanical hamster, but had to write this one himself because Dennis ran off to spend several weeks with a young lady related to the author's girlfriend.

THE LAST CHANCERS
by Gav Thorpe

Across a hundred bloody war-zones, the convict soldiers of the 13th Penal Legion fight a desperate battle for redemption in the eyes of the immortal Emperor. In this endless war, Lieutentant Kage and the Last Chancers must fight, not just to win, but also to survive!

Check out 13th Legion and Kill Team, the first two novels in the awesome Last Chancers series!

Available from all better bookstores and
www.blacklibrary.com

INFERNO!™

INFERNO! is the indispensable guide to the worlds of Warhammer and Warhammer 40,000 and the cornerstone of the Black Library. Every issue is crammed full of action packed stories, comic strips and artwork from a growing network of awesome writers and artists including:

- **Dan Abnett**
- **William King**
- **Gav Thorpe**
- **Graham McNeill**
- **Gordon Rennie**
- **Simon Spurrier**

and many more!

Presented every two months, Inferno! magazine brings the Warhammer worlds to life in ways you never thought possible.

For subscription details ring:

US: 1-800-394-GAME
UK: (0115) 91 40000
Canada: 1-888-GW-TROLL
Australia: [02] 9829 6111

For more information see our website:
www.blacklibrary.com/inferno